Submerge

TOBIE EASTON

Month9Books

SUBMERGE by Tobie Easton
All rights reserved. Published in the United States of America by Month9Books, LLC. No part of this book may be used or reproduced in any manner whatsoever without written permission of the publisher, except in the case of brief quotations embodied in critical articles and reviews.

Trade Paperback ISBN: 978-1-946700-27-8
EPub ISBN: 978-1-946700-28-5
Mobipocket ISBN: 978-1-946700-29-2
Hardback ISBN: 978-1-945107-84-9

Published by Month9Books, Raleigh, NC 27609
Cover Designed by Beetiful Book Covers
Cover Copyright © 2017 Month9Books

Month9Books

Praise for SUBMERGE

"Romantic, enthralling, lyrical. *Submerge* is nothing short of magical." — Adriana Mather, *New York Times* bestselling author of *How to Hang a Witch*

"Expansive world-building and heart-thumping romance combine to make *Submerge* a delightful and gripping read. Fans of Tobie Easton's *Emerge* won't be disappointed, while new readers will love jumping right into the deep-end." — Jennifer Brody, award-winning author of *The 13th Continuum*

"Tobie Easton is a master at creating compelling and vivid underwater worlds. Following her lovable heroine through another addictive mermaid tale was a pure joy." — Emily France, author of *Zen and Gone*, and *Signs of You*, an Apple iBooks Best Book of the Month.

"*Submerge* dives deep into exploring right from wrong, good from evil, and the depths of eternal love. Readers will be hooked by the rich and believable Mer-world Easton creates." — Jennifer Bardsley, author of *Genesis Girl* and *Damaged Goods*

To Andrea, the best mother any Mermaid could ever wish for.

Submerge

Chapter One

I can't wait. Months of crossed fingers, doubt-ridden smiles, and whispered worries have led to this day. This sunset. Now that it's almost here, I can't wait. Not any longer.

But I can't control the sun either. I may be immortal now, but I have no true power over time. All I can do is squeeze Clay's hand and feel his fingers interlace with mine.

"Almost," he murmurs in my ear, his breath like the warm California breeze that sweeps over us, rippling the blue water so it glints silver-white in the sunlight.

My family's saltwater swimming pool features a disappearing edge like a waterfall that looks as if it flows seamlessly into the Pacific Ocean below. My sisters and cousin all swim in listless circles, their jewel-toned tails swishing beneath them, their lovely faces creased with concern they try to hide. But I'm not in the pool. I'm sitting on a lounger in my bikini, my legs in place and ready to run down to the beach at a moment's notice. Next to me sits Clay, fully dressed and looking strangely out of place in his trademark ripped jeans, band t-shirt, and Doc Martens.

We both stare at the late-July sun as it starts its slow descent toward the waves. Up here, in the backyard of my family's Malibu estate, we're safe from prying eyes. The beach below may be private, but our neighbors can still see it from their windows, and not all of them are members of our Community of land-dwelling Mer. To stay hidden from our neighbors' view, nothing will rise from the waves until darkness cloaks the sandy shores.

I don't know if the thought of what will happen when something does rise fills me more with excitement or with dread.

My sisters attempt pleasant small talk as the sky shifts from blue to pale pink, then from pink to a brilliant, stabbing orange. The sun dips lower, painting the waves that same orange as seagulls fly by, their black silhouettes floating against the sweeping sky. I can't follow my sisters' conversation—not with my legs jiggling and my stomach jumping. After what feels like hours, the orange fades to deep indigo, and then the only light falling on the water comes from stars that dot the sky like firefish.

Now, no one speaks. Everyone's gaze is riveted to where the water laps at the beach.

My cousin Amethyst, who we all call Amy, is the first to see them. "There!" she shouts, pointing into the darkness.

My breath catches in my throat as four muscled figures emerge from the waves in a perfect line, followed by four more directly behind them. Staying in formation, eight of the largest Mermen I've ever seen march forward out of the water, swaths of wet fabric tied around their waists like sarongs now that muscular legs have replaced their tails. Each one carries a spear carved from walrus tusk.

My sisters make a mad dash out of the pool and into their legs, but I'm already running to the wooden stairs that lead from our yard down the steep hill to the beach. I race from one step to the next, Clay close behind me.

By the time I reach the sand, the lines of soldiers have split down the middle to reveal the two people they have guarded all the way up from the deep.

A huge smile splits across my face. My parents. Finally.

My mother's gaze lands on me, and warmth suffuses her normally reserved expression. I wrap my arms around her, then my father.

"Hey, angelfish," he says, voice as jovial as ever, and squeezes me into a wet hug. It's still strange not to feel the soft cushiness of his potbelly. Stepping back, I'm struck again by how much my parents have changed. In my head, I still picture them the way they were before their immortality was restored. Gone are my middle-aged parents with their crow's feet and worry lines. In their place stand two people who look the way my parents must have looked when they were first married. *This is how it's supposed to be*, I remind myself, but it's hard for me to believe. I grew up thinking all Mer would age and die like humans do because two hundred years ago, the Little Mermaid cursed us all.

Her real story isn't all songs and smiles. She fell in love with a human prince and made a deal with a Sea Sorceress—not to get legs (like humans think) but to permanently banish her tail so her prince would never find out what she was. As part of the bargain, she traded her voice and agreed that if the prince married anyone but her, she'd die at the first sunrise after his wedding day. It seemed like things would go her way, until the prince chose to marry a human princess instead of her. The Sea Sorceress offered the Little Mermaid a chance to restore her tail: She could take the sorceress's obsidian dagger and kill her beloved prince. When his blood dripped onto her legs, they'd transform into a tail and she could return to her family in the ocean, an immortal Mermaid once again. But the Little Mermaid couldn't do it. She loved the prince so much, she chose her own death instead. She dropped the powerful dagger into the sea, and the instant it touched the water, it unleashed a curse. Because the Little Mermaid had valued a human life above her own immortality, she cursed all Merkind with human lifespans.

But this past spring, in an effort to save each other's lives, Clay and

I broke that curse and restored immortality to all the Mer. Including my parents. Centuries ago, before the curse, Mer stopped aging in their mid-twenties, which we call reaching stasis. When we broke the curse, my parents and all adult Mer reverted to their stasis ages. Now, after I've gone two months without seeing them, the changes in their appearance seem even more startling. Thank the tides their smiles are still the same, or I may not have recognized them.

When they see Clay next to me, my father claps him on the shoulder.

My mother surprises me by smiling at him. "It was good of you to come."

I guess risking his life to save mine and breaking a centuries-old curse on our entire species have steered Clay into warmer waters with my parents.

Clay clears his throat. *"Willkime haun!"* He's been bugging me to teach him Mermese expressions, but I'm not the best (or most patient) teacher and, through no fault of his own, Clay's pronunciation is terrible. My parents exchange a confused glance as he reddens, but tries again. *"Wilcom home?"* He pronounces the words more clearly this time, but not by much. Lapis and Lazuli, my twin sisters who have just run up behind us, hear his words and hide identical grins behind their hands. My parents catch on.

"Thank you," my mother says in impeccable Mermese, the lilting words dancing across the night air the way they would through the deep ocean if we were Below. With its combination of melodic sounds that glide along the water and high-pitched notes that pierce through it, Mermese is the only language not muffled under the waves.

"We're glad to be back," my father says, switching the conversation back to English. Clay flashes a relieved smile.

"And we're soooo glad you're back," Amy says, her strawberry blond hair flying behind her as she races toward them next to my oldest sister Emeraldine and demands hugs of her own. I let out a breath as I step back, glad to let the others pull my parents' focus. Once their eyes are off me, I roll my neck to relieve some tension.

While Em pecks both my parents on the cheek and fills them in about what they've missed at the Foundation, Clay whispers, "How was I?" in my ear.

"They really appreciated the effort. I could tell," I say.

"That bad, huh?" He knocks his shoulder into mine and smirks. I knock right back.

"So ... you doin' okay?" Concern colors his voice now. He sees past the welcome-back smile I wear for my parents. I don't trust myself to answer him without my façade crumbling like a sandcastle in the surf, so I just nod. I'm happy to have my parents home—I really am. But Clay and I both know what their return means. Now that they're here, there's no putting it off any longer.

"Shall we?" my mother asks, nodding toward our house, with its clean, white lines and huge windows that overlook the ocean.

"What about the stud patrol?" Lapis asks, her blue eyes straying to the eight guards, not for the first time.

"They'll be staying with us, at least for the next few weeks," my mother answers, leveling Lapis and Lazuli with a firm, no-funny-business stare.

"Just until things calm down and we can ensure we all don't need extra protection." My dad directs this at Amy, who's the youngest at fourteen.

"Or until we know we do," Em mutters. She usually has such a knack for keeping her inner cool, but today even Em is as nervous as the rest of us.

Lazuli cracks a smile. "Hey, I, for one, am not complaining." She winks at the handsome young guard with a cleft in his chin. He stares straight past her, scanning the surrounding area, his composure and his spear unwavering. Amy laughs, and the tension dissipates, at least for the moment.

As we head toward the house, Clay says he should get home, that his mom's expecting him. Really, he just wants to give our family some space to be together for the first time in months—and maybe the last time for even longer. Everyone says goodbye to Clay, and I walk him out.

"Be back sometime this week, Lia," Amy calls after us, even though it's only been seconds.

I roll my eyes at her before Clay and I leave my family on the back porch and slip through the sliding glass doors into the living room. Our goodbyes have been getting longer lately. It seems like every night, it's harder to watch him leave. I want to spend every minute with him.

I can feel my family's eyes on us through the floor-to-ceiling windows as we walk from the living room through the entrance hall to the front door. Only once the door closes behind us and we stand outside the front entrance are we truly alone. I'm glad my family—and the entire Community—knows we're together. Finally having my feelings for Clay out in the open means the ocean to me, but sometimes a girl just wants some privacy with her boyfriend. Boyfriend. I *love* that word.

I turn to face the boy in question and he looks oh-so-handsome standing there, with the lights that illuminate the burbling fountain in our house's circular front driveway playing off the planes of his face. I have no words, so I go with the first one that pops out. "Hi."

"Hi, yourself." He gives me that little half smile and my insides warm. The night settles over us in quiet stillness.

We make our way down the long, winding gravel path toward the iron gate that marks the end of my parents' estate. Our clasped hands swing between us, palm-to-palm, and the closer we get to the end of the path, the tighter I want to hold his hand. Saying goodbye to Clay is never easy, but tonight is different. Because as soon as I say goodbye, the night's really over. That's one more night gone before …

"Thinking about Friday?" he asks as if reading my mind. Friday. The day after tomorrow.

"Trying not to." I bite my lip. "I don't know if I'll be able to handle it."

"It's going to be especially hard on you," he says. "I mean, I'll be shirtless all day. I don't know how you're going to focus." His self-confident smirk suffuses his smooth voice. "We both know how much you love ogling my chest, Nautilus."

"I do not ogle," I say, my mock-offense threatening to transform into a peal of laughter.

"Oh, you ogle."

"Anyone ever tell you you're ridiculously arrogant?" I ask.

"You know you love it," he says. I smile, but even as we joke, unwanted thoughts of all that Friday will hold cloud my mind. If even thoughts of Clay's abs aren't enough to distract me, I must be worried. Yes, Clay will be shirtless all day, but only because he'll be at a formal Mer gathering and, out of respect, he'll need to follow the expected dress code for Mermen, no matter how obvious it will be that he's not one. The day after tomorrow, Clay will spend the whole afternoon among every Merman and Mermaid in the Community, along with all those who have come to visit from Below. We both will. And so much could go wrong.

When we reach the gate, Clay spins me around to face him before leaning in close. "It's going to be fine," he says in a soothing whisper as he runs his hands up and down my bare arms. Standing here with Clay whispering in my ear makes a memory rush over me. A memory of me whispering in Clay's ear by this same gate. A memory of the night I found out I had the power to protect him from another Mermaid—an evil Mermaid who had enchanted him to love her so she could kill him in an ancient ritual to alter the curse. I stopped her, but only by brainwashing him to love me instead. Clay and I had stood by this gate when he placed my hand on his heart through the bars as he tried to profess his love for me. I wanted to weep then because what the magic made him feel for me wasn't real. Now, as I stare up into his clear, hazel eyes—eyes unclouded by the haze of magic—I know every word he speaks is his own.

That's why I melt when he says, "No matter what happens on

Friday, we're in it together." He tucks a strand of my long, brown hair behind my ear, and I lean into his touch. "Lia, I love you."

Clay doesn't say the words often. I think they still scare him, just a bit. But he says them now with a certainty that soothes and strengthens me. "I love you, too," I whisper. I've loved him for so long.

"You're not alone in this, okay?"

I nod, but it shouldn't be his job to be the strong one. Sure, he says he's fine. That he doesn't want to talk about all that time he was brainwashed. That we should move on. But with everything he's been through ... "You're not alone, either, y'know. How are you feeling about ... " Should I say it? "... Friday?" Coward. I swallow, try again. "Are you going to be okay seeing ... *her*?" This Friday, the day after tomorrow, Clay will see that same Mermaid who brainwashed him—who played with his heart and mind—for the first time since she and her father tried to kill us both. There's a reason my parents have returned, a reason Mer from Below are flooding into our Community in droves. They're here for the most important and scandalous event in modern Mer history. They're here for the trial.

At the mention of seeing someone who hurt him so much and who he'll now need to testify against in a court filled with Merpeople, a flicker of something shines in Clay's eyes, something raw. But he blinks, looks away, and whatever it was shutters off. A halfhearted chuckle escapes his lips and his smirk slides back into place. "Didn't anyone tell you, I'm pretty tough?"

"Clay ... "

"We'll get through it. We'll get through all of it. And then it'll just be a memory that we can put behind us."

He's right, I suppose. No matter what happens Friday or in the weeks ahead, I'll have Clay and he'll have me. Nothing can change that. I breathe in the jasmine-scented night air and let the thought comfort me.

"You should get back," he says, nodding up the winding path

toward my house. I punch in the security code, and he pushes open the gate. It scrapes through the gravel until the opening is just wide enough for him to step through. But he doesn't. He stands there, waiting under the white, bell-shaped blossoms of one of our brugmansia trees. I place my hand over his on the iron gate as I step in close. Clay brings his other hand up to my cheek, stroking it with fingers calloused from his guitar strings, drawing me closer still. His handsome features—so familiar and so astonishing—gleam in the moonlight, then grow so near they're indiscernible. I let my eyes flutter shut. Let myself taste Clay's lips against mine. Get lost in the richness of every touch, every press of his tongue and graze of his cheek.

A suspiciously familiar, syrupy voice lurking in some hidden crevice of my mind asks me if I really think I'm doing this right. If maybe he's comparing me to *her*. Surely she must have been a better kisser. But I push that voice back into its dark cave as I wrap my arm around Clay and he brings his hand back to cup my head, tangling his fingers in my hair as my chest presses against his.

Finally, in a flurry of breathless, whispered goodbyes, our mouths come together and apart, together and apart, until he slowly pulls himself away and down the street. With one final flash of hazel and a promise to see me in the morning, he disappears around the corner.

Later, after several hours of carefully smiling while catching up with my parents, I lie in my sea sponge bed in the hidden grottos beneath our house and try to sleep. As a layer of satiny salt water covers me like a blanket, I force myself to replay tonight's kiss instead of imagining what risks the next few days will bring.

Chapter Two

It's my last day of normal, and I plan to enjoy it. While my parents are getting caught up at the Foundation, I plan to sit right here, all snuggly on Clay's couch and not think about what's coming. Not think about how tonight, more Merfolk from across the ocean floor will surface here in Malibu. Not think about where I'll be this time tomorrow.

Nope. All I'm going to think about is Clay and maybe how I can get to know his lips even better. I scoot closer to him on the couch, rest my head on his shoulder, and inhale. He played me one of his new songs on the guitar earlier, and the cinnamon scent of his guitar polish still lingers. He strokes my hair, and this den—his den, with its overstuffed, checkered furniture, humming AC, and glowing television—turns into the most relaxing place in the world. Sitting next to Clay, I can forget for a few minutes that I'm a Mermaid and just be a normal girl.

"Lia, can I … can I see your tail?"

Or not.

I sit up so fast, Clay's hand gets tangled in my hair. Ow. "You've seen my tail plenty of times," I say as he works his fingers free.

It's true; he's seen it whenever he comes over and I'm swimming in my pool with my sisters or spending time in the grottos with my parents. But now that we're alone and there's no water in sight, deliberately transforming into my tail just so he can look at it feels like putting myself on display.

"I've never seen it up close," he says, twisting his thumb ring around in a circle. He's right—and that's on purpose. I've been making a point of keeping our alone time as human as possible. We hang out at the pier, walk on the promenade, grab sushi or burgers—y'know, normal stuff. Clay's a human guy and I just … I don't want … it's a lot to take in. What if I scare him off? What if up close, he thinks my tail's gross, that I'm gross?

Since I haven't said anything, he pushes on. "Every time I see you with your tail, we're around your family, and I feel like I shouldn't stare." He lets his fingers sweep through his own dark hair, then claps a hand on his denim-clad leg. "It's just, it's a part of you. This beautiful part, and … but if you don't want to, that's cool. If it's weird or whatever … "

I raise my gaze from my lap. "Did … did you say beautiful?"

The corner of his mouth quirks up. An expression I know well. "Oh yeah."

I look down at my lap again, and he rests a hand on my thigh, the heat of his palm warming my skin through the thin jersey of my skirt.

"I think *you're* beautiful," he says.

All of me? I want to ask. *Even the parts that are more halibut than human?*

I love my tail, but it's always been this secret part of me, the part I have to keep hidden. How will this human boy in front of me—this handsome, patient human boy—react to seeing it up close? I guess there's only one way I'll find out.

I glance at the door to his den; it doesn't lock, but it's shut tight. "What about your mom?"

He gives my leg a reassuring squeeze. "She's writing at that café around the corner. She never heads back before dark." That means we have a couple hours. More than enough time.

I swallow. "Are you sure you want to see?" I'm officially stalling.

Clay nods. "I want to see you. To look at you. Really look." He tilts his head so he can catch my gaze again. "But Lia, if you're not ready, that's—"

"No," I say, too quickly. His face falls, but he nods again. "No! I mean, no, I'm not *not* ready," I rush to explain. "I'm ... " I take a deep breath so I can say the words with the decisiveness I wish I possessed. "If you want to see it, I want to show you."

Excitement lights up his face.

He opens his mouth, closes it. "So ... how ... "

"So, yeah ... um ... " If I'd known I was going to do this today— going to show my human boyfriend my tail, oh tides—I'd have thought my outfit through on a whole different level when I got dressed this morning. Maybe worn a wrap-around skirt like I do when I'm at home. Still, it could be worse. My current skirt is loose and flowy, so at least it won't rip when I transform.

If I can transform at all. Usually, releasing my tail is the most natural act in the world for me. But with Clay next to me ... See, not to get R-rated or anything, but the only reason Mer have legs at all is for ... well, mating. Under the ocean, that's the only thing we'd need them for (which is why we don't get our legs until we hit puberty). So, if I'm thinking even the teensiest bit about ... um, *being* with Clay ... it's hard to get rid of my legs.

I look pointedly down at where Clay's strong hand still rests on my thigh. "I'm gonna need you to—"

"Oh! Right." He lifts his fingers up one at a time and moves his hand away. "Better?" he asks as he gets up to perch on a nearby armchair.

Better for my focus? Absolutely. But I miss the warmth of his touch.

I slip off my flip-flops, then scoot to the corner of the couch so my back's against the armrest and my legs stretch down the length, across the cushions. Okay, no more stalling. I said I was ready to do this, and damn it, I'm ready. *Clay's your boyfriend. You trust him. He said he thinks you're beautiful. Beautiful, not abnormal.*

My eyes lock onto Clay's hazel ones. I read anticipation there, but also a promise. A promise that we'll both still be us. Some of the tension melts from my shoulders as my eyes drift closed.

Transforming without water nearby is strange, so I conjure an image of the ocean in my mind, letting its rippling waves whisper to me. I imagine the call of the ocean that all Merfolk hear, the one luring us out to sea and down into the deep. As I inhale, I can almost smell the harsh, clean bite of salt water.

Then I feel it.

The familiar pushing and pulling sensation of invisible tides crashing against my legs.

My bones and muscles dance under my skin, shifting and fusing in metamorphosis. It's the deepest, most satisfying stretch imaginable. I drop my head back and let it wash over me. When the tingle of enchanted tides recedes, I open my eyes. There, on Clay's checkered couch, lies a long, golden Mermaid's tail.

"Whoa." Clay jumps off the armchair in surprise. At the awe on his face, my nerves undergo their own transformation as a thrill shoots up my spine.

He's staring at me—all of me—and he's smiling. More than smiling. He's grinning, his eyes the size of sand dollars.

"That was the coolest thing I've ever seen."

He comes to kneel next to the couch and runs his gaze up and down my tail, angling his head this way and that, like he's examining each golden scale.

My face heats, but the open-mouthed appreciation gracing his features keeps me from ducking my head. I feel like I'm shining from the inside out.

"Can I?" He reaches out a tentative hand, but doesn't touch.

I swallow again, then nod. When that hand touches my tail, I almost gasp at the newness of the sensation. His fingers skate from one scale to the next, emblazoning a path down the length of me. When he reaches my fin, he traces the edge of it with one curious fingertip. "Can you feel this?" he whispers.

"Of course. Can you feel it when I touch your toes?"

"This is so many more degrees of awesome than touching my toes." He's experimenting now, holding the tip of one of my fins between his thumb and forefinger while he exerts a gentle pressure. It feels *good*. Like a massage somewhere I didn't know I needed it.

I force myself to focus on our conversation. "I like your toes. I like every part of you."

Next, his hand moves back up, sliding along a surface smooth enough to slice through waves without resistance. I fight to keep my breathing even, to keep my tail in place under his touch.

"I never realized how many different shades of gold there are," he murmurs. "How is this possible?" He's moved alongside the couch, and he kneels by my torso now, looking up into my face with such wonder, such reverence. I lean down as he leans up, and I can see the gold flecks in his eyes, the ones I've always thought match my tail perfectly. I should tell him that, but all I can think about is how close his lips are to mine, how easy it will be to—

I jerk when his hand slips down to the side of my tail, my fin smacking against the couch cushions. He jumps back, his eyebrows shooting up.

"Ticklish," I say.

I may have been admiring his eyes a second ago, but now I don't like the gleam sparkling in them. "Claaay!" I squeal as he wriggles his fingers up and down the sides of my tail. Soon I'm doubled up with laughter, fighting to catch my breath, my fists and fin pounding against the couch as I squirm every which way. But while my tail is agile in the water, moving it nimbly on land proves impossible, and before I know it, I'm tumbling off the couch with no way to stop myself.

Instead of landing with a thud on the hardwood floor like I

expect, I land somewhere soft, but firm. Clay's lap. An arm wraps around my upper back, holding me up, holding me close. Suddenly, I'm breathless for an entirely different reason.

"Thanks," I say, wondering in the back of my mind if my tail makes me too heavy for his lap, if I'm going to make his legs go numb. I tuck an errant strand of hair behind my ear, shifting my weight in a way I hope is subtle.

Then Clay's hand is on mine, sweeping all my hair to the side. What's he doing? Why is he ... my gills! He's staring at the gills visible on my neck now that I've transformed. And just like that, all my nerves rise up like it's high tide. A tail is one thing—at least people see Mermaid tails in paintings and the movies and water bottle commercials. But gills? There's no way a human, even one as completely cool as Clay, will think that's anything but gross. County fair, carnival freak show gross.

Sure enough, his hand is leaving mine.

"I should get up," I say, trying desperately to move off his lap but only managing to flop my tail back and forth. "I'm sure you don't want—"

"Shhh," he says. "I'm busy." And then his thumb is stroking my neck right below my ear, where small slits flutter with my breaths.

"You don't have to—"

"I like every part of you," he says, echoing my earlier words.

I would smile, but Clay chooses that instant to press his lips to mine.

We've never kissed like this before, with me in my true form. In its own way, it's a first kiss.

And it feels like one. Slow and sweet and swirling to ever-increasing depths. I forget everything else. My gills, my tail, the school of fish swimming in my stomach. All I'm aware of now is the place where our lips meet. The world shrinks down to the two of us, holding each other on the hardwood floor. It's just Clay and me and the cinnamon air stretched tight between us.

Until the door to the den swings open, slamming against the wall. And all at once, it's me and Clay—and Clay's mom.

Chapter Three

She stands in the doorway, mouth hanging open wide enough that a koi fish could swim right in.

My hands fly to my tail in a ridiculous attempt to block it from view. When my palms meet human skin instead of slick scales, confusion and relief flood my consciousness in equal measure. My tail was in place a minute ago. How did I transform without even realizing it?

The kiss. Of course! I was so wrapped up in the kiss, I didn't notice my body responding to it, to Clay. All I can do now is thank the current it did.

But if a Mermaid tail in the middle of her living room isn't what's put that look of utter shock on Clay's mom's face, what has?

The way Clay's head snaps to the side in his rush to avert his gaze gives me a clue. Swallowing my dread, I glance down. The transformation into my tail and back again has left my skirt all rucked up around my waist. Clay's mom must think we were ... no! No, no, no!

The same truth must have dawned on Clay, 'cause he looks about as mortified as I feel. I tug my skirt down with frantic hands and we both scramble to our feet, nearly tripping over one another.

It's been mere seconds since Clay's mom opened that door, but I'm as winded as if I'd dodged a tiger shark. She stands there, her laptop still under one arm, and finally closes her mouth as she runs a hand through her short, dark hair. It's the same rich color as Clay's, except for the big, blond streak she's added right in the front. I can never decide if it makes her look like a cartoon skunk or a total rock star. I've always liked Clay's mom. She never forgets to ask me how my day was and she listens to the answer and she laughs easily and she even started buying those packs of roasted seaweed sheets once she found out I like them. She has no clue I'm a Mermaid, but other than that, she's gotten to know me pretty well. And now she must think I'm … Why did she have to come home early? Why didn't we go into a room with a lock on the door? Seriously, how stupid can we be? What in the Seven Seas are we supposed to say to her now? *It's not what it looks like, Mrs. Ericson. I was just showing your son my golden Mermaid's tail.* Please. Even someone like her, who writes fantasy novels for a living, wouldn't believe that one. We are so screwed.

She clears her throat, and we both freeze.

Taking a step back, she places a hand back on the doorknob. Slowly, deliberately, Clay's mom pushes the door as far back toward the wall as it will go, until it hits the springy doorstop. "This," she says, nodding at the door, "stays open." She levels us with a say-you-understand-me stare, and we dip our heads up and down in agreement, neither of us daring to say a word. I'm still smoothing down the sides of my already-smooth skirt; I can't stop fidgeting. She turns to leave the den, then looks back at me over her shoulder. "It's nice to see you, Lia."

"Y-you, too, Mrs. Ericson." Well, what else am I supposed to say? Sorry you think I was doing something I wasn't but I really can't explain?

With the door now wide open, she walks out of the room. There's nothing but our stunned faces and the echoing of her footsteps down the hallway until she calls out, "That café is getting awfully crowded.

I think I'll be writing at home from now on."

Clay tries to say something, fails, and tries again. "Sounds good, Mom."

Once we're alone, we both sink back onto the couch. Clay's face bears no trace of his trademark cocky smirk. "She thinks ... "

Covering my face with both hands, I shake my head. Then I take a deep breath and peek at him through my fingers. "Still, it could have been worse. A lot worse." She could have seen my tail. I don't need to say that part—Clay knows. But I do say, "We have to be more careful."

He takes my hand and squeezes. "Yeah." A long pause. Then, "Should I not have asked you?"

Now, it's my turn to squeeze his hand. "I'm glad you did."

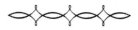

We've migrated to Clay's dining room table. Twenty minutes and two mom check-ins after ... the incident ... we decided hanging out in the most open, visible spot in the house was a much-needed gesture of goodwill. We've even left some space between our chairs while we play Uno. Clay taught me last month and I totally sucked at first, but I've gotten the hang of it. I'm thinking about laminating a deck so I can play in the grottos with my family or my best friend Caspian. Then again, I doubt there's enough strategy or skill involved to hold Caspian's interest.

Clay's hand brushes mine as I reach for a card, and when he smiles, just a trace of smirk slips through. Well look who's already recovered from the mommy-induced embarrassment.

I slam down a yellow two and do a little victory dance in my chair as I call out, "Uno" while watching Clay draw one card after another from the deck. This is my last day of normal, and I'm going to get it back on track. Just watch me.

For the rest of the afternoon, I plan to play Uno, veg out in front of bad reality T.V., maybe find some of those seaweed sheets in Clay's pantry. Yep, I'm determined to have fun.

"Hey, Lia?"

"That's your serious voice," I say.

"Maybe." He fiddles with the corner of one of his cards but doesn't put any down or pick any more up even though it's still his turn.

I level him with a mock-earnest expression that makes him chuckle. Then his brow creases, and he glances over his shoulder, checking that his mom's out of earshot.

"So ... my ... " He mumbles something and I miss it. Clay never mumbles.

"Sorry, what?"

He grits his teeth, tries again. "My ... dad called."

"Oh." That all you got, Lia? Real eloquent response. "Um ... that's good, right?"

"Yeah, it was actually. It's the first time *he's* called *me* in ... yeah, so, it was good. He wants to get dinner."

"That's huge," I say, letting myself smile now that I know it's good news. Clay's dad is in the Navy, and after the divorce, he moved down to the base in Point Loma, got a new girlfriend, and stopped driving up to Malibu to visit. Clay considered it a good year if he got a birthday card from him. But a few weeks before school let out for summer (right after Clay and I saved our lives, broke the curse on Merkind, and had our first real date), Clay started playing gigs at clubs around town. He hadn't played in public since his dad—the one who first taught him to play the guitar—left town, so it was a big step for him.

An even bigger step was the day in mid-June when Clay invited his dad to come watch him play. When he called me later to tell me his dad actually showed up, he sounded a whole different kind of happy. Little boy happy. So happy that I may have encouraged him to keep calling his dad and start talking to him on a regular basis again. But if Clay's dad called *him*, this marks the first time he's initiated the contact. And if he invited his son out to dinner, it means the guy's trying.

"Pretty huge," Clay agrees. He puts his obscenely large pile of cards down on the table and looks straight at me. "Which is why I want you to come with me."

"Out to dinner?" I try to keep my eyes from popping like a spookfish's. I've never met Clay's dad.

"I know the timing is bad with the trial and everything, but he wants to go on a Sunday, so we won't have to worry about being in court," he messes with the frayed hole in the knee of his jeans. "I thought we could drive down in the afternoon, get an early dinner, then drive back up before it gets too late and, I don't know, maybe get some frozen yogurt somewhere just the two of us."

He's thought this through. Maybe even practiced that speech in his head a couple times. I knock my knee playfully into his. "Tempting me with dessert? You must really want me to go, huh?" He doesn't answer, just stares up at me with hope-filled eyes that contradict his studied, casual expression. I place my hand on top of his. "I guess it would give us a chance to spend some time together. I'd like that."

"Really?"

"It's just … "

"What?" His body tenses, like he's ready for a blow. Or a disappointment.

"What if your dad doesn't like me?" I don't know why I care what Clay's dad thinks of me. It's not like I have a high opinion of him. But he *is* Clay's dad. I'd be meeting my boyfriend's father for the first time. It feels important.

"That's what you're worried about?" His shoulders relax as he shakes his head. "He'll definitely like you."

"How do you know?"

"Well, for one, my mom really likes you, and—"

"Not after today, she doesn't."

He raises an eyebrow at me. "She caught us all … " he moves both hands in big, obvious gestures, "and she didn't even tell you to go home. Trust me, she likes you."

I hope he's right. "Oookay, but that doesn't mean your dad will. He doesn't know me at all."

"He doesn't know me either." All the humor disappears from his voice. "Not really." His eyes cloud over for a second, but then he shrugs and says, like it's no big thing, "I'd just rather have someone at that table who does."

I study him, listening to what he's not saying. That he's not ready to spend the whole night alone with his dad. That he's afraid once the crowds and the music and all the other distractions he could rely on at a gig are gone, he and his father won't have anything worth talking about to fill the silence.

He's slumped in his chair now, the posterchild for cool nonchalance, but keen eyes follow my every reaction as he waits for my answer.

Less than an hour ago, this boy kissed the heck out of me while touching my gills. I know a good thing when I have it. And I want to spend every day showing Clay exactly how much I appreciate having him in my life. I lean in so our noses almost touch. "Of course I'll go."

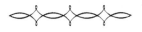

"Hey, um, what's it like not seeing your parents for so long?" I ask Amy that night. "I mean, you haven't seen them in … what, six years?"

"Seven," she says, stopping to let our puppy, Barnacle (who we call Barney for short), sniff a nearby tree. It's still a little strange to see Amy walking. She only got her legs last year, so I'm more used to her long, light purple tail. "That was the last time it was safe enough to visit. Even then, they probably shouldn't have taken the risk." See, I think of Amy like a sister. Her parents sent her up here to live with us when she was a baby so she'd be safe. They felt it was their duty to fight in the wars, to protect families from violent looters who swept through towns after every battle. My aunt and uncle have done a lot of good Below. They've helped people arm themselves and taught them how to fight so they could defend their children. But they've sacrificed a life with their own daughter in the process.

"So, what's it like?" I ask again. I need some insight or I might end up making this whole dinner with Clay's dad even more awkward.

"Uneven is the best word to describe it, I guess. Sometimes, when I get a shell call from them, I spend the rest of the day wondering about them. Picturing what they might be doing, wondering if they're safe. Y'know, that kinda thing. Wishing I could talk to them in person without a seashell pressed to my ear." Barney looks up at her, big brown eyes peeking through scruffy tan fur, and yanks on the leash with all six pounds of his puppy weight. We start walking down the block again.

"Then other days … I don't think about them at all," Amy continues. "A day'll pass, sometimes even a couple, then somebody will bring them up and I'll realize I haven't been thinking about them. I've just been living my life up here." She sweeps some of her strawberry blond hair over her shoulder. "I used to feel really guilty when that happened, like I was forgetting them, but now … " She shrugs.

"I bet they probably want it that way. Not that they want you to forget them," I backpedal. "I just mean, they sent you up here so you'd have this safer, better life. If you're enjoying it so much you're not thinking about them every second, well, that's probably what they'd want for you."

"I hope so."

We walk a few minutes in silence. I wonder if Clay spends some days never thinking about his dad and other days really missing him.

We turn left at the next corner, heading back in the direction of my house. Whenever we get there, both my parents will be waiting for me. The surety of that knowledge settles like hot chocolate warming my stomach. It's a feeling neither Clay nor Amy gets to have.

"What about now that they're coming back?" I ask. Since the undersea wars are over and my parents have ensured the journey is safe, Amy's parents will travel Above as soon as they finish helping rebuild a village destroyed in one of the final battles. That's the reason I felt like it was okay to have this conversation with Amy. I've never asked her any of these questions before because I didn't want to make her sad when there was no chance she could see her parents anytime soon. No certainty they'd be safe. "How are you feeling about finally getting to see them after all this time?"

"I can't wait. I'm so excited." Her teeth sparkle white in a huge smile, and her eyes shine overly bright in the light from the nearest streetlamp.

It's the same reaction she's given every time anyone's brought up her parents' impending visit. "Great job," I say. "Very believable. Now, real answer."

She bites one of the lips that, just seconds earlier, turned upward in an exuberant smile. "I *am* excited to see them. Really, I am, but," her gaze darts down to the concrete, then back up to my face, "it's … it's a lot of pressure, y'know? What if we have nothing to talk about? They don't even really know me." I remember what Clay said about his dad not knowing him. "What if … what if … " The next words escape in a whisper, "they don't like me anymore?" Once the words are out, her entire body deflates. Her shoulders shake and tears run down her cheeks, transforming into teardrop-shaped pearls on their way down. She grabs as many as she can before they hit the pavement but can't help more from coming. Barney paws at her and nuzzles her leg.

I pull her into a hug, and her head falls to my shoulder. She's my height now, but she's only just turned fourteen, and what she's going through would be hard at any age. As I hold her and stroke her hair, I wonder if Clay is afraid his dad won't like him. I squeeze Amy tighter.

"Of course your parents will like you," I tell her. "Of course they will. What's not to like?"

"But they're so strong and brave," she says into my shoulder. "They spend all their time risking their lives to save other people. And I'm just me. Here. Going to school in the grottos. Sometimes I don't … I don't feel like I'm their daughter." More tears come, so I hold her and rub her back. I use my best soothing voice to tell her how amazing she is, how there's no way they won't see that, how they'll be so proud of her.

"You really think so?" She sniffs as she untangles herself from my arms and straightens her crumpled shirt.

I put my hands on her shoulders and step back, meeting her eyes with mine. "I know so."

She gives me a small smile. This one is genuine. I smooth her hair, and we both kneel to pick up the pearls that fell to the sidewalk. Giving my top a shake releases a few that dropped down my V-neck.

"Sorry," Amy says with a little laugh. It's a good sound.

"No prob," I say, stuffing pearls into my pockets. Maybe I can use them to make her some hair accessories or an ankle bracelet.

"I wish it wasn't so dark," Amy says as she squints at the grooves in the cement, searching for more. "But at least the streets are empty. I guess I'll have to learn not to cry in public places before I'm ready to start human school." While she's still kneeling, she scratches Barney's head. "If I start human school." She falls silent again.

Amy has looked forward to starting human school once she got her legs and learned to control them ever since I can remember. But now that the wars are over, no plans are certain. "What if, um, what if your parents insist on taking you back Below? Do you know what you'd want to do?" A lot of the families in our Community are facing similar decisions. I don't want to overwhelm her, but I want to give her the opening in case she needs to talk about it. Plus, I've been curious for months.

Amy shakes her head. "I love the idea of spending more time with them, but … "

"But this is the only place we've ever lived," I finish. Tempting as it is to return to the ocean, it means leaving behind everything familiar, from shoes and s'mores to books and birds. "You've got it harder than I do, Aims. At least no one'll be asking me to decide soon."

After Clay and I first broke the curse, I got my parents to promise that no matter what happens Below, I can stay up here until I graduate from high school. That gives me one more year. One more year to convince them to let me stay longer—because I'm not leaving Clay.

And I'm not the only one determined to stay. Lapis and Lazuli will be commuting to college at Pepperdine once the fall semester starts, and they've said they have no intention of missing out on keg parties at frat houses to go live in an ocean that's not even safe yet. Ironically, Em (the only one of my sisters who was born Below and can't wait to return there with her fiancé, Leomaris) has to stay on land. Now that she's graduated from college, she's basically running the Foundation that governs our entire Community while my parents devote all their energy to installing law and order Below. They've spent the last two months at sea so they could work with all the surviving Mer nobles to create a police force and make the oceans a safe place to live again, starting with the most populous Mer towns and villages, and spreading outward from there.

But that's not the only reason my parents spent time under the waves. They're also quietly rallying support. Since my mother is the infamous Little Mermaid's closest surviving relative, my parents are next in line for the throne.

They haven't declared their intentions of claiming it—not yet. But as the two people who've led our Community of Mer here on land since the beginning, they're the most qualified to help the oceans recover after two centuries of warfare and anarchy.

"So much is changing," Amy says.

"Yeah. Kinda scary, huh?"

She doesn't answer, just picks Barney up and hugs his wiggly body to her chest.

"Do you know if Staskia's family is planning to stay?" I ask.

"They haven't decided," Amy whispers. "If I go with my parents and hers decide to stay ... Lia, I can't even ... "

"I know," is all I say. "I know."

"We haven't told anyone other than you about our relationship yet. It's all so new. Stas and I are still best friends. We're just more than that now, too."

Amy takes a few steps down the sidewalk, and I follow. "If ... if I do go Below, I'd have to leave Barney." As she says the words, Amy hugs the puppy even closer. "I know I'm supposed to want to live in the ocean ... " Her face scrunches, like she might cry again.

"Haven't you noticed, I'm not very good at 'supposed to' lately, either. I mean, falling for a human?" I nudge my shoulder against hers as we walk.

"That's true," Amy says. "And it worked out for you." She looks at me with the same admiration—the same hero worship—so many Mer look at me with nowadays. It makes sand crabs skitter under my skin.

I can tell the idea that it's all worked out for Clay and me gives her hope. But it hasn't worked out for us. Not really. Not yet. Amy thinks it has because there's something she doesn't know. Something our entire Community doesn't know: The only way I saved Clay was by committing the worst, most despicable crime known to Mer. I used ancient, dark magic to steal his free will and siren him.

If Amy knew, would she understand why I did it? Or would she think I'm a monster? I wouldn't blame her if she did. A part of me still thinks I am. Clay has forgiven me for what I did to him, but that doesn't mean I've forgiven myself. After all, just because everyone in my family and my Community thinks I'm a hero, doesn't mean I am.

I swing my arm around Amy's shoulders as we walk toward the front gate of our house, and she smiles at me.

All I can do is hope she never finds out. All I can do is hope she doesn't find out tomorrow.

Chapter Four

The man who tried to kill me smiles from across the room. I stop dead in the arching entranceway, my every instinct screaming at me to flee.

"Chin up, Aurelia," my mother whispers, squeezing my hand. She knows what I know. Everyone is watching. Em swims up to my other side and touches her emerald green tail to my gold one under the water in a reassuring gesture. We're at the entrance of the Foundation's impressive courtroom. The Foundation is the closest thing our Community has to a government. To a human observer outside, the building looks like any other modern high-rise. Its stories of blue-green glass appear elegant, but unremarkable. Little do passersby know this building extends nearly as many levels underground as it does above.

We're on one of the lower floors, deep underground. Despite the fact no actual sunlight reaches down here, the backlit blue glass walls ensure the seamless design of the building, with the lower floors like this one retaining the same bright appearance as their upstairs counterparts. But there's one major difference. This room, like many on the lower floors, is filled partway with salt water. Mer swim back and forth, their tails completely submerged while their torsos remain above the waterline.

I barely see them. I'm still staring at the smiling man near the front of this huge courtroom. The man who, not so long ago, wrapped his thick fingers around my throat and tried to strangle me. I swallow. His face is more drawn than it was the last time I saw him and, because the curse has broken, he now looks about two decades younger. But his angular features are as sharp as ever, his eyes as cold. What the hell does he have to smile about?

Em's tail presses against mine again, nudging me forward. She's right—I can't stay here frozen when all the Mer in this room are waiting to see how I'll act. They'll use this trial as a way to not only judge me, but to judge my family. To judge whether Merkind should trust my parents to be their next queen and king.

I force my eyes to flick from the man's disturbing smile to the two guards, one on either side of him, who hold him up. Gripping him above his elbows, they turn him around, and I take in the bronze cuffs locking his wrists behind his back. A chain hangs between his bound wrists and connects to another, larger cuff around the base of his tail. The position forces his tail up and back, immobilizing him. Reminding myself that he can't move, that he can't attack me again, allows me to drag my gaze away from him and propel myself through the entrance to the courtroom.

Still, I'm aware of his presence the whole time, growing nearer to me as I swim down the central aisle between the rows of raised white marble seats that protrude up from the floor and end just below the surface of the water so that when Mer sit on them, our tails remain submerged. I hold my breath as I reach the end of the aisle. He's just to my right now; I can feel him.

"Over here, Lia."

I turn to my left at the sound of Lapis's voice. She nods toward the seat at the very end of the first row, farthest away from him. She,

Lazuli, and Amy are already seated. As Em takes her seat next to them, I realize my family has placed themselves between me and my attempted murderer. At their show of solidarity, I release the breath I've been holding and settle into my seat.

I can still feel him wading there, and a part of me is screaming to find out where she is. His daughter. The other person who tried to kill me. But I don't look for her. Instead, I make a mental game out of spotting the eight guards my parents brought with them from the deep. They sit unobtrusively in seats scattered throughout the courtroom, blending into the crowd but prepared to protect the members of my family at a moment's notice. Once I've found all eight, I avoid the temptation to crane my neck around again looking for her. I focus straight ahead, where a gleaming emblem of a starfish—the ancient symbol of balance and justice under the sea—hangs from the front wall above seven empty, stone seats. They're made of the same white marble as the stool-like seat I sit on, but they're carved to look like seven identical white thrones standing out against the blue glass of the wall.

Normally, my parents would occupy two of those seats, but not today. Not for this trial, where their own daughter is the star witness to the crime. I watch my mother as she swims over to the private box she'll share with my father. It protrudes from the side wall like an opera box, the kind reserved for V.I.P.s. They may not be passing judgement on this trial, but my parents still hold a place of honor. My father, his typical lighthearted smile nowhere in sight, nods solemnly at my mother as she sits, her back straight, her hands folded in her lap, and her opalescent tail glistening under the water.

I do my best to mimic her posture, her confidence. As I'm elongating my spine, the room erupts in whispers when someone walks in.

Yes, walks. Not swims.

Clay's wearing the forest green swim shorts I picked out, and he has a strand of limpet shells strapped diagonally across his bare chest, same as all the Mermen here wear on this formal occasion. But he doesn't pass as a Merman. Since he's not floating in the water, but walking along the floor like he would in the shallow end of a pool, the waterline that hits all of us at the waist, hits him several inches above his belly button. I'm struck with admiration at the calm, determined expression on his face as he walks alone up the central aisle, one foot in front of the other. My parents decided it was better for him to walk in alone than with our family. They said his testimony would be more trustworthy if he appeared strong and self-reliant. They knew everyone would stare at the human in our midst anyway, so there was no point trying to hide him among a crowd of my sisters.

Still, something swells in me when I notice who's swimming at a measured distance behind Clay, keeping an eye on him.

Caspian. My best friend. As he sails down the same aisle on his silver tail, his ocean blue eyes meet mine, and my face splits into a smile. His presence—so sure, so steady—comforts me even here, even knowing what's coming.

Clay turns into the row right behind mine, stands next to the seat right behind mine. In an instant Caspian is beside him, and in one subtle gesture, he offers Clay his hand under the water. Clay grasps it and, muscles flexing, Caspian supports him as Clay raises himself in the water onto his seat.

"Thanks," Clay says, voice low.

"Hey, it's nice having them whisper about somebody else for a change."

Clay smiles, but it's tight-lipped. Caspian's words remind all of us what's at stake. If what I did to save Clay—what I really did—comes to light in this trial, the same crime that ruined Caspian's family's reputation for a century will stain my family's. Will ruin my sisters' futures. Will destroy any chance my parents have for the throne.

See, Caspian's great-great-aunt was a siren.

And so am I.

I'm afraid that's why the man who tried to kill me is smiling. He knows my secret—and he'll be testifying in his own defense. Maybe he's smiling because he's planning to tell every Mer here exactly what I've done.

Or maybe she is. The Mermaid currently being led through the back entrance of the courtroom by two muscular, female guards. Not only did she attempt to kill me, but she did even worse to Clay. The sight of this beautiful, teenage girl with her sleek black hair, sapphire eyes, and sharp cheekbones fills me with revulsion.

I'd hoped the months that have passed since I've seen her—months she's spent in a Federation jail cell—would have lessened the effect she has on me. But, nope. At the first glimpse of her, my insides burn with an anger I've never felt toward anyone else. The things she did … the things I did because of her … Not even the bronze chain bending her slender coral tail backward and connecting it to her wrists makes me feel better. On her, it manages to look more like a piece of jewelry than a punishment. She's not smiling like her father is, but she holds her head high. How can she look so unruffled? I glance up at the starfish emblem again and hope with everything I have she doesn't find some way to slither out of getting what she deserves. She couldn't, could she?

A hush descends as the arched door next to my parents' box opens, and seven stately Mer swim through it. I recognize four of them as the Mermaids and Mermen who sit on the Community board with my parents. Because I haven't seen most of them since before we all got our immortality back, some of them look years—even decades—younger, but they're still familiar. The other three I've never seen before.

"They're representatives from the three most powerful noble families under the sea," Em whispers to Amy off to my right. "If we want the sentencing to be upheld both Above and Below—if we want to start any kind of reunification—it has to be this way."

More whispers arise behind me. "Is that like the jury?" Clay asks Caspian.

"More like a jury and judge combined," Caspian says. "That's the *domstitii*—the Tribunal. See the strands of trochus shells wrapped around their arms?" Caspian nods at the lengths of small, iridescent seashells that wind tightly up the forearms of all the Tribunal. "They're an ancient symbol reminding everyone here that the *domstitii* are bound to carry out justice." Leave it to Caspian. Even I didn't know that one.

Each of the seven Tribunal members takes a seat in one of the seven thrones lining the front wall; their bright tails stand out like an array of jewels against the white marble.

When the Mermaid occupying the center throne speaks, her words echo off the walls and water. *"Maids and Men, today is the saddest of days. We gather here because heinous crimes have been committed. Crimes that should never have disrupted our Community,"* she gestures to the members of the Tribunal visiting from Below, *"either of our communities."* Behind me, Caspian whispers an English translation of the Mermese into Clay's ear. *"Crimes the likes of which we thought we'd seen the last of,"* she continues. All over the courtroom, people offer solemn nods of agreement. *"However, let us not forget that today is also the happiest of days, for today we gather here to mete out justice so we can put these crimes behind us and move forward,"* another inclusive gesture, *"united."* That last word in particular seems to reverberate off the water surrounding us.

One by one, Mer in the gallery begin repeating it, until the chant of *"united, united, united"* rises to the high ceiling. For longer than I've been alive, the notion of all Mer, those from Below and those from Above, being united once again has been a dream. The idea that it's actually happening—that we're helping to make it happen here, today—clutches at something in the hearts of every one of us.

She raises her tailfin and taps it against the surface of the water, calling for order. Once silence settles over the crowd, she says, *"Let us now hear the recitation of criminal acts."*

The two guards who hold Mr. Havelock bring him into the aisle so that he's directly across from the center throne; since I'm in the first row, if I turn to my right, I can glimpse his face. And, damn him, he's still smiling.

"Begin," all seven of the Tribunal members instruct in unison.

"My name is Filius Havelock, and I am charged with the crimes of planning and attempting to carry out the murder of both a human and a Mer while practicing illegal dark magic," from every direction, eyes dart to Clay and me, *"and of teaching a siren song to my daughter."* As soon as he utters the word "siren," there's an audible intake of breath from the audience.

Beginning a trial with a recitation of crimes is a way for the accused to experience the shame associated with their actions. Whether they are guilty or not, the shame of being accused will stay with them, with their families. If they are guilty, the recitation is a time for them to show remorse. But I don't see a trace of remorse on Mr. Havelock's face.

The Tribunal seems nearly as disappointed by his persistent smile as I do. A few of them scowl in disapproval.

"Is that the full recitation of your crimes?" the Mermaid on the center throne asks, following procedure.

"It is."

"Very well. May justice be your adversary and your advocate."

The guards on either side of him pull him back to where he waited before. As they turn him around, he looks straight at me and winks.

I shudder. I barely have time to hope no one saw me because, at that moment, two other guards bring *her* to the center to replace him.

"Begin," the Tribunal members say together for a second time.

"My name is Melusine Havelock," her syrupy voice makes my skin prickle, and the sound of her name makes me sick, *"and I am charged with the crimes of attempting to carry out the murder of both a human and a Mer while participating in illegal dark magic conducted by my father, and ... "* the air grows thick with tension as everyone in attendance holds their breath, *"of sirening a human."*

Glancing behind me, I see people avert their eyes to the ground as they gasp. Even though every person in the courtroom knew what she was charged with, hearing her say it aloud confirms what they've wanted so much to deny: For the first time in a hundred years, they have a siren in their midst. What would they say if they knew they had two?

When she recited the last crime, Melusine's voice broke, and now she too fixes her gaze on the ground. This response meets with nods of approval from the Tribunal.

Oh no. Is she going to fake remorse and hope they go easy on her? It won't work. It won't.

"Is that the full recitation of your crimes?" asks the Mermaid on the center throne.

"Will I ... have more time to explain?" Melusine asks instead of answering the question.

The central Mermaid shifts slightly, uncomfortable with this deviation from the traditional script. Melusine lifts her gaze to the woman's face, her sapphire eyes pleading and vulnerable. The woman's expression softens. *"You will."* Returning to a more formal tone, the woman repeats, *"Is that the full recitation of your crimes?"*

"It is." Melusine's voice, normally so full of confidence and mocking, sounds subdued.

"Very well. May justice be your adversary and your advocate."

As the guards escort Melusine back to her place, she too stares right at me, just for a second. But I can read nothing in her eyes.

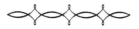

The first Mer to testify are the Foundation authorities who investigated the case. They've used a combination of magic, logic, and human technology to analyze all the events that occurred the day Melusine and her father kidnapped Clay with the intention of killing him in an ancient ritual. One by one, three different investigators describe finding both Melusine and her father knocked out at the crime scene, where they also found the cursed obsidian dagger with its hilt covered in the Havelocks' fingerprints.

An assistant with a tail all the colors of sunset brings that same dagger up to the Tribunal in a clear glass box so it can be entered into evidence. Others shift in their seats in hopes of getting a closer look, but from my place in the front row, nothing obstructs my view. A view I wish I didn't have. A view of the spiny black blade that was once coated in Clay's blood.

In a flash, I'm back under the waves, fighting to pull an unconscious Clay to the surface while he bleeds and bleeds and bleeds. All that blood snaking into the water around us still stains my mind a gruesome red.

As the investigator describes how he linked the illegal potion ingredients for the spell back to Melusine's father, I can't help stealing a glance behind me at Clay, just to reassure myself he's all right. It's silly, but seeing his healed, smooth abdomen makes me feel better. Like I can keep breathing.

One of the investigators describes each ingredient as its remnants from the crime scene are entered into evidence alongside the dagger.

"This was an intricate, premeditated, and malicious crime," he says in closing. *"My colleagues and I urge the Tribunal to issue the harshest of sentences. Thank you for your time."*

Good. Good. We're off to a good start. Caspian translates the last sentence for Clay, and the three of us share the same hopeful smile with each other.

When Caspian swims up to face the Tribunal and takes an oath swearing on the safety of the seas and the power of the current to tell the truth, it's my turn to translate for Clay. I don't do a very good job.

"They're asking him all sorts of questions about how he got

involved with rescuing us."

"And?" Clay whispers back, "What's he saying?"

"He's telling them about finding those ancient Mermese symbols in Mr. Havelock's office while he was interning for him."

"I know written Mermese," Caspian says. *"Studying it is a hobby of mine. I like languages."*

A few eyebrows rise amongst the Tribunal. Mermese has been a strictly oral language for centuries—ever since we learned to seal our voices in seashells and stopped needing written records, which were hard to create underwater. Now, only the highest-level linguistic scholars know how to write in Mermese. *"Can anyone present today verify you know written Mermese characters?"*

Several hands around the courtroom lift into the air, including those of Caspian's parents, his grandmother (who, at ninety-four, doesn't look a day over thirty thanks to her newfound immortality), and my parents. I, too, lift my hand in the air.

"Why are you raising your hand?" Clay whispers. "Should I raise mine?"

"No," I say, "don't worry about it. We're just verifying a minor fact so the court doesn't need to further investigate it."

"Weird."

The Tribunal member who posed the question has us recite our names for the record. Then she turns to Caspian and says, *"Very well. Please continue."*

Caspian takes a deep breath. *"When I found the ancient Mermese symbols in Mr. Havelock's office, I copied them down out of curiosity and started working on translating them. A few weeks later, on the morning … the morning everything happened … I went to Clay's house because I thought Lia might be there. The door was unlocked, and when I went up to his room, it looked like there'd been a fight. There was blood on the sheets, and all over the walls, someone had drawn those same ancient symbols. By then, I'd studied them enough to know how to translate them. They mapped out coordinates. It was part of the spell—marking Clay's bedroom with the place under the sea where he would sleep forever in death.*" Caspian runs a hand through his blond hair, sweeping it back from his face. *"I knew Lia must have gotten there before me and gone after him. That's when I went home and grabbed the kit of healing potions my grandmother keeps for emergencies. I knew where Mr. Havelock kept the keys to his boat, so I took it and headed out to those coordinates. That's how I was there in time to pull Lia and Clay out of the water after the Havelocks tried to kill them, and that's how I had the potions with me that … that … saved them.*"

He looks from one member of the Tribunal to the next, his rich baritone deepening even further with the seriousness of his next words. *"I know I should have gone to the Foundation authorities, asked for help, but there was no time and honestly … I was too scared to think straight. Too scared that she'd … that they'd die.*"

The Mermaid on the central throne offers him a sympathetic smile. *"Considering how close they came to meeting that fate, I'd say your quick response, albeit unorthodox, proved necessary. We're all very grateful to you.*"

The water around us ripples as Mer swish their tails in applause. The lightest of blushes creeps into Caspian's cheeks.

"What's happening?" Clay asks.

"Caspian saved us."

"Duh."

"Just one more question, young man, and then you may take your seat," the Mermaid at the center says to Caspian. He straightens, ready. *"What made you so sure Aurelia Nautilus had gone after the human Clay Ericson? How would she know where to go?*"

Caspian keeps his gaze steady, his face impassive, but I see the muscles in his throat working as he swallows. He's nervous. I doubt anyone else in the courtroom notices, but they don't know him as well as I do.

And I'm nervous, too. So far, every word out of Caspian's mouth has been the truth. But now …

I knew where to find Clay because we shared a siren bond. We still do, and we probably always will. It means I can trace him, feel him, no matter how far away he is. I haven't used it since that day, when I traced him to the ruins of the castle deep in the ocean where Melusine held him captive. But there's no way to explain the bond without revealing I sirened him.

Caspian has lied for me before, but never in a court of law. Never after swearing an oath to tell the truth. The punishment for lying under oath is imprisonment—and now that we're immortal, imprisonment terms start at fifty years. I don't want Caspian to risk that for me. Protecting me's not worth that. Before I can do anything—interrupt, intervene, anything—Caspian's talking again.

"*I knew she'd gone after him because she could read the symbols, too. I taught her how when I first translated them.*" And just like that, Caspian—noble, moral Caspian who a few months ago had probably never told a lie, and certainly never when it mattered—has risked his very freedom.

"*Can anyone present today verify you taught her the symbols?*"

Slowly, I raise my hand into the air. With a knowing look in my direction, so does Caspian's grandmother, the woman who convinced me not to confess in the first place and explained the damage clearing my conscience would do to my family.

Seeing our raised hands, Clay whispers, "Now what?"

The words stick in my throat, along with the tears of gratitude I can't shed. "Caspian saved me."

Just then, my best friend glances back at me, and when his cobalt gaze meets mine, I pour all my energy into conveying to him how much his words, his sacrifice, mean to me. His small nod tells me he understands.

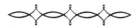

The next woman to testify is a Mermaid I don't recognize.

Not only do I not recognize her, she looks like nothing I've ever seen. Her pale, nearly translucent skin tells me she's visiting from Below. That skin, along with her beautiful, doll-like features, makes her look like someone carved her out of porcelain. Tiny pieces of the clearest crystal sparkle around her eyes and up into her hairline, glittering like diamonds.

But that's not what startles me, not what takes my breath away as she swims up the aisle toward the front of the room. The white-blond hair that runs in loose, lustrous waves down to her waist is streaked with ice-blue strands that perfectly match her tail.

I'd heard that could happen Below, that when Mer spend all their time in the farthest reaches of the ocean, sometimes their hair begins to grow the same color as their tails. But I'm not sure how, and until now, I'd never seen it. I'm not even sure if I believed it. As she floats through the water, tall and graceful, with tendrils of her blue-streaked hair skimming the surface, it's like gazing at an illustration come to life.

She's a mythical creature, a Mermaid straight out of a storybook. So fantastical, so surreal, I get the feeling if I reached out to touch her, she'd turn to sea foam.

"Wow," Clay says, not even bothering to whisper.

I'd tell him to pick his jaw up off the floor, but mine's right there next to his. I've never seen anyone who looked so … magical.

How did I not see her before? Was she sitting way in back? Was she late? Whatever the reason, she's front and center now, and everyone is waiting for her to speak.

A guard swims over and presents the same conch shell, large as a cantaloupe, that Caspian and the investigators used earlier during their oaths. Now, just like he did, she takes it and places the opening of the shell against her heart.

"Upon this symbol of the almighty waves, I swear by the power of the current and for the safety of the Seven Seas to speak only the truth." Her

words glide out in the smooth, swift rhythm of a native Mermese speaker, and although her voice is airy and light, it manages to resonate throughout the cavernous room.

"Please state your name for all assembled," instructs a member of the Tribunal.

"Ondine. Ondine Naiad." As the sound of her name clinks against the blue glass walls, she pauses as if mustering the fortitude to say whatever comes next. *"I'm a cousin of the Havelocks on my mother's side. I've come to offer insight into their character and upbringing for the court."*

This woman—this fairytale princess—is related to Melusine and her eel of a father? Distrust now taints my awe.

"As many of you here today may know," she continues once the Tribunal instructs her to proceed, *"the Havelocks' family—my family—has long held a reputation for being udell."* Udell is an ancient word meaning human-hater. I used to wonder if Melusine and her father were *udell*; now there's no doubt in my mind. Is this woman *udell*, too? *"After rigorous study of both human ways and our own Mer history, I have come to disagree with my family's beliefs."* Has she really, or is she lying? *"Humans have a great deal to teach us. But I know for a fact my cousin Filius doesn't think so. When he first moved up to the surface, claiming to have renounced his antiquated beliefs, I'd hoped ... but he fooled me the way he fooled the authorities here. He hadn't changed. And he hasn't changed. He's udell."*

She's stating something everyone already knows, or at least strongly suspects. She came all the way from Below just to tell us that?

"You may be asking yourself why I'm bothering to tell you that at all. I'm telling you because it matters. Motives matter. I know my cousin. He's going to come up here in a few minutes' time and swear that the crimes he committed, he committed for all of you. So you could regain immortality, glory, and strength. But the truth is, he doesn't care about your glory. All he cares about is his own.

"For us Mer who have come here today from Below, and who have never so much as laid eyes on a human like this young man here," she extends a willowy arm in Clay's direction, *"it may be easy to believe that my cousin's plan to sacrifice an unending stream of human lives in exchange for Mer immortality made sense, that his actions were warranted by his desire for the greater good. But I'm here to tell you they weren't. I knew his parents growing up; he was raised to hate humans, to blame them for all the troubles our kind face. When he performed that ritual, he planned to capitalize on that hatred, to bring himself power by making all of us indebted to him. By making our very lives dependent on his rule, his dynasty."* She turns outward to address the gallery. *"Whatever he tells you, please remember that. He didn't intend to be your savior. He intended to be your dictator. And for that, he should be punished."*

I don't know if I've ever heard someone so dainty and soft-spoken infuse her words with so much power, so much confidence. My distrust fades. I like her. I like the unwavering glint in her eyes that says she knows she's right. There's a fearlessness there.

I wish I felt it, too. Because as afraid as I am that Mr. Havelock will try to manipulate the court by saying all the things she just warned us about, I'm much more afraid he'll say something else. Will he try to turn the court's focus away from him and his daughter and on to me and my crime? Surely he doesn't think anyone would believe him. Right?

I must get lost in thought because I don't hear what the blue-haired Mermaid—was it Ondine?—says next. I don't tune back in until Amy elbows me in the ribs from where she sits next to me, distress written on her face.

"While I beg the court to punish my cousin Filius, I beg them to have mercy on Melusine. I don't deny what she did is unquestionably disgusting and disturbing, but please remember this is a teenage girl who lost her mother less than a year ago to the same wars that have killed the loved ones of so many here today, leaving her alone with a manipulative,

human-hating father." Ondine turns back to face the Tribunal, fixing her gaze on each of them in turn. *"Remember she's just a child."*

Please. She's a child like I'm a child. Why is it adults think seventeen-year-olds can't think for ourselves? Turning eighteen—or even twenty, as dictated by Mer culture—and suddenly not being considered a child under the law anymore isn't the same as getting legs for the first time. I'm not going to magically transform. No insta-adult logic is going to spring into my brain the way toes sprang out of my tail when I was fourteen. Claiming Melusine did what she did because she's a child is a cop-out. If that were true, it would basically mean nothing I've done yet in my life matters. And it does. The good, the bad—they matter. And they should count. I'm glad Caspian has taken back the responsibility of translating for Clay because I'm not sure I could talk without yelling right now if I tried.

I don't care what reason this woman has for appealing to the court on Melusine's behalf. That so-called child spent weeks brainwashing the boy I love more than anything—oh, and tried to stab both of us to death. She deserves to be thrown in a cell for the rest of her immortal life.

Anyone who could do what she did is dangerous.

I feel something brush against my sides. A glance down tells me it was two somethings. Caspian and Clay must know her words upset me, because they've both leaned forward and stuck a hand out on either side of my lap from where they sit next to one another in the row behind me. My head moves from left to right before I take one hand in each of mine. When Ondine glides back down the aisle on her ice-blue tail, I level her with my worst glare.

But soon glaring won't be enough. Soon even the comfort of Clay and Caspian's hands in mine won't tame the clashing waves of fury and fear roiling within me. Because the Tribunal has just called for the last testimony of the day. Within moments, Mr. Havelock is holding the conch shell to his heart and swearing to tell the truth.

Chapter Five

At least his cousin's words have wiped away Mr. Havelock's smile. Still, he doesn't look scared or even bitter as he wades before the Tribunal in his wrist-to-fin cuffs. Instead, he's eerily calm.

"Filius Havelock, you have recited the crimes of which you are accused. Do you deny committing these crimes?"

"It would be foolhardy to deny them when your experts," Mr. Havelock says the word experts like he'll never trust it, *"have provided you with a pile of evidence to the contrary—and when, before this trial is over, you'll hear the sob stories of two sniveling teenagers telling you I tried to kill them."* Despite how low he has seemingly fallen, Mr. Havelock speaks with the same haughtiness he did the night I met him at my parents' sparkling gala. His confidence makes my palms itch. *"No, I won't deny what I did. I will, however, deny that anything I did was a crime."*

Scandalized murmurs sweep through every row.

"I assure you, Mr. Havelock," says the Mermaid on the central throne, her tone brimming with censure, *"attempted murder, unauthorized use of restricted dark spells, and teaching sireny all qualify*

as crimes of the highest order. By denying that fact, by not showing appropriate remorse, you'll only force our fins and earn yourself the harshest of sentences."

"Ancient magics, the ones you call 'dark' and 'restricted,' are not subject to your authority," Mr. Havelock replies, staring down his nose at her. *"Such magics are the only way to tap directly into the power of the ocean. As a child of the ocean, accessing that power is my birthright. And all of yours."* He turns out to face the Mer who've come from far and wide to see him punished. *"No court has the authority to deny that birthright, for the ocean is mightier than any Tribunal, mightier than any law or any ruler."* Something sinister creeps into his voice now, blackening the edges of his words. A frenzied tension coils beneath them. *"Do you want to know the real reason monarchs outlawed these magics in centuries past?"* He lowers his voice to a conspiratorial whisper and, all over the room, Mer lean forward in their marble seats to hear him—fish biting the bait. *"Because our monarchs were afraid."*

He stops scanning the crowd and lets his eyes rest right on mine. *"They knew what most today have forgotten. That ancient dark magic— like the ritual I performed or, say, a siren spell—plants something inside the person who cast it."* Now, his eyes bore into mine, burrowing deep. *"A spell like that, why, it leaves a little seed of darkness that never goes away. And over time that darkness will grow and grow until—"*

The central Mermaid slaps her tail against the water's surface to silence him. *"That's quite enough. Regardless of what you believe or don't believe, Mr. Havelock, this court does indeed have the jurisdiction to restrict such magic, and we'll take every legal step to do so."*

She continues with a series of questions about how he managed to find a siren song to teach to his daughter even though authorities had seized and smashed all shell recordings of such songs over a hundred years earlier. I barely listen as he explains how generations of his family passed the song down in secret; instead, I replay his earlier words in my head.

When I sirened Clay, did I plant a seed of darkness within myself that's still growing? I think about how hard it was for me to let him go ... how tempting it had been to siren him again the day I knew he was finally safe from Melusine's spell. Was that because of some dark impulse budding within me? What if it's still in me right now? What if it's been festering in me all this time and I didn't even know it?

What if it's the real, selfish reason I haven't come clean to my family?

Lost in these dark thoughts, I nearly jump out of my scales when fingers grip my shoulder from behind. "You okay?" Clay whispers, his thumb moving in a soothing circle against the base of my neck. I nod, but only because I can't speak.

Several members of the Tribunal pose their own questions to Mr. Havelock, and he answers with that same eerie calm. Then the central Mermaid, whose tight lips and narrowed eyes say she's ready to see the guards carry him away, asks, *"Is there anything else you think the court should consider while coming to our decisions in this case?"* Her tone conveys it's a routine question, one to which she doesn't expect an answer.

But he gives one anyway.

"Why, yes. Just one more thing." Mr. Havelock's eyes land on me again and he says in a voice as smooth as seasilk, *"I'd like to share something about Miss Aurelia Nautilus."*

Chapter Six

All over the cavernous courtroom, gazes leap from Mr. Havelock to me, searing into every visible part of me. My breath quickens to shallow pants as I hold my body stiff as a coral rod.

Still, he doesn't speak, the silence stretching tight.

"We're waiting, Mr. Havelock," the Mermaid on the central throne says at last. *"What is it you'd like to tell us about Miss Nautilus?"*

His shrewd, sharp eyes lock onto mine, and my whole life narrows to the words leaving his mouth. *"She'll make an excellent ruler one day."*

A smile—the same smile he wore earlier—curls his thin lips. His eyes continue to pierce me, and his words spark instant realization. I know why he's smiling.

Whispers erupt all around me. No one has said anything openly yet about my parents' possible rise to the throne. Until now. Everyone in my family and on the board of the Foundation has carefully—strategically—avoided the topic and kept the focus on fostering peace and reconstruction Below.

Even if my parents did take the throne, that wouldn't make me a ruler in my own right. I'd be a princess (which is way too weird to wrap my brain around … me, a princess? So surreal), but I wouldn't be directly in line for the throne because I'm not my parents' firstborn. Now that we are once again immortal, the traditional laws of the monarchy would apply.

Each Mer reign would last 300 years, a period long enough to ensure each ruler had time to accomplish something tangible that could propel society forward, but not indefinite to guard against corruption and to allow for a fresh, innovative perspective. That means my mother would pass the throne to Em, her eldest child, after she and my father reigned for three hundred years. Then Em and Leo would reign for three hundred years (three hundred years!) before passing the crown to their eldest child.

That's when it dawns on me. While I might not be a queen, as a member of the ruling family, I would be a ruler (a *riliika* in Mermese, the word Mr. Havelock used) once I turned twenty because I'd serve as an advisor to the crown and would be able to effect change.

That's what Mr. Havelock is counting on! That's why he won't utter a word about my sireny; he's trying to buy my allegiance with his silence. Of course. If he accuses me of sireny—even if the Tribunal believes him—it won't stop them from finding him guilty on all counts and doling out the life sentence he deserves. He's too smart to choose vengeance against me when my goodwill could someday mean a transfer to a nicer cell with more lenient guards, better meals, or maybe even a shorter sentence.

Why didn't I see this plan coming? Before my brain has even formulated the thought, I know the answer. Having been raised in the human world, I think too much like a human; Mr. Havelock was raised Below, and unlike me, he thinks like a Mer through and through. He's playing the long game. After all, what're a few centuries to wait when you face an immortality behind bars? He's using the only leverage he's got and hoping to win my favor. He isn't just smiling—he's smiling at me.

It won't work. His decision not to rat me out isn't going to make me so grateful that I petition for his freedom when—if—my family takes the throne. But I don't have to let him know that. I refuse to smile back, but I don't scowl either. With our eyes still locked, I keep my face impassive. Let the sea slime interpret that however he wants.

I'm not the only one keeping my face impassive. My parents sit in their side box looking unruffled by this unexpected allusion to their possible ascendancy. Only I (and I'm sure my sisters sitting stiff as sandstone at my sides) can see how much effort they're putting into this appearance of calm. As my parents must have known would happen, the Mermaid on the central throne checks for their reaction, as does nearly everyone on the Tribunal who isn't currently staring at me. Recovering quickly, she slaps her tail against the water again, silencing the gossiping voices of the onlookers. *"Whatever destiny awaits Miss Nautilus,"* she says the words slowly, diplomatically, *"all evidence suggests your actions nearly robbed her of it. You're lucky she's alive today, for your own sake as well as your daughter's. If you've nothing to add in your own defense, you can return to the gallery."*

She's good. She neither acknowledged my parents' right to the throne nor refuted it. That's not the issue up for judgment—at least not today. As the guards lead Mr. Havelock away from the center of the room, I breathe a little easier for the first time in weeks. Whatever he might expect of me in the years ahead that I would never, could never, repay, I've averted the dangers his testimony posed. Today's threat has passed.

But from the edge of my vision, Melusine seizes my attention. Those sapphire eyes glare at her father with anger, with a pent-up fury as sharp as the blade of the cursed obsidian dagger that's now being carried off and locked away as evidence.

Is she angry with him for not accusing me? For not saying anything in her defense like her cousin did? For something else entirely?

The relief that slowed my breathing moments before vanishes as I try to imagine what Melusine will say when it's her turn to testify. I have no choice but to wait to find out. The Tribunal calls the first day of the trial to a close before gliding through the water into their private chambers. Like all Mer trials, this one began at the end of the week to ensure everyone in attendance—especially the Tribunal members—has time to reflect on what they've heard. But I've been reflecting on these events the whole summer, so for me, the Tribunal's exit is a promise that, until Monday at least, I can try to put Melusine and her father out of my head.

Two days later, after spending Saturday trying (and failing) to relax in my pool with my sisters, another father occupies my thoughts. Clay's. If you can even call a man who barely spoke to his own son for six years a father. *Stop*, I tell myself. Feeding my anger at him won't make this any easier for Clay, and isn't that the whole reason I'm going? To support Clay. Besides, it seems like, for the first time in a long time, his dad is trying.

I remind myself of that when, after three and a half hours in Clay's blue Mustang, I sit across the table from a man with a weather-beaten face and a permanently stern expression that he's forced into what he must think is a welcoming smile.

After the initial pleasantries, we fill the ensuing awkward silence by staring at our menus.

Clay clears his throat. "This place looks great."

It doesn't really. The overly elegant tablecloths and overly chic waitstaff tell me this is one of those California Italian places where no one orders the pasta because they're either a.) not eating carbs or b.) aware they'll get only a meager, artsy serving of noodles with even less sauce.

"Never been here before myself," Clay's dad says, rubbing a hand over his clean-shaven jaw. "Tash recommended it." At least she had the good sense not to come tonight. Having a double date with my boyfriend's father and his girlfriend? No thank you. "I told her you like Italian?" Clay's dad turns his sentence into a question at the end, like he's not sure his intel is current.

"Yep, Italian's great."

"And Lia? You like Italian?"

"It's great," I say. Not that this will be anything close to actual Italian.

"Great," he says as he drums his fingers on the tabletop.

A waitress wearing too much lip liner saves us and, since I don't trust the pasta, I order the sea bass. If nothing else, I'm going to get some omega three out of this dinner.

"I'll do the same," Clay tells the waitress.

"Really?" Clay's dad shakes his head. "When you were younger, you wouldn't touch fish."

Clay's eyes shift over to meet mine as he smirks, and I have to hide my snicker behind my menu. When the waitress takes it, I'm still blushing at the memory of Clay's hand on my tail, his long fingers splayed out against the gold.

"So, Lia, do you know where you're applying for next year?"

Mr. Ericson's question snaps me back to reality. Why is it that the second you're a senior, all anyone wants to know is what colleges you'll be applying to? It's like all other aspects of your life cease to exist.

At least I have an answer all prepared. "I have a list of schools, but I'm hoping for Pepperdine. It's where my sisters go. And my oldest sister just graduated from there." I don't mention they all chose it so they can commute from home and still spend nights and weekends letting their tails free in our hidden grottos and on our private beach.

"Family tradition," Mr. Ericson says in an approving voice. He turns his attention to Clay. "You know, both West Point and Annapolis are still accepting applications. I'm sure I could help rustle you up a nomination from a congressman or..." He trails off but keeps his gaze focused on Clay, steady, like he's used to offering his son help. Like it isn't the first time in years.

"Thanks," Clay says, meeting his eyes and staying just as steady. "Really, thanks." From the brief cinching of Clay's brow and set of his mouth, I know the offer surprised him—that it meant something—and for the first time since we sat down, I'm glad we came. "But I'm set on music theory and composition," Clay finishes. As Clay's dad asks him about his list of schools, I fight to keep the smile plastered on my face.

Northwestern, Curtis, Cornell—all excellent music programs and all thousands of miles away. I'd be rooting for USC's Thornton School of Music if I really was planning on Pepperdine myself, but I'm not planning on anything. I have no plan. How can I? I was confused about my future before this whole immortality/could-live-in-the-ocean/might-become-royalty shebang. Now that I'll ... live forever ... (how is that even possible?), I could go to college any time. I could go ten times. But what's the point of going at all if I wind up living in the ocean floating in some castle? Every question leads to a string of twenty more, and I don't know the answers to any of them.

All I know is I won't leave Clay. Not after everything we've been through to be together. But I won't stand in the way of his dreams, either. That's not what love is. That's why I've spent the last two months since school got out (and we became incoming seniors) encouraging him to apply to all those faraway colleges—all those places so far from the beach that I could never live in them. I've insisted he can't tether his future to mine when mine is still drifting with the current. Because, unlike me, Clay can't go to college ten times. This is his shot, his life. His one life. He's not going to ...

Every time he wants to talk about it, I put him off. With the trial looming and the threat of my sireny being revealed, he's let me. But now that the trial's in full swing, now that I might come out of it unscathed, the conversation's coming. He won't let me put it off forever. He doesn't have forever, so—

Clay's knee knocks mine under the table and I refocus in time to see his father shoot me a questioning look. Great, way to be on top of things, Lia. "Sorry?" I mumble.

"Your major? Just wondering if you're musical like my boy … like Clay here." Right. The dreaded question requiring all seniors to narrow their lives down to one set path, one pre-drawn line in the sand.

"I'm deciding between undeclared and maybe marine bio." I know what you're thinking—more lies. But if I do end up going to college, Pepperdine does have some cool opportunities for biology majors to study marine organisms, visit intertidal sites, and get involved in ocean conservation. I know I could never major in business the way Em does, and Lapis and Lazuli are majoring in poli-sci and international relations, respectively, which are both kind of interesting. Politics has never been my thing though, because, well, I've never had a thing. With marine bio, I could learn more about the world I come from, about myself, about … I don't know … how I connect to it, maybe.

"Oh, that's right. I should have guessed marine biology. I keep forgetting you're *that* Nautilus. Your family runs the Foundation for the Preservation and Protection of Marine Life." I nod. "I'll most likely be meeting one of your parents this coming week. I have an appointment with the board over there."

"You do?" I know the Foundation has met with naval representatives before, but usually that's handled by people lower down in the P.R. department so someone in a uniform can get some pictures shaking hands with charity representatives, maybe smiling next to a dolphin. Clay's dad's an officer. Why would he meet with the board? "Why are you meeting with the board?" I ask, keeping my tone light.

He straightens in his seat, his expression unreadable. "Collaboration. Keeping communication open. Very typical." He takes a sip of his water, then asks, "I assume you'll be joining the family business after you graduate?"

"That's kind of T.B.D.," I say, as the waitress sets down plates of overly precious food decorated with dainty curlicues of unidentifiable sauces.

Clay must realize how much I hate this discussing-Lia's-future conversation because his hazel eyes meet mine, offering a reassuring gleam before he gestures to his food and says, "Looks fantastico," in a too-loud Italian accent. Some of the more uppity patrons turn to stare, and the corner of Mr. Ericson's mouth quirks up in a smile. In that second, he looks so much like Clay that I can't help the surge of emotion in my chest telling me to like him. But then my brain remembers how much pain he's caused Clay, and I remind myself it's so much more complicated.

As we eat, we cover all the remaining basics: school, Clay's upcoming gigs, my Austenian number of sisters. I smile big and try to keep the conversation light and sunny, to make this a nice memory for Clay. He can use as many nice memories with his dad as he can get.

By the time the check comes, we're tapped out of small talk. When the waitress brings back Mr. Ericson's credit card, Clay and I are ready to thank him for dinner and spend the rest of the night just the two of us. Considering the portion sizes here, I'm hoping some of that time will be spent eating our weight in frozen yogurt. The silence drags, and there's something in Clay's expression—in the way his lips fold in on themselves and the brief sadness in his eyes—that makes me wish we didn't want to leave. What must it be like to run out of things to say to your own father? Maybe the fro-yo will help soothe Clay's disappointment.

But the second Clay shifts in his chair like he's getting up, his dad's hand lunges across the table onto his, holding him in place. "Wait."

Clay freezes, and so do I, my bag midway to my shoulder. Aside from an awkward half hug when we arrived, this is the first physical contact they've had all night.

"Wait," Mr. Ericson says again. He takes his hand off Clay's, and claps it on the tabletop a couple of times. Clears his throat. "I, uh ..." His gaze slides over to me before shifting back to his son. Whatever he wants to say to Clay, he wishes I weren't here, wishes they were alone. I'm about to excuse myself to the ladies' room when

Clay squeezes my knee under the table, a silent plea for me to stay. Whatever Clay's dad might want, I'm not here for him. I'm sitting at this table for Clay, and I'll stay sitting here however long he wants. However long he needs.

Clay's dad flicks his nose with his thumb and gazes at me once more before settling his eyes on Clay and setting his shoulders. "I wanted to say ... that is ... I asked you to get dinner so I could ... tell you ... "

Clay squeezes my knee again, clutching me, and I rest my hand on top of his tensed fingers.

His dad's gaze glues itself to his own large hands resting in front of him. "Stuff with your mom got ... hard. It was easier just to—but I shouldn't've." His posture stiffens further as he clears his throat. "I should've come up more often. I told myself you were busy with school, probably didn't want to see me—"

"No, I—" Clay stops, the words catching in his throat.

"I should've come up more," his dad repeats. "I know you'll be heading off to college, and I don't want ... " As he shakes his head, his features pinched, this large, tough man sitting across from me looks suddenly small. "Maybe we can do this more often until you go. Dinner or a game maybe."

Clay doesn't really watch sports, but he's nodding anyway. "That'd be nice."

Even though Mr. Ericson's spine stays ramrod straight, something in his face, in his breathing, sags with relief. "Good." He reaches through the distance across the table and claps a firm hand on his son's shoulder. "Good."

◁◇◇◇▷

Clay stays quiet for most of the car ride home. I leave him be, giving him space. It isn't until the beachfront restaurants and storefronts along the Pacific Coast Highway start looking familiar again that he speaks. I expect him to say something about dinner, about his dad. Instead he says, "I want to stay in California. For college."

My jaw drops. I recover enough to ask, "Is this because of your dad?"

"No. Yes. Not the way you're thinking." He stops, but I force myself not to bombard him with the zillion questions now splish-splashing around in my head. After what feels like forever, he starts talking again. "I want to believe my dad'll follow through, I do, but …"

But he's not ready to get his hopes up. "I know," I say.

"If he does, staying in California would mean getting the chance to see him, which would be great, but that's not why I want to stay. I think of all the time he wasted." We reach Sunset Boulevard right as the light turns red. Clay uses the opportunity to face me. "I refuse to waste time. I'm not going to live forever." The words hang there between us, heavy and cold as glaciers. "I know you want me to apply to all those East Coast schools because you don't want me to give anything up for you. You don't want me to stay in California just for you. But I wouldn't be staying for you—I'd be staying for us." Emotion swells inside me as the light turns green and he steps on the gas.

"And for me," Clay adds, voice low. "You haven't wanted to talk about it, so I haven't pushed you, but I've done a ton of research, and some of the top music schools are right here." I stare at his profile as he watches the road. Have I been so determined not to stand in the way of what he wants I've stopped listening to him? Maybe what he wants has changed. I listen now. Really listen.

"Besides," he says, "I made that list of schools two years ago. There's more I want to do now. I've … I've been thinking about taking scuba lessons."

His quiet words fill the entire car. "Really?"

He nods, stealing a glance at me before focusing back on the traffic. The fact that I'm grinning like a parrotfish must embolden him, because he releases a breath. Soon, that familiar smirk graces his lips. "Like I was gonna let you have all that fun late at night without me."

He's talking about my late-night swims in the ocean, but when he raises an eyebrow suggestively, my face—no, my whole body—heats.

As the traffic around us lightens, his tone turns more serious. "I want to see as much of your world as I can. To really understand it."

Am I dreaming? Did he just say ...

"Somehow, I think I'll get more out of scuba diving in California than I will in Pennsylvania or upstate New York. What do you say, you think it would be all right with you if I stay put?"

Thank the tides we've reached another stoplight, because I throw my arms around him and smatter the side of his face with kisses until he's laughing, rich and deep. Once the car's moving again, I sink down low in my leather seat and stare out the windshield. Headlights, streetlights, the illumination from bustling, roadside restaurants—all of it blends together against the deep blackness of the street and sky, swims in my vision as my eyes brim over with tears.

I'm so happy.

Early the next morning, I cling to that happiness with everything I have as I swim back into the courtroom. But as soon as I'm seated and court's in session, piranhas bite into the pit of my stomach. Today—mere minutes from now—Melusine will testify.

Chapter Seven

I should be scared she won't be as strategic as her father and will reveal my sireny. I should be scared she'll say something that will hurt Clay, who, whether he admits it or not, is still affected by what she did to him, how she violated him. I should be scared of both those things—and I am. I'm terrified. But what scares me the most, what's causing this gnawing in my stomach and constriction in my throat, is me. I'm the most afraid of myself. Because I might lose control.

The instant that … that bitch starts talking, I don't trust myself not to snap. My parents are counting on me to keep my cool, my entire Community (along with all the visiting Mer nobility) will be watching, expecting some regal, heroic reaction, and most importantly, Clay will need me to be strong. But what if I can't be? What if I can't be any of those things because the sound of her voice—the thought of what she did—makes me ill? In the controlled bastion of propriety that is this courtroom, what if I start screaming at her or, worse, burst into tears? Loud, sloppy, gasping tears I can't stop? All of it—the sneering disgust, the white-hot fury, the raw hurt and pain—it presses right up against the surface, a tsunami I'm afraid is too powerful to stop.

The guards escort her to the center, in front of the Tribunal, and I grit my teeth. Just for today, I've forgone my seat in the front row with my sisters so I could sit one row behind with Clay as she testifies, protocol be damned. Now, we reach for each other's hands at the same instant and clasp them together under the water.

The slick syrup of her voice sticks in my ears and throat as she takes her oath.

"First and foremost," the Mermaid on the central throne intones, *"do you, Melusine Muriel Havelock, deny any of the charges brought against you by this court?"*

"No." How could she, with all the evidence against her? *"I admit to everything I've done."* Gone is the anger with which she glared at her father last week. Instead, she's composed, controlled, the way I wish I could be. The very sound of her voice turns my insides volcanic.

Melusine takes on a faraway, almost disconnected tone while she recites her crimes for the court records. Even Caspian, as he whispers a translation from where he sits on Clay's other side, says the words with more feeling than she does.

Various members of the Tribunal ask her questions, probing into when her father taught her the siren song he testified had been passed down through generations of their family, when she'd first sirened Clay, how she and her father had drugged him with a potion to keep him alive underwater, what details she knew about the ritual and the dagger—the one she rammed into Clay's stomach.

She answers each one in that same disconnected voice. When the flood of questions ceases and a lull hangs over the court, she says in her articulate, slanting Mermese, *"Now, may I explain?"*

"The floor is yours," says the central Mermaid, *"as is your right."*

Why does she even get to explain? Don't her actions speak for themselves?

Melusine twists her hands, and the sore, red marks where her bronze cuffs have rubbed her skin raw stand out against her pale skin.

"I knew what I was doing was illegal, but," she pauses, *"I thought it was right."*

I expect some kind of uproar from the audience at this, or at least more shocked whispers, but the room remains silent save for Caspian's quiet translations.

"From the time I was very small, my parents told me tales of how life was before the curse, of how our kind should be the majestic, immortal beings we once were, but had been robbed of the life we deserved by one foolish mistake. The Little Mermaid condemned us all when she threw that dagger into the ocean. I grew up, the way I know many of you did, feeling cursed, broken, grieving each second of my shortened lifespan as it slipped through my fins with me powerless to stop it."

In front of me, my sister Em glances back to where her fiancé Leomaris sits behind her before returning her eyes to the front. I know both of them felt that way. Since I was raised in the human world, I never expected more than a human life. But Em and all the other Mer who were born Below or raised by more traditional parents than mine (or even, in Em's case, subjected to a very traditional grandmother before moving Above), grew up feeling cursed and powerless.

"That overwhelming sensation of powerlessness only grew as the violence of the wars forced my family to leave our home in a city I loved, in the dead of night, swimming down the only streets I'd ever known and seeing them littered with bodies and blood. We moved in with one relative after another, each time somewhere more remote, more removed from the fighting. But the violence would spread, and we'd leave again, my father always fearing for my safety. By the time I turned twelve, we'd moved seven times. As a little girl, I used to beg my mother for a baby brother or sister, so I wouldn't be alone when we packed up and left." For a fraction of a second, her sapphire eyes flit to where my sisters sit next to each other in the front row. *"I suppose I wanted a friend I wouldn't need to leave behind. But once I got older, I understood why my*

parents never had another child—worrying about keeping me safe was hard enough."

The way my father shifts slightly in his seat tells me he just might be pressing his copper-colored fin against my mother's opalescent one behind the walls of their private box. They moved up here and started our entire Community for that very reason. They were determined to live in a world where they could raise their children in safety—even if that meant the human world. If they'd stayed Below, Em's childhood might have been scarily similar to Melusine's. And I might never have been born. I swallow. Many throughout the gallery must be thinking the same thing about themselves and their own families because a strange sadness settles over the courtroom, thick as morning fog over the ocean.

"*So, my parents were all I had,*" Melusine continues. "*And, despite the moving and the hiding—or maybe because of it—we were very close.*" She moves her head like she wants to look back at her father, but stops herself. "*Very close. Then ... then one day early last year,*" her smooth voice catches in her throat, "*my mother ventured out of the decrepit old manor house we were staying at way out in the country. She swam to the nearest village to pick up some sweet shrimps. I'd complained I was bored cooped up inside, so she said we'd make crustacean cakes together to keep my mind off things. There hadn't been any raiders anywhere nearby for months, so she thought she'd be safe.*" Melusine shakes her head. "*She didn't come home that night. I waited up for her until my eyes stung ...* "

Melusine falls silent. No one on the Tribunal makes a sound. It's so quiet, the swish of her coral tail under the water slushes in my ears. "*... but I must have fallen asleep at some point, because when my father woke me up,*" her tail, her whole body stills, "*he told me he'd found her body in the village square. There'd been a skirmish; she must have gotten in someone's way.*" The next words tear through her, ripping through the silk of her voice: "*They'd cut her throat. Left her to die.*"

Melusine doesn't sob. She's not a slobbering, blubbering mess the way I'd be up there if I had to talk about my mother being murdered by some stranger in a violent mob. In fact, her tears don't make a single sound as they slide from her sapphire eyes down her face, glistening against her cheeks in the simulated brightness of the underground chamber. But even she can't control the gentle *plunk, plunk, plunk* of them as they solidify into pearls and hit the water one by one, floating away from her and down the aisle, on display for the entire court. Something inside me rebels at the idea of looking at them, so as the tiny, cream-colored drops float toward where Caspian sits at the end of our row, I turn away.

And my gaze lands on my mother. Tears threaten to spill from my own eyes.

No. No! I'm not going to let that monster do this to me. Instead, I focus on how devastated my mother would have been if Melusine had succeeded in stabbing me and leaving me for dead at the bottom of the sea. There's no excuse for everything she's done.

I hope the Tribunal knows that. Their stony faces betray nothing.

"*Miss Havelock,*" says an older Merman on the Tribunal, "*many, if not all, of us here today have lost loved ones in the war.*" I don't recognize him; he must be one of the representative nobles from Below. Caspian leans back in his seat and meets my eyes, guilt written all over his face. Neither of us has lost anyone we've cared about. Everyone we love lives safe on land.

The Mer noble continues, "*To save this court any more pain and emotional bias, please focus your testimony on the crimes put before us in this case.*"

Melusine nods, flicking away her remaining tears with delicate, purposeful fingers. "*A week after … we found my mother … my father sat me down and told me about something he and my mother had been planning before she died. They had wanted to move Above, to move here, where we could all live in safety. At first, I didn't believe that he and my mother would ever consider living among humans. They'd always taught me that humans were part of the problem. They polluted our home and forced us to keep our existence a secret. But then, my father explained he and my mother had another reason for wanting to travel to land, a nobler reason. They'd found a way to use ancient magic to reverse the curse—to give our entire kind back our immortality. Even though she was gone, he wanted to continue the plan they'd made together. But he said he'd need my help."*

She looks up into the faces of the Tribunal members, her blue eyes wide. *"Please understand. Before I came on land, I'd never even seen a human. All I knew of them was what my relatives told me—that they contaminated the oceans without a care and forced us to live in hiding, that they spread across the planet like … like toxic algae, that they wasted resources and spread disease to one another, acting out their animal urges until they got too old and died. When my father told me the details of the ritual and what I'd have to do, he said since humans had no connection to the ocean's magic and, unlike us, weren't meant to live forever, they were lesser life forms. That their short lives weren't worth as much as ours."*

I'm going to be sick. Lesser life forms? I shift to my right, feeling the press of Clay's skin against mine, arm to arm, leg to tail. How can she sit in a courtroom, a place dedicated to justice, spewing such disgusting, archaic—

"How can I even say that?" she asks, arching one thin eyebrow. *"I know now that's not what everyone's taught. I know maybe it's … wrong … "*

Maybe? Maybe!

" … but before I came on land, it was all I knew. When my father told me taking the life of one human now, and then only one every hundred years, would mean saving the lives of our entire species—lives like my mother's—and would put an end to the wars once and for all, it seemed like it was for the greater good. I'm not saying I didn't know the ritual and sireny were illegal. I did. But … I thought they were right."

"And now?" questions the Mermaid on the central throne.

Now she'll say anything she has to for the whole court to feel sorry for her. She's not some brainwashed victim; she's a calculating criminal in a pretty, wide-eyed disguise.

"Now I … " her graceful shoulders slump, and Melusine grimaces as the movement jostles her fin-to-tail cuffs. But, a second later, she pulls herself upright. *"Now I know how wrong I was. I had a chance to get to know humans for the first time when I went to school with them. I even made friends. Now I know human lives are valuable, and I regret all the terrible, prejudiced choices I made."*

Liar! I want to scream. I know she's lying. I can tell by the way her eyes narrow, like she's scrutinizing how each of her words lands. She hasn't changed. She never made friends. She was too busy manipulating people, like she's doing right now.

If her lies are making me bristle, I can only imagine what they're doing to Clay. Even Caspian wears a pained face as he translates them. I put a comforting hand on Clay's tensed shoulder, but he shrugs it off, staring straight ahead at nothing.

"I'd like the court to know," Melusine turns around and looks from face to face around the room but doesn't glance anywhere near Clay or me, *"I need you all to know how sorry I am."*

Sorry my fin. She's not sorry about anything but getting caught. The question is, how many people in the court—how many members of the Tribunal—know they're being played.

Chapter Eight

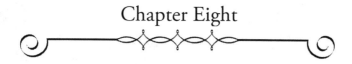

If I never heard Melusine's cloying, candy-coated voice again, it would be too soon. Her testimony has dragged on for what feels like hours, until every one of my nerves is as frayed as an old fishing net. Just when I think the guards will lead her back, a small, mousy-looking Mermaid sitting on the throne at the very end of the Tribunal pipes up. *"If you've finished stating your piece, Miss Havelock, I have one remaining question to determine if another charge is relevant to this case."*

Another charge? I search the other faces in the courtroom. Many look as confused as mine must, but a few have darkened and others have twisted with distaste, Caspian's among them. Clay still stares straight in front of him, his face blank as windswept sand.

"Clay?" I whisper.

His jaw tenses.

The mousy-looking Mermaid, who I recognize as a member of the Foundation's board, says in a voice with more strength in it than I expected given her diminutive stature, *"I ask the court's pardon for the indelicate line of questioning on which I am about to embark. Miss Havelock, we need you to explain for the recordings of these proceedings, the extent,"* she emphasizes the word, *"of your relationship with the mortal Clay Ericson."*

Melusine's entire face shrinks. Her voice comes out in a small whisper, unlike anything I've ever heard from her, *"You mean, how far did we ... go?"*

Tides.

My hands and fins go numb, and I feel like I can't swallow. I didn't think they'd bring ... that ... up. Sireny is the higher offense, already punishable by immortality in prison. They don't need to ask about this. Why are they asking about this?

Clay still won't look at me. I press my side against his again, trying to offer my support, but he scoots in the other direction. The scant centimeters now separating us stretch for miles. What am I supposed to do? What can I do to let him know I'm here for him, no matter what she's about to say?

Because I don't know what that is. Clay hasn't told me much about ... the time he spent spelled into thinking he was Melusine's boyfriend. He hasn't wanted to talk about it, so I haven't asked because I didn't want to push.

No. That's only half the truth. Maybe only a third of the truth. Because most of the truth is I didn't want to know. Didn't want to have to think about it, about the constant comparisons, once Clay and I felt ready to ... That's not fair, I know. But it's true.

Now I'm going to find out—whether either of us wants me to or not.

An uncomfortable silence settles like a cloud of squid's ink, staining all of us.

When the small Mermaid prompts her, Melusine opens her mouth to answer. She shuts it again. I've never seen her at a loss for words, her smooth, easy eloquence cracking. *"I ... didn't ... it didn't. Go far, I mean. We didn't."* Now the words rush out. *"We kissed, a lot, often, but I didn't take it any further, ever. Clay was sirened so he wanted to—"* Clay bites his lips from the inside so they all but disappear, and I want to strangle her even as I cling to her every alleviating word. *"—and my father told me to because it would help ensure Clay loved me for the ritual."* A horrified gasp dominoes through the room as exactly what that means hits the assembled Mer. *"I'd never disobeyed my father before, but I ... and I told myself and my dad it was because Clay was human, because I hated humans, but really ..."* She shakes her head back and forth, almost violently. *"I couldn't. I couldn't do it."*

"You stupid girl," her father sneers from where he waits on the sidelines between two guards. *"Pitying a human. Jeopardizing everything we have worked for."*

The central Mermaid slaps her tail against the water again and gestures for the guards to escort him out.

"I couldn't," Melusine repeats, and breaks down in sobs. These aren't the delicate, pretty tears that glinted on her cheeks earlier. These are heavy, heaving sobs that wrack through her body. As the two female guards assigned to her start leading her out now that there's nothing more for her to say, she turns her head so she's facing Clay and me. "I swear," she says in English. Her eyes lock onto mine. Fierce and terrifying. Terrified. Then the guards pull her away.

That's it—her testimony is over. Had she been planning to reveal my sireny on the stand and not gotten the chance before she broke down? Or did she avoid the topic out of self-interest, like her father did? I guess I'll never know. I should be soaked with relief, but all I can do right now is worry about what Clay is feeling.

The central Mermaid says, *"Can anyone present today verify Miss Havelock's statement?"* Before Caspian can translate the words, she repeats them in English, her voice not unkind.

Clay's hand rises in the air.

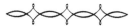

We sit on the bed in my upstairs bedroom. Clay can't go home yet and risk his mom seeing him this upset after what she thinks was a lazy day at the beach. My own parents wouldn't normally let us stay up here alone with the door closed when the rest of my family is down in the grottos, but they didn't object when I led Clay up the stairs. They trust me enough to give us the space we need after today.

I've scooted back into my typical position against the pillows, but Clay's sitting on the end of the bed and the space between us feels wrong, unnatural. I want the gulf of silence to disappear, but I don't know what to say to make it better.

"I don't know what to say."

"Me, either." He doesn't sound upset, just ... exhausted.

"Maybe we should have talked about it earlier." I hate that she's the one who set the tone of this conversation. Now, it feels stilted and awkward—so unlike the *us* feeling I'm used to sharing with Clay. Like we're in sync, swimming with the same current. I hate that now she controls this moment.

I'm not going to let her. I'm not going to let her control one more memory Clay and I share. We need to make this conversation ours.

I want to ask why he couldn't talk to me about what went on between them—especially now I know they never slept together—but I'm afraid it'll come out sounding accusatory, so instead I settle on, "How are you feeling? Really?"

"Honestly? I don't know. A huge part of me is relieved. I was pretty sure we hadn't ... I mean, I remember her stopping things a couple times before they could get ... yeah, so, yeah. But there are so many places where my memory is fuzzy or just," he pauses, shakes his head, "blank. That's why I didn't tell you. In case I was wrong. It's like I couldn't trust my own mind."

"But you believe her? What she said today?" We've been in the dark about this long enough. The truth is what matters now.

"Yeah, I do. I wouldn't've verified it in court if I didn't. It gels with everything I do remember so, yeah, I guess it's over. Now we know." He shrugs his broad shoulders, and stares out the window. "Like I said, a big part of me is just really relieved."

I nod. But I can tell there's more. "And?" I keep the word quiet, gentle.

"And … " Clay picks at one short, clean fingernail. "Naw, forget it. It's stupid."

"Doubt it," I say.

That gets me the barest hint of a smile. But his next words are anything but happy. "There's a part of me that feels grateful." He barks out a bitter, dark laugh. "And I hate it. M—she doesn't deserve my gratitude. Yeah, nothing happened. But I hate that something … anything … could have without me even really knowing. God—" His hands jerk in a sharp, violent gesture, like he wants to hit something. "I'm just so angry."

Hazel eyes plead with me to understand.

"Me, too." It's true. "I'm angry, too. Knowing … what we learned today, it makes it better, but it also doesn't. I'm angry, too."

Clay sighs, deep, and I wonder if I've said the wrong thing. Then he collapses next to me against the pillows. I rest my head on his body, in that safe nook where his shoulder meets his chest. He lets me lay my arm across his torso and hold him tight.

Hours later, after the sky turns purple-black and Clay drags himself away to get home before curfew, I still lie on my upstairs bed. I can't seem to make myself head down to the grottos. The rich cinnamon scent of Clay's skin clings to my sheets and pillows, and I hold on to it, just as I held on to him, hoping it will calm me, center me, the way holding him centered both of us.

While he was here, my every thought narrowed to how to take his burdens, make his cargo lighter. Now that I'm alone, and the focus is gone, my thoughts float along tides I don't want them to travel. Of course, I'm overjoyed at what I found out today. Learning Clay wasn't violated any more than I already knew he was means I can let out a breath I've been holding for months. But if Melusine held herself back from doing that with Clay, the same way I did … a slithering, sneaky voice in the back of my mind stabs at me, taunts me, tells me I'm no better than she is. Right when I want to jump out of my own skull, something hard hits my window pane, clattering against the glass.

And again.

And—I open the window in time to catch the next small, round object aimed at the glass.

A pebble? No. A small, beige button shell. On the moonlit lawn below, cloaked in silvery shadows, stands Caspian, cupping a handful of what must be more button shells.

It figures. Caspian would never pick up whatever pebbles were lying around. He'd come prepared.

A smile shines across his face as he catches sight of me, and he climbs up to my window, quick hands pulling themselves up the bougainvillea-covered trellis. Just as he usually does when he's in his legs, Caspian wears nothing but a pair of loose-fitting swim trunks that ride low on his hips. If any of my elderly human neighbors happen to be watching his 6'3" shirtless frame slip into my bedroom window, I can only imagine what they must think. I laugh as I grab his tan forearm and hurry him the rest of the way inside.

"What?" he asks, pulling up his trunks. They immediately slide back down to sit below his hip bones.

"Nothing. It's really good to see you." And it is.

There's that smile again.

"Why'd you come in this way?" I ask, though I have a sneaking suspicion. Caspian always comes through the underground entrance in the grottos.

"I needed to talk to you without your parents overhearing." He rubs the back of his neck. "Without them knowing I'm here." He fingers the shells still cupped in his palm before stuffing them in his pocket. "I remembered you had a trellis near your window and thought I could come see you this way."

I'm tempted to make a joke about how stereotypical it is that he climbed a trellis to sneak into my room, but since Caspian's family is more traditionalist than mine, his parents don't let him watch many human movies or T.V. shows. As far as Caspian's concerned, he's the first one to ever think up this plan—and pride paints his boyish features. All I say is, "Pretty smart."

He beams.

I usher him farther into my room, and he sits in my spinny desk chair, his massive, muscled chest and long legs completely dwarfing it. I perch on the end of my bed, facing him.

Caspian hasn't been in this room for years, not since we were guppies and I'd insist on showing him some human toy or other. Having him here now—in this dry, human place—strikes me as strange. The same way I feel when Clay goes down to the grottos.

Like my two worlds are colliding.

"What's so scandalous you had to come here in secret?" I joke, shaking off the weirdness. Although I bet I know the answer.

"You're testifying tomorrow, and I just wanted to make sure you don't do anything … "

"Stupid?"

"That you'll regret. Forever." He thinks I'm going to confess.

"Casp, I'm not an idiot."

He leans forward, resting his arms on his knees. "No. You're brilliant." The conviction in his voice, the certainty in his clear blue eyes startles me as much as the words. Caspian, who understands the intricacies of our government better than I ever will and who can learn any language and who listens to classical *konklilis* for fun called me brilliant. "And you're brave. And you're—" he clears his throat "—a good person. A good person who's sometimes too hard on herself."

"No, I—"

"Yes." He puts so much vehemence behind the word, I don't disagree again. "You put too much pressure on yourself. You always have. If I know you—which I do—" it's not a joke but an honest, straightforward statement of fact "—you're spending tonight feeling guilty. Maybe even comparing what you did to what Melusine did."

He does know me.

"You're blaming yourself." He looks down at his bare feet before raising his pale blue eyes to meet mine. "And I haven't helped."

"Caspian, you—"

He holds up a hand. "I said terrible things to you about being a … about what you did to Clay."

Caspian still can't utter that word. Siren. The word I'm branded with in his eyes. "They were true. The things you said." I flash to that night, to me crying, kneeling in my gravel driveway and begging Caspian's forgiveness after he'd uncovered the truth; to him yelling at me for the first time ever, calling me a monster no better than the siren aunt who destroyed his family's reputation, saying a part of me liked what I'd done, liked having Clay want me. Each accusation had stabbed into my heart. "They were true."

"They were mean." He runs a hand through his dirty blond hair. "I was angry. I was just so mad at you for—"

"You had every right to be," I say. I can't listen to a litany of my sins. Not from Caspian. "I'm glad you said everything you said that night. I needed to hear it."

"But you don't need to keep repeating it to yourself now." In one smooth motion, he wheels the chair closer to me. "And you don't need to repeat it on the stand tomorrow," he says, his words firm as granite.

"But," my voice is small enough to fit inside a clam shell, "don't I kind of deserve to go to prison?"

He doesn't scream the word "no" or praise my good intentions the way Clay would. Instead, Caspian levels me with a thoughtful, serious expression. "I've considered that." Of course he has. Of course he's weighed every option, clear-headed and rational. "The reason to put someone in prison is to keep them from repeating their crime. Melusine might very well siren," the word sticks in his throat before slipping free, "again, so she deserves to be there." He spells out his logic like he's presenting a lesson to the class in school. "But there's no reason for you to be there because you won't do it again."

"No, I won't." There's nothing that could ever make me go anywhere near sireny again. I am not a siren.

"I know. I trust you." A tentative hand settles on my shoulder. His touch anchors me. "It's over, Goldfish. You've got to put it behind you. For your family. For … me."

I sigh and let my head fall forward. "Thanks, Casp. What did I do to deserve a best friend like you?"

He shrugs, and something sad flits over his face. "You have me, y'know. Always." The words fill my whole room, and even though we're in this dry place, I feel like I do when we're underwater, out in the briny ocean just the two of us.

When he lifts his hand from my shoulder and wheels the chair several feet back, away from me, I snap to the here and now. He gives me the precocious smile I know means a joke is coming. "Besides," he says, "I didn't go to all that trouble to save your tail just so you could end up in some jail cell."

It isn't until the laughter shakes its way through my chest that I realize a good laugh with Casp was exactly what I needed.

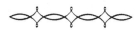

"Upon this symbol of the almighty waves, I swear by the power of the current and for the safety of the Seven Seas to speak only the truth."

With the conch shell pressed against my heart, I state my name for the record.

My own testimony swirls by in a blur. I've recounted the story so many times by now, I'm starting to sound like a *konklili* (a Merbook recorded inside a seashell) that's set on repeat. I detail everything for the court. Except my own sireny.

I try to keep the end of the story—the part where Clay and I break the curse and I carry him to the surface before he drowns—brief, but the Tribunal members ask question after question. When I finally finish, the water around me rolls and splashes as all the assembled Mer swish their fins through it in applause, including my sisters and parents. No one on the Tribunal stops them—even the Tribunals' faces beam at me in admiration.

Guilt rises like high tide. My throat tightens, and my cheeks burn.

It feels like forever until the applause recedes. When it does, the Mermaid on the central throne asks the customary final question: *"Is there anything else you think the court should consider while coming to our decisions in this case?"*

Yes! It's only now, with the entire Community and all the visiting Mer nobility staring at me like I'm some kind of savior, that a realization crashes over me: All this time, a tiny, secret part of me wished Melusine or her father would reveal what I did. That they'd take this choice away from me.

But they didn't. And now it's up to me. It's up to me whether I swim out of this courtroom a free Mermaid or am dragged away in chains. Should I really keep the illegal, immoral, disgusting thing I did a secret?

Movement catches my eye. Caspian raises his arms over his head, pretending to stretch. As soon as he sees me looking, he drops his arms and holds my gaze, then nods at the row ahead of him.

Em. Lapis. Lazuli. Amy. Amy, whose heart-shaped face splits into its sweetest, most encouraging smile the second she notices me looking at her.

If I'm honest with the court now, I'll condemn my entire family to the severest shame. For something they had nothing to do with. My sisters' children, grandchildren, great-grandchildren will all be shunned because of me. My gaze shifts to my parents, watching me from their private box. My parents, who gave up their entire world to keep me and our kind safe, who are the best chance the Mer have to escape total anarchy—and who will never see the throne if I tell the truth now.

I swallow.

"*No,*" I answer. "*There's nothing else I'd like to add.*"

Relief washes over Caspian's features, but my focus stays on my parents. The pride on their faces stings like the worst jellyfish. I decide to make them a promise. Right now. I may not be able to tell them the whole truth about saving Clay, but this will be the last time I hide something from them. I look from one to the other.

I will never lie to you again.

Chapter Nine

What I wouldn't give to get out of this courtroom. The blue glass walls, the starfish emblem, the uncomfortable marble stool I'm sure has left a permanent imprint on my tail—all I want is to say goodbye to them forever. I think of the postcard I just got from Kelsey, my closest human friend. Her parents took her to Paris for the end of summer vacation. What I wouldn't give to be able to see the Eiffel Tower and the Louvre and to go shopping. To try real baguette and *pan au chocolat* and *escargot*. Instead, I'm here in the courtroom, where I've been for days on end. I guess it's not like I could ever go to Paris anyway—that much time in a plane, that far away from the sea ... the call of the ocean would drive me mad. At this point, I'd settle for a trip through the exit door.

Soon enough, I tell myself. After all, today is the last day of the trial, and this is the last testimony.

Clay walks to the center of the room to stand before the Tribunal, and the assembled Mer do nothing to conceal their stares at the human in our midst. As is customary in Mer trials, the victim is the last to testify. Experts testify first, then less involved witnesses, followed by more involved witnesses, the accused, and the victims of the crime. It's an order established to keep the court as objective as possible by saving testimony more likely to be emotional until after all the facts and evidence have been presented.

When a court official hands Clay the conch shell to place against his heart, the central Mermaid begins the oath in English.

But Clay recites it back in Mermese.

As the lyrical, lilting language leaves his lips, my eyes widen. His pronunciation isn't perfect, but it's damn good. Mutters of approval spread through the assembly. How did ... ? My gaze lands on Caspian. I raise an eyebrow.

"What?" Caspian whispers. "He begged me. Like I could ever turn down someone who wanted to learn."

"Why didn't he ask me?"

"The word 'impatient' might have come up." Caspian smiles, and I elbow him in the ribs. "Besides," he adds, "I think he ... wanted to impress you."

"Thanks for helping him."

"Oh, you know me ... "

After the oath, Clay continues in Mermese: *"Good afternoon and thank you to the court for welcoming me here today and for seeking justice in this matter."* Clay clears his throat and says in English, "Well, that's all I've got."

Several people chuckle, including two members of the Tribunal. "Thank you, Mr. Ericson," the central Mermaid says warmly. "We'll continue in English, shall we?"

With a Foundation employee translating, Clay tells the same story of Melusine's sireny and the day he was kidnapped that I've heard him tell over and over. When he reaches the part where he swam in front of the cursed dagger to save me, risking his life and breaking the curse with his love and sacrifice, he, too, gets a round of applause. Tails swish back and forth through the water with vigor until the Tribunal follows up with questions.

After they've asked for every detail he can remember about his interactions with Melusine and her father, they change course.

"How long have you been aware of the existence of Mer?"

"Since the day Mel and her father kidnapped me," Clay answers honestly. "Lia never would have told me if Mel hadn't held that dagger to my throat and threatened to kill me if Lia didn't confess." I want to throw my arms around him. Clay's just made sure the Community won't look down on me or my family for revealing our existence for the first time in modern history.

"Have you told anyone else about our existence? It is of paramount importance that you answer truthfully."

"No, I haven't told anyone. I swear. And I never will."

"Does anyone close to you suspect?"

Why are they interrogating him? Clay's the victim here.

"Does anyone close to me suspect my girlfriend's a Mermaid? No," he says, in a voice less sarcastic than I would use. "Even my mom would never believe that unless she saw it with her own eyes, and she makes a living writing fantasy books. She noticed I was acting weird last year, but she figured it was because I was unhappy dating Mel and now that we've ... broken up ... and I'm with Lia, she thinks everything's back to normal. My friends do, too."

"And your father?"

"My father wasn't around last year to notice anything was weird." Clay keeps the words even; I doubt anyone else hears the undercurrent of hurt running through them. "He's in the Navy, so he isn't around much," he says, like he's trying to excuse away his dad's behavior. "I've only just started seeing him again."

The Mermaid on the central throne exchanges a look with the petite, mousy Mermaid on the end, then with a member of the Tribunal visiting from Below. "And you are quite certain you've never confided anything in him that would make him suspect?"

"I'm sure. Very sure. My dad's a straight-and-narrow kind of guy. He wouldn't believe in Mermaids if they invaded his naval base.

Lia's met him—she can confirm for the court how … conventional he is."

"Miss Nautilus has been on a naval base?" The central Mermaid's nostrils flare as her volume increases. My mother shoots me a look brimming with a mix of so much anger and fear it makes my breath catch. She's gripped my father's hand so tightly her knuckles are as white as a crested wave.

I shake my head right as Clay says, "No, of course not. I'd never take her anywhere near a Navy base."

An audible exhale echoes around me, and the members of the Tribunal visibly relax. My mother loosens her grip, leaving my father to shake out his hand. How could she think I would be so stupid?

"And there's no one else who could pose a threat?" The central Mermaid has returned to a normal volume, her face composed once again. "A sibling or—"

"I'm an only child. There's no one. I will keep your secret until my death."

Clay's death is something I don't let myself think about because I'll go out of my mind, but it was smart of him to say that. Every one of the immortal creatures now gazes at him with some degree of sympathy—and gratitude for eliminating their own deaths with his bravery. No way they'll interrogate him further.

As if to prove me right, the Mermaid asks the standard final question, "Mr. Ericson, is there anything else you think the court should consider while coming to our decisions in this case?"

He pauses, then straightens his shoulders. "*I would like to thank all of you for trusting me,*" Clay says in his accented Mermese, "*and for welcoming me into your world. I have so enjoyed learning about your rich history and fascinating, beautiful culture. I look forward to learning more. Thank you.*"

All over the gallery, Mer are smiling at him. He walks back toward me through the water with his head high as the Tribunal declares the official end of all testimony.

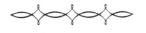

The verdict should be in by now. It's been six days since Clay testified. Melusine and her father are clearly guilty. All the evidence points to them; it should be a quick decision. What's taking so long?

With each passing day, my nerves have tightened like fishing wire. I can't sit around the grottos waiting and wondering for another minute. That's why when Clay texts to ask if I'd like to hang out on the beach together, I can't say yes fast enough.

When he arrives at my front door, he carries a bag full of brand new snorkeling equipment. "I thought this could tide me over until my scuba lessons start. What do you say?" He holds up an eye-and-nose mask. "Want to show me your ocean?"

More than anything. "But it's still light out," I say, nodding at the sunny, California sky. "You know I can't go swimming in the ocean until after dark."

"You can if you wear a bathing suit instead of your tail." He smiles like he's the smartest guy in the world. And like he knows it.

Then again, maybe he is. That rule is so ingrained in me—and I've been working so hard to follow every one of the Community's rules to kind of make up for breaking so many to save Clay—that it didn't occur to me I now have enough leg control to go swimming in human form. I kept my legs while I was fighting off Mr. Havelock on the sea floor, didn't I? When I really needed to, I kept my legs in water even though I thought it was something I could never do; that moment last spring showed me I was capable of it if I really tried, so I've been practicing regularly since then. For years, I had told myself I couldn't do it, so I have to admit, my progress over the last few months is something I'm proud of.

And with Clay by my side in nothing but his swim trunks … I don't think I'll have a problem maintaining my legs today. I kiss him—fast and frenzied and full of the promise of more—then run upstairs to change while he heads through the house to the beach.

Fifteen minutes later, we're gliding through open ocean together.

"Luu ah dish," Clay blurts excitedly around the mouthpiece of his snorkel, pointing below him into the water. "Luu ah dish!"

My vision isn't as sharp underwater as it would be if I had my tail in place, but it's still as sharp as any human snorkeling mask—or so I'm assuming based on the level of detail I can see that Clay still misses (even after using several coats of the anti-fog liquid he bought at the Surf & Snorkel shop to clean his mask). I take in the sight of the neon orange garibaldi fish with their iridescent blue spots swishing toward us, and I flash Clay a thumbs-up under the water.

Clay stays still as a stonefish while the creatures flit around us, weaving between our limbs before melding back into formation as soon as they've passed us. His face breaks into a huge smile as he grabs my arm and pulls me into a patch of emerald green kelp where dozens of slender, silvery queenfish munch away on spiraling, leafy stalks.

Clay's snorkel, paired with the mask, makes him look like a cross between an insect and an alien. *My alien,* I think, before scolding myself for being so stereotypically swoony. A spotted stingray the size of a tennis racket swims five feet below us and Clay practically vibrates next to me, pointing with one hand and squeezing mine with the other. No wonder he makes me swoon.

We swim farther out, but stay close enough to the rock formations along the coast to ensure there are reefs to see. I can't get used to swimming in legs. They flop all over the place when I try to kick them the way Clay does. Things get easier when I decide to pretend they're a tail; I hold them together, point my toes, and use an undulating motion to propel myself forward. Much better.

Hand in hand, we careen through the calm sea, admiring purple sea urchins, calico bass, and even a moon snail. Right when I can tell from the disbelief on Clay's face that he thinks it can't get any better, we glide alongside an ancient sea turtle who scowls at us skeptically until I show Clay how to gain its trust by scratching gently along its shell. Clay's eyes shine with glee, and I revel in it.

The longer we're in the water, the more adventurous he grows, swimming faster and diving deep before spiraling back up to suck in air through his snorkel.

When he surfaces after an especially long dive, Clay pulls off his mask and mouthpiece and smooths his wet hair back with one hand, his chest rising and falling with his breath. He throws his head and arms back, letting the sun warm him. "This is such a blast."

My eyes follow the rivulets of seawater that gleam in the sunlight as they trickle down his biceps, down his shoulders and chest. He catches me staring, and I blush so hard I probably look sunburned. But I don't think he minds because a predatory smirk dominates his face as he slides toward me through the water. Strong arms grab me and pull me against him, my wet body pressing against his. "You're so warm," he whispers, and our faces are so close now that the words skate across my cheek. I don't feel the cold the way humans do, so my body must indeed feel warm against his ocean-chilled skin. He holds me to him even more tightly, and I wind my arms around his neck. Droplets of water from his face collide with mine as he takes my mouth in a kiss as sweeping as the sea breeze itself.

His lips taste salty as only the ocean can make them, and his skin smells like brine and sea air. There's something so natural, so *right* about kissing him like this, out in the blue, with Clay anchoring my body to his as the waves rock and swell against us.

Under the sun, out in the surf, it's the perfect moment.

Until shouts pierce the summer sky, cutting through the calm.

"Lia! Lia!" Arms wave at us, and then two blond heads bob toward us through the waves as Lapis and Lazuli slice through the current at top speed despite the use of their legs.

Usually, I'd be embarrassed if the twins caught Clay and I kissing and annoyed at the teasing that would follow (hey, it's not like it hasn't happened before—they get too big a kick out of it if you ask me). But this time, the urgency on their faces wipes away any emotion but alarm.

"Lia!" Lazuli shouts again, "They're back. The Tribunal's back."

"Come on!" Lapis yells, gesturing for us to follow as she and Lazuli head back the way they came.

Clay's face bares all the anticipation and anxiety I feel. With his hand gripped in mine, I speed us through the waves toward the verdict.

Chapter Ten

"*This Tribunal, consisting of representatives from both the Community of Landed Mer and the noble families of Below, and endowed with authority by the almighty ocean, does hereby decree the fates of defendants brought before this court.*" All seven members of the Tribunal recite the words in unison, causing them to echo throughout the cavernous chamber.

Mr. Havelock wades before the panel of enthroned Mer, his jaw clenched and his face blank. But genuine fear mars Melusine's sculpted features, her sapphire eyes wide with worry.

Good. She should be worried. She brainwashed Clay and tried to kill us both, and now she's going to prison for the rest of her immortal life. Where she belongs.

"*The fate of Filius Havelock is as follows: Filius Havelock, for the crimes of planning and attempting to carry out the murder of both a human and a Mer while practicing illegal dark magic, and of teaching a siren song to a minor, this Tribunal finds you guilty. You will spend the remainder of your immortal life imprisoned under highest security.*"

Deep inside my chest, something loosens, and I let out a breath.

Now that his official fate has been intoned by the entire Tribunal, the Mermaid on the central throne explains the details of his sentence. *"Due to the udell leanings of your family and the precarious state Below during this time of rebuilding, you will remain in a cell Above for the time being to prevent illicit aid or attempted escape. Relocation to a cell Below in the high security caves at a future date remains at the court's discretion."*

I guess that makes sense. Historically, anyone convicted of sireny or the instruction of siren songs served out their eternal sentence in a Mer prison of the highest security. That meant living out your days trapped in a tiny, isolated cave in a desolate region of uninhabited ocean. The only light came from nearby underwater volcanos and the only company from some of the sea's deadliest predators. These conditions were reserved for the most dangerous criminals—and those spreading sireny definitely qualified. But right now, in the aftermath of the wars, resources are spread too thin Below as it is to maintain security.

Two guards lead Mr. Havelock through the exit—his face twisted with venom and his narrowed gaze glinting with a determination I don't like—while two others bring Melusine to replace him at the center.

As I watch her swim forward, a glimpse of ice-blue catches my focus. On the opposite side of the courtroom sits that Mermaid from Below—the one with the blue streaks in her white-blond hair who looks like an engraving from a fairytale book. Odette? Ondine? Something. She hasn't attended the trial since she gave her testimony, at least not that I saw. She must have come today to hear both her cousins' sentences. Her plea for mercy on Melusine's behalf swims across my memory. Well, she'll be disappointed; the sentence for sirens is always the same.

As if to prove me right, the Tribunal recites its second verdict: *"The fate of Melusine Havelock is as follows: Melusine Havelock, for the crimes of attempting to carry out the murder of both a human and a Mer while participating in illegal dark magic and of sirening a human, this Tribunal finds you guilty.*"

The words I've waited months to hear sound more soothing and more final than I could have imagined. So sweet is the relief of those few words that, despite the somber feeling soaking the courtroom, I turn light as seafoam. Like I could float up from my seat all the way to the ceiling.

It isn't until Caspian eyes me cautiously and Clay squeezes my hand that I realize the Tribunal hasn't yet decreed her sentence. Why have they stopped talking?

Murmurs spread throughout the gallery as, one by one, people notice what I just have. The noise halts just as abruptly when the central Mermaid clears her throat. *"As all assembled here know, the sentence for those found guilty of sireny has always been immortal imprisonment. However—"*

No, no, no …

"—never before has there been a case of a siren who was still a minor when she committed the crime," continues the central Mermaid. *"Or a case of a siren with any motive beyond cruelty and self-service. While this court in no way questions the illegality, immorality, and utter repugnance of Miss Havelock's crimes, it is our judgment that being a minor, she was wrongfully coerced into her misdeeds by her sole parental figure. Therefore, while we do indeed find her guilty, we also deem it necessary to amend the expected sentence."*

Is she pausing just to see if it kills me? Tides! I focus hard on keeping my breathing steady as I concentrate on the central Mermaid's next words.

"After much deliberation, this Tribunal has decided the following. Melusine Havelock, you will, first and foremost, be forbidden from any contact with humans as you have proven yourself a danger to them. You will live under Foundation surveillance in a secured facility of the Tribunal's choosing for three years, during which time, you will participate in mandatory counseling and instruction in human sensitivity, which

will continue for two years following your release. All your movements are hereby restricted to the grotto network for three months, after which time you will be permitted to travel underwater only while meeting specific terms of an eighty-year probation period; furthermore, you are barred from ever venturing into the human world for any reason without prior Foundation approval. Any instance of noncompliance with these restrictions will lead to immediate and permanent imprisonment."

That's it? That can't be it. A few years of surveillance—not even imprisonment!—and some restrictions she's no doubt cunning enough to break? What's to stop her from sirening all over again?

Similar thoughts must plague Clay because fear tinges the set of his mouth, the corners of his eyes. "What if she does it to someone else?" he whispers as much to himself as to me.

"While we do not believe, given your age and motives, that long-term imprisonment is justified in your case, you have nonetheless proven untrustworthy and thus we deem severe repercussions warranted as both a punishment and a precaution. Therefore, this Tribunal is including one more provision to your sentence to ensure you can never again commit the high crime of sireny."

Now that the Mermaid on the central throne has explained the reasoning, all the voices of the Tribunal join for the pronouncement of Melusine's fate: *"Melusine Havelock, you will henceforth be stripped of your voice."*

As gasps fill the room, Clay whispers in my ear, "C-can they do that?"

"Well, the magic exists, but I haven't heard of anyone using it to take a Mermaid's voice since ... my mother's cousin's."

"Your ... ? Oh. Right."

The Little Mermaid. Humans may get a lot of the details of her story wrong, but they're right that the Little Mermaid gave up her voice as payment to the Sea Sorceress. Like I said, she didn't do it to get legs (she got them at puberty like every other Mer), but to *keep* her legs permanently so her prince would never find out what she was, and the two of them could live a human life together on land. When Hans Christian Andersen wrote down her story, he said the Sea Sorceress cut out the Little Mermaid's tongue as part of the bargain. But why would she resort to something so bloody and gruesome when Mer magic would do the trick? The truth is, the sorceress gave my ancestor a potion that took her voice away. Every Mer knows that. But the idea that the court would use one now as a punishment? Using a potion to take someone's voice may be less gory than cutting out her tongue, but it still seems barbaric.

Then again, if anyone deserves it, I guess it would be Melusine. Even thinking her name brings back the tsunami of sharp fear and seething hatred. Still …

The central Mermaid slaps her tailfin against the water to regain the focus of the crowd, many of whom have started whispering amongst themselves. Once they fall silent, she says, *"The aim of this court is not cruelty. It is not our goal to leave you without any form of verbal communication. Therefore, the Tribunal has consulted with several potions experts to craft a draught that will only remove Miss Havelock's voice while she is above water. She will thus be able to speak to other Mer when she is submerged but will be unable to speak in the human world, rendering her incapable of sirening again."* The Mermaid nods at a court employee who disappears out a side door and returns balancing a silver tray upon which stands a small glass vial brimming with steaming, inky potion.

"Now?" Melusine screams from her spot before the Tribunal. *"You're going to do it now?"* Her careful composure cracks as panic seizes her, contorting her face into something wild. She writhes violently in her bonds, the metal chain clanking against itself as she pulls it this way and that, twisting her body away from the potion on the tray that glides closer to her by the second.

The guards clamp their fists around her upper arms in bruising grips, but she doesn't stop thrashing.

"Be still, Miss Havelock," says one of the nobles on the Tribunal.

"Your fate has been intoned, and so shall it be."

But Melusine continues to buck like a bull shark. *"Stop! Not my voice. I'm not ready! Don't do this!"* As two other court employees join the one carrying the tray, Melusine snaps her mouth shut and turns her face from side to side to avoid the vial. With an exasperated sigh, one of the them grasps her jaw in his large hand and pries her mouth open.

Her scream fills the courtroom.

And then it doesn't. Not because she's stopped screaming—her head remains tilted back, her eyes welling with rage, and her mouth moving—but because the potion has hit her tongue.

The instant her screams die away, shock passes over her face. She tries again, to scream, to speak; when no noise meets her ears or any of ours, a flash of helplessness overwhelms her face that makes me want to ... no, she deserves this. She deserves it.

The expression vanishes as she swallows and stills, correcting her posture and lifting her chin in what could either be dignity or defiance.

Flanked by guards, she exits the courtroom in silence.

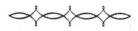

"That was kind of brutal," Caspian says, staring at the now-closed exit door.

"At least it's done with," says Em in a voice meant to be comforting but that comes out unsettled. I nod.

Beside me, Clay exhales. "It's over. It's really over."

I lean my head on his shoulder, and he rests his on top of mine.

Mer shift all around us, preparing to leave. That is, until the slapping of a fin against water yanks everyone's attention back to the front.

"Before we call this trial to a close, there remains one more matter to be decided by this court."

My head snaps up at the same time Caspian shoots me a questioning look, schooling his features to hide his alarm. One more matter for the court? Foghorns blast their warnings in my mind. Is this about me? About my sireny? Maybe they've found out, and now they're going to take my voice. My hand clutches at my throat.

"The Tribunal has made a decision in regards to the human, Clay Ericson."

Chapter Eleven

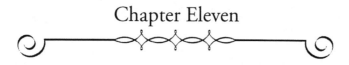

"They can't do this!" I shout from my spot at the dining room table. We all gathered here instead of in the grottos after leaving the courtroom so Clay would be more comfortable. Like anything we do now would make him more comfortable when he's being treated like sea scum. "Clay was a victim in this whole thing. Why are they treating him like a criminal?"

"Now, let's not overreact," my father says, trying to smile. "No one on the Tribunal or in the Community thinks Clay is a criminal."

"They're going to force him to drink a potion. Who else did they do that to? Oh yeah, Melusine—who is a criminal."

"They're not taking away Clay's voice," my father says.

"No," I throw back, "just his memories."

"*Some* of his memories," Em says in her let-me-correct-you-because-I-know-everything voice. "The potion the Tribunal is requiring him to drink will only get rid of *some* of his memories. That's what they said. Just the memories about Merkind. Just seeing us with our tails, that sort of thing. I'm sure it won't be that bad."

I scowl harder than I've ever scowled. She looks away.

"I mean, the Tribunal knows what they're doing," Em continues, but with every passing word the confidence seeps out of her voice. She's trying too hard to make sense of this, and she knows it. "They're not forcing him ... exactly. They gave him tonight to adjust to the idea, and tomorrow he'll come forward to drink the potion willingly." Now Em doesn't look either me or Clay in the eye; she sees the flaw in the logic even if she doesn't want to say it, doesn't want to believe it.

Lazuli says it for her. "Yeah, but you heard what they said. If he doesn't drink it willingly, they'll have someone from Ocean's Intelligence slip it to him over the next week."

"Talk about a violation of his rights," Lapis says, echoing my thoughts.

"Technically it isn't." Em says. "According to Community bylaws, in extreme situations deemed a significant threat to Mer safety, the court can authorize the covert use of noninvasive magic against a human if doing so protects Merkind." Em rattles the words off like a *konklili* recording on the Mer legal system.

"And that sounds like a fair law to you?" I challenge. How could it? Clay doesn't have a real choice. Either he opts to take the potion or they force it on him. The only reason they're even giving him the illusion of a choice—the only reason they didn't shove the potion down his throat in the courtroom today the way they did with Melusine—is to keep up appearances. Our entire Community and the Mer Below see Clay as the hero who broke the curse, so treating him the same way they would treat a criminal would be too unsettling for Mer to witness (especially because most Mer in that courtroom have spent decades Above, living and working among humans). Giving Clay this extra day to consider his non-existent options is a way for the Tribunal to save face and maintain the façade of civility—for our legal system to seem fair and just when what they're doing is not only unjust, but despicable.

If he agrees and drinks the potion "willingly," the Tribunal can smile, pat themselves on the back, and tell everyone he consented because he acknowledged that sacrificing his own memories was the right choice; if he refuses, they can vilify him, claiming he put his own selfishness above Mer safety and that they have no other recourse but to force the potion on him as a last resort. Either way, they win and Clay loses. We lose.

Em shoots a helpless glance at me, then Lapis, then Lazuli, then Amy, hunting for an ally. "The law allowing them to do this was written to keep us safe. You heard what the Tribunal said. With Clay's dad in the Navy, they consider it a threat to our Community, and to all the Mer Below, that Clay knows about us. I mean, I think they would let it go if his dad held a lower rank, but he's in naval intelligence. And they said the Navy's already been poking around our operations, questioning the Foundation about sonar reads from China that picked up unexplained movement around our facilities because of all the visitors from Below. The rest of the board were already worried about Clay knowing about us, but once they found out about his dad, and that you met him—that someone in naval intelligence sat face to face with a Mermaid across a dinner table—"

"In a crowded restaurant," I counter, "in my human form, away from water, away from the naval base. Don't try to anchor this on me."

"They think it's too big a risk for us, especially now that we're going to have more activity back and forth between our Community Above and the Mer Below as we rebuild."

"Do *you* think it's a risk? You know Clay. Do you really think Clay would ever say anything to his dad to put us in danger?" I pin her with my glare so she can't wriggle away from this. Her eyes dart to Clay where he sits next to me wearing a stony expression.

Seconds tick by.

Em sighs. "No." She crumples into her chair and doesn't say anything else.

"None of us think Clay would ever do anything against us," Amy says, voice quiet but firm.

"Thank you, Amy," Clay says. They're the first words he's spoken since we all sat down in the dining room. Hearing his voice robbed of all its usual mirth scares me. Amy scoots her chair closer to Clay's and crosses her arms in front of her chest. I couldn't love her more.

Now that it's obvious she and the twins are on my side, and even rule-follower Em's arguments have been silenced, everything's in place. I turn to my parents. "Mom, Dad, you can stop them, can't you? You can both make statements about Clay's character—make the Tribunal realize this isn't necessary, right?"

Of course they can. What good is having parents who run our entire Community—who are in line for the throne, for tides' sake—if they can't pull rank in a situation like this?

"I wish we could, angelfish," my father says, leaning toward me across the table, "but we—"

"We can't, Aurelia," my mother finishes, voice crisp. "To be frank with you, we've already tried. That's why the Tribunal took six days to return with the verdict. It's why your father and I haven't been home much this week."

"I ... thought you were working."

"We were," my father says. "We were working on negotiating with the Tribunal. Because of our position in the Community and the possible roles we may take on soon, the Tribunal shared their decision with us first as a courtesy. We've spent the last five days straight trying to convince them Clay can be trusted, but seashell, they just won't budge. Not now that the Navy has started setting up all kinds of meetings with the Foundation, asking questions about increased, unusual underwater activity in the area."

"If the Tribunal was comprised solely of Foundation members," my mom adds, "we may have had a chance at persuading them, but the Mer nobles are naturally distrustful of humans because they live in deep, unexplored regions of the sea and have never known any. Clay is a foreign entity." My mom smiles at him, but it's a sad smile. "Not to us, of course."

"That's it?" I can't believe it. "You're just going to let them do this to him? After everything he's been through?" I'm shouting again.

"Tone," my mother warns. Seriously? My tone? *That's* what she's thinking about right now? "For your information, young lady, part of the Tribunal's original decision was to forbid you from seeing Clay after he drank the potion and forgot you were a Mermaid." I gasp. "Your father and I convinced them that wasn't necessary. That it would be too traumatic for Clay to have his supposedly-human, normal girlfriend break up with him out of nowhere, and that it would make him unnecessarily curious about you and what might have changed your feelings. Then he might question the memory loss."

"We tried, Lia," my dad says. "We're not on the Tribunal, so we don't have any legal standing to question the verdict. That's the very best we could do." His expression begs me to understand, but I can't. Earlier, in the courtroom, I was furious the Tribunal could make such a ruling, but I was sure my parents could get it overturned, or at least get it postponed until we had a better plan.

"This can't be happening." I don't know whether to scream or cry. Lapis and Lazuli sneak worried, sidelong glances at me; their determination has evaporated now that they know my parents already tried.

Already failed.

Even Amy has uncrossed her arms and stares hopelessly at her lap.

"At least … " Em searches for something, anything, to say to make it all okay. "At least, the Tribunal thanked Clay for all he did to help break the curse and even said they regret what they have to do."

"But they're still going to do it," Clay says, the words settling over the table like sand after a storm. He doesn't say anything else, and I know it's for my sake. He doesn't want to say anything that would offend my parents, doesn't want to speak against my culture, but all the anger lurks just beneath the surface. I can sense it, and it makes me feel so helpless. All I want to do is soothe it for him, make it better.

"You're always saying you want a normal relationship," my mother says to me, trying for genuine comfort. "Maybe you can look at this as your chance. At least this way, you and Clay can enjoy each other's company without so many concerns looming over you." She doesn't have to say what concerns she's talking about. We all know: whether or not I'll leave to live in the ocean, and how we'll ever be together long-term when I'm going to live forever and he's going to … well, not live forever.

"You think that makes this okay?" I ask. "How can you make it sound like I was asking for this?"

Em jumps in before my mother can respond, "Aurelia, she didn't mean it that way, and you know it. Try to calm down."

"Calm down? Calm down! Em, what if it were Leo? What if they wanted to just erase some of the memories you two have shared? Who knows what Clay will forget?"

The other day in Clay's den, when he saw my tail up close, when he stroked it before kissing me, gills and all … will that memory just be wiped out? How is that fair? It makes me glad I didn't use my tail when we went snorkeling; at least he'll remember that. My mind reels as it sifts through our time together, cataloguing which memories will get to stay and which will melt away. He'll forget the grottos, but at least we haven't spent much time down there. I'm suddenly overjoyed that until that day in Clay's den, I'd insisted on keeping our time together so human. He'll remember our sushi dates, our visits to the pier, our trip to the guitar shop in LA, all the makeout sessions after his gigs. And obviously, all the time we spent together before he learned I'm a Mermaid.

That's something, but it's not good enough. Not when everything was finally out in the open. I spent so long hiding who I was from Clay. Being honest with him brought our relationship out of the dark, made it real. I won't go backwards with him. I can't.

So I come up with a plan.

"What is it you want to tell me?" Clay asks once we're alone. "Does it have something to do with why you stopped fighting with your parents?"

"It's almost scary how well you know me," I say.

"Well, I knew you wouldn't give in unless you had some idea how to fix this." My worry must show on my face because he adds, "You did a good job of continuing to put on a show. Your parents thought they finally calmed you down. Your whole family did—except maybe Amy. I never really know what she's thinking, but she'd never rat you out. So, what's the plan? I know you've got one." He cocks an eyebrow at me and waits.

"It's not a very good one," I say. The guarded hope in his gaze makes me afraid I'll disappoint him. "I can't stop them from making you drink the potion. If my parents, with all their clout, couldn't convince them to change their minds, no one can. They must be really freaked out about our kind being discovered."

Clay swallows and fights to keep his face from falling. "Why did I have to mention my dad at all? Damnit." He kicks a stone hard as we continue walking along the deserted beach.

"You couldn't have known," I say. But I should have. I wasn't thinking when I agreed to go to that dinner. All I thought about was that Clay wanted me there.

Before Clay or I start swimming in a guilt swamp, I push on. "Since we can't convince the Tribunal it's safe for you to know about Mer, we need to make them—make everyone—think we've come to terms with wiping Merkind from your memory. We should give my parents some kind of talk about how even though we're still upset, we understand why keeping Mer existence a secret is so important. We'll say we've talked it over and we're willing to make the sacrifice."

"But I'm not willing to make the sacrifice. Not when it's completely unnecessary. Lia, I would never, ever tell anyone. I would never put you—or any of you—in that kind of danger." Hurt at being accused of such a thing simmers beneath the surface of his words.

"I know that, I do. But see, if we keep fighting them, they won't trust us. And then we'll never be able to pull off the next part."

"Which is what? Because you're saying I still need to drink that potion, so I don't know what kind of plan this could be."

"You'll drink the potion and forget about the Mer," I say. "But not for long. Tomorrow night, we'll spend some time alone, and I'll tell you everything you've forgotten. If you don't believe me, I'll show you my tail. It worked the first time." A memory of Melusine forcing me to confess I was a Mermaid and show Clay my tail rises in my mind. "Then I'll take you memory by memory, filling in the blanks. We'll stay up all night if we have to. Your mom will still be up in Monterey, right?"

"Yeah. She left for her book signing yesterday. But, Lia, if your plan is to tell me about all the memories they take from me … " He stops walking and turns to face me, then tucks a strand of my hair behind my ear. In a quiet voice, like he's afraid to shatter my hopes, he says, "Don't you think everyone might worry that you'll do exactly that?"

"The Tribunal will make me swear not to, they said so this morning—it's what gave me the idea."

"Even so … "

"I know. That's why you're going to decide you want your memories of the Mer to go away. You're going to give a speech about how much you just want a normal relationship with me … and most of all, how painful it is for you to think about Melusine sirening you. How you have nightmares about it and about her and her father trying to kill us. You're going to say losing your memories of the Mer

97

will be a relief. Then later, I'll cry to my parents about how much it hurts me to know you were suffering and how *of course* I'll respect your wishes because it's your mind and they're your memories. By the time we're done, everyone will think we've found the good in a bad situation and have accepted what needs to be done."

"You mean I'm just supposed to walk up there tomorrow and gulp down some potion that'll alter how I remember our relationship?" He stares out at the ocean with eyes that could burn. When he turns back to me, something naked, something painful etches itself onto his face. "Lia, I've learned so much about you, about your culture … I don't want to forget that."

"Are you saying you won't like me anymore if I'm just the cute girl from your history class?" I'm hoping the joke will diffuse the tension and make him smile, but as soon as the words leave my mouth, they feel wildly inappropriate. "Sorry," I mumble. I don't want to diminish how he's feeling. He has every right to be upset, even to explode if he wants to.

He shakes his head. "You could never 'just' be anything to me. And you know I loved you before I had any clue you were a Mermaid. I could never not love you. But we're more than that now. You and me, we're … " His eyes search mine, as deep and vast as the ocean that crashes behind me.

"I know," I whisper, stepping closer. He rests his forehead against mine, and I close my eyes. His breath caresses my skin. "That's why I won't let them ruin what we have. I'll tell you about every memory."

"It's not the same. It won't be the same." I don't know whether to be relieved or crushed at the resignation slipping into his voice.

"No, it won't be." Now that resignation fills my voice, too. Using every grain of my strength, of my belief in us, I replace it with resolve. "But it's the only way they'll leave us alone, so we're free to make new memories." I want to cry. Instead, I say, "What's losing a few months compared to the lifetime ahead of us?"

He doesn't lift his head from where his forehead still exerts gentle pressure against mine. And he doesn't open his eyes, either. Just places his large hands on my waist, not pulling me in, but holding on to me, like I'm an anchor. His anchor.

Will he forget this, too? The thought makes tears sting my throat, but I push them down. I've never needed to be stronger than I do in this moment.

We stand like that in silence as the sun sinks lower in the sky. I know with each passing second, he's coming to terms with it. With letting them steal into his mind. He must see what I do—that it's our only real option aside from giving up. Finally, he whispers, in a voice choked with more emotion than he probably wants me to hear, "Then here's to making new memories."

Now he does pull me in, pressing my body flush against his and seizing my mouth violently with his. There's a wildness, a fervor, in his kiss I've never felt before. Like he's searching. Desperately.

So I push back with equal ferocity. *I'm here,* I tell him. With lips and tongue, I make him believe me. And he takes it, gripping my waist even harder before thrusting his hands into my hair and locking us together. It's the fiercest, most loyal kiss we've ever shared.

When we finally rip our mouths apart, both gasping for breath, clarity careens into me. I know everything.

I know what I want.

I know what our first new memory needs to be.

And I know now's the time to make that memory. But not here. Not on this beach. Not anywhere near the grottos or my family or anything Mer. Because this is going to be a night to remember.

❖❖❖

"You what?" With a sharp yank on the steering wheel, Clay pulls his Mustang off the road and onto the shoulder.

"I want to. Tonight."

Clay stares at me, stunned. The sunset paints his face in orange and blue shadow. "But the potion … "

"It'll only take your Mer memories," I say. "That's why I wanted to leave the beach. If we go to your house, your room … " Sure, I showed Clay my tail in his den but never in his bedroom. "We've only ever been human in your room. It'll be like our sanctuary." It always has been.

"I-I thought you wanted to wait."

"I did. But that was before a group of judges who I didn't choose decided to capsize my entire life." I unclick my seatbelt so I can turn to fully face Clay. "I wanted to wait because I thought we had time."

"We do," he says. So many emotions play across his face, but he keeps landing on concern. "No matter what I forget tomorrow, I won't forget I love you." He reaches out a hand to cup my cheek, and I lean into his touch. "I'll never forget how much I want you."

"I believe you," I say. "But that's just it. After tomorrow, you won't want *me*. Not the real me, anyway. Because it won't be all of me. I'm going to do my best to narrate every memory you lose, but it won't be the same, not really. Even once you know I'm a Mermaid again, we'll never have these months back, so there'll always be missing pieces. Missing moments. You'll never have all of me again—not the way you do tonight."

A tear rolls down my cheek, and Clay catches the pearl between his fingertips.

He pulls his hand away so he can stare at it, and my cheek feels cold. I can see his mind working as he rubs that pearl between his thumb and forefinger.

"Lia, you know I want to. God, I've wanted to for … but not if you're not ready."

"I appreciate that, I do. But who says I'm not? Hearing what you said in that courtroom about my Community, my culture … seeing what you're willing to go through just to be with me … " Another tear threatens. "Clay, I've never loved you more."

Our lips meet then, tender and sweet. "You mean everything," I whisper. "Everything." And this time the kiss is deeper, so deep we both get lost in it. "This is our last chance to have all of each other," I say, pleading with him to understand.

"I-I just don't want you to do anything you'll regret." The sun has disappeared behind the ocean, and darkness presses in from outside the windows, surrounding us as we huddle close together in the shelter of Clay's car.

"I could never regret being with you."

"But—"

"Listen to me." Now it's my turn to touch his cheek. I place my hands on either side of his face and lock my intent gaze on his. "Not ever. You are the one for me. You know that and I know that. This is what I want."

As sure as I am of my own feelings, fear and self-consciousness suddenly seize me—what if this isn't what Clay wants? This is all *a lot* to deal with. I let the next words spill out of me in a rush, "But if it's all too complicated … " I swallow and say the thing I don't want to say. "If *I'm* too complicated and you want something," someone … "simpler—"

He doesn't let me finish. "I don't want simple," he says, staring right at me. Then he smiles, and it's *so* genuine. "I want magical."

His words touch something deep inside me. "This is what I want." I say again, more sure than ever. "You're what I want."

Clay's eyes close as he bites his bottom lip. When he opens them again, desire darkens the hazel. I've never seen such naked hunger. "You're what I want," he echoes, voice gravelly and rough. "You're all I want." In that instant, the last of his restraint melts away. This time, the force of his kiss astounds me with its heady mixture of honesty and pure, uncaged ferocity. I push back with lips and tongue, stoking the growing fire between us. Has Clay always tasted this *good?*

When we release each other, Clay presses a button that rolls the convertible's top down, and the sea wind whips my hair in every direction. "Let's make a memory they can't take from you," I say into the night. He revs the engine into roaring life and thrusts us back into the rush of the street, toward his house and all that waits for us there.

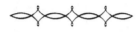

Clean sheets and laundry soap and cinnamon. Clay's room smells the way it always does. The way it did the first day I saw it. Before I knew Clay was sirened, before he knew I was a Mermaid, before I was even sure he liked me. I love this room.

I've been here a zillion times, but tonight … tonight it feels entirely the same as always, and yet completely different. Knowing why I'm here makes the room feel smaller and larger and perfect and entirely surreal. My feet stop in the doorway, hesitating for just a moment at the threshold. Then Clay walks around me and into the room, and the spell breaks. With Clay in it, the bedroom feels like his again. Like a place where I'm welcome. A place I know. I step inside.

Even though Clay's mom is still in Monterey, I lock the door this time—and a thrill bolts down my spine as the telltale *click* echoes through the room.

Clay's guitar rests on his flannel bedspread; he doesn't keep it hidden anymore. But now he picks it up and places it on a nearby chair to make room on the bed.

The bed that stands there, dominating the entire room. Has it always been so big? I swallow. Clay sits on the edge of the mattress, so I join him, like I have a hundred, two hundred times before. Can he feel the new tension wrapped around me like tangled seaweed strands?

We've agreed not to speak once we're in his room so there's no risk one of us will say something Mer-related. Instead, Clay lets his kisses and his hands speak for him.

His palms skim up and down my arms, leaving streaks of exhilarating tingles in their wake from shoulder to wrist. My fingers twine into his hair as our mouths latch together, more lasting and leading than ever before. Then his mouth moves down to my throat and I gasp at its warmth and at the cool heat it creates. I chase the sensation until it's too strong, crashing over me like tidal waves. That's when I pull his mouth, so talented and tempting, back to mine.

Emboldened by the silence and the storminess in Clay's unguarded hazel eyes, I lie back on the soft bedding, feeling one strap of my tank top slip down from my shoulder. I bite my lip, my expression a question, an invitation. He grabs what he needs from the nightstand (and there's something that seems both so comforting and so momentous about that small, foil packet), then he moves toward me, balancing his weight on strong, muscled arms until those same arms wrap around me, and knowing hands slide under the fabric of my shirt, against the bare skin of my back, crushing me against him.

Time surges and crests, and we move with it, holding each other close.

Close.

So close.

Closer than we've ever been.

It's rebellion and solace.

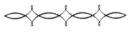

It all goes according to plan. For once. Clay and I told my parents we decided to accept the Tribunal's decision and continue dating with me pretending to be human, just as they proposed. They believed us,

I think because we looked so miserable about the decision. A part of my miserable expression came from the sick twisting in my stomach when I uttered the deceptive words straight to my parents' concerned faces. Was it only last week that I'd sworn to myself I'd never lie to them again?

Then, we headed to the Foundation with my family, where we met with the Tribunal, not in the courtroom in front of a gallery of onlookers, but in a private conference room. They selected a room on one of the dry upper floors that are human-friendly so that, after Clay drinks the potion, I can tell him he was here helping me do some filing for my parents. When Clay and I first walked in with my family, the sight of the Tribunal members seated along one side of the metal conference table wearing business suits—and legs—disconcerted us after weeks of staring at them for hours on end seated on white marble thrones in their jewel-toned tails.

When they asked Clay if he would agree to drink the potion willingly, he consented and began the speech he and I had rehearsed, stating what a relief it would be for him to get rid of his traumatic memories of Melusine and her sireny.

He's still talking now, as I sit here with a carefully constructed expression of compassion and sadness at how plagued he is.

In truth, a large part of me is sad—devastated even—at what's about to happen and about how much work it will probably take for Clay and me to reconstruct his memories, to rebuild what we have. But another part of me can't focus on his words or the Tribunal or the conference room. Because a big part of me isn't even here.

It's back in Clay's bedroom, replaying last night. Replaying the glorious sight of him. The way the sheets crumpled in my palms, the way his caring, comforting sounds caressed my ears, the way his body pressed against mine, taking me somewhere new.

I always thought I'd feel different after, but I don't. And I do. I feel more aware somehow, more awake, but I still feel like myself. I feel *more* myself. Like I did something I'd always known I'd do in a way that made me feel like me. Maybe it's because I love him and he loves me. Maybe it's because I chose when. Maybe it's because it was in a room I love so much or because he smelled so good. I've never been that close to another person. As I look at him now, remembering his breath as it mingled with mine, our bodies intertwined, I know with everything I am that from now on, we'll always be that close. We'll be that close forever.

My attention settles back into the conference room as Clay tells the Tribunal and my parents how much easier he thinks our relationship will be once he doesn't have to carry the baggage of knowing what Melusine did to him, or wondering when I'm going to move back to the ocean, or worrying about how we'll possibly make it work now that I'm immortal.

"It was so much simpler before I knew," Clay says. The Tribunal nod approvingly, no doubt feeling justified and smug. My parents share a knowing look that makes my jaw clench.

I'm the only one who understands what he's really saying and, despite the pain contorting my face, his words soothe some of my tension. I flash back to what he told me so passionately last night: *I don't want simple. I want magical.*

Clay doesn't mean what he's saying now. He meant what he said last night.

One of the Tribunal members addresses him. "We need to search your person to ensure you haven't left yourself a letter informing you about Merkind, in your jacket pocket, for instance. We've already had operatives search your house and automobile."

Clay's jaw tightens, no doubt at the thought of them rummaging through his things without his knowledge or permission, but he drops his shoulders and lets it go. The more he cooperates, the more likely everyone is to believe him.

A male Tribunal member performs a full pat-down, checking inside every pocket. It reminds me of what I imagine airport security is like, not that I've ever traveled. No one asks Clay to take off his shoes like they do at airports on T.V., but they check everywhere else, even his waistband.

With that done, another member of the Tribunal—a hulking Merman who identifies himself as the Foundation's leading potions expert—hands Clay an inconspicuous paper cup filled with a sharp, minty liquid. The potion.

As he raises it to his lips, lips I've so recently marked with my own, his hazel eyes meet mine and I read the promise in them. We're in this together. We have each other.

We do, I try to answer back with my gaze. Always.

He tilts his head back, throat working as he swallows.

No one in the room makes a sound.

Clay wipes his mouth with one hand and stares down into the now-empty paper cup, dazed. Next, he glances around the mundane conference room as if trying to remember how he got here. The Tribunal told us he would be especially impressionable for the first few minutes to help with the transition.

"Clay," the potions expert says, capturing his attention.

"Yes?" he answers, latching on to the familiar sound of his name.

"How are you feeling?"

"Fine, thank you," he says. "How are you?" I let out a breath.

"Do you know why you're here today?"

His gaze moves sluggishly around the room, and he lets out a self-conscious laugh. "Uh ... no. That's weird, right?" He licks his lips, no doubt tasting the minty remains of the potion. "Brain freeze?"

"Do you believe in magic, Clay?"

"Like rabbits in hats? Hey, anything's possible at kids' birthday parties, right?" The self-conscious laugh again. "Sorry. Do I know you?" he asks the Merman questioning him.

"What about spells, magical creatures of any kind? Do you believe in those?"

"Does anybody really? Except maybe my mom, but y'know she has an excuse. Writer," he says with an eye roll. "When did I get here?"

"Have you ever seen anything you think would qualify as real magic or a real magical creature?"

Clay's eyes are open and honest, almost childlike in their gullibility. "No, never."

A wave of general relief sweeps over the Tribunal members. A pang of sorrow hits me. *You planned for this,* I remind myself. *You'll tell him later.*

"That's good, Clay," the Merman says. "You're at the Foundation for the Preservation and Protection of Marine Life. You've been helping to do some filing for your community service hours. Remember?"

"Yeah, that's right. I remember." He latches on to the false memory, and some of the fog lifts from his eyes.

That's my cue.

I step closer to him, rest a comforting hand on his forearm, and say what the Tribunal instructed me to: "Clay, my parents say we're done with all the filing. We can get going now. I'll walk you home."

Clay turns to me and cocks his head. "Who are you?"

Chapter Twelve

My heart stops. He stares down at where my hand still rests on his arm.

"Do I know you?"

"Yes, I'm—"

The Merman slams his palm down on the conference table. "Stop." He holds a hand up in my direction, then addresses Clay. "Do you know this girl?"

Clay stares at me for several long seconds. *Please. Oh, please.*

"No," he says. My heart plummets through the floor, into the dank, hidden waters below the building. *No.* "Is she one of the other volunteers?" He aims a benign smile in my direction as he politely pulls his arm back. There isn't a speck of recognition in his glazed eyes.

Before I even know what's happening, three of the Tribunal members rise from the conference table and surround me. Two grip me by either arm, and one stands between me and Clay. "Hey!"

Within seconds, they've pulled me into an adjacent room. They're all so much taller than I am, so much bigger, that all I can see is the starched gray fabric of their suits. The door clicks shut behind us.

"That's quite enough," my mother's clipped voice says from somewhere near the door. The suited Tribunal members unhand me at once, and my parents are instantly by my side.

"Are you all right, Lia?" my father asks.

"Clay! I need to talk to Clay." I push past my father toward the door, jiggle the knob, harder and harder, but it's locked. "Open it," I say, half threat, half sob.

"We're not going to do that," one of the Tribunal members says. Behind him, one of those two-way mirrors like the kind in a detective show takes up a whole wall. I rush to the glass.

"Aurelia," my mother says, "Perhaps you should—"

"Shhh!" I say.

Clay's talking. His words fill the entire room, like we're inside a *konklili.* They're echoey and strange. This isn't human technology, like the mirror. It's Mer magic.

"Where did those people go? Is something wrong?" Clay asks.

Yes. Everything. Everything is wrong.

"Everything is fine," the Merman says in a soothing voice. "Clay, what school do you go to? Can you describe it?"

"Sure, Malibu Hills Prep. It's a bunch of Mediterranean buildings with palm trees everywhere and all these cool winding paths."

"And what's your mother's name?"

"Andrea Lund Ericson. But she stopped using Ericson professionally after the divorce."

"And what's your girlfriend's name?"

My body inches closer to the mirror. Closer to Clay. I hold my breath.

"D-do I have a girlfriend?" His whole face scrunches up in confusion. It's so similar to the strained expression he used to get when under sireny that an eerie chill skitters down my spine. "I can't remember."

He can't remember.

He can't remember me.

The room—the world—spins. I press my palms against the glass to keep from collapsing. My mother steps behind me and places a hand on my shoulder, but I barely feel it.

"Yes!" I scream as loud as I can. But neither the Tribunal members still in the other room nor Clay so much as twitch. "Yes!" I scream again. They can't hear me.

"No, you don't," the Merman says, in calm, measured tones. "You did. Her name was Lia."

"Leah," Clay says, like he's a toddler learning a new word.

"The two of you ended things because you had nothing in common." How dare he? "Isn't that right, Clay?"

"Yes, that's right. We had nothing in common," he mimics. "So we ended things."

And just like that, my relationship with Clay—the most important, shining thing in my whole life—is gone.

Wiped out like a footprint in the sand.

I shake my head back and forth, back and forth.

"Clay, this is Maribel," the Merman says, indicating one of the other Tribunal members. "She's going to speak with you a bit more and then take you home. Thank you for volunteering at the Foundation for the Preservation and Protection of Marine Life."

"You're welcome," Clay answers, voice polite and detached as he follows his guide out an exit on the other side of the room.

"Stop!" I cry. I can't let him leave, can't let this happen. Can't let him forget me. I pound my fists against the glass. "Clay!" Harder and harder, louder and louder until my hands throb and my throat burns raw. "Clay!"

His name rips through me as tears flood my eyes, blurring my last sight of his back as it disappears through the door.

Chapter Thirteen

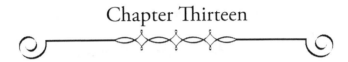

C lay doesn't remember me, Clay doesn't remember me, Clay doesn't—

"Are you hearing me?" my mother asks. "Sweetheart, you've had a shock. Come sit down." Hands steer me into a chair.

When the potions expert walks in, venom shoots through me. "What did you do?" I rasp out, my voice broken. Everything's broken.

He sinks, slowly, into the only other chair in this small antechamber, and the other Tribunal members stand around him in silent support. There're too many of them; I can't breathe.

"Clearly," he says with maddening calm, "the potion was a success."

I balk. "A success? How can you say that?"

"It was meant to eliminate his memories of the Mer. You are a Mermaid. The potion was merely more vigorous than we anticipated."

"We understand how troubling this must be for you," says the Mermaid who occupied the central throne during the trial.

You understand? Really? It takes all my self-control not to fling the words at her. "How do we fix it?" Even as I ask the question, the sickening, devastating answer slithers through my mind, but I can't face it.

"I'm afraid it's permanent, Miss Nautilus," says the Mermaid. "It's a powerful potion with no antidote. That's part of the reason we chose it—to ensure its effects would never wear off."

"You're telling me you're going to do nothing." It's not a question. It's knowledge that leeches into my bones, stealing all the warmth from my body.

"Ultimately," says the potions expert, "the Community and all Merkind are safer this way. That is our primary concern, as it should be."

"And that is why," says the Mermaid, "we need you to take an oath swearing you won't see him again. He won't remember you, and we can't risk your presence confusing him if someone he's with does remember you and knows you were his girlfriend."

Before I can shout my refusal, my father places a hand on mine and says in a sedate voice so rare for him, "It's the only option at this point. If you see Clay in front of his mom or one of your friends, like Kelsey, they'll think he has amnesia or that something is seriously wrong with him. That'll lead to all sorts of questions we can't answer."

"So, what? I'm just never supposed to go to school again?"

"We'll have to devise an alternative now. Perhaps the Foundation's Mer high school in the grottos. You can't risk running into him in front of anyone. It'll be traumatizing for him and dangerous for us," my mother says, staring at me with imploring eyes.

So many words. They bombard my ears with noise. Noise full of reason after reason why I should accept the unacceptable. Why I should curl my tail around me in defeat.

"No."

"No?" The potions expert—*some expert,* I think to myself—arches an eyebrow.

"No." I repeat. "I won't agree to not see Clay. To just give up." On him. On us. "I won't do it."

"Then I'm afraid you leave us no choice," says the Mermaid.

What's that supposed to mean?

Without another word, all the Tribunal members line up in the same order they sat in at the trial, spines erect and eyes staring straight ahead.

"Aurelia Nautilus," intones the Mermaid once again positioned at the center, *"we hereby forbid you from being within sixty yards of the human Clay Ericson or seeking any other means of communication with him. Any violation of this edict will result in immediate imprisonment for not less than the minimum sentence of fifty years and not more than one hundred years."*

And just like that, I can never see Clay again.

Chapter Fourteen

My parents take my phone and all my other devices. They tell me once I figure out how to break the news to Kelsey and my other human friends that I won't be returning to my school for senior year, they'll give me my laptop back so I can send some supervised e-mails. Kelsey'll probably get them once she comes home from France—and she'll hate me.

But at least hate is something. It's more than Clay will feel. Because to him, I'm nothing. I don't even exist.

My sisters aren't going to sneak me their phones, not even Amy. Not now they know I could be imprisoned for sending a single text message to Clay. And even if I could send a hundred texts, it wouldn't do any good anyway. What am I supposed to say? Hi, you don't know me, but I'm in love with you, and just last night we ...

A fresh wave of sobs seizes me by the chest, yanking until I can't breathe. Last night, Clay and I gave something unparalleled to each other. Last night, I shared a part of myself I've never shared with anyone. Last night, we both became something more than ourselves.

And today, every new touch, every gasped breath, every promise-filled gaze has been erased.

Like last night never happened.

Like we never made that commitment, that connection to each other.

Who am I kidding? It's like we never met at all.

The tears don't stop. I don't think I've ever cried this many. They roll below me under the blankets of my upstairs bed, hard pebbles of grief that dig into my skin.

Once my parents have locked up every possible means of human communication in some hidden corner of our massive house (for "my own good"), they return to my room. My mother wears a firm, determined expression I know from years of experience means she's trying to convince everyone—and herself—she's in control of a situation. My father just stares down at his hands clasped in front of him.

The bed dips as he settles himself on the edge of it, my mom standing next to him.

"We're so sorry this happened, seashell," my dad says, patting my hand where it sticks out from under the covers.

"You should be," I say. The words stick in my constricted throat, but I push them out.

My mom's lips tighten.

"Now wait a minute," my dad says.

"How could you let this happen? How could you?"

"You know we don't have power over the Tribunal once they're selected and sworn in," my mother says. "Even if we were already crowned as monarchs—which we're not—our power wouldn't stretch above the rule of law."

"Stop it! Stop reciting legalities like I'm some P.R. assistant at the Foundation. I'm your daughter."

"I know that." My mother's voice is quiet, controlled. The opposite of mine.

"Then how could you let them do this? You've always been in charge of everything. You control the whole Community. Why couldn't you control this?"

"We wish we could," my dad says, still patting my hand.

"Aurelia, we hate how hard this is for you," my mom says. "Try to pull yourself out of this. I know it's hard right now," she places a comforting hand on my head where it rests on my pillow, "but try to focus on all the good that can come out of this. You and Clay will both have clean slates now to date people more … suitable for you."

I jolt to a sitting position, jerking my head away from her and my hand back from under my dad's. "How can you say that? I love him. I *love him*."

"We know it feels like that," she says, her hands making a placating gesture, like I'm some mental patient who needs to be soothed. Like just because I'm young and crying, I'm irrational. "The last thing we want is for you to be in pain."

"We like Clay," my dad says in the same soothing, calm-the-crazy-teen voice my mom is using. The one I'm starting to hate. "He's a great guy. And after he saved you, and all of us, well, we certainly weren't going to break the two of you up, but Lia, you know you two couldn't have lasted. The longer it went on the more pain you'd be in later. Try to understand, honey."

"Being with Clay didn't cause me pain. This does. Having all the memories of me—of us—ripped from him. I'm in pain now. And you let it happen." My voice is shaking as much as my hands. I can't talk to them anymore. Can't look at them. "Get out. Please. Get out."

On top of everything is the new and terrible knowledge that my parents aren't on my side.

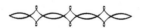

"You shouldn't yell at them," Em says from the doorway. "It isn't their fault." She always sides with my parents. She's the only one of my sisters who was born Below and who has any memories of what it was like to live in hiding, then to flee to a new life here. She was only a toddler, but she remembers the fear and having our mom and dad hide her to protect her from raiders. "It isn't their fault," she says now.

I don't have the energy to argue with her, so I say nothing. Since I don't tell her to leave, she folds the covers back and sits next to me. But once her hand makes contact with the pearl-strewn bed, she hops back up. Without a word, she uses large, sweeping motions to scoop them up, then plucks the ones that are still left from my hair and clothes before depositing the lot into my nightstand drawer.

"You should save these. To make a chain."

The simple, somber words make me grasp her hand and squeeze. Sure, Mer sometimes use the pearls from tears to make frivolous accessories, turning a child's scraped elbow or stubbed fin into a shiny bracelet or headband to make her smile, but those accessories don't stand out in one's memory. Over time, one pearl bracelet looks the same as the next, and who knows if it came from a failed test or a fight with your siblings? Making a chain—an *esslee* in Mermese— is different. That's when a Mermaid or Merman intentionally saves specific tears and uses them all in one long chain interspersed with precious gemstones or carefully selected charms, all meant to commemorate the experience that caused those tears. It means they were shed over something especially meaningful, something life-altering.

We make chains after funerals to commemorate the dead and at weddings, as a gift for the bride and groom—proof of the happy tears given by their loved ones. I've even heard of warriors from Below making chains in remembrance of a limb lost in battle. Such chains are wound in loops around the torso on special occasions to keep a memory alive or used to decorate the home like a piece of fine art or stored and cherished for years to come.

By saying I should make a chain out of these tears, Em is acknowledging the severity of my pain, the severity of what the Tribunal has done to Clay. Instead of trying to sweep what's happened into the seagrass or claiming I'm overreacting, Em is telling me she knows this experience matters.

That's why I don't resist when she takes a clean, loose-fitting T-shirt from my dresser, lifts me up by my arms and wordlessly helps me change, putting the crumpled button-down I wore to the Foundation in my laundry bin. I don't think I'll ever be able to stomach wearing that shirt again.

Once she's replaced my pencil skirt with cupcake-festooned sweat pants, Em scoots behind me against the headboard and uses gentle, experienced fingers to untangle my hair.

In the silence, with Em there coaxing out each snarl, I take my first real breath since I stood in that conference room.

After several minutes of silence, she says, in a voice so quiet I doubt I'd be able to hear her if we weren't sitting so close, "I trusted them, you know. The Tribunal. I never thought they'd give Clay a potion if there was any risk of … this." I feel movement behind me as she shakes her head. "It's so … unfair, so archaic. The kind of extreme, unpredictable potion Mer courts would have used hundreds of years ago."

"That's why I didn't say anything," I tell her, "when I found out Melusine was sirening Clay. I wanted to, but I found out the Mer government Below used to execute any sireny survivors so they couldn't pose a risk to Merkind. I couldn't trust the Foundation not to do the same to him."

"It never would have occurred to me they would do that to him. I've never not trusted the Foundation." Em takes my hair, now free of tangles, and starts putting the strands into one loose braid. "I work there every day and I … I never thought something like this could happen."

Once she finishes the braid, I turn to face her. "If Mom and Dad do … take the throne, that means you'll be queen one day."

Em's eyebrows swim together; clearly this topic has been on her mind. "If you are," I say, "promise me you'll change things. That you'll, I don't know, modernize the laws somehow, to make sure nothing like this can happen again." A fresh wave of tears seizes me. It's already happened to Clay. To me. I clutch on to my big sister's shoulders as my body shakes, overcome.

She holds me tight. "I promise," she whispers.

No sooner has Em left, insistent on making me sugar kelp tea, than Amy comes in balancing a bowl of soup on a tray.

"I picked it up from Sal's on the pier," she says by way of greeting. Her leg control is good enough now for her to walk around the neighborhood, visiting all the places she'd only ever heard about while restricted to the grottos, including Sal's, which makes my favorite clam chowder. The ultimate comfort food. I'm several knots past comfort, but Amy looks so unsure standing in the doorway that I try for a weak smile of gratitude. She sets the tray between us on the bed then looks at me expectantly.

"I'm not really hungry." I stare at the steaming chowder. I'd been meaning to take Clay to Sal's. Now I never will. In my mind's eye, he's sitting at Sal's eating clam chowder and oyster crackers with some simple, boring, pretty, human girl. Playing footsy with her on the sawdust-strewn floor. And he's laughing, happy because he doesn't know what he's lost, doesn't remember me at all.

My expression must register at least some of my regret because Amy's face falls. "Please eat something. You didn't eat this morning." She nudges the bowl closer to me.

"I can't, Aims."

Her gaze wanders helplessly around the room, and she toes her flip-flop on and off, on and off, until a clarity, a decisiveness sparks in her eyes. She picks up the spoon and dunks it in the soup, scooping up a heaping bite of clam and potato.

"Open the stable, here comes the seahorse." They're the same coaxing words I used to use to get her to eat when she was a toddler. She's said the one thing I can't resist. Even though I don't smile—can't smile—I open my mouth and let the seahorse spoon swim inside.

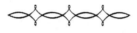

"All I can say," Lazuli says as she and Lapis come in and take up residence on my bed, "is that the Tribunal are assholes."

"Damn straight," Lapis adds before breaking off a piece of the whole wheat roll Amy brought, dunking it in my chowder, and sticking it in her mouth. I rest my head on her shoulder.

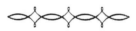

Part of me wants to ask them to leave so I can be alone to … what? Mourn, plot, sleep? I'm not even sure. I feel trapped in some alternate reality that can't be my real life. Trapped and exhausted. That's why I let them stay. Let Em ply me with tea and Amy cuddle me and the twins turn on some brainless comedy on the little-used T.V. hidden away in my bureau.

They stay like that for hours, until all the light is gone from the windows. My eyes, raw and red, droop with the desperate need to close. Other than the one time I caught a human strain of the flu at school and had to stay dry, I've never slept anywhere but on my sea sponge bed in the grottos under a satiny layer of salt water, but I have no resolve to move, to face my parents, to drag myself from this bed where Clay so often held me, laughed with me, kissed me. While my sisters sit finishing the movie, I slip out of my sweatpants and under the duvet cover, letting my tail free as I surrender to a heavy, thunking sleep.

When I wake up to blazing, orange sunlight streaming through the window, warmth surrounds me. Lapis lies on one side of me, Lazuli on the other, with Em draped along the end of the bed and Amy curled up in her arms. My whole bed is a heap of jeweled tails.

I shut my eyes again, willing myself to fall back asleep, to fight off the riptide of my own thoughts. Right now, consciousness is my enemy, but I'm on the losing side of this battle. Instead of receding into a sleepy fog, my thoughts clang against each other like swords.

So I lie there between my sleeping sisters while my own brain wreaks havoc on me. I try every trick to make myself fall into a mindless, quiet sleep, from focusing on my breaths to counting shells, but I can't block out scenes from yesterday as they replay over and over. If I'd knocked that potion out of his hand at the last second, if I'd fought off the Tribunal members, if I'd—

Footsteps clap down the hallway toward my room. Two sets of feet. It must be around six o'clock now, and my parents are leaving for work. Today's another normal day for them.

You're not being fair, the good-girl voice inside me whispers. *They didn't know. They couldn't stop it.*

They didn't want to stop it, another, darker part of me thinks. *They didn't want you to be with Clay. They said so last night.*

When the knob turns, I shut my eyes, pretending to be asleep until the door shuts again. I sigh. Trying to fall back asleep now is useless, so I wait until I'm sure my parents have left, then transform into my legs before extricating myself from the bed, careful not to wake Em, Amy, or the twins. It's partly consideration and partly that I don't want to talk to them or see the pity that's sure to fill their eyes the instant they open them and look at me. I slip on my sweatpants and slip out of the room.

On the entrance hall table sits a note addressed to me in my mother's elegant handwriting. It says how she and my dad know this must be hard for me, how the Foundation is covertly monitoring Clay to ensure his mental and emotional stability so I shouldn't worry, how they love me and trust that I'll follow the Tribunal's order to stay away from him.

They trust me? Then why are four of the guards who have been staying in a completely different wing of our house now stationed at the front and back doors? I bet if I checked, all the other exits, including the one in the grottos, would be guarded, too. Overnight, I've gone from being a lauded savior to a prisoner in my own home.

My parents shouldn't have bothered with the guards. No matter how much I want to, I'm not going to go running to see Clay when he … when he doesn't remember me; any encounter we have now will leave him thinking either I'm crazy or he is. When he doesn't even recognize me, how can I tell him we're in love? Madly, deeply, in every way in love? I can't.

Who are you? The memory of his blank face slices through my heart. I can't scrub away the image of his hazel eyes—eyes that have looked at me every day for months like I'm cherished, like I'm loved—staring at me like I was a total stranger.

When less than forty-eight hours earlier we …

I swallow, refusing to break down again. I grab a blanket from the living room and head to the backyard. A guard eyes me as I walk past him and slip through the sliding glass door, but he relaxes when I settle onto the sectional next to the outdoor fire pit, now empty and cold.

I wrap the blanket around me as much for comfort as for warmth while I sit and stare out at the ocean, a pale grey-blue in the early morning light.

I take deep, full breaths of the salty ocean air, and let myself get lost in the familiar, repetitive rhythm of the waves. I don't know how long I give in to their hypnosis before sharp words pierce through the lull.

"I need to see her," a low, masculine voice says to the guard at the entrance.

My heart leaps like a jumping carp. Clay? Did the potion wear off? Has he remembered and come looking for me?

But no. The voice is wrong—restrained, firm but polite, deferential. I will my heart to beat normally.

"Your orders are to keep her in, correct? Not to keep anyone else out." Persuasive. Logical.

Before he enters the backyard down the side path, I know it's Caspian rounding the corner. What I don't expect is that he's sopping wet, his swim trunks clinging to him and his blond hair dripping onto the patio. "I tried the grotto entrance first, but the guard stationed there said everyone was upstairs. It seemed like a waste to swim home and dry off when I was already here."

I fling the blanket off my shoulders and onto his as I say, "I fell asleep upstairs last night and my sisters … didn't want me to be alone, so they stayed up there with me. They're still sleeping."

Caspian tilts his head, like he's not even sure how I can sleep without being wet, but he lets it go. "Your parents told my parents what happened. I figured you wouldn't be talking to anybody last night, but I couldn't wait any longer than that. I didn't want you to feel alone."

I've been rubbing the blanket up and down his arms to warm him up, but now my hands pause and I peer up into his face, my head angled nearly all the way back because of his height. "Thank you," I say.

Even surrounded by my sisters, I'd felt alone. Now … well, having

Caspian here doesn't change anything, doesn't fix anything, but it does help somehow. Having him close soothes something deep inside me, reminds me that there's someone who's always on my side. "I'm really glad you came." I didn't realize how glad until this moment. It's a moment that stretches between us.

I slow my hands, then pull them away.

"Of course I came." Caspian takes a step back as he starts vigorously drying his hair and ears. "I'm sorry you have to go through this. Is it stupid to ask how you are?"

"I'm ..." What? "... frozen. It's like everything in my life just ... stopped." I sink back onto the sectional. "And I don't know what to do. I thought my parents could help, but they say legally, they couldn't stop it."

"No, once a Tribunal has been selected and sworn in, its members have complete authority to decide any issues, anticipated or otherwise, in connection to a case."

It figures Caspian knows that. I shake my head, "Still ..."

"I'm sure they wish they could have helped."

Do they? "It doesn't change anything either way. Now that Clay's drunk the potion ..."

"There's no antidote," Caspian finishes.

"That's what the Tribunal told them, told all of us, but—"

"No, Lia, there's no antidote. As soon as I found out what happened, I talked to my grandmother about it." Caspian's grandmother knows more about potions than anyone (if she hadn't been a wizened old woman with terrible arthritis up until three months ago, she'd probably be head of the potions department at the Foundation, even with the stain of Adrianna's sireny on her family). Now, I want to smack myself for being so fin-deep in my own pity party yesterday that I didn't think to go to her right away. I grab Caspian's forearm. "What did she say?"

My face must be wild, desperate, because more pity paints his features than ever before. "The court's required to disclose a list of potions ingredients upon request. For public safety, they don't give out mixing instructions or amounts, but she didn't need those. She put in a request yesterday morning, as soon as she found out what happened, and she spent all yesterday poring over that, researching every ingredient." He sits next to me, and takes my hand. "The potion works by constructing extremely powerful wards that completely block Clay's mind from accessing certain memories. Nearly all of the active ingredients were specifically chosen for their permanence." He looks directly at me, speaking slowly, willing me to understand. "My grandmother said no potions mixer, no matter how skilled they were, could create an antidote to the potion Clay drank."

I want to protest, to insist she must be wrong, must have missed something.

Reading my expression, Caspian squeezes my hand where it rests in his larger one. "She's certain, Goldfish."

Those words make my stomach sink like a war-torn ship, taking my hopes with it to the ocean floor. When saving Clay from sireny had seemed hopeless, I'd found a way through endless hours of research and my own will. I hadn't found a good way, but the fact that I'd found a way at all had given me some grain of hope I could find a way to reverse that potion. Research my way to some seemingly impossible answer that brought him back to me.

But Caspian's grandmother has devoted her long life to studying and mixing potions, both Below and Above; she understands them better than I ever will. It's how she saved Clay when Melusine nearly poisoned him to death. I've known her since Caspian and I were guppies, and she's one of the few people whose expertise and fierce protectiveness make me trust her judgment implicitly. If she says the potion is permanent ...

"I'm sorry," Caspian says. "I just didn't want you to spend months trying to find an antidote that doesn't exist."

And I would have. But at least it would have given me something to do. In a few days, I would have fought my way out of this frozen numbness and committed myself to getting Clay his memories back. Now that I know it would be useless—that Clay's memories aren't ... I swallow ... aren't coming back, what ... "What am I supposed to do?" I say the words more to myself than to Caspian, but he answers anyway.

"I don't think there's anything you can do. He ... he doesn't know you anymore." A vision dives into my mind: me, accidentally-on purpose running into Clay somewhere where there would be no one like his mom or any of our human friends to recognize me, then asking him out on a first date and starting our relationship from scratch. We'd fall back in love and, once he trusted me again, I could show him my tail and tell him everything. It would be hard for him to believe, but if he really loved me ...

An obvious flaw slashes its way through the fantasy. I could never spend enough time with him to earn his love and trust without someone seeing us, without getting caught and imprisoned by the Foundation until Clay had lived out at least fifty years of his short, human life, maybe more. By then, he'd most likely be married to someone else and have kids ... kids he could never have with me.

"Maybe it's for the best." Caspian's clear, blue eyes beg me not to get mad at him for what he's saying. "After all, even if the potion had worked like it was supposed to, how long could the two of you have made it work without him knowing you're a Mermaid. It wouldn't have been real anyway."

"We had a plan," I say, fixing my gaze on the patio floor instead of on my best friend's face. "I was going to," I take a deep breath, "show Clay my tail and explain everything he'd been forced to forget, only this time we wouldn't tell anyone that he knew."

"You were going to tell him for a second time?"

"I wasn't going to be in a dishonest relationship. Not again."

Caspian takes this in. "I can respect that. But you would have had to lie to everyone else you care about, so maybe this really is better. Clay will get to have a normal life now. And ... you'll move on, too."

"I won't." I'm not being obstinate, just honest. "I won't ever be able to move on from him."

Something like sadness lances across Caspian's features, but he reins it in, replaces it with a comforting expression. "I know you may feel like that now, but—"

"No. This isn't just some high school romance I'm going to get over in a couple months. You just don't understand because you've never been in love."

His azure eyes widen, "Lia, I … "

"I'm not trying to be mean, Casp. You just don't understand what Clay and I have … had. How could you?" His jaw clenches, and he scrubs a hand over his face. "Even if what we had is … gone," I continue, "I'll never just be over it." My next words are a whisper, "I'll never be over him."

Caspian stands, and paces in front of the fire pit. "But the two of you have no future, so where does that leave you?"

I stare out at the wan, fathomless ocean again. "I don't know."

Two weeks. That's how much time my parents let me keep to myself, wandering around the house talking to no one but Barnacle and trying to drown out my constant, useless, torturous thoughts by binge-watching one T.V. series after another.

After that, they find me upstairs in my room. I'm in bed, half-buried under the covers (like I have been most of the past two weeks) with Barnacle snuggled in a warm, comforting ball next to me.

My mom pulls back the baby pink curtains I've drawn and splashes the room in unwanted, ironic sunshine.

"How's the show?" my dad asks, nodding at the television.

"I don't know," I say as I mute it.

"Your mom and I have planned something for you tomorrow. It should be fun."

I pull my body into something resembling a sitting position. "I really don't want t—"

"You don't even need to leave the house," my mother says, her tone telling me whatever this plan is, it's nonnegotiable. "Just the bed."

"Why?" I ask. "What's happening?"

"You're going to have a visitor."

Chapter Fifteen

Palpable relief paints my family's faces when I come down to the breakfast table showered and dressed in real clothes. My hair's still wet, but at least it's washed and combed, which is better than I've been doing lately.

"Aurelia," Em says on a hopeful sigh, pulling out my chair.

Getting myself out of bed and marginally presentable sapped me of my energy, so I just nod. Once I'm seated, awkward silence sets in. My mother gives me a tight-lipped smile, pretending everything's normal as she passes me my crab omelet, but pity tinges her eyes, like it does everyone's.

"Here, Lia, have my strawberries," Amy says, shoveling them onto my plate before I have a chance to answer.

"So," my father says, clapping his hands and slapping on a grin that makes him look more nervous than happy. "You all know about Lia's guest," he says. Lazuli sneaks a sidelong glance at me like she's wondering whether I'll have a breakdown while said guest is here. "What are the rest of you up to today?" With the twins' fall semester starting next week and Amy's the week after, summer freedom is running out.

"We're heading to the mall with Jen B.," Lapis says, then abruptly shuts up when Lazuli elbows her none-too-subtly. Going with friends to the mall—or anywhere I might run into Clay—is off my list of potential activities. Now, instead of teasing me over breakfast like they usually do, the twins shoot me identical apologetic looks before falling silent and focusing on their food.

"How 'bout you, Em?" my dad asks with an uncomfortable laugh.

"After I go to … work," she doesn't say the Foundation, "I have a meeting." With her wedding planner, I'm sure. Because the love of her life is a Merman, so they get to get married and live happily ever after—forever.

"Amy, sweetheart, what about you?" my mother asks.

"I'm heading over to … a friend's." Staskia's. She's going to Staskia's.

Is this what it will be like from now on? Everyone afraid to be themselves in front of me? Treating me like I'm going to break? It makes me so afraid I will.

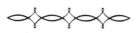

By the afternoon, all I want to do is crawl back into bed. Instead, at my mother's insistence, I change into a formal *siluess*, a garment that looks kind of like a fancy crop top and that Mermaids wear when the bottom half of the body is in tail form. This *siluess* is teal with pearlescent pieces of delphinula shell. Once I'm dressed, I head to the grottos to meet my guest.

My parents have hired me some stuffy, stodgy tutor and expect me to welcome her in style. Because on top of losing Clay, I've lost my school. The friends I've made over the past two years, the classes I've been looking forward to, the teachers I like—all of it gone. Like Clay's memories.

In a few months, I'll be starting at the Mer high school where the Community kids go whose parents are more traditional than mine and favor a Mer education instead of assimilation into human schools. Except while I've been focusing on American literature and A.P. Euro, they've been studying *konklilis* of the classics and interdisciplinary navigation. I'm woefully behind in Mer history, cultural studies, and formal Mermese oration. Not to mention the advanced electives available to seniors like marine botany, Advanced Potion Mixing, and dolphin communication. That's why my parents have decided I'll start mid-way into the semester, once I'm more caught up; until then, I'll spend every weekday studying with some extremely well-respected—and probably extremely boring—tutor visiting from Below. I doubt I'll be able to focus when all I want to do is sneak back up to my room and inhale Clay's scent from the T-shirt he left behind the last time he came over swimming. He's all I think about, but so far, those thoughts haven't gotten me any closer to a solution, a way to help him. Any way at all. And I don't know what kind of future I have without him in it, so why should I care about preparing for a school year—for a life—that doesn't include him?

That's why I'm far from enthusiastic as I move the coatrack in the hall closet aside, step through the false back, walk along the concealed corridor, and head down the winding stairs to the hidden grottos.

Once I'm in the stone entry chamber, I stick my flip-flops on a shelf, hang my wrap-around skirt on one of the wall hooks meant for exactly that purpose, and slide into the canal of silky water that cuts into the middle of the floor and leads around a corner into the rest of the grottos.

When I'm seated, I let my eyes drift closed and allow the sensation of invisible tides to push and pull against my legs as my golden tail slips free in one deeply pleasurable stretch.

Before long, I've swum through the glistening caves comprising the main ballroom, the smaller ballroom, and the formal dining hall before finding my way to the little-used salon my parents have converted to a study for me and this new tutor. Like all the rooms in the grottos, it's a cave filled with salt water up to my waist, so my upper half remains above the water while my tail swishes below. The furniture is mostly made from rock formations along the walls, including a long table flanked on either side by benches with the rest of the room offering plenty of open space for swimming. The walls are studded with opals, and the tabletop is encrusted with an intricate mosaic of a coral reef made from tourmaline of every color.

I've never spent much time in this room before because it's so far from where my sisters' and my grotto bedrooms are, but it's lovely.

I swim over to the table, run a finger along the mosaic, and wait to meet this renowned tutor who will dictate the next several months of my life.

The person who swims through the entrance is someone I never expected to see again.

She glides in on her ice-blue tail, the matching ice-blue streaks in her pale hair skimming the surface of the water. Just like they did in the courtroom, small crystals decorate the skin around her eyes, glittering like tiny diamonds. Her features are delicate, exquisite— like a porcelain doll's. I'm struck once again by the impression that she's some fairytale illustration come to life.

My mother swims in behind her. *"I'm sure you remember each other from the trial, but allow me to formally introduce you. Aurelia, this is Ondine Naiad."*

Ondine dips her waiflike frame forward in the water as her tail flips up behind her, her fins fanning out to face me behind her head; the whole thing looks kind of like a curtsey. It's the traditional Mer introductory greeting used Below. Like every Mer, I learned the same one as a child, but I've known all my parents' colleagues in the Community for so long, it's been years since I've done it. I tip my torso forward and lift my tail in the same formal gesture, but my movements are stilted and awkward, especially compared to her elegant ones. She smiles placidly, but her gray eyes take it all in.

I don't know how I feel about being taught—and judged—by someone who spoke out in favor of a more lenient sentence for Melusine. The woman swimming in front of me is related to the Havelocks. How could my parents have chosen her?

"MerMaiden Naiad is the head of the acclaimed Sea Daughters Academy. Several of the visiting Mer nobles send their girls there." I guess that's why my parents chose her. If Mer nobility send their children to a school she runs, she must have a stellar reputation Below. She *did* say she was disgusted by what the Havelocks did … I'll have to keep an open mind. *"She's taken a sabbatical from her work at the school to come here for the trial,"* my mother continues, *"and she's graciously offered to extend it so she can tutor you."*

"Thank you," I say in Mermese.

"It's my pleasure." Her voice clinks like fine-cut glass, feminine and clear. *"And I'm grateful for the opportunity. I'm afraid my cousins' crimes have put the reputation and fate of my school in jeopardy. This show of faith in my skills as an educator by your family will go a long way toward ensuring Sea Daughters Academy—with its history that stretches back centuries—doesn't close."*

My mother rests a hand on Ondine's shoulder; she and my dad never could resist a good cause. *"Will this room be sufficient?"* she asks Ondine, gesturing around the salon.

"It's lovely," Ondine says, echoing my thoughts from earlier.

"I know you two have a lot to cover," my mother says. *"I'll let you get started."* She swims closer to me and cups my cheek with a comforting hand. *"Learn as much as you can, and try to enjoy yourself, okay?"* Pity soaks my mother's words. She hasn't looked at me the same since the morning Clay drank the potion.

I nod, even though I doubt I'll be able to concentrate on anything.

She drops a kiss on my forehead, then nods to Ondine before she swims out of the room.

And leaves the two of us alone.

Ondine treads there staring at me. She's still smiling—a smile made incandescent by her beauty—but I get the sense she's evaluating me. Right when I think I'm going to start squirming like a fish caught on a line, she says, "Shall we?" and uses a long, willowy arm to indicate the table.

We take seats opposite one another on the benches.

"Now, do you go by Aurelia or Lia?" She's switched to English, a gesture which surprises me, both because she's visiting from Below, and because one of the subjects she'll surely be instructing me in is Mermese.

"Either's fine," I say, "But only my mom and my oldest sister call me Aurelia."

"Lia it is," she says. "And why don't you call me Ondine?"

Call a teacher by her first name? I've never done that before. I can't quite bring myself to say it, so I just nod.

"Now that's settled, let's begin, shall we?" Her Mermese accent makes her English sound exotic and mesmerizing, like a magic spell.

But it's not mesmerizing enough to hold my attention for more than twenty minutes into a lesson on the reign of King Nereus and its impact on Mer art and architecture. I try to concentrate, I do, but all I can think about is how excited Clay and I were when our schedules were posted online, and we found out we were both going to have second period this year with Mr. Reitzel, my favorite history teacher. That's the history class I'm supposed to be in, not here in the grottos by myself learning about Mer dynasties and downfalls. I picture Clay and me, sitting in Mr. Reitzel's sunny classroom, surrounded by our friends. We pull our desks close together, Clay's leg pressed against mine. *Hey, study buddy,* he whispers in my ear before he smirks at me. I can almost feel the warmth of him next to me ...

"Lia?" Ondine raises one colorless, crystal-embellished eyebrow.

Busted.

"Sorry," I mumble, staring at the table.

She stares at me for a long moment. "Don't be sorry," she says at last. "You have quite a lot to face lately, yes?" Of course, she already knows; by now, everyone in the Community and all the visitors from Below know the unexpected results of the potion. "No one can expect you to behave normally."

Really? 'Cause it sure seems like my parents do, setting up these classes and all. And every time we talk, my sisters keep begging me with their big, round eyes to just act normal. Like everything's fine and I'm moving on. But it's not and I can't.

Ondine slides off her bench and swims the length of the room on her frosted tail. Am I in trouble? Is she going to get my mother?

But she swims back toward me, then away again, then back, all the time studying the shimmering walls of the grotto. "This really is a lovely room. And you and I have the privilege of staying here together for the next four hours," she says. "Time is what life is made from. Do you agree?"

Flashes of the first time Clay and I met on the ocean outlook at school, of our first kiss on El Matador Beach, of hours spent talking about everything, of the night we … our last night together. All those moments make up a vital piece of my life. And by stealing those moments, hasn't the Tribunal stolen a piece of Clay's life from him? From us … Yes, time is what life is made from. I nod again.

"Then let us not waste it," Ondine says. "King Nereus is clearly not holding your attention today."

I open my mouth to say I'm sorry, but she holds up a slender-fingered hand. "Do not apologize. Just tell me what will hold your focus so we do not waste the day. We have a lot to catch you up on, Lia. What would you like to learn?"

No teacher has ever asked me that before. Hmm … Anything history related will make me miss Clay and Mr. Reitzel (even if he's never heard of King Nereus), and anything about potions will make me angry or will just make me feel more hopeless. "Maybe, um, deep sea biology." Clay wasn't in my bio class last year and my teacher was boring as a blobfish, so I won't run any risk of losing myself to nostalgia. Plus, marine bio might have been my best subject while I was at a human school, but I know I'm waaaay behind on the intricacies of it emphasized in a Mer education.

"Biology it is," Ondine says as she returns to her place on the bench across from me. "Now, as you may recall, each ocean creature maintains a level of connectivity to the ocean itself, in varying degrees. This explains why ocean plants contain magical properties, as do fish and other sea life, and are often used as potion ingredients as well as in spells and rituals. Merpeople draw upon this same connectivity each time we transform between our tails and our legs. Are you with me so far?" Her eyes narrow—not harsh or critical, just assessing.

I nod. This isn't like my old classes; since Mer culture is built on oral traditions (and on spoken instead of written language), I have no notebook to doodle on while I pretend to pay attention. Even in my old Mer classes at the Foundation school I attended before I got my legs, I could get lost in the back of the classroom if I wanted. But here, with Ondine, I'm the only student, the sole focus, so I can't get away with letting my attention slide. Fortunately, what she's saying now is actually interesting.

It's not until an hour later, once we've reviewed the entire magical hierarchy of sea creatures by genus and she says we should take a break that I realize it's the first time since Clay walked out of that conference room and out of my life that my mind has been fully engaged in anything unrelated to his memory loss.

I spend most of the subsequent lesson on intricate Mermese grammar floating in my own guilt, but I muddle through until I've officially made it through today—my first successful day back as a real, functioning person. Ondine doesn't say anything, doesn't offer me any effusive praise as she hands me a net full of *konklilis* to listen to for homework. But when she dismisses me, she wears a small smile of approval.

Upstairs in my room, I listen all the way through the first two *konklilis* before I let myself miss him again—and burst into tears. Stop it, I tell myself. You're stronger than this. You'll find a way to get through it. Focus on your classes, on your family, on anything but him. Survive. Find a new normal. I force my sobs to subside. I can do this.

I can't do this. Clay's a part of me and, no matter how much I know I have to, I can't just ... so I spend the next week following the same pattern: I throw myself into my studies during the day, then sneak upstairs to my room to cry in secret at night before I go down to bed in the grottos and lie there for hours without sleeping. It's not healthy, I know that, but I don't know how to stop missing him.

I put on a contented mask around everyone so my parents can stop worrying and my sisters can feel okay about enjoying their normal lives. And since I'm doing well in my classes and making myself clean my plate at dinner and contributing to conversations with my sisters that feel as insignificant as daydreams, I have everyone fooled.

Or almost everyone.

Chapter Sixteen

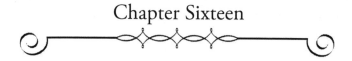

"What is it you're not telling me?" Caspian swims around to face me in his turquoise swimming pool. This is the first time I've been anywhere but my house or the stretch of private beach out back since ...

It feels strange and not strange to be out. Strange that it doesn't feel stranger.

What am I not telling him? Everything. That I'm a mess. That I don't know how to stop obsessing about a boy who doesn't remember me. That without my school, my human friends, or any clear idea of what my future looks like, I don't have a clue how to handle my life right now.

I just shrug.

"That's not an answer." Caspian crosses his large, sculpted arms across his chest and waits. I glance at the two guards who flanked me here on my swim through the grottos, and who now keep watch at the two entrances to Caspian's backyard. I could try to pretend they're following me to protect me instead of to keep me from running to Clay, but the mental trickery takes too much effort. I lower my voice so they won't hear me. "What am I supposed to say?"

"Whatever you want. As long as it's the truth." Despite his insistent body language, Caspian's eyes—as blue and deep as the ocean—are kind. And concerned.

"That I ..." That I'm afraid I'm going crazy? I can't burden him with that. Not after everything he's done for me. He'd spend the next hour—or two, or three, or however long it took—trying to comfort me, but it wouldn't do any good because there's nothing he or anyone else can do to fix it. "That I'm sick of being trapped in my own head. Can we ... can we talk about you for a while?" Now that same concern shining in his eyes creases his brow.

But only for a moment. Then he sighs and musters a half-hearted smile. "Sure." He swims several slow, smooth strokes through the water. "Gemma Auger invited me to her party this Friday."

Gemma Auger. I haven't seen her in a while. She goes to the Foundation's high school with Caspian, so we haven't run into each other much since I transferred to Malibu Hills. She was always nice, though. When we were eight, she let me borrow her starfish hairclips for the class talent show after Lazuli "borrowed" mine the week before and lost them. She's pretty, too. Like, really pretty. With that shiny, shiny hair and those wideset eyes. Is she tall? I try to remember if I've seen her with legs. Why did I never notice whether she was tall? I don't think I like Gemma Auger very much.

"Are you going to go?" I ask.

"Yeah, definitely."

"Oh. Good. That's good. You totally should go. Gemma Auger's really nice."

"Yeah, she is." He takes a stroke toward me. "So, would you like to go ... with me?" He breaks his gaze away, staring at the water. "Because, it would be fun and you should get out, so, right."

"Wouldn't Gemma Auger get the wrong idea if I came with you? I doubt she'd like that seeing as how she invited you and all." Sometimes, Caspian really doesn't get girls.

"Why would she care?" His eyes widen, and he shakes his head. "Oh! No. Gemma didn't *invite me* invite me." The discomfort on his face tells me how much he dislikes such imprecise language.

Caspian's so cute when he gets flustered. It's no wonder Gemma Auger wants to go out with him. A pang of something I can't identify makes my throat constrict, so I clear it before saying, "Oh really? And what exactly did she say when she invited you but didn't *invite you?*"

"She said … " He bites his bottom lip, determined to get every word right. "'Hey, I'm having a party on Friday 'cause my parents'll be Below checking things out. I'd love it if you'd come and … hang'… yeah 'hang with me?'"

"'I'd love it if you'd come and hang with me?'" I raise an eyebrow. "Newsflash, Romeo: she *invited you* invited you." I keep my tone teasing and jokey. After all, this is the first time I've joked about anything in weeks, and it feels nice. A much-needed dose of normalcy and sanity. But there's an undercurrent of sadness I can't shake. Is it guilt for joking around when I still have no idea how to get Clay his memories back? The shocked expression on Caspian's face almost makes me feel as carefree as I'm acting.

"But … Gemma …" He sighs, then stops swimming when he's right in front of me and straightens his shoulders. "Well, it doesn't matter what she meant. She wasn't clear why she was inviting me, and I want you to come, so I'm inviting you."

"Are you *inviting me* inviting me?"

I let the words hang there between us as long as I can before my straight face crumbles and I smile at my own joke. Like he'd ever.

Caspian doesn't smile. He stares right at me—right into me— with earnest blue eyes.

This just got way too real.

"Casp … I … I'm not ready to … go to any parties." I peer up into his face helplessly, pleading with him to understand. Clay may not remember me, but I can't forget him. Can't forget that I'm in love with him. I'm not ready to let that go. I can't imagine I ever will be.

But I can't risk losing Caspian's friendship—being with him is the only time I feel like I'll be able to stay me.

We swim there, inches and miles apart. The clear water stays so still around us, as if it too is afraid to move. "Is that okay?" The words slip from my lips in a whisper.

His fingertips skim the surface of the water, creating ripples between us. "Of course," he says, but his face says different. It says he's hurt.

"I'm sorry," I say. "I can't—"

He holds up a hand.

But I can't stay quiet. "Please don't let anything have changed." The words come out loud, desperate. I can't take anymore change. I can't.

Caspian looks at me long and hard. "So, how are your classes going?"

Thank you. Thank you, Casp, I want to shout. It's the safest, most normal question he could ask. The most Caspian-like question. With my expression, I say thank you. And with my mouth, I say, "They take a lot more focus than I'm used to. I've never had to pay more attention in a class in my life." I don't mention I like it because it forces my brain to take a break from agonizing over … everything.

"That's good, though. It means you'll get caught up fast."

"I hope so, but not everyone can be all scholarly like you."

As if to prove just how scholarly he is, Caspian says, "I'd give my fin for a private teacher. What's it like having class one-on-one?"

"She's …" I shrug. "She knows her stuff." It's only been a little over a week, so we've barely started swimming toward the surface, but already I can tell she knows more about Mer culture, history, and politics than could fit in a hundred *konklilis*. "And she seems nice enough, but …"

"But what?" he asks like he knows the answer. How does he when I don't?

"Well," I draw figure eights in the water with my finger. "I want to like her, but I don't know if I can. I don't know if I can trust her. She's Melusine's cousin, and—"

141

"And you're the Little Mermaid's cousin, and I'm the great-great-nephew of a siren. The Havelock's crimes are *not* her fault," he says with a finality bred from years of having his family shunned for Adrianna's actions. "Are you going to judge her for what they did?"

"No!" I rush to explain. "But she testified to keep Melusine out of prison."

"Ah."

"Yeah," I say as I lean back and let my body float on the water on my back.

He does the same, floating next to me. "So … you think Melusine should have been sentenced to immortality in prison?" he asks. Ever since the last day of the trial, all the attention has centered on the surprise verdict about Clay. No one has asked me what I think about what happened to Melusine.

"I thought I did," I say. "When the Tribunal determined she wouldn't face immortal life in prison, I was furious because I wanted her to get the harshest punishment possible for what she did." I stare up at the cloudless sky as I drift on the water's surface, and my mind conjures a picture of Melusine's silent screams as they forced that potion down her throat. "But then when I watched them strip away her voice … that was …"

"Barbaric," Caspian says.

"Yeah."

He's silent for a moment, and I know he's pondering. From the corner of my eye, I can see his blond hair circling his head in the water like a halo.

"How well does your new teacher know the Mer legal system?"

"Really well," I say. It's one of the subjects she's teaching me, and she seems to be a bottomless chasm of information on past cases and judgments.

"Then maybe she knew that even if they didn't imprison Melusine, the punishment would still be harsh and would stop her from sirening again."

"Maybe," I say. I hadn't thought of that.

"And even if she hadn't … Lia, what if it were Amy? She's your younger cousin. If she'd committed a crime, even a terrible one, would you testify to try to keep her from being imprisoned forever?"

"In a heartbeat," I say without hesitation. I sigh. "So, you think I should let Ondine off the hook?"

"I think you're a good judge of character, and if you want to like her, you should let yourself like her."

I think about that. I've never had a teacher who asked me what I want to learn before, who cared so much that I stay interested. With all the mess in my life, she's the only one who spends every day insisting I can … do more. I really want to like her, but I've been holding myself back. I haven't been fair to her. "Why do you have to be so smart all the time?"

"It's my burden." A smile permeates his words.

I splash him in the face, and his resulting sputters make me laugh. When was the last time I laughed? Really laughed? It feels indescribably good.

We're both swimming upright again as he splashes me back. I push my palm through the water, sending a wave of it right into his mouth, and he lets it stream back out through his gills, which makes me laugh even harder. When I catch my breath, I look up to find him staring at me again.

That same breath lodges in my throat, and I swallow. As his silver tail glints below him in the water, his soft blue eyes lock onto mine. "Goldfish, I know everything that's happened because of the Tribunal's order is still very new, but whenever you are ready to … go to parties again," he offers a small, sincere smile, "just know I'll be here."

"Y'know, a rebound hookup can be totally hot."

"What?"

Lapis leans in the doorway of my bathroom and watches me paint my nails (an activity I'm hoping will make me feel more normal). "And healthy." Her tone grows more serious when she says, "Much healthier than moping around wanting someone who, let's face it, you can't have."

I know she's trying to help, but I so don't want to have this conversation right now. Or ever. Denial is my safest course of action. "I don't know what you're even talking about." With all the practice I had last year, you'd think I'd be a better liar.

"Oh, please." She waves a hand, dismissing my feigned ignorance. "I talk to the guards." The lift of her eyebrows tells me she's been doing more than talking to them.

Great. Now not only are the guards serving as a daily reminder that my parents don't trust me not to break the law and run to Clay, they're also eavesdropping on me. And apparently on—

"Caspian is gorgeous," Lapis says. "Always has been. You can't deny it."

No, I can't.

"And he's been face over fins for you for forever."

This time I cut her off. "He has not. We're friends and now he just, I don't know, feels sorry for me or whatever." Even as the words leave my mouth, I know they're not true. Maybe I'm not just in denial about yesterday's conversation; maybe it's a pattern.

"Not even you're dense enough to believe that." She rifles through one of my bathroom drawers and steals a lip gloss.

"Gee, thanks," I say as she squeezes some onto her lips.

"The boy likes you, Lia."

For the first time, I don't deny it.

She pockets the lip gloss, and I don't stop her. I never wear that color anyway. "Look," she says, "I know what you had with Clay was … special. More special than anything I've ever had with anyone …" Wow. "But, it's over now. It's not fair, but it's true. And Caspian, he's a good guy, y'know?"

"I know." Boy, do I.

But what she doesn't know—what nobody seems to get—is that Clay and I aren't over. Not to me. Deciding we are would be the smart thing to do, the healthy thing, but it would also mean killing the most precious, cherished relationship I've ever had. Still, as long as I cling to it, I'm not really living. Even if I don't choose today, eventually, I'll have to decide between refusing to let go, and saving myself.

Lapis must notice me shrinking, retreating into my own thoughts, because she says, "Hey." I look up. "Take it from someone older and wiser: Caspian's a really good guy. Just … think about it."

I don't want to think about it. Not about Lapis' unsought, oddly caring advice or about Caspian's words. His kind, touching words. *I'll be here.* Did he really mean—

No. Not thinking about them. I make myself think about his other words instead, about how I should let myself like Ondine.

I think about them now as she tells me about the upheavals that occurred under the ruling family of the Atlian (when the human Renaissance was just beginning on land).

Last week, we finished the reign of King Nereus, and we've moved on to the reign of his successor, Queen Viridian.

"What you must understand," Ondine says from across the mosaicked table in the salon, "is that a lot had changed in the three hundred years since Nereus had taken the throne, so Queen Viridian faced a divided, paranoid people."

As she talks about how Queen Viridian's talent for wards and protection magic led to a sense of security and peace throughout the kingdom, I can't help but admire how knowledgeable she is, how articulate. She speaks like she knows what she says makes perfect sense.

How old was she before the curse broke? It's hard to imagine her as anything but young and impossibly beautiful. But there's a strange wisdom in her eyes. It's intriguing. I do want to like her. I really do.

"One thing you and I and every other student of our history must understand," Ondine explains, "is the crucial role magic has often played in shaping politics, sometimes through carefully planned strategy and sometimes in ways that are unexpected." The crystals around her eyes sparkle as she tilts her head. "Can you think of another example?"

"Um … the Little Mermaid?"

"Is that a question?" Ondine asks in her lilting, accented English. Her gentle smile says she's not angry, just nudging me.

"The Little Mermaid," I say with more confidence this time.

"Good. Why?"

"Well, when she threw the dagger in the ocean instead of killing the prince with it, she unleashed the curse that stripped all Mers' immortality." I try to relate the familiar story to politics. "People got so angry, they blamed her family, dethroned her father, the king, and executed him. The power struggles that followed led to like 200 years of war."

"Precisely. And to escape the violence of those wars, your parents and several others came to the safety of land to start your Community." She gestures around our cozy, grotto classroom. "And here we are."

"All because of one cursed dagger …"

She nods. "You must never forget that one spell or one piece of magic can have far-reaching results. That is a lesson I teach to all my students Below who study magic."

"You teach magic, too?" Wonder seeps into my voice.

"To my advanced students, yes. It's my belief that magic is part of a complete education. But it is also a responsibility." Something dark passes over her face, turning down the corners of her mouth.

"What's wrong?" I ask.

"It is nothing for you to worry about. Only that, because I teach magic, I worry more people will fear me now that my cousins have been convicted. I have devoted my life to teaching and to the school. If parents pull their students out and we're forced to shut it down …" She shakes her head again.

In that moment, Ondine looks so sad it's as if her entire being is tinged the same cold, pale blue as her tail and the streaks in her hair. Guilt rises in my throat. Just yesterday, I lumped Ondine in with her family even though I should know better. That makes me just as bad as those parents trying to shut down her school.

"That's why," Ondine continues, rallying the strength back into her voice, "I'm so *grateful*," she says the Mermese word, which expresses more emphasis, "to your parents for their show of public support. It will go a long way toward ensuring the academy's doors stay open and I can continue to teach there."

While I would never want her school to close, the idea of Ondine going back there to teach—leaving here for that far-off academy out at sea—upsets me more than I would have expected. She's taught me so much already, and her classes are the only part of my day right now I look forward to.

"Either way, today I am teaching here, and you and I have a lesson to continue. Where were we? The influences of magic on history and politics, yes?"

"I mentioned the Little Mermaid."

"An excellent example of magic having unintended political consequences. Now let's look at an example of magic having intended consequences on politics." Ondine swims over to where her bag rests on a high shelf embedded in the grotto wall and pulls out a scroll of red algae leaves, along with two blue larimar stones. From its sheen, I can tell the scroll is coated in magically infused wax. Scrolls like this one used to be for writing, but ever since Mer discovered how to store our voices in *konklilis*, we've only used algae scrolls for art. She unfurls the scroll on the table and anchors it with the heavy stones. The glamorous but stern face of a woman wearing an intricate hairstyle and extravagant *siluess* stares up at me. "Xana." Ondine says before I can ask.

"That name sounds familiar." But I can't place it. "Who was she?"

"She was the niece of Queen Viridian. As part of the royal family, she was made a *daniss*," that's Mermese for chancellor, "and was given a principality to rule in the waters near modern-day Spain. Because she wasn't an immediate family member, it wasn't a large principality, but it was in a beautiful, fertile region of the sea."

I trace Xana's authoritative face on the scroll with my finger. I can see this intimidating, sophisticated woman as a *daniss*, running an entire region of the kingdom. Long before the immortality wars, when the Mer monarchy thrived, the royal family maintained its power across the vast ocean by dividing its empire into regions, with each region ruled by a *daniss* who was a trusted family member or favorite of the royal family. If my parents take the throne, will they reinstate this system? Will I be a *daniss*, entrusted with ruling part of the realm? Butterfly fish swim in my stomach.

"For 150 years, Xana ruled her people well, and her kingdom prospered. Then the human community that populated the coast Above built a piping system that dumped toxic waste and refuse into the surrounding sea. Mer became sick, and no potion known at the time could cure them. That was before the Secrecy Edict required Mer to hide our existence from humans, so Xana went ashore to reason with the young human king." Ondine's soft, enigmatic voice draws me into the story, and I lean in. "There are no surviving records, but according to all accounts, the human king refused her pleas to desist with the harmful practice." Looking again at the face under the coating of shining wax, I can't picture this woman pleading for anything, but I don't dare interrupt.

"When she couldn't reason with him, she did the one and only thing history remembers her for." Now Ondine's voice—her whole expression—turns somber. "She sirened him."

I gasp. "That's why her name sounds familiar. I read a lot of history about sirens last year."

"Xana's sireny is a prime example of magic used intentionally and strategically to affect politics. Once the human was under her control, she had him reverse his earlier rulings, thereby saving her people."

"Wait but, if she was a *daniss* who saved her entire region, why haven't I heard about that before? In the *konklili* I listened to that mentioned her, there wasn't anything about that. There wasn't anything about anything except her being an evil siren."

Ondine steeples her long, delicate fingers. "Yes, well, even though at the time, sireny was perfectly legal, because of its subsequent status as a high crime, Xana's memory has been convicted in the court of public opinion and widely vilified. Still, many Mer near the northwest regions of Spain speak well of her to this day and honor her memory, if clandestinely. That's where this scroll is from."

"You mean, she wasn't evil, even though she sirened someone?" I keep my tone light, indifferent, but my breathing has grown shallow.

Is it my imagination, or does Ondine look too knowing, too apologetic, when she says, "Unfortunately, after he reversed the order, Xana was still bent on revenge, so she used the siren bond she shared with him to sense when he was alone and to call him to her so she could murder him in cold blood after making him—"

But I've stopped listening.

The siren bond.

The siren bond!

Even after I stopped sirening Clay, the bond between us remained. It was much weaker than when he was still under my spell, but it was enough for me to sense him, to find him after Melusine and her father kidnapped him. How did I not think of it before? *Because you and Clay purposely didn't use it so you could have a normal relationship.* But we don't have a normal relationship now, nor any hope of one. Not when I can't even contact him. And the bond we share now isn't a true siren bond—it's the unexpected remnant of one (unexpected because Clay is the first human on record to outlive sireny for any significant stretch of time). I don't need to use any sireny to activate our bond now. Caspian's grandmother explained to me that when my sireny wore off and Clay survived, our bond morphed into something never seen before, something that will always connect us. If I could use the bond …

I bolt off my bench seat. "I'm sorry, Ondine, but I'm not feeling well. Can we end a little early today?"

Now that I know I might be able to sense Clay … to see him even … I can't wait another second to try.

"Lia, do me the courtesy of not lying to me." Her words are calm and even, not angry. "Hold yourself to a higher standard."

"I … " What am I supposed to say? I can't exactly tell her I want to go test out the remnants of a siren bond. But she's trusting me not to lie, and for some reason—maybe because she's been so straightforward with me, treating me like an adult—I don't want to lie to her. "I have something I need to do. I can't tell you what, but it's important. Can we end early today?"

She holds my gaze, her expression unreadable for a moment before she says, "Absolutely," like she trusts my judgment, trusts me without question. I thank her and rush from the room.

Within ten minutes, I've locked myself in the bathroom off my upstairs bedroom and am lowering myself into a steaming tub, hoping the water will help me focus. I close my eyes.

I'm so keyed up with anticipation, it takes several long, slow breaths before my mind calms, and the heat seeps into my tense muscles.

It's been nearly four months since I've done this. I conjure an image of Clay in my mind. The first one that occurs to me is of his face on that night, our last night together, right before he leaned in to kiss me, to brush his lips against mine. The memory of that night that was everything I'd ever wanted it to be when I still had Clay in my life has mutated into one that taunts me now that we've been ripped apart. The pain it brings with it blurs my focus.

I push it out of my head and turn the water hotter before I lie back down, close my eyes, and select another memory. One of Clay playing his guitar for me, sharing a new song as he did so many times, his face alight with excitement. Now that I have that image, I concentrate on sensing where he is. I reach out with my mind, searching for the pull in my center linking me to him.

Nothing.

Could the potion have blocked out our connection along with his memories?

No. I refuse to believe it. From the oyster shell soap dish on the bathtub ledge, I grab my favorite bar of soap. The one I barely use. The one I've been saving because it smells like cinnamon. Like Clay. I bring it to my nose, and as the familiar scent washes over me, I focus again on my core and ask myself where Clay is.

A tug—so slight I almost miss it. But there it is, thin as the thinnest thread but pulsing with life. A half sob, half laugh rips through me.

When Clay was under my siren spell, I could access the bond in an instant and use it to see him as though he were right next to me, to sense his every emotion as though I were a part of him. What I wouldn't give to have that back, to feel what he feels, to know if he's truly okay. Now, all that remains is a glimmer of the bond, but it's enough to tell me something vital: Clay and I are still connected. In a way the Tribunal doesn't know about and the potion didn't destroy.

After Melusine was first arrested, magic experts at the Foundation tested her with a spell to see if she still held a siren bond over Clay.

When she didn't, they concluded her bond ended when her siren spell wore off—they didn't know the real reason she had no bond with him was that *my* bond took over when my sireny conquered hers on that boating trip.

Right after Caspian's grandmother told me not to reveal my sireny so my parents would have a chance at the throne, she said the bond between Clay and I was unprecedented. If there's no record of a bond like this one in history, then who knows what magical properties it has?

The Tribunal, the Foundation experts, my parents—everyone— said there's no way to reverse the potion Clay drank. But none of them knew about the bond. Is there a way to use this secret, strong magic connecting Clay and me to restore his memories?

My fins curl with excitement. I could hug Ondine for reminding me about the siren bond, even if she didn't know what she was doing. Okay, maybe not *hug* her—I don't know if someone that regal and enigmatic ever hugs anyone. I try to picture her reaction if I even attempted it, and I erupt into a fit of irrational giggles, my tail splashing water out onto the floor. I can't help it—I feel lighter than I have in weeks. I may not know how to get Clay's memories back, but at least now I know it might be possible. Which means I have a lead to follow.

And that means I have what I've been living without all these weeks.

I have hope.

Chapter Seventeen

By the next evening, my hope has given way to impatience. All I want to do is go find a way to study the bond. I'm itching to learn more about it.

Instead, I'm standing in my backyard waiting for the sun to set. Again.

This time, when the light fades and figures step from the ocean onto the private beach, it's Amy who runs down the stairs, putting her new legs to good use as she takes the steps two at a time.

My sisters, my parents, and I follow, and soon we're all standing on the dark beach in front of the two fiercest warriors I've ever seen.

The man and woman stand tall as the waves crash behind them. They carry kelp-net bags with their belongings, and they've strapped short pieces of dark, rough fabric around their hips now that their legs are in place, evoking the image of ancient gladiators ready to fight to the death. He's all muscle, with arms thick as the thickest seaweed stalks, pecs bigger than my head, and a sharp shard of what I think must be igneous rock piercing his nose.

She too looks like she could break me easily. Tight, corded sinew stands out beneath the squid ink tattoos that cover both her arms like sleeves and spider onto her neck and ripped abs. It's rare to meet a Mermaid who doesn't wear her hair loose and flowing, but this woman wears her dark auburn locks out of her face, in a sleek braid down her back bound with straps of the same shark's leather as the *siluess* that binds her breasts.

Menacing blades made from sharp swordfish bills peek out dangerously from holsters strapped to his bicep and her waist.

"Mom!" Amy squeals, launching herself forward.

"Baby!" The warrior enfolds her daughter in a hug, then strokes Amy's hair back and stares into her face before covering her forehead in kisses.

"Daddy!" Amy says next as her father scoops her up in a massive hug of his own that lifts her off the ground. He spins around with her, making circles in the sand.

The rest of us hang back to let them have their moment, but soon enough we're all exchanging hugs and hearing how much we've grown. "And you," Amy's mom says when she reaches me, "what's it like to be responsible for saving all Merkind, huh? Our very own heroine in the family."

She smiles and hugs me so I don't have to answer. Now that she's closer, I notice the white scar running diagonally across her cheek. She's the real heroine—out fighting to protect people for decades during the wars. But I don't know how to say that, so instead I just say, "It's really good to see you, Aunt Rashell. You, too, Uncle Kai." His hug is bone-crushing. Now that the curse has broken, they both look younger than they did seven years ago.

When my aunt stands in front of my dad, everything goes quiet. And when my dad embraces his little sister for the first time in seven years, tears shine in his eyes. I stare at them, and at Amy, once again clutched in her father's bear hug.

We did this. Clay and I. By breaking the curse, we gave them this happily ever after. And now, it's my job to get ours back.

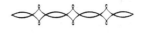

The only trouble is, I have no idea how to do that. Last night, after Amy and my parents took Aunt Rashell and Uncle Kai to get settled in the grottos, my sisters and I went for our nightly ocean swim, and I swam off by myself. Siren magic draws its energy from the call of the ocean itself. Since the bond I share with Clay started out as a siren bond, I was hoping connecting to it while in the ocean would give me some idea about how to use it to communicate with his mind or sense his emotions or … something. But it didn't help. Sure, the ocean made the bond a little easier to get in touch with and even made its pull a little stronger, but only enough to tug me toward shore, back toward Clay's house. Where I can't go.

So that experiment was a total dud. The best thing about the bond is that no one has ever reported anything like it before, so it may be the key to achieving magic everyone has told me is impossible. The worst thing about the bond is no one has ever reported anything like it before, so I have no way to research it. Last year, I listened over and over to all the surviving records about sireny that the Foundation has, and none of them said anything I can use now …

"Where has your mind paddled off to?" Ondine asks in her exotic-sounding English. I've told her I don't mind if she speaks Mermese, but she generally sticks to English when we're not studying Meremse oration or grammar. I'm thankful; it makes our classes feel more relaxed, more personal.

I apologize for losing focus, and she continues the lesson, spreading a large, human map out on the table and pointing out various ocean locations in relation to human cities I know.

"Here," she says, indicating a point off the coast of Denmark, "is the site of the historical capital city of Meris, which served as the seat of the monarchy for thousands of years, until ... when?"

"Um ..." She hasn't taught me this so if she expects me to answer, the correct response must be something logical. "Oh. Until the King was blamed for the curse his daughter, the Little Mermaid, caused and he was executed."

"Good. Nobles loyal to him fled, and angry mobs ransacked the palace, and eventually the city. Your parents are in the process of setting up a new capital here," she points to a location in the Pacific, not too far from California, "in what used to be called Aquinilinus, and what they are appropriately renaming New Meris. Why have they chosen this location?"

"Well, it's not too far from us." I study the map. "Less than a day's swim, so it would be easy for people from the Community to travel to if they wanted."

Ondine nods. "And what about for the Mer already living Below?"

This one's harder. "Is it because a lot of the remaining population is near the U.S.?"

"And up near the human region of Canada, yes. The wars started in Northern Europe, and for a long while, this region was the safest because no relatives of the crown ruled its principalities, which were instead far enough away to be entrusted to nonblood-related allies, making it far less of a target. Since the fighting spread here last, its infrastructure is the most intact and thus the easiest to rebuild. There are still houses and the remains of a marketplace, even a palace—"

"Wait." A marketplace, a palace ... I examine the map. Judge the distance from the Malibu coast. "Is the new capital ... New Meris ... is it where Melusine and her father took Clay? When they kidnapped him?"

"It is," Ondine replies, watching my reaction. How did I not know this? A chill skitters down my spine at the memory of that dreary, haunting place. Crumbling, abandoned houses with tentacles of hidden creatures twisting through their windows. Lonely, winding streets lined with cracked seashells. And a once-splendid palace of crystallized ice and white coral.

My heart drops at the memory of it.

"Filius most likely chose it for the ritual for the same reasons your parents are: proximity, structures intact enough to provide shelter and, in his case, a place to hide what he and Melusine were doing."

That makes sense. "So ... the Foundation is restoring it? Right now?"

"In conjunction with restoration teams from Below, yes. I'm sure your aunt and uncle can tell you about the progress. From what I hear, many individual citizens Below are helping as well, day and night, so the main areas are already livable enough that families have started moving back. In time, we should be able to restore the city to its former grandeur. The palace in what is now New Meris was originally built as a summer retreat for ..."

As Ondine chronicles the entire history of what will soon be the capital city, I'm once again swimming through that silent, ghostly marketplace, the bond tugging me ever onward toward the palace. Toward Clay.

I need to figure out how to use that bond to bring his memories back. I need to. But how can I when no information exists on this type of weird, never-before-seen, post-siren bond? Maybe the key is to research other types of magical bonding from centuries ago, like the kind between monarchs separated by long distances or the ones between indentured servants and their masters. But, there's a major riptide in that plan. Even if there *are* research materials on magical bonds, there's no way I can get to them. Any *konklilis* on magic that powerful would be at the Foundation, and there's no way anyone would trust me in the *konklili* archives again. I can't fake interest in an internship this time, not now that my parents know I used it to access information I wasn't allowed to see. They've let it slide because I did it to save Clay's life, but if I tried to get anywhere near there again, they'd know I was up to something.

If I can't access *konklilis* on magical bonds, then I have to hope someone who knows about them will help me. Could I ask Caspian's grandmother? She knows a lot about magic—mostly potions, but spells, too. She is the one who made sense of how Clay and I broke the curse, after all. But, she's my parents' … uh, what do you call a campaign manager for potential royals? A monarchy manager? Anyway, she's so invested in getting my parents on the throne, I'm not sure what she'd do if I told her about the siren bond. She went from refusing to speak to me for sirening Clay to forgiving me when I brought back her immortality, then convincing me to cover up what I did so the shame didn't hurt my family. If I told her about the bond, she might try to help, but it's just as likely she'd use magic to destroy it (is that possible?) or tell my parents and put a stop to it before I could do anything that might jeopardize their reign. No, telling her is too unpredictable.

All other magic experts who live Above work at the Foundation. Caspian might know a lot about a lot, but I can't throw history or linguistics at this problem, and he's not a magic guru. There's only one person who might be able to help me understand the bond and how I can use it to help Clay.

And she's sitting right in front of me.

Ondine smooths strands of pale blond and ice-blue over her shoulder. "Now Sea Daughters Academy is not far from New Meris. It was founded near Egypt, like many great schools of the ancient world." Her finger glides east on the map. "But while many others closed over time or were forced to shut down during the wars, Sea Daughters moved with the changing political climate. I began working there once it relocated to a deep-sea trench in the Atlantic. The academy thrived there for some time before moving to an island in this region as violence spread along the sea floor. The island is a nature preserve where no humans—save the occasional scientist—are allowed to venture. We cloak our presence there using powerful protection spells cast by myself and the advanced students."

"And … did you teach the students the spells?" Was that subtle?

"I did, yes. They've worked well for us, although we'll be removing the underwater cloaking spells now that the wars are over and law enforcement has started to regularly patrol the area."

"Would you … would you start teaching me magic?" I'm about to rush into some made-up explanation for why I want to learn it but … *Lia, do me the courtesy of not lying to me.* Her words still hover in the air between us. A trust I'm not sure if I'm ready to embrace, but can't break, either. Instead, I say simply, "I need to learn it."

Dozens of tiny crystals glint around her eyes as they narrow. "Your parents haven't added magic to your curriculum." Will she mention this to them? They'll think I'm trying to find a way to get Clay back. "And we have so many other topics to cover."

I don't hide my disappointment. I let it register on my face, my gaze pleading. For her not to tell, for her to teach me, for her to offer me a way to get back everything I've ever wanted.

Her doll-like features study my desperate ones. "Very well. We'll begin your magical education tomorrow."

Chapter Eighteen

Bat only a few hours later, I get an entirely different education. One I never bargained for.

"What do you mean, dance classes?"

"For the wedding," Em says. "We'll all be expected to do traditional dances after the ceremony, and, let's be honest, your dancing could use a little practice."

"Hey!" I say as she half-guides, half-drags me from my downstairs bedroom through the grottos toward the main ballroom. I'm not actually that offended; I would be if her words weren't accurate. Sure, I learned all the traditional Mer dances as a child, and I performed them dutifully at Foundation events for years, but only while I was still young enough that my fumbling could be cooed at as adorable instead of criticized as uncoordinated. Once I hit about ten or so, I let Em, with her expertly executed movements, and the twins with their enviable grace take the spotlight while I floated into the background. I still dance at parties occasionally, but just fun moving-to-the-music, flipping-my-hair-around dancing, not anything formal. "Em, I'm not in the mood for a dance lesson. Can't I just skip the formal songs at your wedding if I promise to be on the dance floor for the more casual stuff?"

"There may not be any casual stuff," she says.

"What do you mean?"

"Mom and Dad are under a lot of pressure to prove to the Mer Below that they haven't abandoned their traditions by coming on land. That they're still truly Mer."

"Of course they are," I say as we swim into the ballroom where Leomaris waits for us. "How could anyone doubt it?"

"Because they left," Leo says. "They came Above instead of fighting in the wars. To their supporters, that's heroic. But to those Below who question whether they should take the throne, that's a sign your parents may have dismissed their heritage."

"That's ridiculous," I say.

"Yeah," Amy says as she swims in from the direction of her grotto bedroom with Staskia at her side. "Aunt Nerissa and Uncle Edmar are the ones who have insisted on keeping tradition alive up here—for the whole Community." Staskia nods at Amy's words.

"I know that," Leo says, "and so do you and so does everyone else Above, but not everyone Below is convinced. We need to do everything in our power to prove your parents aren't too human to be the next Mer monarchs."

"And we can do that by taking dance classes?" I raise my eyebrow.

A look passes between Em and Leo that strikes me as serious, decisive. "Last night," Em says, "Mom and Dad sat Leo and me down. They said all those on the visiting nobles' council and the Community board are pushing to make our wedding a big spectacle, something all Mer, both Above and Below, can get excited about. A show of our family's stability and adherence to tradition. Even MerMatron Zayle is advising them to do it." Em keeps the words even, careful not to betray a trace of how she feels about the idea. She's starting to sound as diplomatic as our mother.

"Your parents offered us the chance to get married any way we want to instead. But we'd need to do it soon, before rumors of some wedding extravaganza spread Below."

"They don't want their political affairs to interfere with our special day," Em says. "I'd been planning to do a human-style ceremony, something simple on the beach so I could invite some of my human friends from MHS and college, then do a Mer reception here in the grottos with the Community. Mom said I can do that in the next month or so, and they'll keep the wedding rumors quiet, but ..."

Leo takes her hand under the water. "But we have a chance here. A chance to help your parents. To help everyone by finally getting leaders on the throne who know what they're doing, who can promote peace."

After two hundred years of war. "So ... a really big wedding's going to save our whole species?" I ask, dumbfounded.

"That would be an oversimplification, Aurelia," Em says, the thinning of her lips letting me know I'm trying her patience. "But, it may indeed help. Since putting Mom and Dad on the throne would mean that one day, I'd be," she swallows, "I'd be queen, this would be a way to introduce me to the people, make them feel involved in my life and connected to our family. Show them our strength and our values. I can't in good conscience pass up that opportunity." Em always sounds like such a grown up. I keep waiting to sound like that, but so far it hasn't kicked in. She looks at Amy, then at me. "But if we're going to do this, it's imperative that while all eyes are on us, each member of our family makes an impeccable impression." She emphasizes the word impeccable, and I shoot Amy and Stas a nervous glance.

"Okay, dance lessons it is," Amy says, smiling one of her giant, bolstering smiles. "Dancing is fun, right?"

Both Em and Leo shift their gazes to me. If Em can hand over the wedding day she's dreamt of since she was a little girl to help our family and our people, what kind of ingrate would I be if I said no to dance classes just because the thought of dancing—of deliberately doing anything fun—feels like I'm betraying Clay by not devoting that time to trying to strengthen the bond. "Oh all right," I say. I swim over to Amy and take her hands, ready to dance. "What are we starting with?"

"Actually," Leo says, "today you'll be dancing with—"

"Caspian? What are you doing here?" I ask as he swims into the ballroom, his wet blond hair smoothed back from his face.

"Um, Em asked me to come. The guards let me in." He takes in the sight of all of us treading around in the giant ballroom cave, then looks at Em. "You said you needed my help?"

I glare at my oldest sister. Why did she do this? Why now, when I'm desperately trying to keep things normal with Caspian. Okay, granted, it's not like she knows what happened between us the other day, but … damn it … I'm blaming her for this anyway. She shouldn't have called him without talking to me.

"Yes, I do need your help. We do." Em explains about her intention to use the wedding to showcase our family, and how she needs to make sure Amy and I are up to the challenge traditional dancing will pose. "I knew Lia would need a partner today—a dance partner—and I thought who better to call than you?"

"Dance partner?" Caspian's eyes dart to me. Does he think I put her up to this? Is he embarrassed? Excited? What?

Before he can say another word one way or the other, the twins glide into the room wearing the skimpiest of *siluesses* and the heaviest of Mer-made, waterproof makeup.

Caspian's ocean blue eyes widen to the size of sand dollars before he clears his throat and looks away.

"Well, we're off," Lazuli says. "Places to go, Mermen to see. Just wanted to tell you two," she looks at Amy and me, "to practice hard and dance pretty."

"Why aren't you staying for the dance lesson?" Caspian asks, careful to keep his eyes on their faces.

Lapis laughs. "Like we need lessons." She meets Lazuli's eyes, and without uttering a word, the two of them swim away from each other and back together in a perfectly symmetrical figure eight before joining hands, twirling together, and then, for the big finish, swishing their tails through the water and sending up two perfect streams that arc above their heads, framing the twins before splashing gently downward.

"Wow." Staskia voices what all of us are thinking.

"See ya later," Lazuli says. On their way toward the underwater exit that leads to the tunnels connecting our grottos to the rest of the Community, her gaze falls again on Caspian. "Em invite you?"

"To help by being Lia's dance partner," he answers.

Lapis turns to Em with a smile, "Subtle," she says before ruffling Caspian's hair.

He's still blushing when the twins leave.

"I should probably head out, too," Stas says. "Aims and I were, um, doing homework, but we're all finished, so ..."

"You're welcome to stay," I say.

"Yes, stay if you like," Em says. "Let's just get started. We'll try an *allytrill* first. Lia, you dance with Caspian, and Amy and I will take turns dancing with Leo. Amy, you first since I've already been practicing. And don't worry," she smiles reassuringly at Amy, "now that we've agreed to make the wedding such an event, it'll probably take another six months to plan at least, so you have plenty of time to figure out which boy from school you'd like to ask to be your plus one."

"For now, I'll try to do you justice," Leo jokes, swimming forward.

"Thanks," Amy says in a quiet voice. "But you can dance with Em, 'cause um," she looks at the water, then at Em, "Stas is going to be my plus one."

I hold my breath.

"Amy, don't be silly. Staskia doesn't need to be your plus one. She and her parents are invited. There's plenty of room on the guest list—you can have a real plus one."

Oh, Em. I try to catch her eye, but she's still looking at Amy. Was I this oblivious before Amy told me she and Stas were a couple? I remember my surprised, sputtering reaction. Yep. Yep, I was. Part of me wants to shake Em, to shout out the truth, but this is Amy's moment.

My cousin's eyes meet mine, and in that instant, I try to fill my gaze with as much support as I can. With a deep breath, Amy swims closer to Staskia, whose dark eyes brim with anticipation.

"Staskia *is* my real plus one," Amy says. She grasps Staskia's hand. The two of them float there in the water looking from Em to Leo to Caspian. "I've given myself until the wedding to tell my parents, and yours. But, Em, I figured you should know—for the seating chart and everything."

Stunned, Em shoots me an am-I-understanding-this? look, and I nod. "Yes. Yes, that's good to know," Em says. "For the seating chart." Em keeps her face composed, but a second later she's hugging Amy. Twice.

And Amy's smiling gill to gill. The next thing I know, I'm smiling, too.

As Em finally lets go, Leo squeezes Amy's shoulder and asks Staskia, "Will your parents mind if you sit up at the head table with us and the rest of the family's dates?"

I've never seen Staskia look more overjoyed. The dusting of freckles across her face dances as she grins. "They'll be glad. They've been wondering ... where I'd be sitting." Before Staskia has even gotten all the words out, Em has wrapped her in a tight hug, too.

"Hey, Amy," Caspian says.

She turns to him, her eyes vulnerable. She's always really liked Caspian. "Yeah?"

"You're still going to save a dance for me, right?"

If possible, her grin gets even wider as a second wave of relief crashes over her. I could hug him. "You bet," Amy says, her hand still holding Staskia's in the water.

Fifteen minutes later, I'm the one dancing with Caspian. Our tails swish in carefully timed, parallel movements beneath us. One of his palms presses against mine, held out to the left side of my body. And his other hand ... his other hand rests firm and warm on my hip, right where the golden scales of my tail meld into skin.

The position puts our bodies close together, his broad, naked chest a hairsbreadth from mine. I'm suddenly conscious of my breaths, afraid if one of them is too deep, my ... bikini top will smash against his bare skin.

Last week, I could have done all this—danced palm to palm and chest to chest with my best friend in the whole world—and told myself he didn't care, that he didn't see me that way. That if I brushed against him or stared up into his blue eyes or inadvertently wet my lips with my tongue while we talked, it wouldn't matter because he would know not to get the wrong idea. Last week, I thought his only feelings for me were ones of friendship.

Now, well ... this is the first time I've seen Caspian since he asked me out. On a date. I want to tell myself he was just trying to get me out of the house, just pitying me and hoping I'd finally have some fun. I want to tell myself he didn't mean it. And telling myself all that would be easy because it's not like I gave him a chance to say the words. He never said ...

But his expression. That raw, open expression when he asked me to go with him to that party. Like he'd mustered his courage, like he'd been waiting for just the right moment. I know Caspian. He's careful with his words, careful with his actions. He never *just says* anything. Him asking me out, that was premeditated and intentional. That was a risk he'd evaluated—and decided to take.

And one that, because of me—because I can't cope with one more thing to worry about, one more thing to have to fix—he probably regrets.

Should I bring it up? Clear the air? I want to. As we dance through the water, I want so desperately for things to be normal between us.

Instead, the space between us feels tight. Charged. But what could I say that I haven't already? I'm still in love with someone else? I need you to be my friend and not demand something of me that I can't give you?

I can't say any of that here, not in front of Em and Amy, Leo and Stas. Instead, I say, "Thanks, Casp. For doing this today. For coming over when Em asked."

"She said she needed me. Besides," his hand exerts a gentle pressure on my hip as he spins me under his other arm, "I'd never pass up a chance to see you." Our eyes meet as I spin back into him, and his are so sincere.

"Casp …" I shake my head, my tone begging him not to say things like that. He never used to. As the music from Em's waterproof player strikes up to a new octave, a thought strikes me with equal resonance. Has he been saying things like that and I just haven't noticed? Haven't wanted to notice? No, I'd have to be as dense as deep-water bamboo. He's saying them now because he must see what Lapis sees, what Em sees … that with Clay gone, now is his moment.

Except it isn't. Knowing I share the bond with Clay has rekindled my faith that we'll find our way back to each other. I can't tell that to Caspian—not only because it's illegal for me to have contact with Clay and anyone I tell has to choose between trying to stop me and breaking the law, but also because I know what Caspian will say. Doubt will darken his handsome face when I tell him I don't have any kind of real plan, and he'll say I shouldn't get my hopes up. But my hopes are all I have right now, and they're swimming higher and higher toward the sky without my permission. So, I don't know how to handle Caspian's interest in taking our relationship … somewhere new.

"Aurelia, what are you doing?" Em asks, swimming up next to us. "You're doing it wrong. Watch Leo and me. See, let Caspian guide you, like this." Leo exaggerates the move so I can see it as he uses his palm to push Em's palm back, guiding her in a dip over his other arm, which extends firmly against her lower back. "If you don't pay attention to the signals he's sending you, you'll miss the dive entirely. All right?"

I nod. She and Leo head over to give Amy and Stas a few pointers as Caspian's palm presses against mine. That same second, he anchors a strong, muscular forearm against the small of my back. Before I can question it, I arch as gracefully as I can, bending my body backward. I inhale sharply as my torso tilts, afraid I'll fall, but right before I hit the tipping point, Caspian completes his end of the transition with perfect timing, moving his hand away from mine and resting it on my chest. With his palm now pressing against my breastbone, fingers splayed and steady, and his forearm still supporting my back, I let out a breath of relief as I once again find my balance. His face, familiar and fathomless, hovers over mine, and trust suffuses me. With Caspian's hand guiding me, I let myself fall.

I extend my arms in a diving position above my head as my body flips over Caspian's arm, and I arch backwards into the silky water. It swallows me, envelops me in a smooth, salty rush and some of my tension, my anxiety, loosens. I focus on the dance, using my abdominals to twist my body around when I'm directly over Caspian's silver tail, which he curls upward to frame me, his fins draping over me like a curtain as I pass underneath them. Moments later, I break the surface again, my long hair flipping through the air in a cascade. That same instant, Caspian's hand returns to my chest, dipping me once more over his arm, completing the circle. This time, my body rises back up as his palm meets mine and we return to standard position, facing each other, his hand sliding from the small of my back to rest once again on my hip.

"Much better," Em says, sharing a smile with Leo, like they're accomplishing their joint goal of ensuring I don't make an idiot of myself. "Although if you want to keep the pace, do the whole thing a little faster next time."

"You did a great job," Caspian murmurs.

I go to say, "We did a great job," but "we" is a dangerous word right now, so instead I nod my thanks. I'm determined to make things more normal between us, so as we transition into another dance—a calmer, slower one called an *allydriss*—at Em's instruction, I transition into a more ordinary topic. "How's school going?" Assuming he hasn't been invited to any more parties he wants to bring me to, this topic should be a safe harbor.

"It's good. It's still strange to suddenly have so many people wanting to swim next to me in class or sit near me at lunch or just be interested in what I have to say, but it's a nice change. And I'm still mostly hanging out with the people who have always been my friends, even when a lot of Mer considered me a social outcast."

"Sounds like a good policy," I say. The desire to ask if he's going to that party with Gemma Auger wriggles out from hiding, but I bury it again; no good can come from asking. And it isn't my business.

"Besides," he says, his voice taking on a bitter edge, "everyone has a new outcast to shun now." Confusion clouds my mind at his words, but then realization dawns, bright and blinding. Something sinks in my stomach at the thought of her.

"You've ... seen her around school?" I haven't asked before now because I shouldn't want to know, should put her behind me, but suppressing my curiosity has never been a strong suit and I've done about as much of it as I can take.

"No one wants to associate with her, not even the teachers. She keeps to herself mostly," Caspian says. "And even when we're in the underwater classrooms where ... her voice ... works ... she doesn't talk. It's kind of ... sad." After watching her silent screams in the courtroom, I sometimes have trouble remembering that her voice still functions just fine when she's underwater.

I have even more trouble picturing Melusine, who had people flocking around her at Malibu Hills Prep no matter how hard she ignored them, as a loner. I don't want to feel sorry for her, but whenever I picture her, an image of her taunting Clay with that dagger wars with an image of her tear-stained face during the trial,

169

and the two push and pull at me like strong, opposite currents. "Well," I say, "she's not imprisoned like everyone thought she'd be, so it can't be that bad."

Caspian's fingertips grip mine as he spins me under our raised arms. "At least if she were imprisoned, no one would taunt her on a daily basis. Some people are even making a game out of it, egging each other on. The crueler their insults, the more popular they get. It's pretty disgusting actually." Caspian shakes his head as he times the strokes of his fins with mine. "One girl even sat behind her in class, just so she could … just so she could pull out Melusine's hair. One single strand at a time. Over and over." His hand tightens on my hip at the memory, and his upper lip rises into a sneer.

"That's … why would anyone do that?" I always think of the Merkids I went to school with before I got my legs as nice, decent, respectful of each other. Some of them might not be my favorite, but I thought all of them were basically good people.

Caspian shrugs. "I don't know. Because they can get away with it I guess."

"What did Melusine do?" I picture her spinning around and unleashing a scathing rebuke at whoever touched her. But … no, she couldn't have. If her head was above water, she couldn't have said a word. The image in my imagination changes to Melusine slamming her tail into whoever it was, turning them into the victim. But … she couldn't have done that, either. One scale over the line and she'd be resentenced to imprisonment. Caspian confirms my creeping suspicion.

"She did nothing. There was really nothing she could do. She just sat there and took it." Now I picture Melusine sitting in class with her spine stiff as a coral rod and her face struggling to stay impassive as someone yanks one ebony hair after another from her scalp. "When she didn't react at all," Caspian takes a deep breath, "I did."

"What do you mean you did?"

"I … I raised my hand and asked the teacher what the penalty was for one student forcing any kind of unwanted physical contact on another. The teacher looked at me strangely because she couldn't see what was going on right next to me in the back of the classroom—it was too subtle, especially since Melusine wasn't reacting—but she gave the answer I knew she'd give. That any student doing something like that would be expelled. The reminder was enough, and the girl stopped. She glared at me pretty hard, and so did her friends, but she stopped."

"Well, that was good of you." Why does he look like there's something he's not telling me?

He takes a deep breath. "I'm going to tell you something, and you're not going to like it. But I'm going to tell you anyway because I don't want it to seem like I'm doing something behind your back."

Whoa. What am I supposed to say to that? "O-okay." The thought flits across my mind that I could use that same line as an opening to tell him about the bond with Clay and my intentions to learn how I can use it to save our relationship. It makes telling him almost sound easy, but I know it won't be, so I focus on his words instead.

"I've been … sitting with her. Sometimes."

I falter, spinning in the wrong direction. From across the room, Em shakes her head and sighs. "You've been sitting with Melusine?" I ask, hoping I've misunderstood him. Since Caspian is Mer, it's not like Melusine could siren him, but the very thought of her near him makes me instantly queasy—and the spinning isn't helping.

"Y'know, at lunch. Just every once in a while, to stop people from messing with her. She wouldn't even look at me at first, but now since the lunch area is underwater, we talk … sometimes."

Right, left, right, left, swish, and spin. I focus hard on the dance sequence to keep from erupting at him. "So, this has been going on a while, then, you and Melusine talking?" Right, left …

"It's not like we're … friends or anything," Caspian says, fixing his gaze over my shoulder instead of on my face. "Not exactly. But we are talking, so I thought you'd want to know."

"Great," I say through gritted teeth. "Glad to hear you're not *exactly* *friends* with the girl who tried to murder me." I'm trying to keep my voice down so the others don't overhear, and my words come out in a sarcastic hiss. "Have the two of you talked about that over lunch?"

"Lia," Caspian says with censure in his voice, "I told you this calmly and openly so we could both be rational about it."

"Rational?" It's getting harder to rein in my volume. "What is rational about you getting all chatty with a criminal?"

"What did you want me to do, Lia? Sit back and let it happen? I couldn't just watch while people said disgusting things to her, while they shunned her." His eyebrows swim together. "I know what that's like."

I rest a hand on his bicep, not worrying if I'm breaking position. "It's not the same, Casp. I admire that you want to help, I do, but when people at your school said those things to you … you hadn't done anything to deserve them. Melusine, she—"

"I know what she did, Lia. I haven't come down with amnesia." His eyes widen. "Sorry!" he says. The reminder of Clay's memory loss—another unforgivable piece of collateral damage caused by Melusine's crimes—stabs into me and twists. "I don't think she's innocent," Caspian continues. "I know she's not a victim here, but she's still a person."

"She's also a siren." I let the word hit, and for the first time, Caspian misses a step. "Since you haven't come down with amnesia, you must remember what you said to me when you found out I'd …" I glance around at the others nearby. "… you know. You yelled at me, told me you could never forgive me—and you walked out of my life." But he's going to coddle and protect Melusine? Why?

"You're forgetting what else I did: came back, apologized." Indignation creates sparks of anger in his voice and both our movements become quicker, harsher, as we dance through the water. "I forgave you. I don't forgive Melusine—she didn't siren him to save his life. And she was willing to kill. I know that. But she also wasn't raised the way we were. She thought what she was doing was for the greater good."

No. *No.* What's happening plays out before my eyes and I want to scream. I inhale, exhale, try to calm down so he'll listen to me. "This isn't personal, okay. I'm not saying you shouldn't talk to her because I don't want you to." I don't want him to, but that is so far from the point. "I'm saying you shouldn't talk to her because she's dangerous."

He shakes his head, opens his mouth to respond, but I cut him off.

"The fact that you would even try to disagree with that, that you would feel safe enough around her to sit and have a conversation without being constantly on guard proves what I'm saying. Don't you see what's happening? She's luring you in."

I let that sink in as we both dive under the water and circle each other, but when we surface, denial paints his features. "She's not, Lia. Trust me. She wouldn't even speak to me at first. She told me to leave her alone."

"She's manipulating you. I don't know why. I don't know if it's because she knows we're close and she's trying to get to me or—"

"Of course it's about you." Now his voice is the one laced with sarcasm.

Ouch. "I didn't say that. Maybe it has nothing to do with me, maybe it's about your new fame for being involved in breaking the curse and her hoping she can use you to worm her way out of ruin. For all I know, maybe she's just bored and wants someone to mess with." A memory of her malicious smile and mocking laughter fills my mind's eye. "Whatever her motives are, she has some."

Sadness stretches across his face. Is he hurt by the news that Melusine is messing with him? At least sad is better than fooled. His next words take me by surprise. "Why do you always underestimate me?"

I shake my head. "Casp, no I don't."

"Yeah … you do. It's like when you thought that I wouldn't figure out … what you were doing to Clay. Or that I wouldn't be able to ensure we had fun together at that party."

"What? That's not it at all. I know we would've had a good time."

"Not good enough for you to agree to go with me ... on a date." Before I can respond, he says, "You underestimate me. And right now, you're underestimating my understanding of this situation. If Melusine had an ulterior motive for talking to me, I would know it."

No, he wouldn't. Not because I underestimate him. Not because I don't think he's smart. But because she's a mastermind. The music swells to a crescendo, and we send up arches of water with our fins. Our movements may be synchronized, but our thoughts aren't. "I'm not underestimating you," I say. "You're underestimating her. Please. Please just stop talking to her, just stop sitting with her. Just, stop."

"No. She's being targeted. I can help her, so I will. It's that simple. And I don't need your permission."

When did I ever say he did?

A glance over his shoulder at Amy and Stas laughing as they start the next sequence tells me we're late for a series of spins. Caspian interlaces our fingers above where our palms meet and stretches out his arm, sending me whirling through the water. I spin back toward him and away, toward him and away. Each time his chiseled, troubled face flashes back into my line of sight, I try to think of something else I can say to convince him. Melusine doesn't do anything by accident. If she's been talking to Caspian—if she's convinced Caspian to talk to her—she's plotting something, I'm more sure of it with every passing second. Whatever it is, it's at Caspian's expense. And if he won't put a stop to it ...

When Caspian pulls me in, my back now firmly pressed against his chest in the dance's closing pose, I'm dizzy. Unsteady.

"All right, that's enough," Em says. "Nice progress. Why don't we switch to a new dance?"

Everyone swims to the center of the room at Em's instruction, but with Caspian's hand in mine, I know I'm going to need to try an old dance. With a most hated partner.

I need to go see Melusine.

Chapter Nineteen

"That's not a good idea," Ondine says as she swims behind me to gaze over my shoulder.

I'm sitting in our grotto classroom, bent over a small terracotta pot of seagrass. I've asked if we can start with something more advanced than learning to just sense energy, but Ondine shakes her head and points to the plant in front of me, saying "Sensing the power of a living thing is the foundation of a magical education."

I sigh. When I woke up this morning and rushed to get ready for my first-ever lesson in magic, this is so not what I imagined. Sensing the energy of some seagrass? Snoozeville. Besides, as soon as class is over, I'm heading straight out to confront Melusine and the thought of it ties my whole body in knots; I was hoping magic lessons would be the perfect distraction until then. It never occurred to me tapping into the ancient power of ocean life could be so, well, boring.

Under Ondine's watchful gaze, I close my eyes and begin.

In and out. In and out. I focus on my breath until my mind calms. Then I reach out mentally, searching for the plant's energy the way Ondine instructed.

Nothing.

I don't sense a single thing except maybe my own impatience and the weight of Ondine's expectations. I'm about to open my eyes and confess that I don't know what I'm doing when I remember something.

The first time I ever did magic, it didn't work at first. I stood on that boat during my biology field trip singing the song Clay wrote in a desperate attempt to free him from Melusine's clutches—and it wasn't working. Her magic was stronger, much stronger. That is, until I remembered reading that siren spells drew their magic from the call of the ocean. I focused on that ocean power to connect to the magic, and that's what strengthened my spell enough to get Clay away from Melusine.

This plant, like every one of the ocean's creatures, has its own inherent magical properties. That's why it could be used as an ingredient in potions or as a component of spells. As a creature of the ocean myself, I should be able to sense those properties since they're innately similar to my own. I focus on myself, sensing my own heartbeat; picturing my entire network of muscles, bones, and veins; imagining the blood coursing through my body like an ocean current. Then I do the same thing with the seagrass, picturing what its root system must look like under the sand in that pot, visualizing the complexity of each blade beneath the smooth, green surface. I reach my mind out again.

This time, the plant's magic emanates a light, steady glow. I can't see it, but I can feel it—just a subtle awareness that it's there, like knowing someone has just swum into a room even though your back is turned.

Excitement swells in me at the new sensation. But then I realize, that's it. The sensation isn't growing any stronger or deeper. All I've done is sensed a plant. If I were learning magic purely for the sake of learning magic, this would be a gratifying moment, but I have a goal. I'm doing this to find a way to use the siren bond to help Clay get his memories back. And no amount of communing with seagrass is going to help me accomplish that.

"What's next?" I say, eager to move on to something more useful.

"You've sensed the plant?" Ondine says, surprise uncurling in her voice.

"Yes. It's like a constant, glowing…" I gesture toward the plant, unable to adequately put the magic into words, "thing." *Real eloquent, Lia.* "What's next?"

She comes around the other side of the table and studies me, eyes narrowing.

I shift my weight on my stone seat. "Did I do something wrong?"

"On the contrary," she says. "I'm quite impressed. I was expecting this exercise to take the rest of the afternoon. I thought you didn't have any magical training."

"I don't." Uh-oh. The last thing I need is for her to get suspicious. "But, I've read a lot about advanced magic and … y'know, witnessed some of it last year." All of that's true. Somehow, though, omitting information feels like lying. Ondine has been so adamant about honesty that I find myself saying, "And I have a little experience."

"You do? What type of magic?"

Oh, you know, just the most heinous and evil type known to Mer. No biggie. "Um, nothing formal."

Those gray eyes scrutinize me again, but when I don't elaborate, she doesn't ask. Instead, she says, "If we're going to continue your magical education," If? "you need to know something. I don't believe any topics should be taboo."

"You don't?"

"Lia, what do you know about education Below?"

Where is she going with this? "Not much. My mom said private lessons like this are more common Below."

She nods, her cornsilk hair catching the light. "That's right. Group classes in schools like the one I run are very small—between 3 and 7 students—and each pupil has several hours of private instruction each week with one teacher, who is responsible for guiding that pupil's intellectual development."

"I never realized it was that different."

"Think of it like the relationship between the human philosopher Aristotle and the leader Alexander the Great. Except Below, such an education in not restricted to antiquity nor to the ruling class."

"The Mer schools up here aren't like that," I say. "I guess because they're supposed to prepare us for human high schools and colleges."

"That's understandable," Ondine says, "but it seems a shame to me. Traditional Mer education ensures each student's potential is fully nurtured, and it's an important part of our culture. In the North Sea, where I was raised, the teacher-student relationship is considered nearly sacred."

I take that in. It makes me genuinely glad I've been taking our classes seriously. Doing otherwise would have been a huge sign of disrespect to Ondine. "Thank you for explaining it," I say.

She smiles again, and it makes her whole face glow. "You're welcome." She nods formally. "Now you'll understand why you should always feel free to confide in me. It's my job to teach you, Lia—and not only about history or grammar. There's nothing you can't come to me with. I want you to know that."

Do I know that? Ondine has been kind to me, patient with me. She hasn't given me any reason not to trust her. And right now, her expression is so earnest, I don't doubt she means every word she's saying. She truly sees me as the Alexander to her Aristotle. Normally, I'd say that's arrogant of her and roll my eyes, but based on all her lessons so far, maybe it's just self-aware. Maybe she just knows she's a good teacher and she's not going to cloak that in false modesty the way others would. The problem is, I'm no Alexander the Great. And if I am honest with her, if I tell her the type of magic I've performed, she'll know I'm not. She'll know I'm an imposter. A criminal.

No matter how understanding she claims to be, it doesn't mean she'd understand why I sirened Clay or why I kept it a secret—why I'm continuing to keep it a secret so it doesn't ruin my entire family and my parents' chances to help our kind. Entrusting her with that secret would give her too much power over too many lives. But my gut tells me I can trust her. I see it written all over her face, etched in her open, imploring eyes. I *feel* it inside me.

When did I become so tangled up in my own deceptions that I had to stop trusting my instincts about who I could talk to? Let me tell you something: It sucks.

And it starts to suck even more as she waits for me to confide in her, her angelic face so hopeful and encouraging. All I can do is sit there biting my lip and trying to convey with my eyes how sorry I am that I just can't make myself trust her enough to say the words.

After a long silence that pulls at me with each passing second, she gives a quick nod, and all that hope on her face gives way to disappointment. She reins it in, closes it off behind a professional mask, but it's too late. I've glimpsed it, and I feel awful. Like I've let her down.

"Well, whatever experience you've had," she says, voice even but detached, "it's helped you. You have a better understanding of magic than most Mer when they begin their formal education."

"Does … does that mean we'll be able to move on to more advanced topics?" Because I need to. Fast.

"Like what?"

Like magical bonding. Like understanding how I can use the unprecedented remnants of a magical siren bond to try to do the impossible and counteract an irreversible potion. "Like … um how magic can connect people or how a spell can leave a mark even after it's worn off." I'm being vague on purpose, trying not to reveal anything that would spark her suspicion.

She cocks her blond head. "What you're talking about is very advanced magic. Don't misunderstand me; I have complete confidence in your ability to learn such magic. Eventually. After we've built your foundation in magics and you've had time to repeatedly put that knowledge to the test."

"Are we talking a month or …?"

"Lia, those types of magic require extensive theoretical knowledge and field training to perform correctly. They're not without risk. The students at my school study magic for a minimum of three years before touching those topics, sometimes much longer."

I swallow. Three years? That's never going to work. I need to have that theoretical knowledge now so I can understand the bond well enough to use it. There's no one else I can ask; no other way for me to access the information I need. "What if I'm super dedicated to learning about—"

Ondine holds up a slender-fingered hand. "I appreciate your enthusiasm, I do, but advanced magic carries inherent risk. As much as I hate to discourage scholarship, I cannot let you swim blindly ahead into uncharted waters." She must sense my growing desperation because her lovely face softens. "I wouldn't be opposed to accelerating your magical studies and devoting additional time to instructing you in them if I could justify that decision with a valid reason for why you need to learn these magics."

I have a valid reason. If only I could tell her what it is.

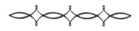

Can I trust her? I'm still mulling over the same question hours later as I swim to the Foundation through the tunnels. When I reach the underwater entrance, I don't have an answer yet, but I do have a sinking sensation in my stomach. The tips of my fins tingle with dread. Right now, I need to put everything out of my mind and focus on the confrontation that lies ahead of me.

Maybe I wouldn't be so nervous if I had a better plan. So far, the only plan I have is to intimidate Melusine into not spending any more time with Caspian. I'm not sure how I'm going to do that (I don't feel very intimidating), but I can't wait and do nothing if she's plotting to hurt him.

Calm down, I tell myself as my breathing gets shallow and quick. I haven't set a scale inside the Foundation since … since the day Clay forgot me, and as the sleek, burnished stone of the building's underwater façade comes into view, I'm repelled by the thought of going into the place I grew up trusting so implicitly. *I can do this. It's just a building.* Yeah, a building with Merfolk in it who ruined my life.

With one last flick of my tail, I propel myself through the large, gold-rimmed porthole that marks the entrance. Inside, familiar blue glass lines the walls of the massive cavern, and a row of receptionists sit in giant, padded trumpet shells, chatting happily amongst themselves or welcoming guests or securing shell messages to trained octopi and sending them off to deliver eight at a time to other departments. A smiling Mermaid in a bright white *siluess* bearing the Foundation's aqua logo greets me in Mermese. *"Hello, Miss Nautilus, what can I help you with today?"* Surprise colors her pleasant words; I don't come here much, and when I do, I normally don't stop at reception, since I know the way to both my parents' offices and to Em's.

"I'm here to visit the residences," I say, forcing a smile. *"But I'm not sure where they are."* After the trial, I overheard my parents talking about the logistical problems posed by Melusine's sentence. She wasn't sentenced to imprisonment, so she obviously can't be kept in one of the Foundation's jail cells. Since her father now resides in one of those cells and she is a minor with no other legal guardian, she couldn't return to the house the two of them previously leased from the Foundation. Because her comings and goings need to be supervised, the sentencing board decided she must live within the Foundation itself where her actions could be monitored. But the only living quarters inside the Foundation other than jail cells are the lavish, temporary residences set up for visiting dignitaries from Below.

Had my parents let her stay in some luxurious suite, many members of the Community would have been enraged—not to mention the same visiting dignitaries would have feared for their safety had their neighbor been a convicted siren, no matter how young. It was Em who came up with the only viable solution: The board took the smallest and most distant of the residence suites, stripped it of all finery, and made sure no other visiting guests were housed in the same wing.

Like I'd hoped, the receptionist assumes I'm meeting one of these other guests. *"Head straight up through the portholes here on the left."* She gestures, and her arm creates ripples in the surrounding water. *"Go up four floors, then take an immediate left and the security personnel will be able to direct you to the proper residence from there."*

I thank her and swim straight up through the first porthole, continuing through each subsequent one as I cross vertically through the vast stories. It's a long way up; no wonder everyone who works in this building is in such good shape. I emerge through the fourth portal and head down a spacious tunnel to my left, where two security guards sit on raised stools behind a marble podium. The female guard is busy both monitoring the screens in waterproof casing that show the video feed from the upper, dry floors and keeping an eye on the bubbles containing the fisheye view of all happenings on the lower floors. The male security guard, who wears an arm strap of striped heliacus shells designating his office, smiles. *"Here for a visit?"*

"Yes. Um ... " I clear my throat. *"Melusine Havelock."*

His eyebrows shoot up. Before he can object, I rush to say, *"She's allowed unscheduled visitors, right? Since she's not under a prison sentence?"*

"Strictly speaking, yes, she's allowed visitors." He says the words with distaste, like he disagrees with the ordinance. When he looks back at me, his face softens into paternalistic concern. *"How 'bout you give me whatever message you have, and I'll relay it, huh? That way, you won't even have to see her and you can head on home."*

He means well. He's probably older—though I can't tell from looking at his immortal face, since he and everyone else now appear forever in their twenties—and he thinks he's looking out for me. But I can handle this. Really, I can.

Even in my head, the words lack conviction, but I force extra confidence into my voice when I say, *"Thanks, but I need to speak with her. It won't take long."*

He shifts on the stool, his rust-colored fins twitching uncomfortably. He has no jurisdiction to keep me out, but his hesitant expression tells me he's floundering to find some. *"Do your parents know you're here?"*

"Of course," I lie. As bad as it's started to feel to lie to Ondine, lying to this man I don't know so that I can help Caspian feels easy enough. If I'd told my parents I wanted to come here, they'd have worried I wasn't moving on, and they probably wouldn't have let me see her. That's why if it somehow gets back to them that I visited Melusine today, I figured it was better to plead forgiveness than ask permission.

The security guard scratches the back of his head, then holds a conus shell to my mouth. *"State your full name for the record."*

"Aurelia Nautilus."

Swimming around the podium, he says, *"Follow me,"* and leads me farther down the tunnel. The walls here are no longer blue glass, but shimmering abalone, no doubt to make visitors from Below feel more at home. Fine-cut pieces of quartz dot the ceiling in an impressive but understated display of elegance. We pass porthole after porthole, each one closed and most emitting a warm glow through their circles of glass, indicating they're currently occupied by one visiting noble or other, no doubt here for logistical talks with my parents and the board. Then we turn a corner to a less-adorned tunnel. All the portholes lining these walls are dark, empty. All save one at the very end.

My stomach splish-sploshes.

"Would you like me to go in with you?" the guard asks in one final attempt to shelter me.

I shake my head. *"I've got this covered."*

With the side of his fist, he knocks on the porthole, which has been stripped of its gold trim. *"Visitor,"* he shouts and, without any further warning, unlatches the round circle of glass before swimming back down the tunnel toward his post.

Before I can shrink away from that porthole, before I can let the anxiety coiling inside me push me all the way back home into the safety of my own grottos, I stretch my arms in front of me and swim inside.

Chapter Twenty

O nce, this place was beautiful. With ceilings more than two and a half stories high, these rooms allow water to flow for five feet above my head—creating an atmosphere where guests from Below would be able to live entirely underwater if they chose, while also creating another space above the waterline, similar to the rooms in my own grottos. Mer visitors or (in times past) newly arrived refugees who had not yet been assigned a house could get a taste of what life is like in our Community by using the top half of these quarters, keeping their tails in the water while their torsos rose above it. To allow the rooms to serve both purposes, there is both furniture here below, and protrusions from the walls above providing additional seating, like two rooms stacked above one another with no floor in between.

Yes, the bones of these grottos are spacious and elegant, but they've been stripped to the bare essentials. Where I imagine shimmering gemstones once decorated the walls and delicate crystals once hung from the arching ceiling, now there is simple gray stone. The few pieces of furniture are sufficient, but simplistic: stools of rough-carved rock, a couch with only the most basic sea sponge padding, unembellished cabinets with locked doors to keep their contents from floating out. Off to the side, I glimpse the wall-mounted utensils and ice cabinet that indicate a kitchenette. To my right, a sheet of course-woven kelp fabric hangs over the entrance to what must be the sleeping chamber.

A hand pulls the fabric back, and Melusine swims in front of me. My eyes dart to the corners of the room, where tiny, floating bubbles reassure me we're under visual surveillance (the audio doesn't work underwater, so the guards back at the podium can't hear us, but they can watch our every movement inside these chambers). Being alone with her—with this lovely-faced monster who tried to stab me to death—makes my blood turn to icy, arctic water. As she stares at me with those calculating, sapphire eyes, my body tenses. But while her eyes are the same, her overall appearance has changed. Instead of the fashionable, revealing *siluesses* she normally wears, she now wears one of plain beige, its cut boxy (have her own belongings been confiscated?). Her sleek black hair has lost some of its glorious luster, and bruise-colored circles rim her eyes, like she hasn't been sleeping. A part of me admits she's as beautiful as ever, but instead of dangerous, she looks fragile. Most different of all is her expression— the confidence, the arrogance I'm used to seeing is gone.

Focusing on these differences—on the tangible proof things are not the same as they were in the ruins of that palace where she attacked Clay and me—gives me the strength I need to speak. But what do you say to the enemy whose father you helped imprison and whose voice was stripped on your testimony?

"*Um ... hi.*" Hi? Seriously? I force my next words to sound more powerful, more decisive. "*I have something important to say to you.*"

She doesn't speak, just stares.

"*I won't be here long.*" Am I telling her or myself?

She still doesn't utter a word, even though we're underwater where she can. I picture her in these gray rooms alone for hours on end. Has she gotten out of the habit of speaking? The tragedy of that strikes me, and I wonder if it's true.

Whatever. You're not here to get caught up in her melodrama, I tell myself. *You're here to protect Casp.* So I say, *"I know you've been talking to Caspian."*

Whatever she expected, it wasn't that. But she covers her surprise quickly, crosses her arms, and says, *"Talking's not illegal."* Then she lets out a bitter laugh at the irony. As if to underline the point, her voice comes out not in the melodic syrup that I'm used to but raspy from lack of use.

"You don't fool me for a second," I say. *"I know you must be planning something, and using Caspian to do it. I'm here to tell you to stop. Now."*

"Oooh, intimidating." Then the mocking tone disappears. *"And what if I'm not planning anything? What if talking to him is … just talking?"*

"Right. Like you'd ever do anything without some kind of malicious intention."

"Like when I told the Tribunal about your sireny?" My gaze flicks around the room at her words, my instincts making sure we're alone, fearing she'll be overheard. *"Except I didn't,"* she continues. *"I didn't say a word."* Another puff of that bitter laugh escapes her.

I falter. That's true. But I'll be damned if I'm going to thank Melusine for anything after what she's put me through—after what she's put Clay through. *"Like that was about anything but your own self-interest. Please."* I roll my eyes. *"You did that for the same reasons your father did: You knew it was doubtful anyone would believe you anyway, and you're hoping when my parents become rulers and I'm an advisor to the crown, I'll commute his sentence or offer you more leniency or a pardon or something."* That must be why she stayed quiet, right? *"You did it out of selfishness, that's all."*

Something passes across her face, turning her mouth down at the corners, but before I can read it, it's gone behind a mask of indifference and a shrug. *"Oh, yes,"* she says, *"that's right, like everyone keeps reminding me. I'm the villain here."*

Duh. What does she expect me to say to that? *"I didn't come here to have a conversation. I came here to tell you to stay away from Caspian."* All I have to do is make my point, then I can leave. It can't come soon enough.

"Does he know you're here? Did he ask you to come?"

"Just because he's too noble to stop himself from standing up for you at school, doesn't mean doing it's what's best for him. I won't let you use him or hurt him."

"And you don't think he can decide for himself whether to talk to me?" She laughs again. Another sound that's gravelly from lack of use. *"And you claim you're done controlling people."*

"I'm protecting him," I say through gritted teeth. Damnit—I shouldn't let her get to me, but she slithers under my skin, like always.

Melusine puts one hand on her hip, right above her coral tail. *"Wasn't that your excuse the last time?"*

My face heats. I want to throttle her. *"It's not an excuse."* My volume rises. *"I'm not trying to control Caspian. Don't you get it? He's spent his whole life having people shun him because of his family, and now he finally has a real chance to be treated the way he's always deserved to be treated."* The way I always knew he should be treated. *"Everyone finally sees him, and spending time with you will ruin that for him."*

She shakes her head. *"I don't—"*

"I know. You don't care. But if you don't leave him alone ..." What? What can I really do? Whatever I say next better sound super convincing. *"Let's just put it this way, my parents care about Caspian. They've known him his whole life, and they love him. If you don't stay away from him, my parents could make life a lot harder for you and your father."* There. Better a vague threat than a specific one she could poke holes in. It works; fear registers in her sapphire eyes.

Then those same eyes narrow. She swims closer to me, too close. *"Just between us girls,"* she doesn't dare touch me, but her words skate along my skin like fingertips, *"are you really here to help Caspian?"*

"W-what? Why else would I be here?"

"Wellll ... " She drags the word out. *"Maybe you don't want to keep him away from me to help him. Maybe you want to keep him away from me, so you can keep him close to you."*

"That's ridiculous." The words come out in a much louder burst than I intended. *"I'm in love with Clay. You know that."*

"And like any sane person, I know you and Clay don't have a chance anymore. I know he's forgotten you, and you can't do anything about it."

Oh yes I can. I wish I could shove the words down her throat. But are they true? Just because I want to use the bond with Clay to reverse his memory loss doesn't mean I can. Still, I have to believe it's possible.

In that disarming, perceptive way of hers, she must read something in my expression, because she says, *"Lia, when are you going to learn that life isn't a fairytale? Not even for you."*

"Stop talking to me like I'm a child." The rhythmic flicks of my tailfin turn aggressive with the force of my anger. *"I am not talking to you about this. And I am certainly not trying to keep Caspian for myself."* I'm not. *"Maybe you can't understand this, but my being here isn't about being selfish. It's about keeping him safe."*

She tilts her head. Instead of matching my volume, her next words come out calm, controlled. *"Tell me one thing, Lia. This version of yourself as Little Miss Moral, as the good girl, is it an act for everyone else or do you actually believe it?"*

"What act?" I square my shoulders. *"Everything I'm saying is the truth."*

"Oh you're sadder than I thought. I wonder when you'll see yourself for who you are. Like it or not, my father was right. When we cast that siren spell, it planted something dark inside of us. Both me and you."

I shake my head, willing her to stop talking, willing myself to stop hearing her. But it doesn't work.

"I can see it in you. That darkness," she says, relishing every syllable. *"In your need to control. It's why you're clinging so tight to this idea of yourself, from when you were good, innocent. When you did everything*

your parents wanted and your life made perfect sense." She leans in impossibly closer, whispers, *"That's not who you are anymore."*

I want so desperately to push her away, but I can't bring myself to put my hands on her. She must sense it because she leans back, her hair floating against my shoulder as she moves. *"Someday soon, you'll get that. You'll do something even your pretty little head can't justify, can't explain away."* A smile twists her cherry lips. *"I just hope I get to see it."*

I flex my fingers to keep my hands from shaking. *"I am not like you."*

"I guess we'll see how long you can keep telling yourself that."

"All that matters is what I'm telling you. This is the last time I'm going to say it:

Stay away from Casp. Or you'll regret it."

"Because I'm poison, right? Because my talking to Caspian will somehow infect him." She doesn't say that last one like a question. She stares off, unseeing, but when her gaze refocuses on me, it's a fierce glare. *"Well, princess, I'll leave that up to him."*

Without another word, she swims back through the kelp curtain and leaves me alone in that gray, stone room, gawking like a gaper fish. I could follow her—there's no door to keep me out—but I have nothing to add to my threat. I said what I came to say, and either it was enough to scare her off (despite her constant bravado) or it wasn't. Nervous energy pulses through me as a new thought strikes me like jagged rocks against a ship: What if now she spends more time with him just to spite me? She wouldn't risk pissing off my family like that. Would she?

As I swim out of the porthole, my mind spins down a whirlpool of worry and, once I've swum farther down the hall, I let myself lean against the wall for several minutes of long, slow breaths. Did my visit do more harm than good? Why do Melusine's words—her very presence—burrow so deep that I can't excavate them? And most of all, was she right when she said—

Someone's coming. I was so lost in my own thoughts I almost

missed the telltale ripples of water signaling movement. Melusine is the only one down this tunnel. Who else could be visiting her?

Determined to find out, I duck around the corner and plaster myself against the wall, peeking out just enough to see who's coming. I hold my breath, then tell myself I'm being silly. It's probably just the guard. *Or Caspian,* a little voice whispers in the hidden tide pools of my mind. *Maybe seeing her at school isn't enough and he wants to visit her now, too.* No, I'm letting my imagination swim away with me. Letting Melusine get into my head. Caspian just feels sorry for her and he's too nice not to stick up for her when she's being picked on. But even as I tell myself this, I can picture his muscular frame coming down that tunnel.

I wait, second after second.

Then someone swims into the deserted passageway, and I gasp.

Chapter Twenty-One

She glides in on her ice-blue tail, and all the air rushes out through my gills.

What is Ondine doing here? Ondine who said she was disgusted by Melusine's crime and who is working so hard to distance herself from her immoral, *udell* family.

I float behind the rock wall, open-mouthed, as she swims through the porthole I just vacated. Into Melusine's rooms.

What is she doing in there?

I should leave. They're family, and Ondine's reason for visiting isn't my business. But I don't. I stay put. Because, in the time we've spent together, Ondine has started to feel like family. She listens like family, accepts like family. Has all of that been a lie? The only reason I let her into my life was that she claimed to be different from the Havelocks, said she rejected everything they stood for. But if she's visiting Melusine in secret ...

Minutes drag by like hours as I wait behind that wall, concocting version after version of the conversation happening within those rooms. Am I being paranoid? Maybe suspecting the worst is part of the … the darkness Melusine mentioned. Are the thoughts I'm having now evidence she's right about me? My stomach curls in on itself.

With a creak, the porthole opens. Ondine and Melusine swim out, hands clasped together like they're the best of friends, and head down a side tunnel where they disappear from view.

Without thinking, without planning, I follow them.

Where are they going? Melusine isn't a prisoner, so she's allowed out to previously sanctioned locations. Surely, the guards can see her on their monitors and wouldn't let her go anywhere unauthorized. But … seeing her moving about freely after everything she's done makes my breath come in quick, shallow pants that send my gills fluttering.

I creep along behind them, hanging back and moving my tail and arms as little as possible so the flow of water won't give me away. Luckily, they're moving so quickly themselves, any movement I do make goes unnoticed.

This side tunnel is narrower, dimmer, little used. At the end is another porthole, this one standing open. Melusine swims into it. But as Ondine swims up to its entrance, she hesitates.

I freeze. Does she sense me? Will she turn around? What will I say?

Her back muscles tense, as if she feels something amiss, but the next instant, she too lets the porthole swallow her.

Now I float at its rim. I could turn around, go home. That's what I should do. But the questions nag at me. Where does it lead? Why is Ondine going there with Melusine?

I flick my fins and cross the threshold, surprised when the water drains away on the other side and I find myself lying on my stomach on wet stone with only a thin layer of remaining water rushing underneath me. And flowing downward.

I now lie on the mouth of a downward slope, like a dark, dripping waterslide tube made of stone. It's one of the express passages, not used by the public. I've never used one before, and I don't know where this one will take me. I gulp and plunge headfirst into the rushing water, hoping I don't collide with Melusine or Ondine at the bottom.

Down, down, down, past grips with exit holes along the sides to various other floors. Should I grab one? No, the barely-there sound of movement ahead of me tells me the two Mermaids I'm pursuing still slide down this tunnel, so I keep hurtling forward.

I'm falling so long, I must be heading to the bottom-most underwater tunnels beneath the Foundation. A suspicion of where we're going seizes my insides and twists. *Please let me be wrong.*

I'm about to find out. A gentle thud up ahead, then another, means Melusine and Ondine have landed. I jerk my arms out, pressing my hands against the stone walls at the same time I flatten my gold fins, using all my strength to jam myself in the tube so I don't land on top of them. Water rushes at me, and my whole body bows against it. *One yellow starfish, two yellow starfish, three yellow starfish …*

I count to twenty yellow starfish before my muscles scream and give in to the onslaught of water. Was it enough? Was it too much? If I didn't wait long enough, they'll see me, but if I waited too long, I'll lose them—and then this will all have been for nothing.

I sigh in relief when I land soundlessly in an underwater chamber. That relief vanishes when neither Melusine nor Ondine is anywhere in sight.

"If anyone asks, don't tell them you were down here," clinks Ondine's glass-like voice from somewhere to my left. I swim after it.

"Like anyone will talk to me," Melusine's drawl answers.

I catch up just in time to see the tips of two sets of fins round another bend. Their voices—one hated, one so nearly trusted—grow louder as they stop moving. I duck behind one of the massive desalination pipes the Foundation uses to pump freshwater into underground labs that aren't on city plumbing schematics. Sticking to the pipe like an octopus, I peek around.

"State your business," demands a guard when Melusine approaches him. He's far burlier and meaner-looking than the one stationed at the residences.

"Havelock to see Havelock. I have an appointment."

That's when my suspicion proves correct. These aren't just any basement tunnels. These are the prison.

Sandcrabs crawl under my skin, and all I want to do is flee.

"You're only allowed in while accompanied by an adult with a clean criminal record," the guard recites.

Ondine swims forward and records her full name into a conus shell.

"Follow me to where you'll both be thoroughly searched before seeing the prisoner. Do you consent to these searches?"

Their confirmations grow quiet as he leads them away.

My mind reels. Not only is Ondine visiting Melusine, but she's enabling her to meet with her father—an attempted murderer who spent years orchestrating an ornate plot to kill humans and seize power over our entire species using dangerous, illegal magic. How can she? How can she help two confessed criminals see each other?

After all those times she said she cared about me, said she wanted to help me learn and reach my potential ... Is she scheming with my enemies? Betrayal slams me in the chest. I can't believe how close I came to trusting her.

I need to get out of this prison.

"How could you?"

Ondine jumps out of her scales at my words. Good. Let her be caught off guard for once. She composes herself when she catches sight of me in the shadows of our classroom grotto and says in her even, controlled voice, "You're here early."

Most mornings, when I come into this grotto, Ondine has already been there for quite some time setting up the day's lessons. But today, I'm the one waiting for her.

Yesterday, after forty-five minutes spent lost in the labyrinthine tunnels under the Foundation, I found a row of portholes back up to the underwater lobby and spent the rest of the night at home trying to soothe the black, bitter anger bubbling up inside me. My efforts didn't do any good. One sleepless night later, and I'm still seething. No one is who I thought they were. My parents—who I always thought could take care of everything—couldn't (or wouldn't? I swallow against the lump in my throat) stop what happened to Clay. Caspian, who has always been my closest confidant, now looks at me like I'm denying him something I can't give. I gaze into those blue, blue eyes—into the new, unshielded question there—and I know it means I can't talk to him like I used to, not when what I want to talk about is how desperate and lost I feel without a way to bring Clay back to me. Even my sisters are so wrapped up with all the exciting new possibilities in their own lives that it wouldn't be fair to drag them into my trench of troubles, not when there's nothing they could do to help.

And now Ondine, the one person I thought maybe I could turn to … I picture her holding hands with Melusine as they swam together in that tunnel.

She says she values honesty? Truth? Let's see how truthful she is now. "I saw you yesterday. At the Foundation. With …" I can't quite bring myself to say her name. Not here, in this room that's become like a sanctuary to me. A place to escape the memories of her.

"Ah." Ondine doesn't look surprised. Does she ever? "I thought perhaps you did."

I'd expected her to deny it or at least defend herself ... something. Her lack of reaction sends my own frustration to new heights. "That's all you have to say? After telling me over and over again how important the truth is and how I shouldn't lie to you?"

"I didn't lie to you."

"You said you thought what your relatives did was disgusting. And now you're visiting them? You're *helping* them see each other?" I shake my head. "I get that they're your family, but ... you should have told me. How could you hide this from me? I thought we were ... friends." Saying it out loud makes me realize it's true. Over the past several weeks, here in this grotto, Ondine has become so much more than a respected tutor; she's been my only real friend. Looking at her now, disappointment washes over me in a rising, uncontrollable tide, and it brings with it everything else that's been coiling up inside me. All my disappointment in my parents, in how I'm handling things with Caspian, in the Mer legal system I wanted so badly to trust, in my inability to fix what's happened—even the irrational disappointment in Clay for forgetting me. I can't hold it in anymore. It splashes over within me until I'm yelling at Ondine. "How could you? I wanted to trust you!" I scream the words in her face.

And then I'm sobbing. Hard. And she's holding me. Tight. And it isn't like the hug my Mer teacher gave me in elementary school when I skinned my scale on a sharp rock or like the one my mother gave after the trial. No, it isn't the hug of a teacher or a mother. It's the hug of a friend. Even as I yell at her, accuse her of being a liar, Ondine hugs me and whispers soothing words of comfort until I collapse onto a rock ledge against the wall, exhausted. She sits next to me, still hugging me until I grow quiet. But once my sobs stop and my yells cease, I gulp in enough oxygen to remember that no matter how good her embrace feels, it might be a lie. I pull—forcefully—out of her hold, and move deliberately away from her on the ledge. My eyes narrow.

Switching from a soothing tone to a more matter-of-fact one, she says, "I did not tell you about my visits to my cousins earlier because I did not think it was information you needed to know. But now, it is clearly time to explain. Melusine needs an adult to supervise her visits with her father. If I did not do it, a guard would be assigned. I know Filius. I know how he operates. If he is planning something and attempting to use Melusine to his own ends as he did before, he will do it in such a way that no guard will catch him. But I will understand his meaning. That is why I must be the one to escort her to those prison tunnels. No one else."

I stare into her face, as if looking at her long enough will reveal her intentions. Is she telling me the truth? The logic of what she's just said fits, and she's never given me any reason to doubt her. Conviction and sincerity dominate her expression, but ... how am I supposed to know what to believe? Could all of this be some ruse she's concocted with her family? If it is what's the endgame? Whatever it might be, letting her close to me—closer to me than I already have—would be playing right into their fins. But there's still a part of me that doesn't think she'd hurt me. "I was so shocked to see you there."

"I was not hiding it from you. However, with everything you are dealing with and all your worries, I did not think it was the time for you to know. You felt betrayed, yes?" she says in her lilting accent.

"Yes." That's it exactly.

"For this, I apologize. But I will not apologize for visiting Melusine because I have a good reason." She looks me directly in the eye. "One should never apologize for actions motivated by a good reason. Remember that, Lia."

Is she right? I sirened Clay for a good reason and I've done nothing but apologize ever since. She probably doesn't mean for something as bad as what I did.

"Since we're being honest with each other," she says, "you should know that I have forgiven Melusine."

And just like that, I want to start yelling again. But I don't want to stay an emotional wreck—some hormonal teenager adults write off—so I try to understand why Ondine, someone I've come to respect, could forgive Melusine. The vile things Melusine said to me in her rooms at the Foundation make that anything but easy, and my voice is still trembly and breathless from my early outburst, so all I manage to get out is, "How?" How can someone who forgives Melusine claim to care about me and be on my side?

"I'm glad you asked," Ondine says. "I know you do not forgive her, and you may never do so." I'll definitely never do so, but the gravity of Ondine's tone keeps me from interrupting. Besides, I need to let her explain to know if, after what I learned yesterday, I can still respect her—and even more importantly, if I can trust her. "That is your choice, and I understand it," she continues. "I have not forgiven her father because, although he had a reason for his actions, it was one motivated by selfishness and a desire for power without the intention to use it for a greater good. But Melusine ..." Ondine shakes her head and sorrow swims across her face. "Melusine thought her reason was good. She thought she was saving lives, lives of people like her mother, who was a dear friend to me after she married my cousin. A friend through ... all number of things that have befallen me." That sorrow deepens, darkening her eyes from pale gray to storm cloud. "Melusine thought she was rescuing her species, myself included, from death. She made countless errors in judgment after that, but that's how it started. And while that in no way dismisses what she did, it does earn my forgiveness."

I roll the words over in my mind. A part of me wants to scream that, like Caspian, another person I admire sits calmly telling me why someone whose eyes glinted with glee as she moved in to stab me deserves sympathy. But a larger part focuses on what Ondine's words might mean about ... me.

"So, you're willing to help Melusine by visiting her and taking her to see her father, even though she did something so despicable? Even though she ... sirened a human?"

"Yes. Not even sirening should render someone past forgiveness."

Those simple words warm me like sunlight after a long, icy swim. A chill I didn't know was plaguing me suddenly thaws. All the while, Ondine sits there with me, her blue fins next to my gold ones in the water.

Yesterday morning, hearing those words from Ondine would have been all I needed to finally confide in her about my sireny. To *finally* reveal what I've done and ask her if she knew a way to help Clay. Now, though ... how do I know she's really my friend? Really on my side? What assurance do I have that I won't get played? I bite my lip, examining her face for the umpteenth time. How can I—

"Lia," Ondine's soft voice cuts off my whirring thoughts, "I can tell by your face you want to tell me something. You have wanted to for a while. And I want to be here for you. I know after what you saw yesterday, you are not certain whether or not you can trust me." She angles herself toward me on the ledge. "What you need to realize is, I am trusting you now, too."

"What do you mean?"

"You know a secret of mine now. Going to see my cousins, facilitating their visits, it isn't against the law by any means, but you and I have spoken about the weight of public opinion. You know how tenuous my reputation has been since the trial. If you made my actions public knowledge, the ensuing damage to my good name would mean I'd never be able to return to Sea Daughters Academy. I'd never be able to teach again, and teaching means more to me than anything." That, at least, is something I can't doubt the truth of. "So you see, if you are still not sure whether or not you can trust me, let's make a deal."

I cock my head. "What do you mean?" I say again.

"I want you to feel like you can talk to me. I promise that, whatever you tell me, I'll keep it between us." Saying that and doing it are two very different things. I raise a skeptical eyebrow, and she adds, "If I don't, you can tell your whole Community and all the world Below that I have been helping Melusine visit her father." I inhale sharply, finally understanding. What she's offering is … "Mutual assurance," she says with a dignified smile. "How about we both trust each other to keep confidences? Deal?"

I sit up straighter, hoping the posture will make me feel more confident about what to do. Telling her my secret is still a risk. Will she keep her word? Even if she forgives me the way she's forgiven Melusine, that doesn't mean she won't feel morally obligated to tell anyway, won't insist I have a trial like Melusine did. But I have more leverage than I did before, and more reason to think she may not blame me for sirening. If I don't say anything … without her help, I have no other way to help Clay. I can stay silent and safe, but it means letting him go. It means letting our love go.

And that terrifies me more than any trial or sentence.

"Ondine, I …" I've never said the words before, not when I didn't have to. Melusine saw me do it and told her father, Caspian and his grandmother figured it out on their own (I remember the shock and hate in their eyes, and even now it makes me feel sick), and I only confessed to Clay once Melusine demanded it with a dagger at his throat. This is different. This is a choice—one I can back out of. Before fear can drown me, I say in a rush, "Last year, I wanted to protect Clay from Melusine and I researched and I didn't know what else to do so I …" There's that fear again, its tide rising. "I …"

Ondine squeezes my hand.

"I sirened him."

Chapter Twenty-Two

As I wait for her reaction, the room grows so silent I can hear the *plunk, plunk, plunk* of condensed water dripping from somewhere on the slick ceiling. The tips of my fins curl and uncurl in the water. Ondine doesn't so much as twitch. Well??

"Thank you for trusting me with this, Lia."

I search her face for some sign of her reaction, but she's retreated behind a pensive mask. At least she's not yelling at me, not mortified into shock—that's ... something, right? Since she hasn't stormed off or started lecturing me about how I'm a terrible criminal, I push on. Once I start, the whole story of my sireny spills out of me. Ondine may not say anything, but she holds my hand through every lurid, disturbing detail. When I'm finished, I'm shaking. But I feel lighter, like I've been weighed down at the bottom of the darkest sea and can finally float up to the bright surface.

I wait. When her continued silence has made me jittery enough to ripple the surrounding water with my restless movement, I ask, "Are you going to tell?" She may have promised she wouldn't, but that was before she knew what I'd done.

My whispered question echoes off the grotto's opal-studded walls; I've never heard my voice sound so vulnerable or pleading.

Ondine places a soft hand on my cheek. "Keeping this from your parents …" She shakes her head and I stop breathing. "I understand why you have done it, but," *please no, please no,* "it is not a decision I take lightly. Your parents have brought me into their home and given me a certain degree of responsibility over your welfare." She drops her hand from my cheek. "In these specific circumstances, however, when you had a truly good reason for your behavior and when it is so vital to our kind that your parents gain approval to ascend to the throne, this information is not something they—or anyone else— needs to know. I will keep your secret between the two of us, as promised."

The relief flooding my consciousness is so strong it blots out my remaining doubts. Almost. Slowly, hesitantly, I wrap my arms around her porcelain-doll frame.

With that hurdle out of the way, the next one dominates my focus. I pull back and bite my lip again.

"I told you about my sireny for a reason. I need your help."

By the time I finish explaining the former siren bond and how I hope she can help me use it to reverse the effects of the potion, I'm vibrating with nervous energy. Her reaction once again hides behind that pensive mask. What's she thinking as she stares unseeing at the satiny water around us?

Then I know what she's thinking. Agreeing to keep my secret is very different from agreeing to help me defy the Tribunal. Why would she say yes? My stomach drops to the grotto floor. I shouldn't have asked her. It's too much.

But after I asked for Caspian's help gathering intel on Melusine last year without telling him all the details, I swore to myself I wouldn't do something like that again. I involved him in something dangerous without giving him all the information, and it wasn't right. I won't do that this time. All I can do now is hope my honesty doesn't cost me the only chance I have to help Clay.

Ondine slides off the ledge and into the water, swimming away from me. She's leaving. And she's taking her knowledge of magic with her. I pushed too far.

But, no … she's stopping. When Ondine reaches the center of the room, she turns back to face me. "Technically speaking, since such a remnant of a siren bond is, as you said, unprecedented, there are no laws to govern it. Thus, what you are asking of me is not illegal in the strictest sense. What troubles me is that a solution would require strong magic, and you are a novice."

"I'm a fast learner." My brain dives from one point to the next, searching for ammunition. "You know I'm a good student, a-and you said I sensed the magical energy of that potted seagrass extra fast."

"That is true, but being good at one simplistic spell does not prove much …" Doubt still mars her beautiful face.

I haven't put everything on the line just for her to say no. "I can do this. I know I can." *Please believe me. Please help.*

She swims away and back, pacing through the water. "How much do you love him?"

The question catches me off guard. I'd expected her to ask what I was thinking, how I could even consider taking such a risk, why I refused to move on. Then again, I suppose she did. I answer honestly. "With everything I am."

The reserve dissipates from her face and shoulders, and she says, more to herself than to me, "That may be something we can use."

"What?" I ask.

Thoughts flit like ghost fish behind her eyes as she calculates something, weighs options, but she doesn't explain. Instead, she says, "I do not know how to use this bond to give Clay his memories back."

My whole body deflates.

"But, I will think on it." She lifts my chin so her pale eyes bore straight into my brown ones. "That I promise you."

I thought I'd feel overjoyed if Ondine agreed to help me, but all I feel is the uncertainty still thick in the air. Will she be able to come up with a solution? And in the meantime, what are the two of us supposed to do, pretend like I've said nothing? Like she doesn't know my deepest, most dangerous secrets?

"What now?" I ask. "We have history class? Or ... grammar?" The thought of having a normal school day strikes me as laughable.

"I may not know how to get Clay his memories back using the bond, but I do know how to strengthen its presence." She skims her fingertips over the surface of the water. "What do you say, Lia? Would you like to see Clay?"

Chapter Twenty-Three

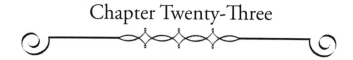

"See him?"

Tears prick my eyes. I haven't been allowed to see Clay since the Tribunal members took him from the Foundation, and no matter how many reports my parents share with me about how "fine" he's doing and how everything in his life is "normal," I can't trust what I can't see for myself. The idea that I could watch over Clay in my mind's eye through the bond, that I could make sure he's truly okay after having so many of his memories wiped, that thought alone wraps me in warmth. We must make this work. "How do we strengthen the bond?"

"The siren song worked because it harnessed the power of the ocean and the ocean's call."

"I remember reading that," I say. "The siren spell uses the call of the ocean that all Merkind hear and directs it outward, calling the human to the siren."

"So," Ondine explains, "if your goal is to use the bond you share with Clay without relying on the siren song, you must learn to harness power on your own, without sireny."

I gulp. "Harness the call of the ocean on my own?"

"I am afraid that much would kill you." My eyes widen and she strokes my arm. "No, you should never attempt to harness more magic than you're sure you can handle, or it will sweep you up like the fiercest current, and leave you decimated. Besides, the only reason the siren spell requires that mighty of a power source is so the siren can brainwash the human, giving commands for him to follow." She raises a crystal-encrusted eyebrow at me.

"That's not what I want to do," I say. "I promised Clay I would never siren again, and I meant it." My words are firm, adamant. Just because Clay doesn't remember what I've done or the promise I made doesn't mean I would ever violate the trust he placed in me.

Ondine nods. Was that a test? "Since you are only seeking to watch over him and not siren him, you can use a much smaller power source. Eventually, once you have learnt enough magic, it will become a constant that flows through you, and you can use yourself as the power source."

"Seriously?" I can't imagine myself—a girl raised on land who often feels so human I'm like an imposter instead of a real Mermaid—coursing with enough Mer magic to fuel the bond.

"Seriously." Ondine smiles at me. "But," she adds, "you will not be ready for that for some time." I try not to let my face fall, but now that I know seeing Clay is a possibility, I can't wait any longer. "In the meantime," Ondine says, "we will use me."

"What?"

"I will be your power source until you're strong enough to be your own." Her words resound off the cave walls.

"You'd do that for me?" I whisper.

"Watching over your young man, it means a lot to you, yes?"

"Yes." So much yes.

"Then I will do this."

It feels like a trick—like an offer too good to be true. But it's also too good to resist. Too good to question. When Ondine gestures me forward, I move so I'm floating right in front of her. "Close your eyes." I do. "Now, sense me the way you sensed the seagrass." I exhale, clearing my mind. With the seagrass, I pictured its root system and individual blades; now I picture Ondine and all her wonderful complexities: bones, muscles, tendons, and the magic I know must flow like her lifeblood through all of it. When I sense that magic, it sends me reeling backward through the water with its force.

Ondine doesn't reach out a hand or say a word, merely waits for me to right myself and return to my position facing her. This time, when I close my eyes and reach out to sense her magic, I think I'm more prepared, but even though the sheer force doesn't throw me backward, what I find surprises me even more.

Her magic has a distinct feel. No, stronger than that, almost a … taste.

"Each person's magic has a unique signature," she says as if reading my mind the way I'm reading her magic.

Despite Ondine's proximity, her words ring out far in the distance, a hum I barely hear as her magic envelops me, entrances me. It's steady and constant, like Ondine. Like the calm, pale sea on an overcast morning. But under that surface lies something deeper I can only begin to sense, a power and a fierceness. It sparkles like crystal and cuts like glass. Her magic lures me toward it as it chills me with tendrils as icy as her tail and hair. This is Ondine.

Once again, the intensity of her power threatens to overwhelm me, but her voice—calm, strong, hypnotic—echoes through the grotto and through my mind. "Hold on, Lia. Grab ahold of my magic and draw it toward you."

"I … I don't think I can. It's too strong." Did I say the words? Think them?

"*You're* strong. You can do it." Her voice vibrates inside my skull now. "Harness my magic, Lia."

I imagine myself twisting those icy tendrils up my arms, clutching that flowing power in my palms and pulling—hard. When I open my eyes again, my consciousness collides back into my own body, but that magic still courses through me. It feels distinctly different from me, foreign, like wearing someone else's clothes. Her magic is a sleek, shimmering dress of the finest, pale blue seasilk. It isn't mine and doesn't quite suit me, but it makes me feel oh-so beautiful. I want to twirl in it and never stop ...

"Lia? Lia are you in control? Can you hear me?"

I force my brain to focus, force my mouth to form words. "Yes. I'm here. I'm holding on. I'm holding on to ... your magic."

"Yes, you are." Ondine rolls her shoulders like she can feel me touching a part of her power. "Once you are positive you can concentrate, you must hold tightly, close your eyes again, and connect to the bond you share with Clay."

I want to—so badly. The idea that I'm seconds away from seeing Clay for the first time in so long ... "Will it, um, will it hurt you?"

Ondine smiles, as warm as her magic is icy. "Not at all. Actually," she lowers her voice in a conspiratorial whisper, "you are only using a tiny fraction of my magic."

My jaw hinges open. A tiny fraction? If this overwhelming force of splendor is a tiny fraction ... I stare at her in awe.

"I will fuel the bond with magic and will give you your privacy as you check on Clay. I won't see what you see. Take your time—I am going to feel along the bond to try to get a sense of it, see if anything occurs to me for how to use it to reverse the potion. Are you ready?"

Am I ever! Infusing every step with purpose, I close my eyes, keep a firm grip on Ondine's cold, glittering power, and reach inward, toward the bond that lives in my center. Now, with Ondine's magic coursing through me, the thread of the siren bond—so spindly and weak the last time I tried this—thickens to the rope-like pull it was when I was a siren. But when this bond was a siren bond, it felt like I could use it to tug Clay toward me, make him obey me. This is different. This bond tugs me toward Clay just as much as it tugs him toward me. It's a stronger, more enhanced version of the same connection that allowed me to find Clay out in the ocean after I stopped sirening him and Melusine kidnapped him. It's a connection linking the two of us.

Without waiting another second, I dive into that connection.

Flannel bedsheets that smell like cinnamon.

And Clay—Clay!—sitting on top of them, holding his guitar.

He runs calloused fingertips through his dark hair and I gasp as I take in his features for the first time in too long. They're so familiar and so striking all at once. The urge to touch him—to press a hand to his lightly stubbled jaw, to trace my thumb along his cheekbone—seizes me. Seeing him like this ... it's too much and not enough. The pink afternoon sun bathes his face in light, and he's so handsome it hurts. His presence warms me, melting the chill of Ondine's arctic magic and making me feel more like myself than I have since the last time Clay held me in his arms.

But something is wrong.

His hazel eyes portray a vague sadness, their spark muted. And his hand rests on the strings of his guitar, but seconds pass, and he doesn't strum, doesn't make a sound. As my initial joy at seeing him ebbs to a more manageable level, I settle into the bond and Clay's emotions fill me.

As high as my spirits rose a moment earlier, now they sink just as low. Deep, desolate sadness weighs down my chest as it weighs down his. It's laced with confusion so thick it's nearly suffocating. He's sad without knowing why, which means he can't shake it. Even after only a few seconds drenched in his emotions and soaking in his thoughts, I know he's been trying. Searching for an explanation for why he feels so dejected, pretending to his mom and his friends that he's fine and hoping with everything he is that one day he'll wake up and it'll be true—he'll feel like himself again. But the days have turned into weeks and the weeks into months, and still something is off, something is ... what? Clay sighs, a frustrated, guttural noise escaping his lips.

It shudders through my own body the way his thoughts pass through my mind. *I should be happy, shouldn't I?* Clay's mind whispers through the bond, all his ideas spiraling toward me at once. *It's my senior year, and it's supposed to be epic. The last rounds of adventures with the guys before we all go off to college next year; classes are pretty good; Mom's making time for us to do stuff together (I think she feels sorry for me after my breakup with Leah, even though I've told her about fifty times it was no big deal)* ... My breath catches, and I tell myself it's just what the Tribunal planted in his head, that he doesn't mean it—but hearing him think it still hurts. *I just can't figure out why I'm so down. Even things with Dad are better than they have been in ages, phone calls and dinners. And Allison just hinted I should ask her out. Why haven't I? Why does considering it make me tense up and want to avoid her? That isn't normal. She's really hot, and she's got those great—*Whoa! So don't want to hear that. I never liked Allison. *It doesn't make sense. I should be flying high. Instead I feel so ... empty.*

Since he doesn't understand—can't understand—why he feels so upset, his confusion mounts to anger. Discordant strumming hacks through the silence, then stops as abruptly as it started. He tries again, fingers moving furiously over the chords as he seeks out a harmony he can't find. Over and over until he throws the guitar down on the mattress. He grabs his car keys off his perpetually messy desk and lets the door slam behind him.

When he drives in his bright blue Mustang down the PCH, I pretend I'm sitting next to him in the passenger seat instead of spying on him using magic he doesn't even remember exists. I pretend I'm a normal girl enjoying a drive with her boyfriend.

But his tensed shoulders, the tic in his jaw, and the worry lines furrowing his forehead ruin the illusion. What I wouldn't give to comfort him. Wait ...

If I can hear Clay's thoughts through the bond, maybe, just maybe, he'll be able to hear mine. I don't want him to think he's going totally crazy, so I'll have to go with something vaguely comforting that he could be thinking himself. I decide to start simple: *Everything will be okay.* I hope it's true—I'll do everything I can to make that true. Taking a deep breath, I pour every drop of my focus into sending the message to Clay through the bond. *Everything will be okay, everything will be okay, everything will—*

But it's not working. While his thoughts and feelings still flow at me, mine collide with an invisible barrier, like ships bashing against unseen but deadly rocks. Damn it! I guess without the siren spell funneling the call of the ocean into the bond, our magical connection isn't strong enough for me to link my thoughts with his when he isn't even aware the bond exists and isn't listening for it. After three more fruitless tries, I go back to passive observation, unable to help as Clay sits behind the steering wheel sinking into deeper, despondent confusion and fighting to bring himself out of it—all alone.

He drives until he reaches Zuma Beach, then parks on a side street. I think maybe he's planning to take a walk to clear his head until he pulls a beach bag from the trunk and unzips it to reveal a towel and sunblock along with his snorkel and mask. My mind flashes to him taking it off his face in the waves, pulling me to him with strong arms, holding me close in the sparkling sea, and kissing me in the surf. Another memory he's lost.

Clay grabs his stuff, and I notice the shorts he's wearing are swim trunks. Sand already dots the bottom of his canvas beach bag and lines the inside of his trunk. How often has he been coming here?

On the path to the beach, he walks with purpose. This isn't a leisurely, meandering stroll by the water to clear his head. This is something else entirely.

Clay pulls his shirt off. Drops his bag. Dons the snorkeling gear. When I check in with his thoughts, they're muted, like he's let his conscious mind succumb to a routine so ingrained he can get lost in it.

Soon, the waves lap at his bare feet. He doesn't hesitate or inch his way in, allowing his body to adjust to the temperature slowly, the way most humans do. No, even though the day is thick with clouds and that water must be freezing to him, he dives right in, using his muscled arms and legs to pound his way through the wan, colorless waves.

He swims farther and farther out, setting a punishing pace. It's nowhere near as far or as fast as my sisters and I swim, but for a human it's … intense. Too intense. This isn't impressive—it's frightening.

My own energy depletes as holding on to Ondine's power and pushing it into the bond grows more and more challenging the longer I do it. Since it's just my first try at this, I should end it here. Let go. After all, it's not like Clay feels my presence. He doesn't even know I'm here. But I can't leave him, not when he's frustrated and lonely and confused. Gritting my teeth, I keep our connection going so I can stay by his side. For what must be an hour, Clay beats back his sadness as he beats his way through the current, his face twisted with emotion he no longer hides now that he's cloaked by the waves. Then, exhausted, he lets himself float.

Purged of the pent up, unexplained feelings he masks from everyone during the day, Clay lies on his back, staring up at the outstretched sky, soaking in the last rays of sun as the ocean carries him to and fro. When he turns his body over and floats on his stomach, observing the fish and kelp through his snorkeling mask, a familiar spark lights his eyes. It's a ghost of the one burning there when we snorkeled together, me without a mask and him pointing out everything he saw with such excitement and curiosity. Seeing that spark now reminds me he's still Clay—still curious and forward-thinking, still determined and daring. He's doing everything he can think of to fight against a moroseness he doesn't understand. And I'm fighting, too. He may not know who I am, he may not feel me here next to him, but I'm fighting just as hard, and now that I have Ondine and her magic on my side, there must be a way. I'll bring him back. Bring us back.

That's a promise.

Chapter Twenty-Four

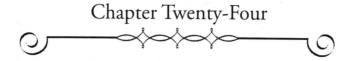

I stay with Clay until he's safely out of the ocean and wrapped in his towel. Then, heart heavy at his lingering sadness but lighter at my own renewed determination, I finally follow the gentle tug of Ondine pulling me back to my own reality. With one last, longing glance at the boy I love, I release my grip on Ondine's icy magic. I pry open my eyes after what feels like days, my head spinning as I stare at the grotto ceiling.

The ceiling? It's only then I realize I must have lost my balance and fallen backward, because I've collapsed into Ondine's arms. She holds me, gentle but firm, until I sit up and she helps me onto a stone stool.

"We will need to practice letting go more slowly," she says, voice quiet and even, like she knows anything louder would hurt all my senses right now.

I nod, but the movement makes me dizzy.

"It will get easier once you're used to it. Think of it like swimming against the current instead of with it. Before, you swam *with* the current; you had the siren spell pushing you forward effortlessly.

Now, you have to swim forward by yourself, without sireny pushing you along and with all that new magic pushing against you, so it's straining all your muscles. Once you develop those muscles with practice, you'll be able to handle that magic."

How does she always manage to phrase things in a way that makes sense? I wish my words came out like that. Right now, no words come out of me at all—I feel like I left them all with Clay.

Ondine rubs soothing circles onto my back. "I am impressed, Lia. I did not expect you to hold on so long on your first try. Your potential for magic is strong." Something lights in her eyes—a genuine happiness—and pride swells inside me, replacing the magic's chill. "How is your young man?" she asks.

Another kind of chill creeps up my arms and tail. "Not so good. He feels that something is off, something is wrong, but he has no way of knowing what that is. He's putting on a brave face for everyone else …" He's done that with me so many times, when he's talked about his parents' divorce or what Melusine did to him or what it felt like when his dad missed a gig. "It's just this … mask of normal. I felt what he's feeling and …" My voice catches.

"Are you not happy that he feels the loss of you, even without knowing it?"

I shake my head. If you'd asked me this morning, I would have thought I'd be overjoyed to learn Clay had some awareness that something was missing—that I was missing—from his life. I would have thought him moving on, maybe dating another girl and being happy, was the worst possible fate. But after watching him today, after *feeling* him, I know there's something much worse. "He's desperately trying to make sense of this deep sadness inside him, but he can't. He thinks he's going crazy." I can't let him suffer like that. I can't.

Ondine doesn't bother with comforting platitudes. Instead, she says, "While you used the bond, I had time to study it. It is unlike anything I have seen. The remnant of a worn-off spell, but still so powerful. I do not yet know how we can use it to return Clay's memories, but there is no denying the connection between you is strong. With it, we can find a way."

No matter the risk, with those words, Ondine goes from being my tutor and friend to being my greatest ally.

I'm excelling in every subject. History, geography, marine biology, culture, even Mermese oration and grammar—I've never done this well. Then again, I've never had such strong motivation. The faster I master the day's material, the sooner we finish our formal lessons and begin our secret ones. I spend each day waiting for Ondine to swim to the center of the classroom, gesture me over, and say, "Close your eyes." Tapping into her power gets a little easier each time, and closing my eyes means seeing Clay.

I stay with him for as long as I can each day, and Ondine never complains, never pulls me away before I'm ready. For that, I'm so grateful.

Sometimes, with my body still in the grotto classroom, I let my mental presence linger in his bedroom while he does homework or scribbles furiously in his leather songwriting notebook before crossing out most of the new words in frustration. Sometimes I watch him with his mom or his friends; those days are the best because every once in a while, someone will say something that catches him off guard, making him laugh, and his smile will finally—finally!— meet his hazel eyes. Those moments bring palpable relief, streaks of sunlight that pierce the dark cloud clinging to him. But they're short- lived. Most days, I follow him to the beach and into the waves where he swims until the sorrow seeps out of him and into the sea. Those are the days I want to hold him most.

It twists my insides to see him every day without being able to hold him like I want to, to have him hold me. I can't talk to him or kiss him or tell him I love him in any way that he can hear. Reaching out for the bond each day is self-inflicted torture. But not seeing him every day, that would be worse.

When I slide back into myself and into the grottos, Ondine often looks tired. She spends every second I'm with Clay studying the bond. Testing it with different spells to see how it reacts. She's even had me try a variety of ways to transfer a thought from my mind to Clay's, but nothing has worked. So far, we're no closer to an answer. But she promises she won't give up until she finds it.

After we've settled into a routine and the overwhelming novelty of being able to see Clay has calmed enough for me to hear my own curiosity, a question bubbles up to the surface one day before we start our lessons. I shouldn't ask it, but I do anyway. "Why did you agree to help me?"

I expect her to say something about wanting me to be happy or respecting the love I have for Clay or even just being a good friend. Instead, her answer surprises me.

"I cannot tell you that. Not yet. But I have a good reason. Do you accept that condition?"

I bite my lip. "If you have a good reason, why can't you tell me?"

"Because you're not ready to know."

Curiosity burns inside me and that creeping sense of mistrust flares again, urging me to argue, to push for an answer. Instead, I close my eyes and tap into her power again so I can visit Clay.

Saturdays, which used to be my favorite day of the week, are now the toughest to slog through. No lessons with Ondine means no practice using magic, which means no chance to see Clay for two whole days. My skin prickles and my mind itches. Sometimes, I try to use the bond myself. Ondine says my magic is developing nicely, which explains why the thread of the bond feels less spindly than before, but it's nowhere near strong enough for me to see Clay without the aid of Ondine's magic. I sigh. Will I ever be that powerful?

Dwelling on it isn't healthy, so I put on my happiest bikini top—bright pink sequins—along with my wraparound skirt and head down to the sun-drenched swimming pool that wraps around nearly two sides of our house. The pool's waterfall edge makes the sparkling water look like it flows seamlessly into the Pacific Ocean below. I'm less surprised than I should be to find it empty. My sisters and I used to spend every Saturday sunning ourselves in the pool, enjoying an entire day in our tails in the safety of our backyard. No hiding. We'd spend the whole day talking and laughing and swimming and splashing.

Now those Saturdays are sporadic at best. Everyone's gotten so busy. With my parents focusing on building security Below, Em has taken over most of their duties in the Community. And even though the twins don't have classes on weekends, they usually spend them on campus with their cool, new college friends. I sigh. I can't fault Amy for not being here. Since she has school in the grottos during the week, she's been using weekends to take her parents sightseeing up and down the coast. Still, I was hoping somebody'd be around to swim with. I sit along the edge of the pool and transform into my tail before removing my wrap-around skirt and scooting into the water.

I could invite Caspian to join me, but we'd end up talking about Melusine. Probably fighting about Melusine. I shell called him a couple times this week, trying to keep things normal. He never had time to talk for more than a couple minutes, and we didn't get into anything serious before he had to go, which was kind of a relief. Option one: Melusine told him I tried to make her stop talking to him and now he thinks I'm controlling and obsessive. If that's the case, he's waiting for the chance to see me in person so we can have some overblown, serious discussion about how I have no business deciding what choices he makes or who he spends time with. Option two: Melusine was adequately intimidated by my threat to get my parents involved and she's stopped talking to him. Even though that's the outcome I wanted, Caspian's smart enough to question the timing. And if he asks me if I had something to do with it, I'm not going to lie. I'm done lying to Casp. That means he'll want to have a serious discussion about how I have no business deciding what choices he makes or who he spends time with.

Maybe he'd be right. Maybe I never should have gone to see her. It scares me that Casp doesn't see how manipulative she is, and I want to protect him, but ...

Her words play through my mind as if my skull were a *konklili* with her voice trapped inside: *"You claim you're done controlling people. I wonder when you'll see yourself for who you are. Like it or not, my father was right. When we cast that siren spell, it planted something dark inside of us. Both me and you. I can see it in you. That darkness. In your need to control."*

She's wrong. She has to be wrong. Still, the memory of her words clenches my stomach. Caspian has always been smart—way smarter than I am; maybe a better person would trust him to protect himself instead of letting distrust of her win out. Does that count as giving into darkness? Did the siren spell really plant something inside me?

In my mind's eye, tendrils of darkness uncurl deep within me where I can't see them, can't claw them out. A wave of nausea makes me grip the pool's edge to steady myself. Ever since I confessed my sireny to Ondine, I've wanted to ask her about what Mr. Havelock and Melusine said, about whether it's true that by sirening Clay, I've unleashed something inside myself that I can't stop. Some residue of evil I can't wipe clean.

But I'm afraid of what she'll say.

I don't invite Caspian over because I don't want a serious discussion. It feels like that's the only kind I have with anyone lately. What happened to shoe shopping and carefree Ferris Wheel rides on the pier? I don't think I could enjoy those things now if I tried, not after everything that's happened.

That leaves me here, swimming alone in a ginormous pool meant for seven people. The Saturday sunshine beats down on my shoulders, and I wonder why it doesn't feel warmer.

"Aurelia, I was hoping you'd be out here." A smile spreads across my face as my mom walks into the backyard, my dad next to her. My hopes leap like flying fish as I picture my parents slipping into the pool for a Saturday swim. But my mom's wearing a business suit, not a *siluess*, and the grim expressions on both their faces tell me I'm in for one of those serious discussions.

Once inside, we head toward my parents' office—the one in the human part of the house, not the one in the grottos. It's a room I barely visit. Even when we're all in human clothes and want to stay dry, we generally hang out in the living room or at the breakfast table. Their office, with its large glass desks and sleek, white leather chairs, feels too formal and foreign.

"We need to talk to you about something, angelfish," my dad says as we enter the office.

In one of those white leather chairs sits Ondine.

She's wearing clothes. Not a crystal-frosted *siluess* but a long, white maxi dress. The kind you can find at any beachy boutique in the neighborhood for the over-fifty crowd to throw on over a swimsuit under the guise of fashion. She stands when we enter and on her it looks regal, even though she's shorter in her legs than I would have imagined. Only a couple inches taller than me and noticeably shorter than my mother. Even with her ballet flat–clad feet planted on the hardwood floor, her slight frame still gives the impression she's floating.

What's she doing here, in the dry part of the house, dressed in human clothes, on a Saturday? It's a weirdness overload. I freeze where I stand. Did my parents find out we're practicing magic? Did she tell them? Did she tell them about my sireny?

I search her face, but it reveals nothing.

"Ondine, thank you for coming in on a weekend," my mother says. "Edmar and I knew everyone would be out of the house today, and we wanted to give Lia some privacy for this conversation."

Her tone is too polite for her to know about the sireny. Even with my mother's diplomatic abilities, that one would send her into a tailspin. I breathe a steadying sigh of relief and let my dad usher me into the chair next to Ondine. Maybe my parents just plan to ask us about the magic. I run through all the possible comebacks in my head for why we need to continue, why stopping us would mean limiting my Mer education.

My parents each take a seat on the other side of my mom's desk, since my dad's is farther away by the window. Sitting with the desk between us gives me the stomach-flipping sensation of being in the principal's office.

My dad is smiling, but it's his keeping-everyone-calm-in-a-tense-situation smile. I swallow. "As I'm sure you know," he says to Ondine, "my sister Rashell and her husband Kai have recently surfaced and are staying with us."

"Yes, I met your sister a few days ago on my way in," Ondine replies in her tinkling voice.

"Good, good," my father says, like we're all at a gala in the grottos making small talk.

"Kai and Rashell aren't only here for a visit," my mother says, speeding toward the point. "They're here primarily to see their daughter, but they also came to deliver information in person. Shell messages traveling from Below are still being intercepted and can't be trusted with anything confidential."

"My sister and brother-in-law spent the wars teaching civilians to protect themselves and their families, and they've spent the months since the wars ended travelling from village to village, helping to rebuild," my dad says.

"Their actions have gained them the trust of Mer they've helped all across the ocean floor, from those in remote cave settlements to those moving back into major cities. People have spoken to them candidly." My mother steeples her fingers on the desk. "From community to community, people have told them how they feel about us claiming the throne."

Oh. Amy's parents have been my parents' secret canvassing team. My mother keeps her words even, uncolored by emotion, but the slight pucker of her lips tells me whatever my parents are about to tell me isn't entirely good news.

"Overall, most people like us," my dad says with another big smile that should be reassuring. "After so many years of violence and people fighting over one ruler after another, none with any legitimate right to the throne, Mer are in favor of finally uniting behind a family with an undisputed claim."

As someone raised in America, I still balk at the idea that my parents have a claim to rule the entire ocean just because my mom is the distant cousin of the former ruling family, and any closer relatives died during the nearly two hundred years we've spent at war. But as a Mer, I understand the unrest and chaos people have endured and how rule by a queen and king in combination with a council is the only kind of government they've ever known, so they're putting their hopes behind leaders they think will finally last.

"People are ready to join together in support of a strong monarchy again," my dad says.

"But, they question whether we can be that monarchy when we've lived so many years Above," my mother says.

I jump in, glad to have something to contribute when for the past few minutes, I felt like I was sitting twiddling my fins at the kids table during an adult conversation. "I thought Em's wedding was going to fix that. Y'know, prove we still hold fast to our Mer traditions." Isn't that why I had to twist my tail learning all those traditional dances, and why Em's still making me practice with her, Amy, and Leo at least once a week?

"Emeraldine's wedding will be helpful," my mother says. "But if we're still living Above, the Mer Below will continue to question our allegiance to them and to our culture."

That's when I get it. They're moving Below. My parents are leaving me here while they move Below. But why is Ondine here? Are they going to ask her to stay with me while they're gone?

"The Mer here on land know we're capable leaders," my dad says. "But if we ever want the Mer Below to entrust us with their welfare, we need to live among them."

I give myself an imaginary pat on the back for figuring it out and keeping my cool.

My mother trains her gaze on me. "And we want you to come with us."

"What?" My heartbeat jitters against my ribs. So much for keeping my cool.

My mom speaks slowly, as if the longer it takes her to explain, the longer she can stave off my freak-out fest. "Your Aunt Rashell and Uncle Kai said the concern people expressed to them over and over was that now that the wars have ended, they see us keeping our children on land as a sign we hold ourselves and our family apart. Rashell is convinced if your father and I move Below and leave all you girls up here, people will see it as a ploy to win their favor. It could easily backfire."

"Taking you with us will show them we're serious about committing to the crown and to life Below, where we would need to live if we became monarchs," my dad says.

The tides are crashing all around me, sweeping in and out far too fast, threatening to pull me under. "Wait … we're all moving Below? That won't work. What about the Foundation?"

"We won't all be moving Below. Em needs to stay here to represent our family on the Community board and continue running the Foundation in our absence. If she's going to be queen one day, getting that kind of hands-on leadership will be a help to her. We're hoping the people will see that and will be satisfied that she's planning her wedding Below."

"And after the wedding, she and Leo will take an extended honeymoon Below," my dad adds. "Kind of a See the Sea while You're Seen tour." He chuckles, his eyes beseeching me to join him, but I can't, not when questions swim laps around my head.

"So, Em is staying here and the rest of us are moving Below? When? How soon?"

"Well, seashell, it's not that simple. You know we see Amy as another daughter, but people Below don't know us and don't view her that way, which is just as well since we think she should stay up here for the time being. She'll finally get to spend some real alone time with her parents, who will stay here with her. They'll watch the house and start heading up a new training force for Community members who'd like to enter law enforcement Below. They're the only ones with the appropriate experience to do it." Before I can react to the sea-quaking news that Amy won't be coming with us, that she'll be living apart from us for the first time since her parents sent her to us when she was one and I was almost five, my mother continues.

"And the twins have worked too hard to get into college—I'm not pulling them out no matter how good it will look for P.R."

My father pats her hand and says more to her than to me or Ondine, "They need this time of their lives to grow and figure things out. Besides, spending the next few years studying human politics and government procedures can only help them."

My stomach sinks like an overburdened ship. "Wait. Wait. If Em's not coming and Amy's not coming and Lapis and Lazuli aren't coming, that means … that means …"

"It would be you and us moving Below into the palace at New Meris, the new capital city. We'd still come back to visit here, and everyone would come see us there, but we'd be the ones living Below."

"If everyone else gets to stay here and keep their lives the same, why can't I?" A whine stretches my voice. It makes me sound like a petulant second-grader, but I can't make myself care enough to stop it. The idea of being separated from my sisters strikes me as impossible, like being separated from my tail. I've never lived away from them. I've never even gone to sleepaway camp because of the whole transform-into-fins-while-you-sleep problem. To be living in the ocean while they're up here … Tides! To be *living in the ocean*. I know, I know, I'm a Mermaid who's only ever lived on land because violence kept me away from the sea, so finally living in the ocean should be a dream come true. But land is all I've ever known. The human world is my home. Moving to a foreign, undersea city where I know no one and nothing … fear surges inside me, tightening my chest. "Why can't I stay, too?"

"We need to bring one of our daughters as a sign of goodwill and trust," my mom says.

"And you're the one the people want," my dad says. "You broke the curse. You gave them back immortality and ended the wars. You represent the hope for the future each one of them wants to see when they look at their new ruling family."

"It's essential you look like you're invested in that future, too, and that means embracing a more traditional Mer lifestyle by living Below." My mom says it like it's already decided.

My next words come out strangled by that pressure in my chest. "You refuse to pull the twins out of college, but it's okay for you to pull me out of my entire life?"

"Seashell," my dad says, "we thought you didn't really …"

Have a life?

"… have anything keeping you here anymore," my mom finishes with a stern look at my dad. "You're not attending your school anymore, and because of the Tribunal's order forbidding you from seeing Clay or anyone close to him, you've had to give up all your human friends and most of your favorite places where you might run into him."

"You hardly ever leave the house, kiddo," my dad says. "It's not healthy … Your mom and I thought this could be a great new stage for you. You could get some distance from … here … and have a fresh start where you're not bogged down by everything you've had to face recently."

They think they know everything about my life, but they don't know the most important part: I haven't given up hope of getting Clay back. Even though I can't go near him, just knowing he's close by, that I haven't really lost him, keeps me going. Of course, it's not like I can tell them that when they think I'm moving on.

"I do have a life here," I argue. "I might not leave the house much right now, but that's because I'm studying. I'm studying—" I catch myself before I can say magic, which is the subject I've been pouring myself into more than any other. "—so hard." But then I realize that my argument is flawed. Continuing my studies isn't something I need to stay on land to do. Ondine's presence in the chair next to me makes sense now. "Ondine's here so you can ask her to come with us, isn't she? So she can keep teaching me in the capital city?" At least if I have to go, I'll have one familiar face there, and Ondine and I can keep studying the bond in secret. I cling to the thought with both fins.

My parents share a look that's equal parts surprise and regret. "Ondine has been gracious enough to take time away from the school she runs so that she could teach you. Our numbers are small on land, and all the qualified teachers up here are busy teaching at the high school set up by the Foundation. Once we move Below, there will be plenty of excellent teachers to choose from, and you're much more caught up than you were before, so you don't need her expertise any longer. We asked Ondine here today to let her know she'll finally be able to return to her school."

I turn to Ondine, who has sat silent throughout this conversation, observing us. I know how much she loves that school, how hard she's worked to keep it open in the face of all the violence and turmoil Below. My mind conjures an image of the young Mermaids who study there, girls like me but who have been raised Below, always focusing on the subjects Mer culture deems important. Perfect Mermaids who speak perfect Mermese and dance perfect, traditional dances and cast perfect, advanced spells. Jealousy spikes inside me, sharp and bitter. Ondine taught those girls for years before she met me. Surely, she cares more deeply for them, and who could blame her?

The reason she agreed to teach me in the first place was to counteract the potential damage to her reputation caused by the Havelocks so that she wouldn't lose control of that school. And now my parents are offering her the perfect way to return there with them singing her praises.

But if she takes it, she'll take my chances of getting Clay back right along with her.

No other teacher my parents find for me will be as skilled in magic, and even if they were, there's no way I'd trust anyone else with my secret. No, all my hope for finding a way to return Clay's memories lies in one person—and she may be about to swim out of my life.

"I won't go!" The words burst out of me before Ondine has a chance to respond. "Not if it means I have to stop studying with Ondine."

"Aurelia." From my mother's scandalized expression, you'd think there was nothing worse I could do in all the Seven Seas than talk back in front of someone she considers a guest. What she doesn't understand is Ondine stopped being a guest weeks ago. With everything she's agreed to do for me, in some ways, she's closer than family. And I won't lose her.

"I mean it," I say. "You want me to move Below? Fine. You want me to leave Em, the twins, Amy, Barnacle?" My dad winces as my volume escalates. "To leave our Community for some underwater city filled with Mer I've never met? Fine. But only if Ondine stays with me." Only if we can keep working on a way to help Clay.

"Young lady," my mother says. "You will stop speaking in that tone." She waits, daring me to say something else. I don't say another word. I tell myself it's because I'd already finished and not because of my mother's steely expression. "We know we're asking a great deal of you," she continues, "but we're not asking it for ourselves. If we can get people to accept us, it will be the first time the Mer have been united in two hundred years. We can make real change and hopefully usher in a lasting peace." She leans forward, her eyes locking with mine. "You can help with that."

Putting up any more of a fight would make me seem like the most selfish Mermaid in the world. What am I supposed to do?

"If I may," Ondine says, her calm voice managing to slice through the tension in the air. "I'd be happy to travel with you all to New Meris and continue Lia's studies, since that's clearly what she wants."

Yes. Yes!

"We wouldn't dream of asking you to do that," my mother says. "Not when your school and your other students mean so much to you."

No, no.

"You've sacrificed too much of your time to help us already," my mom continues. "Aurelia understands that."

Aurelia understands that you're taking away the one person she needs right now. But I can't tell them that without arousing their suspicions about how one person, who until recently was a total stranger, could possibly be so important.

I throw Ondine a pleading look. She's the only one in this room besides me who knows what's at stake.

Before she even opens her mouth, my dad says to her, "We're hoping you can make some recommendations for other great teachers who aren't committed to a school so we can find someone Lia will love." He gives me a wink I know is meant to be comforting. It makes him seem far away. "Can you recommend anyone?" he asks Ondine.

"I recommend ... an alternative solution."

My mother tilts her head. My father raises his thick eyebrows. I hold my breath.

"I understand it is essential that Lia move Below when you do to show your family embraces a traditional upbringing, but she and I have an excellent rapport and I can see why she'd like to continue under my tutelage when so much else in her life must change." Wow. Ondine knows what she's doing; hints of guilt pull down the corners of my parents' eyes. "It is true I am eager to return to my school. Therefore, I propose Lia comes with me, as the newest student at Sea Daughters Academy."

Chapter Twenty-Five

Sea Daughters? Me at Sea Daughters? I try to picture it as my parents ask Ondine a jillion questions. Turns out, since the school moved to a remote island nearly two decades ago during the wars and is thus far away from the ocean floor, it's safer than even the newly renovated, guarded palace in New Meris. Ondine points out that, had I been raised in the ocean, I may very well have attended a school like hers all along, so those who question my parents' loyalties will see my attendance there as proof they're fully embracing Mer education and hoping to integrate their daughter back into a traditional undersea life.

"And your critics aside," Ondine says in her captivating accent, "being amongst girls her own age would be much healthier for Lia than studying alone with another private tutor."

Please say yes.

"I suppose we will be busy once we move Below ... " my mother says.

"Meetings and appearances ..." my father adds. "We'd hate to leave Lia alone all that time."

"Still, she's never lived away from us before." My mother focuses all her attention on me. "What do you want to do?"

The question rushes at me like an unexpected tidal wave. What do I want to do? I want to go back to Malibu Hills Prep and spend my last year of high school going to pep rallies and spending senior ditch day with my friends and making out inappropriately with Clay at my prom while I dance expertly in high heels. But since none of that's an option, I make the choice that will allow me to keep studying magic so I can get back what the Tribunal stole from Clay and me. "I want to go to Sea Daughters Academy."

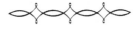

"It's not like I want to leave here," I say, rushing to explain. "The choice was either move Below to live in the new capital city or move Below to live at Ondine's school."

"I just … can't believe you're moving away." Caspian's arm muscles tense as he swings his body up onto the cave ledge and into a sitting position. I've brought him out to Star Cave because it's the only place I'd ever think to break news like this to Casp. We discovered this place as children, and after taking one look at the patchwork of purple, pink, yellow, orange, and red starfish covering the walls, we gave it its name. Humans never come here because the cave is only accessible from underneath, and it's never been off limits because it's within the Border line. Star Cave has always been our secret hideout from the world.

Caspian now sits on the rocky platform that runs along one side of the cave. "I can't picture your house without you living in it." He flicks his silver tail in and out of the water, and it shimmers in the moonlight that streams in through a crevice in the mountainside.

231

"You've lived there my whole life."

"I know," I say, resting my forearms on the platform as my tail wades beneath me in the water. I gaze up at the plains of his face, a face I've known so well for years. The thought of not being able to see it for months at a time … Tears prick behind my eyes, and I turn away. "I'm sorry." I don't know what I'm apologizing for, not really, but I feel sorry all the same.

"Hey, Lia? Are we … okay? I mean, we're okay, right? I know you got mad at me for talking to Melusine." He holds up a hand. "And I get why. I know how you feel about her and everything she's done. But I also have to trust my gut when it comes to the right thing to do."

Is he bringing this up because he knows I went to see her? Does he think I'm being controlling, just like she does? "I don't want to see her hurt you."

"I know. And that means a lot to me." He smiles, and I smile back. "Besides, it doesn't matter now, because she won't talk to me anyway."

"She won't?" Yes! Maybe going there wasn't a brainless mistake after all. Maybe the thought of angering my parents scared her off. "Did she say why she stopped talking to you?" Did she tell you it's because I went and threatened her?

He shrugs. "Just that we weren't friends and we shouldn't act like we were. And that we have nothing to say to each other." He tries to hide it with a dismissive smile, but hurt lurks behind the expression. Was he starting to consider her a friend? If he was, I'm glad I did what I did. It was even more necessary than I thought.

I rest my hand on his. "I need you to promise me you'll stay away from her while I'm gone." He hesitates. "She isn't some charity case. She's a villain."

That's right, like everyone keeps reminding me. I'm the villain here. Melusine's voice coats my memory in its thick syrup. Well, she is. I raise my eyebrows at Caspian, demanding an answer.

"I just said I'm not talking to her anymore, Lia." Actually, he said *she* wasn't talking to *him*, but pointing that out will make me sound juvenile—or worse, jealous—instead of clear-headed and reasonable. "I promise I won't let her hurt me." That's not the same as promising he'll stay away, and we both know it, but I'm afraid to press the point. Afraid we'll get in some big, blowout fight before I leave. Before I move away.

I never used to worry about fighting with Caspian. He's always been the person I could say anything to. My safe place. But when he first found out I'd sirened Clay … no one's ever yelled at me like that. No one's ever been that angry. That disappointed in me. He had every right. He *was* right to be angry, and I was wrong. But that fight made me realize that what Casp and I have, it isn't unbreakable. And I cherish it too much to ever risk breaking it again.

I'm going to have to trust him on this one. Luckily, Caspian makes trusting him easy. I nod and all the tension breaks, dissolving away in the water between us.

"This school you're going to, it's maids-only, right? No Mermen allowed?" It's a half-joke, accompanied by a half-smile. "It's probably just as well. My parents have said over and over that they won't disrupt my education to move Below. Coraline's only in elementary school, so if it were just her, they'd probably have moved already, but since it's my final year …"

Caspian's parents have always been more traditional than mine, which is why he attends the Mer high school set up by the Foundation instead of going to a human school. Still, if there's anything his parents value as much as staying true to their Mer culture, its education. "You think after the school year ends, you might move Below?" I can't help it; hope blooms open in my chest like a beautiful, fire-colored anemone.

Caspian runs an anxious hand through his blond hair. "I don't know. I always thought I'd move on to advanced studies in linguistics under Foundation scholars, but if I moved Below, I could specialize in different Mermese dialects—there's so much to learn there, and now that the wars are over and reunification is going to be so important, maybe I'd have more to contribute that way."

"You'd be so great at that," I say.

"Thanks." His eyes, a deep azure in the dim light, meet mine. "And we'd both be living Below."

The way he says the words—like there's a "finally" after them, like we'll finally be living the way we were always meant to—steals my breath. "Casp ... I don't know how long I'll be staying Below."

It's like he doesn't hear me—or chooses not to. "You know what? I've decided I'm not going to be sad about you moving. You're going to have an adventure! You deserve one, and I'm going to be happy for you." I'm about to thank him for being so thoughtful and trying to make it easier for me to do what I have to when he adds, "I think getting some distance will be good for you."

Distance from what? Distance from Clay? Is Caspian so optimistic about my moving Below because he thinks it'll make me accept that Clay and I are over? Does he have some vision of him and me swimming off into the sunlit waters together?

No, even thinking that makes me feel conceited. But I did tell myself I'd stop being naïve about his feelings for me ...

Even I have trouble mustering that naiveté as he slides off the ledge and into the water in front of me. "We won't be apart forever." He says the words like a pledge, but I don't know if he's pledging them to me or to himself.

I should swim backward, put some distance between us, but the intensity in his expression catches me up in its grip, holding me in place. "Things are changing," Caspian says in that rich baritone I've always found so comforting. Now it sounds strong. Resolved. "We shouldn't fight them. We need to adapt."

Is he still talking about moving Below?

He leans toward me, and my pulse skyrockets with nerves. I picture my hands coming up against his chest to push him away, picture myself telling him again that I can't give him what he wants. But as the distance between us dwindles to nothing, his muscular arms wrap around me. He doesn't try to kiss me. He just holds me. And I don't have to push him away. I just let myself collapse into him.

It feels good to let my best friend hold me. Like maybe we can get normal back.

Wrapped in Caspian's arms, my cheek resting against him, I don't know what I'll do without him when I go off to Sea Daughters. If I lived in the capital with my parents, there'd be a good chance I could convince Caspian's parents to move Below, educational interruption be damned. But if I want to have any chance of getting Clay's memories back—of putting an end to his confusion and deep sadness, and to my own—I need to stand by my choice of going to Sea Daughters, which means Caspian won't be coming with me. Something inside me aches.

Knowing I have to leave him makes me cling to him more tightly, my hands clutching his broad back. "I'll miss you so much."

"I'll miss you, too, Goldfish." He breathes the words against my hair.

We stay like that for a long time, with him hugging me in our hideout, starfish of every color enveloping us the way he envelops me in his arms. When we pull apart, this place that felt so cavernous to us when we were children now feels so much smaller.

"I'll come visit you," he says. "Even if my parents insist I bring twenty guards."

"Promise?"

This time, he doesn't hesitate even for a second. "I'll be there."

It's late when I swim back from Star Cave, transforming into my legs as I approach the shore. I slide into a pair of bikini bottoms I left in the zipped-up canvas bag my sisters have anchored under some distinctive rocks for just this purpose. On the off chance a human finds it, it'll look like someone's beach bag floated out to sea and got stuck. (Em's idea, of course.) When I step out of the waves and onto the damp sand, a warning shoots up my spine.

Someone is watching me on the dark beach.

Every muscle in my body tells me to run—or to dive back into the waves and flee. But before I can do either, the shadow moves toward me across the sand. A flowing, white dress catches the moonlight, and I sigh as my tension washes away with the tide.

Ondine's hair flies in the wind sweeping in off the ocean. She holds up the soft towel I left farther up on the beach, and when I move closer, she wraps it around my shoulders before stepping back.

"You were waiting for me?" I ask, rubbing the terry cloth against my skin. Sure, she's staying close by, in one of the houses owned by the Foundation, but she's never come to see me outside our lessons before. Except for today's earlier, life-spinning conversation in my parents' office.

She nods. "I need to speak with you about something."

What does she need to tell me that couldn't wait until Monday's class? Did I do something wrong? Did she change her mind about having me attend her school? Is she taking back her offer?

"About what?" I ask, trying to keep my tone respectful and only mildly curious instead of borderline desperate.

She glances over her shoulder at my house. "Walk with me."

I wrap the towel more tightly around me as we walk along the shoreline. It's colder than usual tonight.

While we walk, I steal glances at Ondine, but she keeps her focus forward. After several minutes of silence, we both start talking at once.

"What do—"

"Lia, I—"

"Sorry," I say. "Go ahead."

"I am glad you chose to take my offer and enroll at Sea Daughters Academy." She doesn't sound glad. She sounds serious. "But I must tell you something that I could not say in front of your parents."

Ondine stops walking and faces me, her pale eyes colorless in the moonlight. "My invitation for you to study at the academy comes with a condition."

"What condition?"

She holds up a slender hand. "It is not my intention to put any undue pressure on you. If you do not accept my condition, I will understand. We will simply tell your parents you've decided you want to stay with them instead of live far away, and I will recommend an excellent tutor to continue your education at the palace in New Meris. You and I will part as friends."

I'm having trouble focusing on her words with my pulse pounding in my ears. "What condition?" I ask again.

Her lips purse as if she's analyzing whether I'm ready to hear what she's about to say. "If you choose to come to Sea Daughters, you must tell the other girls studying advanced magic alongside you about your bond with Clay. And the past actions that created it."

"You want me to tell them I sirened him?" I feel like the waves crashing behind me are about to sweep forward and pull me out to sea.

"It is not that I want you to. It is that I need you to," Ondine says. Is she intentionally cryptic or is it that her lilting voice makes everything sound so mysterious? That voice continues. "Because you're going to need their help."

She starts walking again, her steps measured and even. "I've been thinking a lot about the bond and about the nature of magic as it pertains to memories. I must do some more research once I'm back at Daughters, but I believe I may know a ritual we can use."

I stop dead and grab her arm. I can't help it; I need to make sure

I'm understanding her instead of just hearing what I want to hear. "You know a ritual we can use to give Clay his memories back?"

"I think so, yes."

They're the most beautiful words—the ones I've been waiting to hear for months. They make me want to kick up the sand and run singing into the ocean.

"But," she says, "the ritual I'm thinking of would be a modification of a very powerful spell. It requires too much magic for you and me to perform alone. We would need the others to help us."

"But you're like the queen of magic," I say. I think back to the icy well of her power I've drawn upon to strengthen the bond. "I've felt how much power you have."

"That is true. I have spent decades studying and practicing magic, and I have indeed accumulated quite a lot of it. But taking too much power from any one Mermaid poses too high a risk. Your magic is rooted to who you are, and when you cast a spell, you unleash it outward, pushing it out into the universe to do what you want it to. That is why Mer who practice magic often feel drained after an intense casting. They have overextended their own power."

The wind whips my hair against my face and I tug it out of the way, listening intently.

"That is also why most modern Mer don't practice much magic—with the wars and the constant need for people to defend themselves and their families, no one could justify engaging in a practice that would leave them weak and vulnerable. Strong magic takes sacrifice, and over time, Mer have become less willing to make that sacrifice. Modern spells require far less energy than ancient magic, but they're weaker as a result. The strongest magic is now done with potions, which take most of their energy from their ingredients and usually only a miniscule amount from the Mer doing the mixing. They require great knowledge and skill, but very little magical output."

Since we don't use much Mer magic on land, I've never learned a lot about how it functions. "But magic is supposed to be … magical."

Yep, I'm super eloquent, I know. "I mean," I try again, "if it's magic, why does it make a Mer weaker to cast powerful spells?"

"Magic is just energy, Lia. For spells, that energy comes from the Mermaid or Merman who casts them. Using some magic is fine because when you send your magic out for a simple spell, it only requires a small amount of energy for your body to regenerate that magic. But send out too much, and you'll feel the effects because it will take too much of your energy to replenish your magical stores. That is the reason bigger spells rely on ocean magic to supplement them, but tapping into that is not a simple act and still requires a sizeable magical output from the Mer casting the spell. There are even tales of Mer in olden days who used so much magic—sent so much outside themselves—that their bodies couldn't regenerate it."

"What happened to them?"

"According to legend, some lost their magic for good. Others died as their bodies fought to restore it and lost the battle."

Wow. If death is a consequence of using too much magic, it's no wonder modern Mer society has adapted to use less of it.

"That is why I've been so careful not to let you practice any magic you are not ready for."

I offer a heartfelt smile, trying to show her my gratitude.

"That is also why I haven't been able to give you more of my magic so you could try to communicate with Clay through the bond. Even though I am admittedly very powerful, it would expend too much of my magic for me to let you take that much."

"I understand," I say, reaching out to squeeze her hand so she knows I don't blame her. I'd never want Ondine to take that risk for me. The gesture seems to mean something to her because she returns it before letting my hand go. "But there's one thing I don't understand," I say. "How come I was able to cast the siren spell on Clay without getting weaker? If anything, I felt more powerful, stronger." My words taper off to a whisper. Even now, it's hard to admit how *good* sireny made me feel—victorious, like I could conquer the world. Scary and exhilarating all at once.

"Siren songs are one of the most powerful spells ever created by Mer—that's one reason they're so dangerous and were once so revered. They don't rely on the Mermaid as a power source, so they don't take your energy. Instead, siren songs harness power from a deep, primal source innate to all Mer."

What … oh! "The call of the ocean." Duh. I knew that. Sireny draws its power from the call of the ocean, the whisper that thrums through the veins of every Mer like a heartbeat, making us naturally long for the sea. The research I did on sireny last year said as much. That's why I could siren without getting drained.

"The ritual I have in mind to restore Clay's memories would require a great deal more energy than sireny does. I think I can successfully modify it to help him," those words hang in the air like sparkling stars, "but casting it will require a group of Mer trained in advanced magic."

Trusting Ondine with the secret of my sireny was hard enough. Can I trust a whole group of girls I've never met with that knowledge?

She must read the hesitance on my face because she says, "It is not easy to qualify for inclusion in my advanced magic curriculum. They are the best Sea Daughters has to offer." She takes both my hands in hers. "I've taught all of them—had all of them under my care—since they were five. Each one is a capable, powerful, caring, young woman whom I would trust with my life."

"How many?"

"We'd need four besides you, plus me to lead. I have three advanced magical students at the school now, and one of the slightly younger girls who is ready to move up." She pauses. "Lia, as I said, I'll completely understand if you decide you'd rather protect your secret and stay in the capital city with your parents."

Four girls. Four girls who'd have the power to destroy me.

Four girls who'd have the power to save Clay.

"I'll do it." I say. "I'll come with you."

The next three weeks are a whirlpool of tearful goodbyes, preparation, and packing. It's not until the night before we leave, when I'm gathering my personal stuff, that everything that's about to change hits me. And when it does, it slams into me like a four-ton orca whale. Looking at the measly pile on my bed of the personal items I'll be taking with me to Sea Daughters Academy makes me realize how much I won't be taking. How much I'll be leaving behind. All my clothes that aren't *siluesses* will need to stay here in my nice, dry closet—all my favorite dresses and shoes. Any jewelry and makeup that isn't Mer-made and waterproof has no place Below. My books and the few stuffed animals I still keep around and my posters and my collection of colorful pens. The backpack I've used for the past couple years, with its buttons and iron-on patches. I tuck it snuggly under my desk to wait out my absence.

I slide my desk chair into place and glance around me—at my dresser, my shelves, my pale pink curtains, and my baby blue bedspread. This room will lie quiet and empty in my absence, silenced and sleeping, like it's under a magic spell. Awaiting my return to come back to life.

What if I don't come back? What if I don't find a way to get Clay's memories back? What if something happens and I have to stay Below? Will the gnawing sadness I felt in him through the bond eventually dissipate? Will he learn to live with it? Or will it build inside him, consuming him, drawing him into a void of confusion and despair he doesn't understand?

Thinking of Clay, picturing him here in Malibu while I'm out in some unknown, remote corner of the ocean, it strikes me just how far from him I'll be. Before the thought has even become fully formed in my head, my heart hurts. Even if I manage to strengthen my magic at Sea Daughters and Ondine devises a way to help Clay, it'll still be months until I have any chance of laying eyes on him again. Tomorrow, I'll swim away from him.

Tonight, I have to see him.

It isn't a plan. It isn't a desire or a revolt. It's a need—one that springs from deep inside me, burning and wild and desperate. I can't leave tomorrow—leave everything I've ever known and ever loved behind—without catching at least a glimpse of the person I love more than anything. Even if it's only for a few seconds.

If I had decided to concoct some elaborate scheme to see Clay, I couldn't have planned tonight any better. Since I've barely been leaving the house lately except to go down to our private beach, my parents have relaxed my guard, who now spend more time watching over the house itself than over just me. And tonight, only a few are positioned outside, patrolling the perimeter in shifts while most of them meet in the grottos to go over plans for tomorrow's move.

After dabbing on some of my favorite shimmery lip gloss— something else I'll be leaving behind since it's a human brand that washes away too easily underwater—I stand at the top of the stairs, my ears peeled for movement below. But everyone's busy in their separate rooms, and the downstairs lies quiet. Keeping my steps as light as I can across the hardwood floor of the entrance hall and living room, I make my way to the sliding glass of the back door and wait. If one of the patrolling guards sees me, I'll say I'm taking a walk on our beach, getting some fresh air, but I'd rather avoid them altogether. I keep my body pressed into the shadows of the dark living room until the perimeter guard passes by, looking stern and vigilant, but still slightly uncomfortable as he gives a subtle tug to the shirt my parents have made him wear in case a neighbor happens by. As a Merman from Below, having fabric covering his torso must feel strange. With another tug at the hem, he rounds the corner toward the front of the house. Perfect. I slip through the door, across the yard, and down the wind-beaten, wooden steps to the beach.

I keep my pace leisurely in case a guard spots me.

Who me? I'm just out for a stroll. A stroll that leads me far up the beach and out of sight, where I slip between two houses to the street beyond.

Humans walk their dogs on the wide sidewalks and chat with their neighbors in the warm, evening breeze. I've lived my whole life in this neighborhood, and tomorrow I'll be leaving it for who knows how long.

But not before I see him. Not before I see Clay. I lean against a wall where a mass of the pinkest bougainvillea half-hides me from view, allowing me to close my eyes and focus. I concentrate on my center, finding the cord connecting me to Clay. It's much thicker than it used to be, and stronger, too. Not a weak thread anymore— much closer to a rope. My magic's getting stronger every day, with every hour of practice, but without tapping into Ondine's power, I'm still not strong enough to see Clay through the bond. I can feel him, though, sense his location, just like I could before I went to Ondine for help. The bond tugs me toward him.

This time, I follow.

I move through the residential streets, winding my way downhill, the bond pulling me onward toward the glittering lights of the main road, as it bustles with dinner patrons and couples on dates. I peer into faces, garnering more than a few strange looks, as I search for Clay, but that rope at my center keeps pulling. I'm definitely not headed toward his house. *Where am I going? Where is he?*

I continue straight until a subtle tugging at my core draws me to my right, through the massive, cream-colored gates of the Malibu pier. Once I step through them, the bond changes to a warm, steady pulse. Clay's here! Somewhere ...

I walk farther and farther down the pier, my head moving wildly from side to side as I search the crowd for his face. Each step of my flip-flopped feet down the rough planks heightens my need to see him.

Then a group of guys in matching sports jerseys moves toward the ice cream shop, and there he is. He's gazing away from me, but I'd know his frame, his profile, anywhere.

Clay.

His arms rest on the railing that overlooks the ocean, and he stares out into its tumbling waves of midnight black. Silhouetted against the dark sky, he glows like some otherworldly creature dropped down among humans.

And even without Ondine's magic, I can sense his unhappiness from the grim set of his mouth and the hopelessness stooping his posture.

I rush toward him for several steps, then freeze in place. If anyone from the Community sees me speak one word to him, I'll be imprisoned. Locked away for decades where I'm unable to help erase that sadness etched into his handsome features.

I've seen him. I got the glimpse I came here to get and now I should turn around and go home. But he's so close. He's right there, and I can't tear my eyes away, not yet. The sight of him is cool, refreshing water to a parched throat. It's life-giving.

How can someone I've been so close to—someone I've been closer to than anyone else in my life, someone I've shared my heart with ... shared my body with—be right there and yet still be so far out of my reach?

Standing here staring at him from down the pier doesn't change that. Any second now, I'm going to leave.

Now. I'll do it right now.

But just as I've worked up my resolve to leave (have I?), my world shifts.

Clay looks up and, across the distance and the meandering crowd, his gaze lands right on me. Our eyes meet.

And his face alights with something. He recognizes me! For one glorious, hope-brimming moment, I think it's the truth. That the light in his hazel eyes is recognition. But it isn't.

It's ... intrigue.

His features mold into a question: Who are you?

He doesn't know me, can't place me, but something about me must light a spark within him, because he starts making his way through the crowd, pushing people out of his path.

Even if his mind doesn't remember me, it's like ... like a part of him does.

He's drawn to me like the tide to the moon. Before I can stop myself, I take a step closer to him, then another. Something much, much stronger than the bond pulls us toward each other.

But what happens when he reaches me? He won't know me and I'm forbidden from speaking to him. I picture it not mattering. Picture him reaching me and sweeping me up against his chest and crashing his lips against mine.

But that's impossible.

Reaching me will only plunge him deeper into a trench of confusion, mire him in questions. And if anyone sees us together ...

No. I can't let it happen. *I'm sorry*, I think.

Then, I spin around—and run.

A glance over my shoulder shows me the urgency and desperation that lances across his face like lighting across a stormy sky. "Hey, wait!"

His voice! How I've longed for months to hear his voice. And now I'm running from it, my flip-flops slapping against the pier and my long hair flying out behind me in the wind.

Don't cry, don't cry. It's never been harder for me to keep pearls from falling in public. I weave my way through the crowd, but Clay's taller, his strides are longer, and he's catching up fast. It would be so easy to let myself slow down, let him reach me, grab hold of me. Instead, while he maneuvers around a family of five, I veer to the left, into a group of large surfer-types, then duck into the space between two stores.

Clay stares at the empty place where I stood just seconds before. He stops running, his head snapping in one direction, then the next as he searches the crowd for me. And all the while, I huddle against the stucco wall of the alley, gazing at the distraught look on his face and doing nothing. Once I've caught my breath and stood there drinking in the sight of him as long as I can bear—and still not long enough—I sneak off the pier, back toward my house, leaving Clay standing still in the ever-moving crowd, looking lost and so alone.

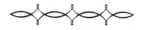

We set out long before sunrise. While it's still pitch black, so our human neighbors won't see us disappear into the waves. With the guards waiting in formation on the sand, I can't help but think of the last time they stood there, when my parents had just returned, and I ran down to this same spot with Clay, eager and happy. I'd worried about the trial but had no idea what lay ahead.

"Can we start the hug parade already? Some of us have dates with the insides of our eyelids to get back to," Lazuli says, running her fingers through her hair, still wet and mussed from sleep on her sea sponge bed.

Lapis, on the other hand, has already combed her hair and put on makeup—and she's uncharacteristically silent. I follow her gaze to where it rests on one of the guards who'll be accompanying us Below and staying with my parents in New Meris. The one with the cleft in his chin. What's his name? Beck? Brook? He returns her longing gaze for a fraction of a second and his shoulders slump before he straightens his spine and focuses forward, blending back into the formation of guards around him.

"It's cold," Lazuli grumbles, filling the silence.

"It's sixty-five degrees," Em says with a put-upon sigh, managing to look dignified even in her bathrobe.

"That's cold!" Lazuli whines, even though we all know she routinely swims in water much colder. I haven't seen her this grumpy since Hard Candy discontinued her go-to nail color; maybe she really will miss us.

She's the first one in my mom's arms when the hugging parade starts. While Ondine speaks with the head guard, all my family members bid each other farewell. Amy's dad hugs me first, wrapping me in solid muscle. "You be careful down there," he says. "Amethyst's pretty attached to you, so you'd better get back safe."

"I'm just going to school, Uncle Kai."

"Still, people know who you are now. Who knows what they'll want from you. You be on your guard."

I'm still somewhat out of it from a night spent tossing and turning before being pulled out of bed in the dark, so I've barely woken up enough to process his words before he's off patting my dad on the shoulder and my aunt has replaced him in front of me.

When she's done wishing me well on my trip, I've come to my senses enough to say, "Aunt Rashell? Um … make sure Amy knows she can talk to you, okay? Just … make sure she knows she doesn't have to be just like you—y'know, some tough girl warrior or … anything—for you to love her." I'm glad she's hugging me so I can say the words into her braided hair instead of to her face, but she looks genuinely grateful when we separate. She thanks me and, once Amy comes over, kisses her on the top of the head before walking over to my parents.

"This is gonna be so weird," Amy says. I couldn't agree more. Then, as if remembering herself, she adds, "But, have so much fun, though." She flashes me one of her encouraging smiles and it almost meets her eyes. "And, make friends, but y'know, ones you don't like quite as much as me."

"You got it," I say. "Play with Barney extra for me, okay? And talk about me with him sometimes, so he doesn't forget me." She nods, then squeezes me so hard I worry about my ribs.

"No pearls," Lazuli says, when it's her turn and she takes in my tearful expression. She hugs me and she smells sugary, like the frosting face wash she likes so much. "Make sure you get in a little trouble."

"I'm going to be cloistered away at an all-girls school," I remind her.

"So start your college experimentation a little early." She winks, and I roll my eyes before Em ushers her off and wraps me in yet another hug.

"I'm proud of you," she says. "You're going to do great." Her embrace is heartfelt, but her shoulders are tense. As soon as my parents swim off into that water, those same shoulders will bear the weight of the Foundation. It strikes me that Em, who has always seemed so grown up, is still so very young.

"I'm proud of you," I say back to her. "You're going to do great."

"Don't forget to keep practicing your dancing."

When Lapis hugs me, she has snapped back to herself. "I'll miss you, squirt."

I nod toward the guards. "Yeah, I'm sure it's me you'll miss."

"Eh." She makes a dismissive gesture with her hand that contradicts her tear-tinged eyes. "Boys'll come and go. Sisters are forever. Like the tides." She shrugs off the sentiment. "Besides, you'll be back annoying me again in a couple of months." But she hugs me extra tight.

Because she knows that none of us are sure when we'll be seeing each other again.

With all the goodbyes finished, it's really time to leave. My mother takes my hand, as she, my father, Ondine, and I all step into the lapping waves, the guards moving to surround us. I take one last look back at my house, white and shining against the dark sky, and at the family I'll be leaving behind. Then, I dive into the sea.

Chapter Twenty-Six

When the sun rises, we're too deep in the ocean to see it. Crossing over the Border line of blue, phosphorescent coral with my parents, the guards, and Ondine by my side struck me as surreal. So much has changed in just the past few months. Everything has changed. My whole life, crossing that shimmering line was forbidden. And these same waters that I'm in now filled me with fear because swimming in them meant entering a warzone.

It wasn't that long ago I covered this same distance alone, from the Border to the ruins of what was once the abandoned village of Aquinilinus, swimming toward Clay and terrified I wouldn't reach him in time to save his life. Now, I swim toward those ruins—renovated into the shining capital of a new era—away from Clay, paralyzed by the thought I won't find a solution in time to save his memories. To save our future.

We move at a quick, even pace, but nothing like the panic-fueled frenzy I forced myself to travel at when I was here last. This time, I make sure to savor each new sight.

Bright fish of every conceivable color, flitting through the water like they're engaged in some intricate dance. The occasional, curious seal eying our traveling party from a distance. Rock formations of sandstone, forming natural archways and tunnels for us to twist through. Seaweed spiraling upward, brushing our bare stomachs.

Something glistens in front of me in the water. A small, circular something.

A pearl.

Tears stream freely down my mother's face, her hand clasped in my father's as they swim. I've been so focused on myself, on everyone I'll miss and everything I'm leaving behind, that I haven't thought how emotional this trip must be for my parents. Sure, they traveled here over the summer for peace talks, but this trip is different. Now, they're moving here—at least for the foreseeable future. Back to the home they left to ensure the safety of our family.

The realization sobers me. I may still harbor anger at them I can't seem to stamp out with logic, but even though they didn't keep Clay safe from the Tribunal, they have kept me safe my whole life. And now, by coming here and making this change, I can help them. Help them help the rest of our kind like they've helped our Community.

The time to do that has come. In the distance, I can just glimpse the glittering tips of the summer palace in New Meris. The one made of crystallized ice and white coral. The one where Clay and I almost died. The one that's been restored and now shines as a symbol of hope to Mer from all over the ocean who have migrated here to see my parents. To see me.

We'll swim together through the streets, so I'm visible to the people. Just as the renovated palace is a symbol of hope, I am a symbol of the immortality I unwittingly helped bring back, and my presence here is a symbol of my parents' commitment to uphold Mer culture and tradition. I've never been a symbol to anybody before. I've never even run for student council.

Nervousness makes my breathing shallow, water flowing in and out of my gills in quick, short bursts. All those strangers staring at me like I'm on exhibit.

"They won't see you," Ondine whispers in my ear in Mermese. *"Not really. They'll see what they want you to be. To them, you are reassurance—in immortality and in your family. Think what these people have been through. Haven't you needed reassurance before? Surely, you can give them that."*

She makes it sound so necessary, and so easy. Her words imbue me with confidence the way her magic so often imbues me with power.

"Will you stay with me?" I ask her before I can stop myself. My parents will be there, but they'll have their public faces on, and they'll be focused on the crowds, as they should be. Ondine can be there for *me*.

"I am not a member of your family, so it would be inappropriate for me to swim alongside you, but I will be there waiting for you at the end of the main street. Then, after you have made your appearance for the people, we will leave together for Sea Daughters Academy."

I have just enough time to nod before the head guard guides our party forward, toward the waiting crowds of New Meris.

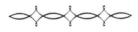

Swimming through the streets is like winding my way through a dream. Surreal and strange. Everywhere I look, I see the city in flashes—both as the ruins it was when I was here last and as the beautiful, bustling place it is now. The residences and buildings I see in my mind as covered in decades of algae now stand proud, their white coral and polished stone restored to a high sheen, their amber windows crackless. No longer do weeds shoot up through the streets as they do in my memory; all the seashell tiles have been re-laid, creating an elegant mosaic. No longer do sea creatures lurk in abandoned doorways; Mer families live here now. Someone calls these lovely houses, with their impressive spires and lovingly laid seaflower beds, home.

With guards and my parents in front of me and more guards behind, I make my way up side streets that must have been cleared for our arrival.

"It's coming along as well as the reports indicated," my mother comments to my father.

Somehow, the remark doesn't strike me as enough acknowledgement of the transformation this place has undergone—from an eerie graveyard of lost splendor to a beacon that will serve as an example to Mer across the ocean of what my parents can help accomplish as long as peace and unity persist.

"Remember, I will be waiting for you at the end of the street. Just swim right to me," Ondine says. I nod, and she squeezes my shoulder before disappearing with one of the guards down an alleyway.

When we enter the town square, my eyes widen in awe at the structure before me, its many towers twisting upward into the calm sea. Layers of grime have been scraped away to reveal a palace of brilliant, gleaming white, so bright it's nearly blinding. Neat rows of oysters line the roof and pathways, fat pearls glinting in their depths.

And all around the palace—filling the square to bursting—swim Mer eager to catch a glimpse of my parents. And of me. The chatter of Mermese dialects I don't recognize along with the vast array of different hairstyles, *siluess* fabrics, skin tones, and fin shapes, tells me Mer have traveled from far and wide to be here today.

I raise my chin and set my shoulders. Was my lilac, pearlescent *siluess* the best choice? My mother would have said something if it wasn't, right? Too late to worry about it now. My parents swim out from between the guards, and the crowd bursts into jubilation. Amazingly, that joyful uproar grows even louder as I swim out behind them. People shout and throw green bubble algae up into the water above their heads in celebration. Several Mermen blow into triton shell trumpets in welcome. But some aren't cheering. Some tilt their heads at us, analyzing us as we move forward. Are they questioning my parents' right to rule? Do I look different to them? Different *from* them because I have been raised Above? Does something about me give me away as not-quite-Mer-enough?

My parents swim forward, but I freeze in place. It's all I can do to keep my head high instead of stare down to remind myself I do indeed have a tail and I haven't shown up in some polyester bikini top. The gap between my parents and me is growing with every flick of their fins. Soon it will be noticeable. Soon, everyone in that crowd will know I've choked and wonder why.

Then magic floods my senses. An icy magic, like frosted winter glass. After hours spent finding and connecting to that magic, I'd recognize it anywhere. *Ondine.* In an instant, the surge she sent at me is gone, just a gentle nudge to remind me she's here. She's here for me. Sure enough, a shimmer of pale blue and a hint of white-blond mean she's waiting for me at the end of the path. I just have to swim to her.

The rest of the procession passes in a blur of staring faces and jeweled tails, of waving hands and pretty words as my parents halt in front of the central coral fountain in the middle of the square to give a speech. With so many eyes on me, I barely hear what my mother says about commitment and hope, what my father says about tradition and education. I let my gaze shift to Ondine, let her presence ground me in the unreality of this day. Of people gaping at me like I'm their savior. Like I might be their princess.

Sure, the idea of being a princess sounds jaw-droppingly awesome. Gowns, glitter, glamor—who wouldn't want to be a princess? I watched movies as a kid and wore scratchy tulle Halloween costumes with plastic crowns just like anybody else, but for someone who's spent her entire life learning to avert attention—to always be careful not to stand out lest I put everyone I love in danger—standing at the center of this crowd throws me. Makes me feel not like me.

So, while my parents do their job by paying attention to the many gathered onlookers, I focus on the only other person here who knows me.

Time drags and rushes until my parents are taking me by the hands and guiding me down the street again while all the Mer around us watch from behind the elegant seaweed ropes studded with crystals.

My parents briefed me on this part during the trip here. This is when they hand me off to Ondine as a symbol to the people that they endorse their child receiving a traditional Mer education—that I am one of them, not some foreign entity living Above. Everyone will watch as I leave with Ondine for Sea Daughters Academy, and they'll feel like they've witnessed me embracing Mer culture. It's a good plan and one that my parents came up with to minimize my exposure. I won't need to make a speech or attend any public parties or give any interviews to the press, sealing my voice in a bubble to be broadcast over the low-frequency waves that cross the ocean. My parents will handle all of that. All I need to do is finish crossing this square and smile as I leave with Ondine for my new school. It's a good plan.

But it means my goodbye with my parents will be public, hundreds of eyes watching. I know there's no other way since the crowds want to see my official hand-off, but ... I sigh, tiny and hidden while keeping a smile painted on my face. We glide through the water, Ondine growing larger and larger in my vision the closer we come to her, until at last she swims right in front of us, her ice-blue tail swishing below her and the crystal shards around her eyes glinting the same white as the grand castle that towers above us.

My mother holds my hand up so the crowd can see her press a kiss to it and place it with great ceremony into Ondine's upturned palm. A cheer spreads throughout the entire square, and many begin singing *Cicereel*, an old Mermese folk song meant to evoke calm seas, that Em sometimes hums while she folds laundry or does my hair. I think our grandmother (the one who I never met and who has long-since passed away) used to sing it to her when Em was a baby living Below. But the tune and the cheers fade into the back of my mind as both my parents turn toward me.

In that second, the polite passivity melts from their faces, their diplomatic smiles transforming into the kind, loving ones we share at home. They stop seeing the crowd and instead see me. They see their daughter, who will be travelling farther from them than I ever have before, swimming off to live away from them for the first time.

The hugs they give me aren't for show; they're warm and close and over too soon. The second Ondine ushers me away and my parents turn back toward the center of the square, I miss them. Even though I can still see them over my shoulder and barely any time has passed at all, I miss them deep in my chest.

"If you're going to cry, can you please do it before we get in the carriage," says a bored, unfamiliar voice in Mermese. *"The last thing I need is your pearls stuck in my hair. Then again. Maybe I could sell them: Princess pearls, ten cowries for a dozen."* Deep brown eyes study me from an exquisite face. I'd been so focused on reaching Ondine, I hadn't noticed the two girls waiting just behind her. Both are my age, maybe a year older. The one who spoke has a shining pink tail and long, straight black hair with two pink streaks framing her face. How did she get those? She wears a silvery *siluess* dotted with opals and a skeptical expression.

"Clam up, Jinju," whispers the other Mermaid. She turns to me and smiles shyly. *"Feel free to cry if you want to. It can be hard. I cried when my parents first dropped me off at Daughters."* She looks down at her turquoise tail, which contrasts beautifully with her dark brown skin, like maybe she didn't mean to let that last part slip. She has a thin streak of matching turquoise in her tight black curls.

"Yeah, but you were five," says the other girl—Jinju.

"Still …"

What am I supposed to say to that? Will laughing it off make me look cool or like I'm trying too hard? One thing's for sure: I *will* look like a five-year-old if I cry. Fortunately, having grown up surrounded by humans, I have a ton of practice not crying in public no matter how badly I want to for fear of someone catching sight of a pearl. But aside from not sobbing like an infant, I don't know how to respond.

Ondine saves me from needing to. *"Why don't we continue this riveting and terribly welcoming conversation with your new classmate once we're all in the carriage,"* she says, eyeing those in the crowd who still watch me.

I nod, trying to look regal and mature while I do it, but possibly coming across as snobby. Then Ondine's words sink in. Carriage? Sometimes I forget that since the wars largely halted innovation and progress, Mer technology Below hasn't advanced much over the past two centuries.

Sure enough, I swim alongside her until a carriage in the circular shape of a moon shell but made of gleaming gold comes into view. Four stunning seahorses—of the giant, deep-sea variety I first saw last year—wade in front of it, in magenta, purple, yellow, and apple green. Two of my parents' guards who will accompany us on the journey grip golden bars attached to the back with one hand, their other hands ready on their spears.

Jinju swims into the carriage through the rounded opening in the side, followed by Ondine. The girl with the shy smile ducks her head and gestures at me to swim in ahead of her. I smile back and swim inside.

Like I'm sure so much will be Below, this carriage is strange and foreign to me. Do we just float around inside it? Won't we bang our heads during sharp turns? A surreptitious glance at Ondine, who has seated herself on a padded bench that curls around the edges of the gleaming walls and is strapping a thick seasilk cord around her waist to hold herself down, tells me what I need to do. I take the spot next to her and do the same. The cord is both strong and soft. No sooner have I secured it than the carriage jolts into motion, speeding through the sea.

Has this thing been crash tested? *No, don't think about it.* To stop myself from getting carsick … seasick … carriage sick? … I stare out the small amber window as the city grows smaller and smaller in its bubbled surface.

"You're away from prying eyes now," Ondine says, although from the way Jinju sizes me up from her seat across the carriage, I'm not so sure. *"How was it?"* Ondine asks, placing a comforting hand on my tail.

"Like getting swept up in a sandstorm," I say, resting my head against the wall behind me. My words echo in the rounded carriage. Down here, I'm the one with the accent. What does it sound like to them?

"But I'm sure you like the attention, Princess?" Jinju poses the words as a question, her eyebrow rising along with her voice. The only person who's ever called me that before is Melusine, and the reminder of our last meeting eels its way up my spine.

"I'm used to a much quieter life." I don't put any bite into my tone. I need these girls to like me. To help me. Plus, I know how I must look to Jinju: like someone who came out of nowhere, stole away her favorite teacher for months, and now plans to infiltrate her school just to make my parents look good. She must see some spoiled, entitled princess. I'm sure she's not the only one. If I want her and my other classmates at Sea Daughters to know I'm not like that, it's on me to show them. Tides, if I thought of me like that, I wouldn't want to like me much either. *"And I'm not a princess."*

"Not yet. But I'm sure you're looking forward to it."

I don't take the bait. Don't let anger creep its way into me. Maybe the journey has been too draining, or maybe leaving everything I've ever known behind has forced some maturity through my gills. *"I'm looking forward to my parents having the authority to help people Below the way I know they can. As for the rest of it … things used to be simpler …"* I shrug. *"So, maybe just call me Lia, 'kay?"*

The corner of Ondine's mouth quirks up before she lets her eyes drift shut for a nap, a clear message that she's leaving us to our own devices.

Jinju tilts her head, studying me with her dark eyes. Before she can say anything, her friend speaks up. *"Hi, Lia. I'm Dionna."* Her smile is less shy now—it stretches up into her cheeks.

I return it willingly. *"Hi, Dionna. That's a really pretty necklace,"* I say, noticing the strand of multicolored quartz beads around her neck.

Dionna lights up like a lanternfish. *"Thanks. I made it myself. I have a bunch of supplies at school. I can make you one, too ... if you want."* Her words turn quiet at the end, but her spark of enthusiasm has already suffused our carriage, making the water around us feel less heavy and stagnant.

"That would be ... " I want to say "cool," but it's not a Mermese word. Above, Mer my age approximate the English version using Mermese sounds, but since these girls have only ever lived Below, they won't know what I'm talking about. *"I'd like that, Dionna."*

Jinju narrows her eyes, as if coming to a decision. Then she sighs and says to Dionna, *"You should use gold beads between some of those midnight blue agate ones."* She looks at me. *"They would look good with your coloring ... Lia."*

"Thanks. So, what should I know before we get there?"

After a moment's pause, Jinju launches into a list of which teachers are more like friends, which ones to be extra respectful with, and which ones drone on and on like grunting sea lions.

The carriage ride to Sea Daughters Academy turns out not to be as long as I feared.

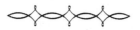

By the time the carriage slows, I've learned Jinju's family is from the Busan Straight—in the waters around South Korea, where Stas' dad's family is from—and Dionna's family has lived near the new capital city for generations. When it was abandoned, they moved from one makeshift settlement to another. Both girls have been attending the academy since they were five.

"It's kept us safe," Jinju says simply. When she glances at the sleeping Ondine, all the former haughtiness melts from her face, and her gaze turns heavy with gratitude.

As the carriage lurches to a stop, my stomach lurches right along with it. I'm about to see the place where I'll be living for the next who-knows-how-long.

I follow Ondine, Jinju, and Dionna out of the carriage, and light assaults my senses.

We're no longer at the bottom of the ocean like we were in New Meris but much closer to the surface, where sunlight filters through the azure water. Once my eyes adjust to the new brightness, a rocky mass fills my vision.

The base of the island stretches up, up, up, disappearing above the water's surface. Lush, green plant life coats whole sections of the rock face in front of us, like moss on a stone wall but wilder.

Ondine thanks the Merman who drove our carriage, and soon he's turning around, taking the guards who accompanied us back to New Meris. When they speed off into the distance, the carriage becoming nothing more than a far-off speck of gold in the blue, it's the first time in months I haven't been under guard. It makes me feel ... almost normal.

Except for the whole going to a brand-new school on a magical island part.

That magic is exactly why my parents allowed me to stay here without the guards. The cloaking spells that hide Mer presence here from humans as well as from unwelcome Merfolk are stronger than any muscles or spears.

As Ondine leads me and the other girls around the island's base, I'm about to become one of the very few who has seen inside those spells. We stop at a craggy spot where a large piece of rock protrudes into the surrounding water.

Dionna and Jinju smile knowingly at each other as Ondine reaches one willowy arm up above her head with purpose, intention.

Nothing changes. And everything changes.

The water around us stays placid, barely moving, but with the newfound awareness for magic I've been building through all those hours of practice in the grottos with Ondine, I sense it as clearly as if I could see it, taste it. The magic swirls around us and skates across my skin.

The reverent expressions on Dionna and Jinju's faces mean they feel it to.

Ondine splays her hand wide, as if she's drawing in the ocean's magic through each of her fingertips, then brings it down to land on the protruding rock the same second she curves her tail forward so both fins unfurl against the rock face on either side of her fingers.

At first, I think whatever she was trying to do didn't work—until Jinju and Dionna swim toward that large piece of rock. Where moments before, the rock's sides melded into the rest of the jagged stone, now one of those same sides has split to create a crevice, half-hidden in the rock's shadow and only big enough for one Mer at a time.

"It's the only way to the island from Below," Jinju says before vanishing into its depths.

"Come on, Lia," Dionna says before she too swims into the crevice.

Ondine squeezes my shoulder and, with a small, conspiratorial smile, whispers, *"Follow me."*

And I do. With a deep breath and a flick of my golden tail, I follow Ondine into the heart of the island.

Chapter Twenty-Seven

I't's dark and cramped, the rocky walls pushing in on me from both sides as I follow Ondine, swimming upward, higher and higher—until my head breaks the surface and the entranceway opens into a cavernous dome. Cool air blankets the top half of my body as I swim waist deep, taking in my surroundings with what I'm sure is wide-eyed wonder.

It's the most beautiful place I've ever seen.

Unlike any of the grottos in the Community, the ceiling of this magnificent room must be above ground because intricately carved openings high up in the arched walls let sunlight stream in. The white-golden light plays off every surface it can reach, making the stone all around us sparkle like it's coated in diamonds. Underneath these openings, water flows in from somewhere outside, creating awe-inspiring indoor waterfalls that punctuate the cavern at various heights and gush down like liquid glass, filling the room with cool mist.

"Welcome to Sea Daughters Academy," Ondine says. *"What do you think?"*

"It's incredible." My voice comes out in a hushed whisper, as if I'm

in an ancient church, but it echoes off the walls and water, bouncing back at me.

Jinju elbows me in the ribs. *"Just wait,"* she says with a wink before she dives straight through a waterfall to my left, the sheet of water parting like a curtain around her pink tail. Dionna follows her, her turquoise fins vanishing just as quickly.

"What the …" That's when I get it. The waterfall conceals the mouth of a cave. A closer look confirms my theory—similar openings lie hidden behind the streaming water of the other falls. Do tunnels wind their way under the entire island?

Ondine leans close. *"Better go."* Her tone tells me she's not coming with me. Now that we're back here, she probably has a zillion headmistressy things to catch up on. The thought that she's in charge of all this jars me. I'd known it in theory, but being here, seeing this place … a new layer of respect for her settles over me. Then she offers that caring smile I've seen so many times in our grotto classroom at home, and I know she's still my friend.

"I'll see you in class tomorrow," she says, and before I know it, I've dived through the waterfall in pursuit of Jinju and Dionna.

Both girls are waiting for me on the other side. *"Figured Ondine'd fillet us if we let you get lost on your first day,"* Jinju says. She and Dionna lead me through a series of downward-sloping tunnels. Right, right, left, right, left … I try to remember so I can do this on my own later, but I eventually lose track and am grateful when we come to a stop. We swim into a room that, unlike the main cavern, is completely underwater. Six sea sponge beds in giant cockle shells line the walls—three on each side—with a seating area at the end made up of large, squishy armchairs in a cozy green fabric that looks like it was woven from manatee grass. Most of the shell beds and the walls around them have been decorated with personal items—shiny bits of sea glass, drawings of *siluess* fashions on waxed algae leaves, hanging conus shells that probably hold the recorded voices of loved ones. But one shell bed on the end remains a blank canvas.

Dionna gestures at it with a little flourish. *"All yours."*

I drop the kelp-net bag of belongings I've been carrying into the empty trunk at the end of the bed, making sure the lid clicks closed so nothing floats back out. I test out the sea sponge with my palm; it's soft. Softer than my bed in the grottos at home.

I glance around at the other beds. Five total. I'd bet anything the other four beds belong to the four girls who study advanced magic. The four girls Ondine thinks can help me restore Clay's memories. That leaves two I haven't met. *"Where are the others?"* I ask.

"In class," Jinju says. *"We got the day off to keep you from feeling like a total loner."* Dionna gives her a "Be polite" glare, so she adds, *"Thanks for that, by the way."* She chants a familiar phrase in Mermese that roughly translates to: Nothing like wandering to make you happy to come home. Caspian could give you a better version. It sounds much better in Mermese 'cause it rhymes. It's strange to me that to these two girls, this place—these shell beds and armchairs and tunnels—is home.

"You girls missed lunch," a motherly voice says from the entranceway. A curvaceous Mermaid with a short, honey-colored tail swims in carrying a covered copper tray. *"Thought you might be hungry after your travels."* She sets the tray down on a low table among the squishy armchairs.

"Yay! I'm starved." Dionna says. *"Thaaank you!"* she sing-songs. It earns her a wink.

"You're a starfish, Gussy," Jinju says.

"And you're a Sea-Monkey," the Mermaid says, ruffling Jinju's hair. Jinju feigns a scandalized look, but she can't hide her smile. *"Lia this is MerMatron Gusseta. Gussy, this is Lia."*

Remembering all the tips Ondine gave me in our lessons in Mer etiquette and culture, I dip forward into a formal greeting, my tail flipping up behind me as my fins fan out behind my head. Phew. I managed that much more gracefully than I did when I met Ondine—and with both Jinju and Dionna's eyes on me, I'm glad I didn't embarrass myself. I want these girls to like me—no, I need them to like me. *"Nii nai sillis suzallis"* I say. A pleasure to encounter you.

"Well aren't you a lovely one." The compliment strikes me as so genuine, I duck my head to hide a blush. *"I'll leave you girls to your day off. Eat up now. I might've snuck something special onto that tray."*

Like all adult Mer now, she looks like she's in her twenties, but something about the way she carries herself and the warmth in her expression when she looks at Jinju and Dionna communicates decades spent as a caretaker. On her way out, she says to me with another wink, *"You need anything, you come find me."*

"What'd she make? What'd she make?" Dionna asks before MerMatron Gusseta is even out of earshot.

Jinju lifts the copper lid. A deep bowl heaps with beautifully sliced, de-spined lionfish garnished with dulse and a green spice rub. In one corner of the tray stands an elegant glass box filled with small, emerald balls coated in some kind of glossy syrup.

"Candied seaberries," Jinju says in a voice that means we totally lucked out. She holds up a fin and Dionna slaps hers against it. I guess that's how they high-five down here. Weird.

"Gussy knows those are my favorite," Dionna tells me.

"How long have you known her?" I ask.

"Oh, forever. She's practically spent her whole life here. She went to school here, then she took the milliki position," that's Mermese for ... it kind of implies chef and housekeeper, in the respectful, BBC sort of way, *"and she's done that ever since."*

"Most of the staff either went here or had daughters who did." Jinju says. *"Or both. It's why they have such high expectations for us."* She rolls her eyes, but it's playful.

"It's kind of nice," Dionna says in a quiet voice.

The girls plop into the armchairs—their tails draped over one arm, their backs against the other—and dig in. I didn't eat anything before the processional in New Meris because I didn't want to have a nervous stomach, so by now I could eat a whole halibut. But I hesitate before my first bite. Above, unless we're eating sushi, we tend to cook most of our fish so we can take it for lunch at school or have human dinner guests without arousing suspicion. I stare down at my lionfish. I've never eaten this much raw fish in one meal before. My body's built to digest it, so I'm not worried about that, but it's so ... foreign.

And it shouldn't be. This is my culture. This is how Mer have eaten for thousands of years. I take a bite. At first, I can't get past the odd sensation of water passing in and out of my gills as I chew. Aside from munching on a kelp leaf here or there, I'm not used to eating underwater. Since I've only ever been allowed to swim in the ocean at night, I'm usually full from dinner. But, I adjust quickly, and soon all I can focus on is the taste. The smooth texture caresses my tongue and rich, varied flavor bursts in my mouth. This. This is what fish should always taste like. *"What's in this?"*

"Good, right? It's called an urtanri rub," Jinju says. *"A local specialty made from ... what is it Di? ... twelve ..."*

"Fourteen different types of local seaweed, all blended together. Gussy makes the best urtanri."

"Have you ever even had anyone else's?" Jinju challenges her.

"No. But how could anyone's be better than this?" Dionna cocks an eyebrow.

"Point," Jinju agrees, taking a huge bite.

I have to agree, too. This is just ... wow. Soon, I've finished every bite and am wondering about the etiquette of licking my fingers before the salt water washes away those last precious molecules of *urtanri*.

After we've finished, Dionna grabs the candied seaberries for us to share, and the two of them take me through the tunnels and caverns, pointing out everything from where my different classes will be the next day to where students usually eat and where they hang out in the evenings. With everyone else in class, stillness and quiet permeate the place, like I'm exploring the chambers of an ancient castle sleeping under an enchantment. As we dive through glistening waterfalls and into hidden caves, it feels like Jinju, Dionna, and I are the only inhabitants of some peaceful, secret world.

That peace melts away when the water around us trembles with the movement of many fins.

"Class just got out," Dionna says as she offers me the last seaberry, then pops it into her mouth when I shake my head. We're swimming in a cave the girls described as a student lounge, filled with low, comfortable couches, glass cabinets with *konklilis* and whalebone styluses for studying, and a large *spillu* board set up. Within seconds, the room floods with students. Girls ranging from around ten to fifteen years old swim into the lounge in groups of three or four friends at a time. A few shoot me curious glances when my unfamiliar face catches their eye, but before I can even think about introducing myself, Jinju and Dionna usher me back the way we came. We pass a group of younger students—five- to seven-year-olds, maybe?— swimming with a teacher in the opposite direction, all carrying brushes made from maiden's hair algae and jars of what looks like sea snail paint.

"Where are they going?"

"Up top," Dionna says.

"You mean … on the island?" I ask. I thought I'd seen everything on the tour they just gave me.

"We had to save something for tomorrow," Jinju says, looking very pleased with herself. I like how confident she is.

I feel anything but confident the second we arrive back at our room and she says, *"Ready to meet the others?"* Am I? Am I ready to meet the other girls who will decide my future—and Clay's?

Chapter Twenty-Eight

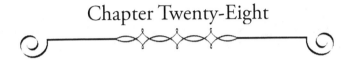

"*C*an *I hug you?*"

"*Um … sure?*" And that's how, before I've even swum fully into the room, I find myself hugging, um …

"*Nixie, this is Lia. Lia, Nixie,*" Dionna says.

"Hi, Nixie," I say.

"*Hi,*" she says, still hugging. Several seconds later, she pulls back enough for me to see her. With her pale blond hair and waiflike frame, she reminds me of a younger Ondine. Except for her tail, which is the color of fresh-cut grass, and the dusting of freckles across her nose. "*I've been so looking forward to meeting you. Thank you. Thank you so much.*"

"*Sure.*" I smile weakly. "*Um, for what?*"

"*For saving all of us,*" she says like the answer's obvious. I guess it kinda is. "*My aunt was going to die. She had scale sepsis. There was nothing else we could do for her. My parents were killed in the wars when I was a baby, so she's all I have. Well, except for …*" she glances around the room at the other girls. "*Anyway, when you broke the curse and gave us all our immortality back, you saved her. So … thank you.*"

Wow. I mean, I guess I knew in theory I'd saved people's lives, but hearing about a specific person—someone so loved by the Mermaid swimming right in front of me—makes a smile start in my chest and spread across my face. *"I'm so happy she's okay."*

"You gonna let her in the room now?" Jinju jokes since Nixie has stopped me practically in the entrance.

"Sorry," Nixie says as she swims to the side, leading me into the middle of the dormitory, between the two rows of shell beds. *"Lia,"* she says my name like it's something shiny and new, *"this is Thessa."*

"Nii nai sillis suzallis," says the girl introduced as Thessa from where she sits on her bed, a large *konklili* in her lap. Her bright white tail compliments her olive skin. She suffuses the formal words with respect and offers a solemn nod. *"Should we be addressing you as princess?"* There's no mocking in her voice—just a desire to do things properly.

I open my mouth to respond, but before I can, Jinju says with a tone of knowing superiority, *"Actually, Thess, she prefers Lia. She's viriss like that."*

I've never heard the word *viriss* (which means salty) used that way before, but from the context, I can tell it must be a slang word Below for cool. Jinju drapes an arm around my shoulders and all the other girls visibly relax, like I've been vetted and accepted for membership. I guess Jinju thinking I'm salty is like getting a celebrity endorsement.

Nixie is younger than the rest of the girls, maybe sixteen or so. *"I'm in the bed next to yours,"* she says, sounding like she's never heard better news. *"I just moved up here, too. From another dorm. Now that I've progressed to advanced magic."* Her chest puffs out with pride.

I wonder how much of her promotion happened because the ritual Ondine is trying to modify for me and Clay requires five other casters. The thought that everyone in this room will know what I did … that I committed sireny … I swallow. Ondine hasn't told them yet, so for tonight, I should try to let myself relax. *Maybe if they get to know you …* I can't picture any of them not balking at me the way

Caspian did when they find out. I can't picture them being anything but shocked, angry, and scared. But Ondine seemed to think telling them was an option, so I have to trust her judgement. That's hard for me to do, but it's brought me this far. *"It's really nice to meet you both."*

"Um, I could ... I could do your hair before dinner," Dionna *offers. "Give you a little sparkle?"* She picks up a handful of golden beads from one of three vanities the girls seem to share and shoots me a small, quizzical smile.

I twirl a lock of my hair in my fingers as I nod and settle in front of her on her bed. Every one of the other girls has something I don't: startlingly beautiful streaks of color in their hair that match their tails. They don't look like Ondine, who has nearly as much ice blue as blond in her hair. Each of these girls has only one thin streak somewhere amongst an otherwise typical hair color, except for Jinju, who has two long, pink streaks, one on each side so they frame her face. Even Nixie, who's younger than the rest, has a wispy strand of shimmery green growing in.

"I've never seen hair like yours until the first time I saw Ondine," I say to them. Well, aside from on rocker chicks and glamazons coming out of those blaringly loud salons on Melrose in West Hollywood. But on these girls, the color looks like a natural extension of themselves. Vibrant and alluring. *"I thought Mermaid hair like that was some old-timey myth."*

"It is rare," Thessa confirms. She's abandoned her *konklili* in favor of our conversation. The white in her hair looks like a streak of liquid pearl.

"It comes from practicing ancient magic." Jinju says. *"From tapping into that inside you and strengthening it until it manifests."* If that's true, Jinju is the most powerful Mermaid in the room; no wonder the other girls were quick to accept me once she did. When Ondine's not around, Jinju is their leader.

Once the topic of magic comes up, eyes sparkle and enthusiasm suffuses the room. Nixie, Thessa, Jinju, Dionna—they all come to life as they tell me how long they've studied under Ondine's careful training, and when she finally let them begin ancient, more powerful spells. Each one has a few favorites she's eager to tell me about as Dionna braids the small beads into my hair.

"Now we're even skilled enough to help keep up the wards that protect the island," Dionna says, her nimble fingers finishing their work. *"There. Look."* She holds up a highly polished, silver mirror that looks like it came from an 18th century shipwreck.

I've never seen my reflection underwater before. Don't laugh, but I look like … a Mermaid. A real Mermaid, living Below the waves, gills fluttering and hair swirling around me in the water. I take the mirror, turning my head this way and that.

The other girls gather around to see. With the gold beads strung into one strand of my hair right at my temple, I almost look like one of them.

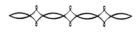

Later, once night falls on the island, the quiet presses in on my ears. After each girl has said goodnight and pulled down the top half of her shell bed as if she's sleeping inside a giant clam, I no longer have other voices to distract me from how much—and how suddenly—my life has changed. What a difference one day can make. This morning, I woke up in the same grotto bed I've slept in my whole life, with my sisters and my parents in the next rooms, in a human house, in a human beach town on land. My home. Now, miles of ocean stretch between me and that life.

Miles of ocean stretch between me and Clay. I haven't been this far from him since the first day we met. And it hurts. It's been so long since we've spoken, so long since he's held me.

An image of him running after me on the pier fills my mind to overflowing. Was that really just last night? From where I am now, inside a seashell hidden under a remote island in the vastness of the Pacific Ocean with nothing but the open sea for miles, that pier feels so far away, like it's in another life. Like it's in a dream.

But I came here for Clay. For us. Because I refuse to give up on our love if there's any chance at all I can save it.

That chance is here. It's the hope of getting back what we had that's brought me so far from it. No matter how awe-inspiring this place is with its waterfalls and magic, I can't forget for a second why I'm here.

I let my mind conjure up another image of Clay—a happier one of his laughing hazel eyes and knowing smirk—and hold on to it as I try to drift off. At home, the pillow of my sea sponge bed rests above the waterline, with the water covering me like a blanket; here, closed up in the quiet darkness of this shell, all of me—my nose, my mouth—is underwater. It's strange in its newness, and even though I can breathe this way just fine, some part of my brain panics, jerking me awake whenever I'm about to finally doze off.

But finally, with thoughts of Clay and waterfalls and golden beads swimming in my mind, I fall asleep, completely submerged.

Chapter Twenty-Nine

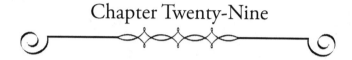

Classes zoom by like speedboats, leaving a white, cresting trail of new teachers to remember and new facts to learn. I'm infinitely grateful I've spent the last couple months brushing up with Ondine. Otherwise, I'd never keep up. I manage pretty well in everything except Mermese oration. Since Mer culture is oral instead of written, proper oral communication is highly valued here. While my Mermese isn't as flawless as Caspian's, I've always thought it was decent. But I guess I infuse it with what the teacher here calls "surface slang" a lot more than I realized.

Still, no one criticizes me or laughs. If anything, the other girls seem eager to offer creative tips for me to improve my pronunciation, and as soon as class is over, they all ask me to explain my English-inspired expressions. They're not mocking me—it's genuine interest.

And I'm interested, too. In Tidal Patterns & Impact, Intermarine Relations, and Classical *Konklili* Studies. My classes here come alive with discussion and debate in a way they never did on land. Now I finally understand the feel Ondine was striving for when we studied together, but which was impossible to muster one-on-one.

All of my classes here are with Jinju, Dionna, Thessa, and Nixie. They've known each other for years and are comfortable disagreeing and pointing out flaws in each other's logic without anyone getting offended. I'm hesitant to speak up at first, to interrupt their rhythm, but the teachers facilitate my entrance into the discussions and the girls ask me questions until I'm verbally sparring with the rest of them—and it's fun!

Fun enough that I'm able to forget what lies ahead at the end of the day. At least for a little while. But then, all my other courses are over and my stomach tangles as my tail turns to lead. Time for my first official advanced magic course, which means ...

As we swim down a new tunnel that leads toward our class, I peer into each of the girls' faces. Will those same welcoming, joking expressions twist with judgement and rage when they learn I committed sireny? When I agreed to tell them, they were hypothetical students at some distant academy, not real people, not ... potential friends. I don't know what it is about these girls—maybe their readiness to be kind to me?—but I like them. They seem like people I could get close to given enough time, but not if their acceptance of me is replaced with blind hatred before we even get to know each other.

Breathe. You said you'd do this, and you will. If I told Ondine I wasn't ready, that I wanted more time before divulging my darkest secret, she'd respect that. She'd give me all the time I needed. But in that time, Clay would be suffering. After seeing his grim, lost expression before he noticed me on the pier, and his confused, desperate one afterward, I understand that more than ever. Any time I spend wallowing in selfish waiting while I protect my secret is time stolen from his life. I can't do that to him.

And in the end, it won't matter how well these girls know me when I tell them. Either they'll understand and agree to help me or they won't. Caspian has known me my whole life and he still recoiled from me when he found out what I did. All I can do now is hope they understand why I did it and forgive me, like Casp did when he came around.

My pondering tapers off as we swim deeper and deeper into the labyrinth of tunnels under the island. Soon enough, no younger students or other staff mill around us anymore. Detailed paintings of elegant Mermaids on old-looking algae scrolls stare down at me from the walls. The stern bone structure of one such painted Mermaid catches my attention. That's Xana, the chancellor Ondine taught me about. I don't recognize any of the others along the wall, but the cold, sapphire eyes in one of the beautiful paintings remind me so much of Melusine's, I have to turn away. Then the five of us swim around a corner, and I gasp.

"Amazing, right?" Jinju whispers, taking in my awed expression.

Shells. Millions of them. All a creamy white. They cover every surface of the chamber we've just entered in gorgeous, elaborate patterns. Most form arches and geometric shapes, but there's also a motif of ... is that leaves? Feathers? I run my fingertips along the walls, tracing the intricate detail, the artistry.

And something else. The magic.

The whole chamber radiates with it. Like a glow I can feel instead of see.

"This is a sacred space," Ondine says, appearing through a seashell-encrusted arch on the other side of the room. *"A place where magic itself is worshipped."*

I jerk my hand back, like maybe my touch will sully the pristine power of this place.

Ondine shakes her head, smiling. *"You can touch it. Every student committed to the study and reverence of the old magic is welcome here."*

All the other girls have fallen silent, their playful banter halted, their heads bowed in respect.

"We have an important undertaking ahead of us," Ondine tells them, her voice both quieter and more endowed with authority than I've ever heard it. *"Before we begin, Lia has something she needs to*

confide in you. Something I trust all of you to hear without judgement or fear."

I wait for my own fear to squeeze my chest, tighten my throat. For dread to drag down each word of my confession.

But it doesn't come.

I don't know if it's Ondine's familiar presence warming me, or the open, patient expressions of Jinju, Dionna, and the others bolstering me, or the palpable serenity of this place calming me, but for the first time, the words pour from me without stammering and guilt.

I tell them about seeing Melusine sirening Clay, about researching a way to stop her and finding nothing, about singing Clay's own song to him on that boat to keep Melusine from luring him in again. About all the days afterward. I expect gasps and shocked faces, but instead, the girls stay silent and their heads stay bowed, like the hush of this sacred grotto has settled over them. *Didn't you hear me? I said I sirened someone. I sirened.* I want to shout or to shake them until they react, until they decide to criticize, ostracize, or exorcize me. How are they so calm? They wade there, listening. I breathe in the quiet, the lack of judgement, and it gives me the courage to continue. I tell them about the bond. About what it could do while my sirening was active, how it changed but didn't disappear afterward, and how Ondine and I have strengthened it.

Then I tell them that we want to use it to do the impossible: to counteract the irreversible potion that blocked Clay's memories.

Jinju is the first to speak. *"Can that even be done?"* The know-it-all tone that usually permeates her voice has been replaced by earnest curiosity.

The other girls' gazes echo her curiosity as they fix them on Ondine, waiting for an answer. Before she can give one, I say, *"You guys don't ... hate me? For being a ... "* No matter how many times I say it, I almost can't believe it myself. *"... a siren."* Something quick and unreadable passes over the girls' faces, like they're communicating with each other silently, the way the twins do.

This time, it's Dionna who speaks up. *"You explained to us that you had a good reason, so we understand why you felt the need to do what you did."*

"You learned that from Ondine," I say. Of course. She's mentored these girls their whole lives—it makes sense they'd examine a serious matter the way she's taught them. Still, all it will take is for one of these girls to slip, to tell a family member or …

I guess that's why they call it trust. As if reading my mind, Ondine says, *"Nothing will strengthen the magic you do with others the way true trust will. Now, you have proven that trust both to our circle here and to yourself. Which means,"* Ondine glances around at us, *"you're ready to begin working magic together."*

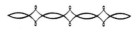

As much as I hoped our doing magic together meant Ondine had finished creating the ritual to restore Clay's memories, she explained it was too complicated a spell for her to perfect so quickly.

"Watching how you girls work together today on something simpler will help me understand how to make that ritual work. It will, in fact, help me see if the ritual will work at all."

Under her direction, the five of us form a circle in the center of the grotto. *"Until now, Lia has tapped into my power so she can strengthen her bond with Clay enough to check on him. Now, I'd like to see if you all are able to achieve the same thing working together without me as an active participant. That will show me if your magic is compatible enough with one another's for all of you to attempt something stronger together. It will also give you girls a chance to get to know Lia's magic—because in the end, if I am able to create a ritual that works, I won't make any of you participate. It will be up to each one of you to decide whether or not you'd like to help."*

Gee, this little exercise doesn't have any stakes at all, does it? I try not to let my nerves show on my face.

"Now close your eyes."

Under Ondine's instruction, I reach out with my mind like I have so many times to tap into her power. Only this time, when I open myself up to it, new magic floods my senses. It swirls all around me.

Dizziness overwhelms me, and a moment later, hands grip my shoulders.

"Whoa there. I've got you."

I open my eyes to find myself floating on my back in the water, with Thessa guiding me back upright. *"Are you okay?"*

I nod, but bring my hand to my head when the movement threatens to worsen my sudden dizziness. Tides, I couldn't even handle myself in their circle for five minutes. I must look like such an amateur to them. Now they probably won't think I'm worth helping.

"There was just ..."

"A lot of magic," Dionna finishes my thought.

"It happened to me the first time I tried to connect to the group," Nixie says, her cheeks turning pink.

"Really?" I say. Even Nixie, who's newest to the group besides me, has been studying basic magic at Sea Daughters since she was a small child.

"It happened to all of us." Jinju says after a moment. That eases some of my embarrassment. *"You'll get used to it,"* she adds. The words are an invitation for me to continue trying, and I nod my thanks.

"Stay focused this time." Ondine's clinking voice takes over from where she watches us outside the circle. *"See the magic for what it is instead of as one overwhelming mass."*

I don't 100% understand what she means. Okay, I don't even 75% understand what she means, but I've embarrassed myself enough already, so I might as well learn by doing. I brace myself for the onslaught as best I can, close my eyes, and open my mind again.

The magic's there, swirling all around. This time, instead of marveling at it the way I want to, I force my attention back to my breathing until I know I'm steady enough to keep my balance. *See the magic for what it is.* With a clearer head, I look at it again, look closer. Ondine's right—it isn't a mass. It's ... how do I even describe it? It's an intricate braid. Different strands weaving into each other around a central strand of familiar, icy blue to create something stronger and more complex.

By itself, each strand is far less powerful, and less overwhelming. I smile; I know what to do.

I take my time, familiarizing myself with each one individually. Each girl's power has its own unique trace. I try to identify each. It's like going to a fro-yo shop and trying out all the flavors in one of those tiny taster cups even though the snooty salesgirl says you're limited to two.

Patience has never been my strong suit, so now that I can identify each strand of magic, I'm eager to do what I've set out to do: tap into the group power and test out the bond with Clay. I haven't seen him since I left him all alone on the pier, and the thought that if I can make this work, I'm only seconds away from feeling like I'm sitting right next to him sends a tingle from the top of my head to the tips of my fins.

With my mind, I seek out a place where all those strands of power overlap, and I grab hold of that the way I've done so many times with Ondine's magic. Once I have a firm grip on it, I call up the bond.

I want to cry with happiness at the familiar comfort of Clay's room. I can almost smell the laundry soap and cinnamon. His messy desk, his flannel sheets ... with so much distance separating me from land, from Malibu, this feels like going home.

Seeing him gives me that rush of warmth and electricity and joy and love it always does. But it's followed by the pang of sharp worry I'm getting far too used to every time I see the sadness ingrained on his handsome face. He's sitting on the edge of his bed, staring down at his cupped hand. My worry only intensifies when I see what he's holding. A small, white bottle with one of those childproof caps. That brand name plays in TV commercials. Those pills are antidepressants—strong ones with a whole host of side effects. Clay's thoughts fill my head. *What if they make me feel … not like me? But I don't feel like me now. I haven't in a while.*

What Clay doesn't realize is his depression isn't chemical or hormonal. It's magical, so those pills won't help. He stares at them for a long time before putting them down on his nightstand and picking up his leather, songwriting notebook. The last few times I've seen Clay trying to write, he's been blocked and frustrated, crossing out lyrics as soon as he writes them before giving up. Now though, he begins writing right away and continues furiously, only stopping to strum a chord, rub his stubbled jaw, and write some more. He looks like he hasn't slept.

Every cell in my body longs to cuddle up next to him. To sweep his dark hair out of his face and sweep his sadness away with a kiss. To take care of him the way he hasn't been taking care of himself.

Instead, all I can do is watch helplessly as he rubs exhausted eyes and reads whatever lyrics he's written over and over, with that same obsessive frenzy.

After several more minutes, he drapes the open notebook over his denim-clad leg and picks his guitar back up.

His hands coast over the worn, smooth wood, and I get lost in their movement. When his long, calloused fingers press down on the chords, knowing so instinctively what to do after years of practice and passion, a sense of awe suffuses me. I love hearing him play.

But as he strums, I know this won't be one of the hope-filled ballads or get-stuck-in-your-head-in-the-best-way rock songs I've come to expect from him since we got together and he started writing more.

These notes are drenched in a low, hopeless longing.

His rough, beloved voice rumbles through me.

"A wicked mystery,
A half-forgotten dream.
Running away on a midnight tide
So far away from me."

He hits an intentionally discordant note, jarring in its sharpness.

"When I close my eyes, she's still here
Haunting my thoughts
Girl on the pier. Who are you?"

That's me! He's thinking about me. He's been thinking about me enough to write a song about me after he'd been blocked for months. My breath and heartbeat quicken. It must mean something, right? Does it confirm everything I've been wishing for—that our connection is stronger than any potion the Tribunal forced down his throat? Stronger than magic?

As if in answer to my question, he starts the chorus, his voice rising to a crescendo that threatens to break but holds strong.

"Girl on the pier,
Girl on the pier.
Where are you and why do I care?
Girl on the pier."

An image of myself standing on that pier flashes into my mind. Vivid and crackling in its intensity. It's Clay's memory of me through the bond. I see myself the way he saw me: windswept and wild, my hair flying around me against the night sky. It's nothing like what I see in the mirror at home. Here, through his eyes, I'm a force of nature. Striking, powerful, alluring even. And something else. Beautiful.

It disarms me. But not as much as the pain that laces each lyric as he continues to sing, losing himself in the up-swell of the music.

"No matter how fast I run, how far I reach,
I can't catch you.
I can't catch me.
Did I disappear," his voice finally breaks, the next part quiet.
"just like you?
Girl on the pier."

He sings the chorus twice more, and I choke back tears at the anger and anguish pouring off him. As much as I want to be happy that seeing me meant something to him, it also clearly unleashed something. Something deep and instinctual—and torturous in its elusiveness. He's so lost, it feels to him like he's ... disappearing. And it's all my fault.

When he stops, the last melancholy chord still lingering, his eyes are wet.

So are mine when I open them and find myself back in the mystical, shell-studded grotto.

The other girls glance at me, some with sheepish expressions, some with unmasked curiosity. Wait a minute ...

Nixie breaks the heavy silence. *"That's what a human guy looks like?"*

"You all saw that?"

"We kind of couldn't not *see it,"* Dionna says.

"Only someone with a lot more experience and raw power than us is strong enough to not get sucked into a tap that powerful." Thessa finishes.

I glance over my shoulder at Ondine, who's wading behind me, ready to catch me if I would have fallen backward again. All those times I used her magic for the bond and she not only ignored what I was seeing but conducted her own diagnostic spells to study the bond at the same time—she must be even more powerful than I imagined.

But Nixie, Jinju, Dionna, and Thessa did see Clay. I watched him while he was in his bedroom playing a song he thought was for his ears alone—and they were there with me, watching alongside me.

My face flames. It was an intimate moment.

"Question: Who was that song about?" Jinju asks, but her expression says she already suspects.

"Me," I say, fighting my blush as I tell them about the night on the pier—going to Clay, finally catching a glimpse of him after so long apart, and having to run away and leave him.

"And now he can't stop thinking about you ..." Dionna says, her voice breathy. Like she's reciting the next line of a fairytale. The girls release a swooning sigh that might as well have been synchronized. Nixie's is practically a squeal.

"Seriously, though," Nixie says, curling the wispy green streak in her blond hair around her finger. *"Is that what a human guy looks like? Because ... wow. Anyone else thinking maybe the Little Mermaid's been misjudged?"*

"Nixie, that's highly inappropriate." Thessa says, wearing what seems to be a forever-serious expression. Then she tilts her head. *"Although, I will admit he was quite handsome."*

"And those legs ..." Nixie trails off, her face nearly as red as mine. *"He just ... has those all the time, right?"*

Suddenly, I'm glad Clay was wearing jeans instead of shorts or swim trunks.

Before I can answer, Ondine takes back control of the conversation. *"Ladies, may I speak with Lia in private?"*

Nixie is still whispering to the others about Clay as they leave. As soon as we're alone, Ondine asks, *"Lia, was the bond as strong and vivid as when you tapped into my power?"* When I nod, relief sweeps over her face before she replaces it with placid composure. *"Good,"* she says. *"That means your magic is compatible with the group's. Together, we should all be able to perform the ritual I've been researching."*

I want to shout with glee and do a backflip in the water!

"In time," Ondine adds.

In time? What does that mean? *"What does that mean? How much time?"*

"*That,*" Ondine answers, "*depends largely on my spell writing abilities, and,*" she swims closer, "*on you.*"

"Me?"

"*I'm basing the spell on an ancient ritual that requires strong magic. You're not powerful or experienced enough yet to attempt it.*" It's not an insult; it's a fact.

"*What can I do to make sure I can handle it?*" I ask, my fins fluttering with nervous energy.

"*You've been raised in the human world, largely disconnected from your own magic and with no opportunity to study the rare, ancient spells we teach here. The next step for you is simple: Study magics with us, Lia.*"

And that's exactly what I do.

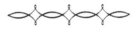

It's much easier than I expected to do what Ondine advises and settle in to a life on the island. Especially once I've gone up top.

I don't know what I thought the surface of the island would look like; when I heard this place was a California nature preserve, I pictured some dry shrubs by a rocky beach and maybe a few old turtles. Boy, was I wrong.

Maybe the periphery of the island by the shore looks like that, but that isn't where we spend our time.

Every other day here, classes end early, letting out midway through the afternoon. That's when the other girls and I head for the island's surface. We swim through an underground tunnel that lets out at the very center of the island.

In the most breathtaking lagoon I've ever seen.

Seriously—it's epic. Lush green mountains and trees work along with the cloaking spells to hide a natural pool of the bluest water from passing ships or the occasional visiting scientist. Many of the cascading crystal waterfalls I've marveled at in the caverns beneath the island originate here, flowing down from the mountains and into the rippling water, creating caves in secret pockets behind.

Wildflowers of every color line the banks, and species of sea birds I've never seen before soar overhead or nest in the island's tall treetops. Like Ondine herself, this lagoon strikes me as something straight out of a storybook. Mermaids play tag beneath the waterfalls or sun their jeweled tails on the rocks peeking through the water or bask on the banks while they run white fishbone combs through their shining, long hair.

As fantastic as our swimming pool is at home, this? This is better. Never before have I been allowed to release my tail under the sun out in nature before, warming my golden scales in golden rays and soaking up that warmth until it drives me to dive into the cool, refreshing waters of the lagoon. It's like travelling back in time through the centuries, to before Mer hid our existence from humans, when Mermaids could lie out on ocean rocks and be admired by passing sailors who'd go home and regale townsfolk with stories of the beautiful maidens they'd seen at sea.

Today, as I lie out on such a rock in the center of the lagoon, I gaze at my tranquil surroundings and reflect on how peaceful and natural my life is here.

Flipping onto my stomach and spreading out my fins, I lean over the blue water to practice the spell I learned during class in the shell grotto yesterday. With a delicate, careful flick of my wrist, I summon up a thin layer of water and wrap it around air to create a perfectly spherical bubble, turning it just so, making its rainbow surface glint in the sunlight. A dorky smile spreads across my face. I made that! Even after three weeks here studying with Ondine and the other girls, magic astounds me.

"*Decent work,*" Jinju says with an approving nod from where she lies next to me, idly bouncing a gleaming white pebble from one of her pink fins to the other.

"*That spell's not easy,*" Nixie says. Of course, she's probably been able to do it for ages, but she's too polite to say so. "*You're catching up.*" She dives into the water to examine my bubble from underneath, and when she's right up close, I flick it so it pops against her nose.

"*Hey!*" She bursts out laughing.

Sitting up, I create another bubble and splash it at Dionna, who retaliates. Some of the younger students gather to gaze at the magic they hope to learn someday. Smiling, I call up a whole slew of rainbow bubbles and float them around all of us, slowly rotating them so they shine. The magic drains some of my energy, but the beautiful floating spheres make all the girls smile and laugh, so I keep it going as I lean back, dip my fins into the lagoon, and enjoy the moment of simple bliss.

With one sentence, life on the island goes from simple to thrilling.

"*The ritual is ready,*" Ondine says one night after she's gathered the six of us in the shell grotto. It's late, and the rest of the school is sleeping in their shell beds, but I'm suddenly wide awake. "*The potion the Foundation gave Clay didn't eradicate his memories; our memories are too essential to who we are to be forcibly removed without killing us. So, the potion shielded his recollection of you under wards, much the same way our island is shielded.*" That's right—Caspian's grandmother said his memories of me and all other Mer were warded by the potion. "*Now, because those wards were designed to be permanent, it will take very strong magic to break through them. Very strong magic.*"

A mixture of fear and excitement glints in the other girls' eyes.

"*To achieve that level of magic,*" Ondine continues, "*I have based our spell on the most powerful ancient ritual I could find—one I'd wager all of you have heard of."*

"A famous one?" Dionna asks.

"An infamous one." Ondine lets what she's said register before finishing. "*If you choose to participate, we'll be performing a ritual based on the one the Sea Sorceress used to curse the obsidian dagger.*"

Chapter Thirty

What? How? My mind races to review everything I know about the spell that cursed the dagger. In exchange for banishing the Little Mermaid's tail and giving her permanent legs, the Sea Sorceress struck a deal with her. Either the Mermaid got her prince to fall in love with her and marry her, or—if he chose someone else—she'd die the sunrise after his wedding day. When the prince chose to marry a human princess instead of her, the Little Mermaid's sisters went to the Sea Sorceress to beg her for mercy.

That's when the Sea Sorceress created the dagger. She gave it to the Little Mermaid along with simple and terrible instructions: Use it to kill her beloved prince as he slept in his marital bed on his wedding night, and when his blood spilled on her legs, they'd turn back into a tail. She'd be an immortal Mermaid once again, capable of returning to the sea. But when she couldn't bring herself to kill him—when she chose to save a human life over her own immortality—she dropped the dagger into the ocean and died. The instant that blade touched the waves, it stripped all Mer of the very immortality the Little Mermaid had failed to value and cursed us all with human lifespans.

That's one powerful dagger. But how did the Sea Sorceress make it that powerful? I thought the answer was a secret lost to time.

"How do you know that ritual?" My voice comes out much quieter than I expected, but Ondine hears me in the hushed grotto.

"I have devoted my life to protecting ancient magics that would otherwise be lost to Merkind, so we have access to them in case we need them someday. I consider it a sacred duty."

A glance around at the solemn but unsurprised faces of the other girls tells me they share in this sense of duty, that they too are committed to the protection of ancient magics.

"Whatever her methods and motives, the Sea Sorceress was a genius when it came to magic." Ondine says, *"In the thousands of years she was alive, she devised some of the most powerful spells in history. That magic deserves to be protected so we can learn from it. That's why I have spent decades tracking down her spells from the farthest reaches of the oceans and the oldest families, and studying their intricacies."*

My intake of breath echoes off the shell-encrusted walls. The information Ondine has just trusted me with could land her in prison; since I've told her about my sireny, knowing this secret makes our relationship feel even more equitable somehow, more balanced.

Still, I can't help but ask, *"Isn't it ... isn't it dangerous for anyone to know those spells? What if ... they get in the wrong hands?"*

"Magic doesn't work for us, Lia. We work for it. Preserving it, protecting it, ensuring it endures so it can protect us. I pass these spells down with the utmost care," Ondine says, running a hand down Jinju's hair and looking around trustingly at the other girls. *"And I'd protect them with my very life."*

Doubt must still mar my face because Ondine swims closer to me, putting her cool hands on both my shoulders. *"Lia, the law would have us blindly destroy all this magic we may someday need instead of preserve it. When has destruction, instead of knowledge, ever been the answer?"*

Those are words I can't argue with. In fact, I don't know what to say at all.

It's Jinju who asks, *"How does the ritual work? I thought you said we'd all need to cast it together, but,"* she clears her throat, *"the Sea Sorceress imbued the dagger with power all by herself."*

"Did she now?" Ondine raises an eyebrow, and the crystals around her eyes glint in the low light.

We all nod. That's how the story goes. *"Didn't she?"* I ask.

"Well, do you know how the Little Mermaid's sisters got her to agree to create the dagger?"

"Sure," I say. *"Even some humans know that part. They traded their hair for the dagger."*

"And why do you think she wanted their hair?"

"Um ..." I've never thought about that. *"'Cause she was gross and evil?"* I try.

"That seems to be the subconscious assumption that allows most to dismiss this detail of the story. But let me ask you, what do you know about a Mermaid's hair, Lia?"

And just like that, I feel like we're back in the classroom under my house and she's testing me on Mer customs.

"Well ... I know Mermaid hair contains trace amounts of magic." When the twins were freshmen and had already started at Malibu Hills prep, they'd heard about a charity drive at school to donate their hair so it could be made into wigs for children with cancer. But no matter how much they pleaded with our parents, my mom and dad said they weren't allowed to participate. My mom complimented them for wanting to, but she explained their hair had magical properties. Nothing easily discernable, but she didn't know how it would react to the heating, dying, and processing needed to make it into a wig, and it wasn't a risk worth taking. The twins were majorly P-o'd until Em suggested they organize a toy drive for the children's hospital instead. I gave them my favorite, rainbow Chinese jump rope, still new in the package since I'd been saving it for when I got legs. *"Our hair's like our fins, right? A reflection of our inner magic?"*

Ondine nods. *"That is why when a Mermaid practices the most powerful spells, her hair reflects it,"* Ondine says, fingering one of her own blue strands. *"The Sea Sorceress didn't require the Little Mermaids' sisters to provide their hair because she was cruel or evil. She did it because she needed some of their magic to create an object as powerful as the obsidian dagger."*

"But couldn't she just do it herself?" I ask. *"I mean, she was mega-powerful."*

Ondine's lips form a slow smile. *"She was indeed. But remember what I told you about how expending too much of one's own power means you can risk losing it? Not even someone as powerful as the Sea Sorceress was immune to that rule. She needed something from each of the Little Mermaid's five sisters that would allow her to use their magic in her spell. In our ritual, I'll embody her role, and the five of you,"* she looks at all of us, *"will serve as the five sisters."*

"Does that mean we have to chop off our hair?" Nixie asks, looking horrified. A few of the others gasp, their hands flying to their long locks.

"No," Ondine says. *"The Little Mermaid's sisters didn't know enough magic to actively participate in the spell, but you do, so you'll cast it with me instead of giving me your hair."*

"Hang on ... if you're performing the Sea Sorceress's role," I say to Ondine, *"and the rest of us are taking the place of the five sisters, how does Clay fit into all this?"*

Ondine's pale eyes meet my gaze. *"What would the Sea Sorceress have been without the dagger?"*

Silence permeates the grotto.

Finally, I manage to choke out, *"Clay's going to take the place of the dagger?"*

The same dagger that—because of this ritual—ended up cursing my entire species?

"The same dagger that almost killed him?"

"That's what gave me the idea, and it is precisely why this ritual stands a chance of working," Ondine says. *"The obsidian dagger nearly*

killed him. That forges a magical bond with such a powerful object. He may have survived, but Clay is now inextricably linked to that dagger."

The other girls nod at the logic of this. I guess I still have a lot more to learn about magic. *"That is good news for us,"* Ondine says. *"It means Clay can stand in for the dagger. And just as the Sea Sorceress combined her magic with the sisters' magic to imbue the dagger with power, we can combine our magic to imbue Clay—with his memories."*

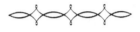

I can't stop smiling. I'm smiling the entire time Ondine explains the intricacies of the ritual to us. I'm even smiling while she emphasizes how dangerous a spell this powerful can be, how it can have unforeseen effects, and how carefully we'll need to perform it. I can't help it—the more I hear, the more her plan makes sense and the surer I am it will work. Clay will get his memories back. He'll get his happiness back.

He'll get himself back.

I'm still smiling as I lie in my shell bed with the lid closed and no one there to see the unabashed joy on my face.

When Ondine had finished explaining the ritual, she looked around the circle from Jinju to Dionna to Thessa to Nixie and asked if they would agree to perform it with me.

I'd been so sure they would say no. These girls barely know me. Ondine told me performing ancient magic this powerful drained a Mermaid of energy and left her weak. Not to mention this spell defies the spirit of the Tribunal's order, even if it doesn't violate the letter of the law. Sure, these girls have been super nice, but why would they agree to help me with something this complicated?

A subtle shift had rippled through the water around us as the other girls looked to Jinju. Her spine had straightened with authority. *"Learning to complete a spell so ancient and so complex can only strengthen our magic, both individually and as a circle. We'd be honored to take part."*

After Jinju'd spoken, the other girls had smiled enthusiastically. Even the earnest, reserved Thessa saw the logic of her words and nodded in approval.

These girls hold their duty to strengthening and preserving magic above all else. It's something I'm only just beginning to understand.

A soft knock on the outside of my shell accompanies a whispered question, *"Lia, are you awake?"*

I lift the lid to reveal Dionna, shy smile in place. At my nod, she sits on the bed, settling her turquoise tail beneath her. *"I figured you'd still be up,"* she says. *"I just wanted to tell you, I'm really excited you're going to be joining our circle."* She runs a hand through the turquoise streak in her springy black curls. *"I think the others are, too."*

So far, I've been learning magic alongside the girls, but I've been like a visitor. For the ritual to work, Ondine explained I'll need to be an official member of their magic circle. I'll take a blood oath binding my magic to theirs the way they've bound theirs to each other.

Ondine said formally joining their group isn't something I should do lightly, and I'm not. If these girls are willing to do so much to help me and Clay, then despite some nerves, I'm honored to be part of their circle. We'll perform both the oath and the ritual in a week, once Ondine has triple-checked her final modifications.

I squeeze Dionna's hand. *"I'm excited, too."*

That excitement only grows when I return from my classes the next day to find a conus shell waiting on my bed. It's a message from

Caspian! His low, familiar baritone washes over me as I hold the shell to my ear. He has a school break and his parents have agreed to visit mine in New Meris, which means Caspian can spend a day visiting me here at Sea Daughters Academy before he takes tours of a few places Below where he can do specialized dialects training next year. Eeee! Four days from today, Caspian will visit, and a week from today, Clay will get his memories back.

Chapter Thirty-One

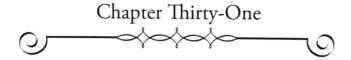

"And this ..." I yank on Caspian's forearm as we swim out into the sunshine, "is the lagoon." I've saved this spot for the grand finale of our tour.

His jaw drops as he takes in the pristine nature all around us. "You're absolutely sure it's safe to be out here in our tails?"

I nod, and enjoy not only his awe, but also the experience of speaking English again after so long. "It's under strong protection wards."

"Wow." Calculating blue eyes sweep the expanse of rippling water and gently swaying trees. "These must be stronger wards than even the Foundation has access to."

"Impressive, huh?" I'm bouncing with giddiness I didn't expect at seeing Casp again and at showing him my new home away from home—because that's what Sea Daughters Academy feels like to me now.

"Um ... yeah." He's still taking in every detail, his gaze narrowed. We're alone out here while everyone else is in class. I'm excused because I have a visitor. (Caspian didn't like that his visit was pulling me away from my studies, but when I told him how well I'm doing in my classes here, he seemed appeased.)

"We can stay up here until dinner if you want," I say. "I can't wait for you to try the food. And meet my friends." The girls are going to flip when they see him.

"You seem happy here."

"I am," I say, the sentiment resonating in my chest. "Don't get me wrong, I miss my family and a certain blond, silver-tailed Merman A LOT, but I am happy." Especially because the people here are the ones who will help me get Clay his memories back.

I have to tell Caspian about the plan. I'm not going to tell anyone else, but Caspian has proven how trustworthy he is over and over. He's also made it clear to me he doesn't want to be shielded from information for his own protection. I remember how hurt he seemed during our dance lesson when he told me I underestimated him; I don't want him to feel like that again. Now that I have a set plan to restore Clay's memories, Caspian deserves to know.

He's already updated me on what my sisters are up to and filled me in on news from the Community. We've covered every other topic. Well, except for whether Melusine is still staying away from him. Part of me wants to ask—especially now that the three-month restriction limiting her to the grotto system is over and she's allowed to move about more freely. The thought alone scares me and makes me even happier I'm on this island, far, far away from her. No, I won't ask him if he's talking to her again. I refuse to let the mention of her cause another fight and ruin such a perfect day—not when I have such limited time to spend with Casp as it is.

But that means there's only one thing left that we need to talk about. Now's the time to tell him about the ritual; I can't put it off any longer.

"Casp, I nee—"

"Oh! I almost forgot to tell you. Leomaris asked me to be one of his *lenlitli*." That's kind of like a groomsman.

"*Viriss!*" I say.

"Salty?" He raises an eyebrow.

"Uh, sorry. It's an expression here. Like cool."

Caspian doesn't look like he approves.

"Did you say yes?" I ask. Okay, I'm officially stalling. Of course he said yes to Leo.

He echoes my thought, "Of course. I know how important this wedding is for your family."

"Thanks," I say, "And thank you so much for coming here." I didn't realize how much I missed him until I saw him get out of the carriage this morning.

"I would have come even sooner if I could have, Goldfish." He looks down into the clear water then up into my eyes. "You mean a lot to me."

"You mean a lot to me, too." I don't know if I've ever said those words to him before, even though nothing's been truer my entire life. "That's why I need to tell you something."

Hope paints his unguarded face. I better do this fast. But even though we're alone, the middle of the lagoon feels way too out in the open for such a secret. "Come here." I guide him behind one of the crystal waterfalls. "Casp ..."

"Yeah?"

The cave behind the fall is smaller than I expected, and Caspian and I wade right up close to each other behind the cascade of water.

"I found a way to get Clay's memories back."

Even in the small space, Caspian manages to reel backward. "What?"

"Well, I should say Ondine found a way." I tell him everything—and I mean everything, from confessing my sireny to Ondine all the way up to our plan for the dagger ritual. I won't keep Caspian in the dark—not again.

Once I've finished, he's quiet for a long time. "Lia ..." He stops, tries again. "Lia ... I understand how badly you want Clay to remember you—"

"It's not just about me. Clay ... he's in a bad place—"

"I get it. I do. You want to help him and get back what the two of you lost." Sadness passes over his face; then he sets his jaw. "But Lia, you absolutely cannot do that ritual."

"What? Why not?"

"Why not?" He looks at me, incredulous. "Forget for a second that you're talking about an ancient spell that would almost undoubtedly be illegal if anyone knew it still existed—"

"Oh, 'cause the laws are so fair and just," I say, thinking about how those same laws allowed the Tribunal to mandate that Clay drink that potion and left us with no legal recourse to fight them.

"Just because one law is wrong, doesn't mean they all are," Caspian says. "But even putting aside the legal issues, ancient rituals like that aren't used anymore because they were too dangerous. They took too much power."

"Ondine explained that to me," I say, validation welling inside me. "Don't worry—that's why we're going to be so careful. And that's why we're going to combine all our magic." It's sweet of Caspian to be concerned, but he doesn't need to be.

"No!" He shakes his head. "That's why you shouldn't even be considering it. You can't combine your power with these girls. You'd be giving them full access to your magic—to *you*. You barely know them. You barely even know Ondine."

"Yes I do!" Hot anger begins to rise, and I fight to keep it at bay. "Ondine and these girls are the only ones who have been willing to help me. Truly help me. Everyone else—my parents, my sisters— they've pitied me, sure, but they expected me to just move on."

"That's because you should," he shouts. Then he repeats more calmly, "Lia, you *should* move on." He swims closer again. "I know it's not what you want to hear, but just listen to me for a second. If you give Clay his memories back, you'll plunge the two of you right back into all the problems you had before. He's human, Lia. Human.

No matter how much you want that to work, it never will. He's going to age and die, and you won't. You can't have a future together; you can't ever have children—"

"You think I don't know that? You think I haven't thought about all of this a million times? Now who's underestimating who? If Clay wants to break up with me because we don't have a future, that should be up to him. Not to some Tribunal."

"I know you've thought about it. I just don't think you've thought about it enough. Things are different now that you broke the curse. Things have changed. If you keep clinging to Clay and the human world, you're … you're going to trap yourself in limbo where you could never really be happy."

I hear everything Caspian is saying, but … "I couldn't be happy without him."

"Yes, you could. You can." He pauses, takes a deep breath. "We can. You've stopped me from saying this so many times—"

"Casp," I warn.

"No. No. You don't get to be the one who decides what I can and can't say. You asked for time? I've given you time. Tides, have I. But now I need to say this—and you need to hear it before you make a mistake. A dangerous mistake."

He sets his shoulders, which are even broader in this small space. "Lia, I love you." He looks straight into me with the bluest, most honest eyes. "I'm in love with you. I have been for years. Having you gone these last few weeks … not having you there to talk to, to laugh with, I've hated it."

I've hated it, too. I've really missed Casp.

"I want to be with you, Lia. We can have it all now. Don't you see? With the curse gone, we can have the life we were supposed to have. I can convince my parents to move to New Meris sooner and you can move into the palace with your family. We can live Below like we were always meant to." He takes both my hands in his larger ones. "I know it's scary and new, but we can face it—together. Just imagine it. I love you," he says again, stroking the tops of my hands with his thumbs. "Choose me. Please. For once, just choose me, and we can have everything. We can have forever."

He's offering me the life that just a year ago was the stuff of dreams. It's beautiful. Magical.

But …

"I can't." Silent tears stream down my face, and pearls fall into the water between us. "I love you, Casp, I do. But I'm not in love with you." A part of me wishes I was. It would make all this so much easier. "I'm sorry."

He pulls his hands back. The mist from the waterfall lands on my face, mingling with my tears.

"I'm so sorry," I say again. "I can't. It wouldn't be fair. Not to Clay, not to me. And not to you." I reach out to touch his arm, but he moves backward. "Casp, you deserve—"

"I don't get what I deserve," he says. "But what else is new?"

"Please—"

"I get it. You've made your choice." His jaw clenches and he swallows, eyes shining. "And it isn't me." He turns, ready to swim off.

Then he looks back at me over his shoulder. "Is there anything, anything at all, I can do to stop you from going through with this ritual?"

"Nothing." It's the surest word I've ever spoken.

"But—"

"You said you're in love with me? Well, what if it were us … if we were together and they took me from you? Would you risk it, risk everything, risk granting access to your magic and performing some ancient ritual to get me back?"

He doesn't need to say the words. We both know the answer.

All he says is, "Please be careful." Then he disappears through the waterfall.

Chapter Thirty-Two

With Caspian gone, the island feels emptier, colder, lonelier. That's ridiculous, I tell myself. He was only here for a few hours and there's no reason for you to be lonely. You're surrounded by friends.

But Caspian is your best friend.

No. I refuse to wallow. Instead of going to my shell bed to cry, I head straight for Ondine's office off the school's main cavern.

"I can't wait anymore," I say when she welcomes me inside. *"I want to take the oath and do the ritual tonight."*

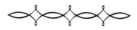

My hand shakes around the sharpened shard of cockle shell.

"Lia, it's okay if you're not ready," Dionna says, clutching her already-bleeding palms. She, Jinju, Thessa, and even Nixie who's younger than I am have all managed to do what they had to; tendrils

of red uncurl from their palms into the surrounding water.

"No, I'm ready." I hope that by saying it out loud, I'll make it true. There's no reason for me to hesitate. These girls are kind and willing to help me and committed to magic.

You barely know them, Caspian's voice rings out in my head.

They've been here for me. They're here for me now. Sacrificing their time and their magical energy. Even their blood.

Seconds pass.

I grit my teeth, push down on the shard, and drag its sharp edge along my skin. Pain lances across my palm and I hiss as my blood forms a crimson cloud in the water. The second one is easier.

Ondine's voice fills the sacred shell grotto. *"Only through blood magic can we forge new links to fully access new power,"* she intones in formal Mermese. *"Today, we welcome such new power into our circle—and into our blood."*

"Into our circle, into our blood," the others repeat, the words becoming a chant that rises up around us. *"Into our circle, into our blood."*

At the same instant, Jinju grabs my left hand and Ondine my right, their palms pressing to mine, linking me to Dionna, Thessa, and Nixie. Bringing me into their circle.

"Into our circle, into our blood." My voice joins the chant.

"Into our circle, into our blood." I close my eyes as the strands of my magic twine with theirs, becoming part of that strong, intricate braid.

"Into our circle, into our blood." Our volume escalates, the chant encircling us, enveloping us as it reaches a crescendo. We raise our joined hands.

"Into our circle, into our blood."

I feel ... strong. Like I'm part of something ... bigger.

A sense of belonging seeps into me, settling deep. I relish it, letting it wipe away any fear I might have felt as I mount one of the giant sea horses the school keeps for long journeys. The carriage that brought me here belongs to the palace, so that option's out. I've never ridden a seahorse before, but right now, with the magic from the ritual still thrumming through me, I feel like I can conquer anything.

Even a midnight journey across the ocean.

If the ritual works—no *when*. When the ritual works and Clay gets his memories back, I'll need to be there for him. We have to perform it as close to Malibu as possible while still being far enough out that we don't risk seeing swimmers or scuba divers.

That means we're headed for the Border. At sunset, surrounded by my new circle, each one mounted on her own majestic seahorse, I depart the beautiful island I've come to cherish. As the waters around us grow dark, my seahorse turns from periwinkle to deep purple.

Soon, the island is a speck behind us. Then it disappears altogether. The seahorses pick up speed, racing through the current so fast, all I can do is hang on, pain pulsing in my injured palms as I cling to my stallion's strong, spiny neck.

After the sheltered tunnels and secluded lagoon of the academy, the vastness of the open ocean strikes me as frightening and thrilling in its freedom.

I'm not alone in the feeling. Somewhere in the pitch blackness next to me, Jinju screams, *"Woohoo!"* and unleashes wild laughter. With my seahorse speeding into the cool current, water streaming across my face, my hair whipping behind me, I toss my head back and let out a wild laugh of my own, giving in to the exhilaration as I ride into the night.

Hours later, the blue illumination of the Border punctuates the dreamlike darkness. It catches me off-guard. How is it I feel so much older than I did the last time I was here? Across that line lies my Community with its ever-present promise of safety. But to save Clay, I need to stay on this side and embrace a spell so powerful, knowledge of it has been cloaked in secrecy for over two hundred years.

Soon, we've found a trench by the border and have left the seahorses to graze in the nearby kelp stalks. Anticipation tingles up the tips of my fins as we form a circle, clasping hands for the second time as, together, we speak the opening words of the ritual.

Chapter Thirty-Three

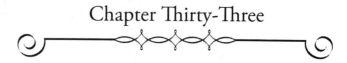

The ancient Mermese spell words taste like the sweetest, darkest chocolate as they leave my lips, melting into the water around me and swirling with the same words from the others in my circle.

When I sat up at night in my shell bed committing these words to memory, I never expected reciting them would be so … delicious. Indulgent.

I could drown in them as they open my magic to the circle, pouring it into the spell. In a few moments, I'll open my mind the way I've opened my magic, giving the others access to my memories as we send them to Clay. But first Ondine nods to me, and all our combined powers rush into my body, flooding my senses.

Ondine and the girls have given me everything they can. This next part's up to me.

With all the power of the ancient spell flowing into me, I invoke the bond I share with Clay. It's not a thread or even a rope anymore. Now, it's a raging, storming portal. Fear spikes through me. I can't see Clay.

I can't see anything. I—

But I can feel him.

Everywhere.

All around me in the swirling storm.
I can hear his every thought, like I'm … inside his mind.

"No matter how fast I run, how far I reach,
I can't catch you.
I can't catch me.
Did I disappear …
just like you?
Girl on the pier."

The lyrics vibrate inside my whole body. *I'm here,* I think.

Shock—undiluted and terrified—radiates off his consciousness and into me. He heard me.

Clay heard me! The ritual is working—our bond is linking my mind directly to his. It's time.

I draw from the power of the circle, using it to fortify me for what I'm about to do. I conjure up the image in my mind of a turquoise bench and a cliff-top view.

"You're Lia. But you spell it cool."

"Yeah. Lia Nautilus."

"I'm Clay."

The first day we met. I push it from my mind into his. Before waiting for a reaction, I summon up the next memory. Dark hair shining under the fluorescent lights of the gym as he unknowingly saved me from revealing my secret in P.E.

"She can take my spot in yoga. I have swim trunks … I'd rather go swimming."

The two of us in history class, a low whisper and a cocky smirk.

"I'm a prince in disguise."

"Really? I didn't know princes liked to wear jeans with so many holes."

And at his desk in his room.

"Hey, I just thought we were friends, Nautilus, that's all."

"We are friends."

"*Promise?*"

"*Promise.*"

I fling memories at him like cannon balls, one after another. Ondine explained it's the only chance I have to break through the artificial shield created by the Tribunal's potion and unlock his own memories. I keep up the attack, using one treasured moment after another as ammunition.

"*This is a song I've been working on for a while. It's the only one I've finished and I think it really captures ... well, just listen.*"

Clay's calloused fingers strumming the chords of his guitar.

His lips kissing my neck in his sun-drenched backyard.

Exploring that guitar store in L.A.

Running away between the food trucks, trying to escape his ketchup hands.

It's not working. Clay's head throbs against the onslaught—I can feel him kneeling on his bedroom floor, clutching his head in both hands—but his own memories aren't surfacing from beneath the potion's strong shield.

I must try harder. Maybe more powerful memories?

A boat thrown about in the wind. Me singing with all my might and Clay walking toward me across the deck, sirened.

Him, cloudy-eyed and malleable.

Me, letting my sireny wear off on that beach and crushing my lips against his for the very first time. Then running off and leaving him on the shore.

Him and me at the bottom of the ocean.

"*I can breathe underwater because ... because I'm a Mermaid.*"

And later in the grottos with Caspian's grandmother.

"*Only true love—free of uncertainty or hesitation, free of any type of magic—could have broken that spell and given us our immortality back.*"

Days later, out behind my house.

"*I'll be performing next Friday. Would you ... be my date?*"

"*Yes!*"

"Good. Because I wouldn't want to share the night with anyone else. Not now that I know I love you."

The searing pain in his head intensifies and Clay's scream pierces my entire being. Tears stream down my face. I'm torturing him. And for what? This isn't working.

The magic from the ritual begins to drain out of me, and I can feel Ondine and the others straining to keep it going. It won't last much longer. Work, damn it!

"Lia, can I ... can I see your tail?"

My gold fins stretched across his checkered couch.

Both of us, hand-in-hand in the ocean, snorkeling through the waves.

One by one, the other girls let go of the magic, unable to continue. Ondine holds on longest, but finally, even her presence leaves me.

The ritual's magic is leeching out of me—and it hasn't done its job. When it wears off in a few second's time, what will happen to Clay? Having seen all these visions but not having any of his own memories to make sense of them ... he'll think he's gone insane.

No. No! I can't let that happen.

With every ounce of energy I still have, I seize the last drops of the spell's magic and force them behind one last memory that I catapult at Clay.

"I-I just don't want you to do anything you'll regret."

"I could never regret being with you ... This is what I want. You're what I want."

His palms skimming up and down my arms, my fingers twining into his hair, his strong arms wrapping around me, bringing our bodies together. So close.

CRACK!

The force sends me reeling. An explosion from the hidden depths of Clay's mind, every memory the Tribunal restrained gushing forth.

Clay floats in the ecstasy of it all, his pain forgotten.

With one last gasp, my body screams, and I let go.

Chapter Thirty-Four

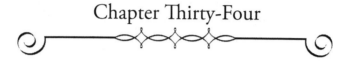

I shouldn't be swimming. After a spell like that, all I should be doing is lying in bed with a steaming cup of sugar kelp tea. But I don't care. I don't care about anything but seeing Clay.

Ondine knows nothing will keep me away now. All she says is, *"Go. The sun will be up soon. You have until tonight, but then you must head back. I'll cover your absence until then with the other staff. Your horse will be waiting for you here. She knows the way to the academy. And remember, you are part of our circle now. You can tap into our magic for protective spells if you need them."*

"Thank you," I say, wrapping her in a hug. "Thank you."

"Be careful," she says. *"Don't let anyone see you together."*

I nod. The Tribunal's order still stands; getting caught with Clay would mean imprisonment. With her warning words still ringing in my ears, I let my adrenaline carry me toward the steady blue light, and I cross the Border toward Malibu. Toward Clay.

For the first time, I use the bond I share with him to not only sense where Clay is but to tug him toward me. Now that he remembers we share this bond, I hope he'll know to follow it.

I use it to guide him toward one of the Community's beachfront estates. It belonged to a family who has already moved back Below, so it's been empty ever since. The perfect hideout.

The closer I get, the dizzier my excitement. My head breaks the surface of the sea right as the sun peeks over the horizon. Its growing light illuminates the outline of a figure standing on the shore, hands in his pockets.

My face splits into an uncontainable smile, and I pick up speed, only pausing to transform into my legs and slip into the pair of teal bikini bottoms I brought with me.

The first rays of morning sunlight bathe the ocean in their pale glow as I step out of the waves and Clay runs to me.

I move toward him on legs I haven't used since I moved Below, and as I launch myself into his waiting arms, I reclaim a part of myself.

I run my hands over his now-damp T-shirt and his lightly stubbled jaw, ensuring myself he's real. This isn't some magical vision of Clay. This is him, holding me in his arms. Before either of us can say a word, he tilts his head down and claims my mouth in a kiss.

I've never longed for anything so much. We press our bodies close as our mouths revel in their reunion. In his urgency, Clay dips me backward, his hands everywhere on my back, on my neck, tangled in my hair.

I give back with everything I have, letting my lips and tongue show him how achingly much I missed him. Our mouths come together over and over as the waves lap at our feet. Only the need for air finally pulls us apart, and only by centimeters. Clay's strong hands come up to cup either side of my face and shining hazel eyes drink in the sight of me.

"There you are, Nautilus. I couldn't find you for the longest time."

"I'm here," I say. "I'm here."

It doesn't take long to find the spare key hidden beneath a stone frog outside the front door. The dark, quiet house welcomes us into its sanctuary.

The family who used to live here took their personal possessions, but all the furniture is still here, barely used, like the display in a department store. Everything just so. They probably spent most of their time in the grottos.

Clay and I close all the curtains, just to be safe, never straying more than a few windows apart. After so long spent away from each other, that's about as much distance as we can bear. While we move from room to room, I tell him about where I've been and the spell I used to restore his memories.

We find a den nestled at the back of the house. Something about sitting on the unused, unfamiliar furniture feels strange, so instead, while Clay lights a fire, I use pillows, couch cushions, and some soft blankets I find in the linen closet to build us a cozy pile in front of the oversized fireplace.

We settle into the cloud of pillows to enjoy each other's company for the first time in way too long.

We do a thorough check of his memory. I ask him every question I can think of, and he remembers everything (well except for the outfits I was wearing at any given time, but odds are he never remembered those). Once we're sure all the moments from our time together are intact, he lies back with his arms behind his head. "I feel like *me* again. Finally. I was so ..." The next word slips out in a whisper. "... scared. There was this gnawing sadness, like every thought I had was wrong. And nothing I did could fix it."

I rest my head on his chest and he brings one arm down, pressing me snuggly against him. "My mom was worried," he says. "She sent me to a psychiatrist. Even my dad said I wasn't acting like myself."

He trails off, and I can tell he doesn't want to say any more about it for now, so I ask, "How are things with your dad?"

"Good, actually. I've even spent a few weekends with him. He set me up in the spare bedroom and everything. It doesn't really feel like home, y'know, but the officers' quarters are right by the pool, and the gym on the base is pretty cool." He stops rambling and lets a small smile sneak onto his face. "It's kind of been the only good thing in my life these past few months. Knowing my dad and I are working on our relationship. Knowing we finally have one."

"I'm so glad," I say.

We lapse into silence again, but this time it's a comfortable one. I drape my legs over Clay's, luxuriating in his proximity and the warmth of the fire. He runs his fingers through my hair, staring at the strands in the firelight.

"I don't remember the last time it was dry," I murmur, my voice languid, lazy.

"When did you do this?" he asks. "I like it."

"What?" I ask.

"This." He takes a strand from the left side of my head and brings it around in front of my face so I can see it. It's gold! Not blond— shimmering, sparkling gold. The same color as my tail.

I run the shiny, metallic streak between my fingertips. "It must have happened during the ritual to restore your memories. That was some powerful magic." I tell him more about the academy, the other girls, Ondine.

"I can't believe you did all that—uprooted your whole life, put yourself at risk like that—to help me."

I rest my hands on his chest, soft cotton over solid muscle. "I would do anything for you."

When they meet mine, his lips create the same slow, constant heat as the fire crackling behind us. I can't get enough.

With the feel of Clay's lips still on my skin and a whole day's worth of new memories to treasure, I oh-so-reluctantly make my way across the Border, find my seahorse waiting in the kelp forest, and begin the long journey back to Sea Daughters, twirling my lock of golden hair.

I arrive with a plan. I'm going to ask Ondine if we can work out some kind of schedule that will allow me to see Clay in secret on weekends. Maybe we can say I'm doing some kind of research project or ... something. But first, I can't wait to tell Dionna, Jinju, Thessa, and Nixie all about seeing Clay. There will definitely be squealing involved.

The wards know me and open for me when I bring my hand down on the protruding rock and splay my fins around it. I make my way quickly through the central cavern and the tunnel system to my dorm.

"Guys! Guys, check out my hair!"

But no one's there.

It's late—way past the school's mandated turn-in time—but each of their shell beds is empty. Something's not right.

Where are they? As my urgency to find them mounts, a wave of dizziness hits me, and I sink onto the bed. A vision flashes into my mind: For an instant, I'm looking right at one of the white walls of the shell grotto, with its distinctive mosaic of seashell pieces in leaf-like patterns. Then, just like that, my mind spins back into place, and I'm staring at the walls of the dormitory again. What just happened? How did I do that?

Relax, I tell myself. It must be a side effect of the blood oath; I can see the other girls in the circle, or more accurately, I can see through their eyes (if the sight of the grotto wall was any indication). How come none of them ever mentioned they could do that? I'll have to add that to the list of things to talk to them about when I find them. At least now I have a good idea where they are.

But I can't shake my mounting unease as I head toward them. What are they all doing out of bed this late? I fly deeper and deeper down the tunnels, past the paintings of Xana and the other elegant Mermaids, into the sacred stillness of the grotto.

My breath rushes through my gills in a massive sigh. They're here. *"You guys scared me when you weren't in our room,"* I say.

"We've been waiting for you, Lia," Ondine says in the formal voice she always uses in this grotto.

"You guys waited up for me? You didn't have to do that."

"Yes, we did," Jinju says. There's a … seriousness in her expression I don't like.

"We need to talk to you about something." Ondine adds. *"But first, did our ritual work? How was your reunion with Clay?"*

"Yes, it was wonderful. Perfect. Thank you." I hope my expression conveys my deep gratitude.

"Good," Ondine says. *"I'm glad we could help you. Because now, we need your help with something, Lia. Something vitally important."*

"Of course," I say, swimming farther into the room and taking my

place in the circle. After everything they've done for me, I'll help with whatever they need. *"What can I do?"*

"The ritual we just used to restore Clay's memories isn't the only spell of the Sea Sorceress's that we could modify to do some real good."

I meet Ondine's gaze so she knows I'm listening as she continues. *"The reason the Tribunal made Clay drink that potion to block his memories of Merkind is that they're scared. They were telling the truth when they said human government officials have begun questioning increased ocean activity, what with all the Mer travelling back and forth between Above and Below now that the wars are over."*

"But the Foundation has started monitoring that more closely," I say, remembering what Em talked about so much over dinner. *"They've set up new travel guidelines and time restrictions—"*

"That is true," Ondine acknowledges. *"But those are short-term solutions. Every day, human technology gets better. Our species has only survived this long because so much of the ocean remains unexplored. It is only a matter of time until that changes."*

"We need a more long-term fix," Thessa says. *"Something that will deter humans from discovering us."*

"And we've found a spell of the Sea Sorceress's to do just that," Ondine says.

"What kind of spell?" I ask.

"What do you know about the Sea Sorceress herself? About her background?"

Her background? *"Nothing,"* I say.

"What about her name?"

I know Ondine well enough to know she won't ask me questions I can't answer. If she's asking, I should be able to figure it out, but I'm drawing a blank.

"Her name," Ondine says in response to my confused expression, *"was Himeropa."*

"Himeropa." The weight of that revelation collides into my chest. *"She was the first siren,"* I whisper.

Now that Ondine says it, a memory bubbles to the surface of my mind, something I heard in one of the restricted *konklilis* I listened to last year that suggested Himeropa and the Sea Sorceress may be one and the same. *"It's true?"* I ask, already knowing the answer in the pit of my stomach.

Ondine nods.

"The spell you want my help with …" I swallow.

Ondine's crystal-embellished eyes bore into mine. *"Is sireny."*

Chapter Thirty-Five

"You ... you know siren songs?"

My question is for Ondine, but Jinju, Thessa, Dionna, and Nixie—they're all nodding.

My breathing grows shallow, and lightheadedness threatens. *"All of you? You're all ... sirens?"*

The scariest part isn't that they nod; it's the pride on their faces while they do it.

I feel sick. *"Do the others know?"* I think of the teachers, MerMatron Gusseta, and the younger students.

"Not about sireny," Ondine answers. *"Some of the staff understand it's taken strong magic to keep us all safe here, but if they wonder if every spell we've ever used is legal, well, they've never asked. Sometimes rules need to be bent to protect innocent people—and keep them protected. If anyone should understand that, Lia, it's you."*

I look anywhere but at her and the others while my brain spins, desperate to make sense of what I've just learned. My gaze lands on the intricate patterns of shells all around me on the walls. When I came in this room for the first time, I'd thought the design was in the shape of leaves. *"Feathers ... "* I whisper.

"In homage to the seabirds Himeropa loved," Nixie says, like she's reciting the answer out of a textbook. Of course. It's the origin of the ancient Greek siren myth—the one about bird women. Himeropa and her siren sisters used to decorate their hair and *siluesses* with feathers; they even let the seabirds they loved sit on their shoulders while they sang sailors to their doom on the rocks of the sirens' island home. An island so much like this one.

"Homage? Why would you want to honor anything to do with Himeropa?"

"She was a magical prodigy," Jinju says.

"She was the worst villain in all of Mer history," I say.

"Come now, Lia," Ondine says, voice laced with disapproval. *"Haven't you learned that nothing is black and white? History has misjudged her, just like it has misjudged Xana."*

Xana, the Mer chancellor from the waters near Spain who saved her people. Xana, who was a siren. Xana, who Ondine taught me about back in the classroom under my house. How long has she been preparing me for this moment? How long has she known she was going to ask me to … siren?

"Don't misunderstand what I'm proposing, Lia. I'm not suggesting you hurt anyone. Just that you discreetly siren those on the highest levels of naval intelligence for however long you have to. You'd learn who's on the verge of any innovations or programs that could lead to the discovery of Merkind. Then you'd siren whoever you'd need to in order to ensure those programs don't happen—the engineers, the scientists, the politicians in charge of funding the projects—and you'd deter them from making progress."

I gasp. *"You can't even be considering sirening that many people."*

"It wouldn't be possible with a regular siren spell," Jinju says. *"But we've been working on this."* She turns to Dionna, who doesn't quite meet my gaze as she holds up a gleaming potion that sparkles like starlight in a bottle. *"We based it on the one the Sea Sorceress used to strip the Little Mermaid of her voice—the same one the Foundation used as the basis for stripping away Melusine's voice. Except this potion will magnify the drinker's voice. Make her siren song stronger than ever.*

Strong enough to siren countless mortals at once. The combination of that ability with the constant flow of power from our circle, and those mortals could be controlled indefinitely."

"That's terrifying," I say. "Even if I could siren multiple people at the same time, I would never do it. Have," I gulp, "have any of you ever actually sirened anyone before?" It's the question I've been afraid to ask for the last several minutes. Each girl shakes her head in turn.

"Not every Mermaid can siren, Lia," Ondine says. "It's powerful magic, usually passed down in families. You must have had an ancestor who could do it whom you've just never heard of. That is why we need you for this to work. I can't siren, and neither can any of these girls. We are sirens because we learn to sing the songs so we can preserve them, but you do not need to fear that any of us could go on land and siren a human—that is not possible."

Relief floods me. Okay. Okay. They know siren songs, maybe they've even sung them in their fervor to learn and preserve ancient magic, but they haven't sirened anyone. Maybe they just don't understand. "You think sirening all those people—scientists, government officials—you think it wouldn't hurt them. But it would." An image of Clay as the empty shell he was while under the siren spell rises to my mind's eye. "It doesn't just affect one or two decisions they make. It strips them of their free will—takes over their lives. You're asking me to keep living, thinking people with families under a siren spell, possibly for years. That's," I don't want to call them crazy. "... inhumane and cruel."

"We're not saying you should do what Melusine did to Clay," Dionna says. "You won't be messing with anyone's heart. This isn't romantic. It's political."

"It's wrong," I say, infusing my voice with pure conviction. "And I won't do it."

I wait, trusting that these smart, skilled girls I've come to know and count as friends will listen to me, will try to understand. Will ask me questions until we're all swimming in the same current.

Ondine's voice turns as icy as her tail and hair. "What makes you think you have a choice?"

Chapter Thirty-Six

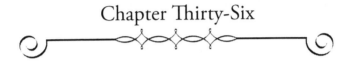

She's never spoken to me that way before, and it's the callous tone as much as the words themselves that stun me. *"W-what?"*

"I would like it if you'd see the logic of this course of action and commit yourself to fulfilling it willingly. But if you don't, we will make you."

My fins flutter, inching me backward, away from her, but Jinju and Thessa move closer together, trapping me inside the circle. I push down on my fear and straighten my shoulders. *"You can't make me. I said I'd never siren again. And I meant it."*

Ondine shakes her head—like I'm a misbehaving pet—and takes on a condescending air. *"When you did the ritual, you unlocked Clay's memories by sending him your own. But you didn't just give them to him. You gave them to all of us. Your memories make you who you are Lia. I told you: The Tribunal shielded Clay's memories instead of destroying them because they knew attempting to destroy even one memory could be fatal. One word from me, and the girls and I can destroy all the memories you gave us."* She swims closer to me through the eerily still water. *"You refuse to do this, and we will kill you."*

My gaze flies from one girl to the next as I wait for one of them to object, to say they'd never agree to kill me for refusing to siren. But no one says a word against Ondine.

"*How can you do this?*" I ask all of them, but it's Ondine who speaks. I shouldn't be surprised. She speaks for all of them. How long have I been letting her speak for me?

"*Don't put this on me, Lia. I want to treat you like an adult. But unlike Jinju, Dionna, Thessa, and Nixie, you refuse to reflect on this situation—and this very sensible solution—from an adult mindset. Your stubbornness and immaturity are disappointing.*"

For one horrible second, shame swims through me, like I should feel guilty for disappointing her. Then I remember what she's asking, and I force myself to glare instead. "*Just because I disagree with you, doesn't mean I'm not acting like an adult.*"

"*Then be reasonable. Think what we can accomplish for Merkind. If you could keep humans from making any serious advances toward discovering us, our whole culture could flourish without fear. Your parents' reign could go down in history as a renaissance.*" She moves closer to me through the water. "*You would be able to spend all your free time with Clay if you want to, and when he eventually ... passes ... well, you would have something fulfilling and important to occupy your time.*" Her tone softens, sounding as understanding as it has so many times before. "*I know you've felt aimless, Lia. Like you don't know what to do with yourself now that everything is changing. Don't you see? This is your purpose.*"

I have so many objections, so many questions. The one that spills out of my mouth is, "*Why me?*"

Ondine smiles her enigmatic smile. *"As I said, not everyone can siren. Originally, I'd planned to have Melusine join us. I knew she had the ability in her because her grandmother on her mother's side was a siren—she was just never caught."*

The painting next to Xana's ... the Mermaid with the sapphire eyes so much like Melusine's ... Does that mean all those portraits are of sirens? I force myself to focus on Ondine's words.

"That is why I provided Filius with the siren song to teach to Melusine, and why I answered his questions about the more intricate elements of the spell he attempted last year."

"You mean the one where your cousins almost killed me and Clay?"

"If they'd succeeded, Filius surely would have convinced Melusine to agree to my plan since it would help sustain the power and success of their dynasty. Their motives for power were petty and distasteful, but they could have ultimately contributed to keeping Mer hidden and safe. I waited for years for Melusine to be old enough to fulfill her role. That is when I perfected this potion." She indicates the sparkling substance in Dionna's hand.

"That's why ... that's why you spoke at Melusine's trial and pled for her to be released. So you could still use her as your siren." I thought it was family loyalty or love, like mine for Amy, but it was something much more sinister.

"Precisely." Ondine nods, like she appreciates my powers of deduction. *"But once the Tribunal stripped her of her voice, she was useless to me. It was a harrowing blow. I thought I'd have to give up on my plan altogether. Until Filius told me during one of my earliest visits to his cell with Melusine that you had sirened Clay to get him away from her."*

"You knew." Ondine wasn't shocked and mortified when I confessed my crime to her because she already knew. *"That's why you were so willing to help me."* I look at all the girls. *"That's why you all were."*

"Of course I knew. It's why I went to your parents and volunteered

to teach you in the first place. Melusine was a fantastic candidate. She had strong leg control and was learning how to mask her Mermese accent so she could fit into the human world. But you," she strokes my hair, and I shrink back, *"you were raised among humans. You've assimilated seamlessly. You're perfect for this."*

"Except I won't do it," I say.

"Yes, you will," Ondine says, gliding elegantly backward as she gestures around the circle. *"Or you'll die."*

She means it. The cold glint in her pale eyes makes me sure of it. But I promised Clay I'd never siren again. I promised myself.

Fear yanks at my insides, threatening to drown me before I can get out the next words. *"I won't do it,"* I say again.

Ondine scowls, and the room goes cold as she draws her magic to the surface.

"Stop!"

Suddenly, someone's in front of me in a flash of silver.

"I'll do it. You leave Lia alone, let her out of your circle, and I'll be your siren."

Caspian. Where did he come from? How long has he been here and how did he get in? All the fear I felt for myself a second earlier, I now feel for my best friend.

"What are you doing here?" I ask, wishing with everything I am he was anywhere else and safe.

"Melusine snuck me a letter warning me about Ondine's plan."

"What? How?"

"She did it using written Mermese characters. She knew the guards wouldn't be able to read it if they found it, but I would. She said since the plan involved you, she knew I'd want to know about it."

I still can't wrap my brain around Melusine doing anything to help me. Did she do it to get Caspian hurt?

I won't get any answers now. Ondine reclaims the conversation. *"This is a private exchange,"* she says to Caspian. *"You're intruding."* With a flick of her wrist, strands of her magic burst from her fingertips and wind their way around Caspian's entire body, binding him in translucent, pale blue ropes.

He doesn't struggle. Doesn't scream. He stays perfectly calm.

"I have something to offer you," he says. *"If you let Lia go—release all your ties to her—I'll be your siren for as long as you want."*

Casp, shut up! Stop saying that!

"You cannot siren," Ondine says.

"Sure I can. You said it runs in families? My great-great-aunt Adrianna was a siren. Everyone knows that. And I was raised in the human world, so I'm just as good at blending in as Lia."

Ondine's eyes narrow. *"And why should I choose you?"*

"Because unlike her, I won't fight you every step of the way. You spare Lia, and I'll do everything you tell me." The other girls look intrigued. I don't think they've ever considered a male siren. Ondine's listening, but she seems far from convinced. *"Plus,"* Caspian says, more urgency creeping into his voice, *"I'm a better candidate. You want a siren who can reach the highest levels of government, science, and politics? In the human world, that's much easier for a man."* Even with everything at stake, he throws me an apologetic look over his shoulder, then winces as the magic ropes dig into him and turns back around. *"It's not fair, but it's true. I'll use less magic and get info faster than Lia could because I'll automatically have better access."*

A slow smile spreads across Ondine's face as his logic hits home.

No. Sireny is everything Caspian abhors. It's against every one of his principles. I can't let him commit his entire life to being a siren just to save me.

With Ondine's focus still on Caspian, I use one powerful kick of my fin to propel myself toward Dionna and snatch the bottle from her hand. Before anyone can stop me, I uncork it and drink down every drop of the sparkling potion.

"There," I say. *"Now you have to choose me."*

What did I just do? Still … it was the only way to save Caspian.

Caspian, who looks horrified. I try to tell him with my eyes that

I appreciate what he tried to do. That he shouldn't worry. That we'll figure a way out of this before I have to siren anyone.

"Let him go," I say. *"I drank the potion. I'm all yours."*

"I have a better idea," Ondine says. *"You prove your loyalty to us or he dies."*

The ropes tighten more and more until Caspian, so strong and stoic, can't help but scream.

"Stop!" Panic and tears fill my plea. *"What do you want me to do?"*

"Prove you're committed to our cause by sirening someone high up in naval intelligence who's already been asking too many questions. Siren Officer Ericson."

Clay's dad. Who Clay is just getting to know. Who he's closer to than he has been in years. I swore to Clay I'd never siren anyone again. It's the only reason he was able to forgive me for what I did to him. All the trust in our relationship is built around that promise. If I siren his dad, Clay and I will be over.

Ondine flicks her wrist again, and Caspian screams in pain.

She raises a crystal eyebrow at me, waiting for my answer.

I have to choose: my relationship with Clay or Caspian's life.

"I'll do it." I say, unable to keep the tremor from my voice. *"I'll be your siren."*

Chapter Thirty-Seven

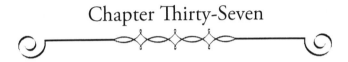

The words echo in my ears, the worst sound I've ever heard. And I've spoken them myself.

I'll be your siren.

How can I? How can I promise to do something that will brainwash an innocent man and break the trust of the love of my life? How can I swear my allegiance to a cause built on the idea of preserving Mer secrecy at any cost, even if that cost is human free will? After I've done so much to get Clay back, how can I do the one thing that will ruin us?

Caspian twists and grimaces in Ondine's magical bonds.

How can I hesitate to do anything that would save Casp?

"Don't do it, Lia," Caspian pleads with me. *"Don't be a siren."* But even as he says the words, his ocean-blue eyes shine with fear. He doesn't want to die.

And I won't let him.

I can't find any words to say to him, but his raw gaze meets mine and we communicate without words, the way we have since we were guppies. He knows I'll save him. His head drops, in profound relief and regret. How did we get here?

The fateful decision made, it's not long before I'm once again riding my tired seahorse through the dark ocean. This time, being surrounded by the other girls in the black water isn't a comfort—it's a threat. Ondine, Jinju, Dionna … they're not my friends; they're my guards. Just as Thessa and Nixie, who stayed behind in the shell grotto, are Caspian's guards. And they'll keep a careful watch on him until Ondine returns. I have until sunrise to siren Clay's dad, otherwise she'll kill Casp.

The sickening, sweet symphony of the siren song fills my ears as we ride. It's the same one Melusine used to ensnare Clay. The same one Ondine gave Melusine's father to teach her. And now Ondine and her creepy cult are teaching it to me. I don't want to learn. I want to stop my ears, block out the seductive music. But they sing it over and over, Dionna's light, airy voice harmonizing with Jinju's throatier one as Ondine's tinkling vocals round out the sound. So tempting. So deadly. By the time we reach our destination and leave our seahorses to rest in a cave, I have every ancient Mermese word of the loathsome song memorized.

Once I sing it, I'll be no better than Melusine. No better than Ondine.

Don't think about it, I tell myself. *If you think about it, you won't be able to do it. And you have to do it to save Caspian.*

Is that me talking … or is it that darkness Mr. Havelock mentioned? The darkness Melusine said is inside me now, ready to manifest and show the world who I truly am?

Horror at the very idea spikes through me. No more thinking. Doing.

Before I lose my nerve, I swim forward toward the giant steel-wire net stretched out as far as I can see. The first of the military defenses that protect the naval base where Clay's dad lives—and the first one I'll need to evade.

I can't wait to put it between me and the rest of them, even if our separation will be temporary.

"We'll be waiting for you," Ondine says. She lifts a hand to stroke my hair but lowers it when I bristle and jerk away from her. *"I wanted this to be your choice, Lia, but you're looking at it all wrong. That's why I'm making the choice for you. In time, you'll see it was the right one."*

"There's nothing right about what you're forcing me to do." Nothing right about stealing a man's free will, about pledging myself to a cult of sirens. *"It's wrong and sick."*

"It's brave," Ondine says, her pale face glowing eerily against the dark water. *"It's a way to protect your entire species from discovery. You'll be our secret weapon."* She smiles at me, and it's terrifying.

I don't want to be a weapon. *"Please don't make me do this,"* I beg, searching her face for a trace of the kind, trustworthy friend I believed her to be. *"Please don't kill Casp."*

Her exquisite features harden to marble. *"Whether Mr. Zayle—or you—die tonight is entirely your decision."* She raises a willowy arm, gesturing at the wire net and the naval base beyond it. *"We'll be waiting for you,"* she repeats before a flick of her ice-blue tail carries her back into formation with the others. They float there, watching me, jewels laid out on rippling black velvet.

I want to cry, scream, bury myself under my blankets and stay there until I wake up to discover I never left home at all.

Instead, I square my shoulders and face the net.

It's meant to keep out foreign submarines and machinery—not Mermaids—so its diamond-shaped gaps should be just large enough for me to fit through if I'm careful. But what other defenses wait for me on the other side?

Only one way to find out.

I extend my arms in a triangle over my head the way humans do on a diving board and flick myself forward with my fins. I bite my lip. What if I don't fit through the sharp wires? Twisting my torso, I make it in past my waist—and get stuck. Cold steel presses into the widest part of my tail, where my hips would be if I were in my legs. Maybe I shouldn't have eaten so many of Gussy's candied seaberries ...

I writhe, but it does no good. Are Ondine and the others still watching me? If I fail to free myself, will they swim over to help? I don't want their help. Not again. Not when everything they do for me has some perverse ulterior motive. I can do this myself.

It's like taking off one of Lazuli's miniskirts, I not-so-successfully convince myself. Then I grab hold of the wires, grit my teeth, and pull down with my hands at the same time I shimmy my lower body forward and curl my fins inward. Steel scrapes against my golden scales and the skin of my palms. It leaves a painful rawness in its wake but no blood.

I pop free, surging into the murky water ahead of me. I did it!

As I exhale, relief fluttering through my gills, I don't let myself turn back to check for the others. Instead I focus forward, narrowing my eyes as I search the darkness for the next obstacle. Now comes the real test.

Sonar. My parents worried about even low-level signals picking up on Mer activity near the Community when Mer swam up from Below in record numbers during the trial; the closer I get to an actual naval base, the more likely it is that sonar swaths the whole area, waiting to pick up anything irregular. What would I look like on their signal? An illicit diver attempting to sneak onto base in an act of espionage? A confused dolphin swimming close to shore? Or worst of all—a Mermaid just begging to be captured and subjected to government experiments?

About 200 feet ahead of me lies the opening of what must be a desalination pipe. It looks just like the one I hid behind at the Foundation when I followed Melusine and Ondine. All I have to do is swim in through that pipe and let myself out once I'm inside the base. But there's no way I can make it that far without the sonar picking up on my unwarranted presence.

That is, unless I can somehow throw off the sensors and confuse the system. But how? My mind spins. What do I have at my disposal?

Nothing, other than the sarong I've tied over my bikini top to use on land. No tools or technology. No potions. No nothing.

Except ...

Of course! When I took the blood oath, I connected my magic to the others'—and they connected theirs to mine. That well of power still lurks inside me, ready for me to call upon.

With a quick flick of my wrist, I conjure a shimmering turquoise bubble the size of my fist, just like the ones I created on the island to entertain the other girls as we lounged on the rocks in the lagoon. A pink one follows it. Then yellow and purple and green. Last week, I wouldn't have been able to manage more than a dozen of these, and even that many would have worn me out. Now, a strange giddiness overcomes me as more and more bubbles take shape around my fingertips, pouring out of that deep reservoir of magic that now resides within me. In seconds, hundreds upon hundreds of rainbow bubbles surround every inch of my body, cloaking my movements to confuse the sonar—I hope.

The rush of power intoxicates me, and a smile stretches across my face as I swim safely forward through the monitored waters to the desalination pipe. But once I reach the circular opening, sharp fear replaces that punch-drunk giddiness as I remember why I have access to such strong magic—and what it's costing me. And it scares me how easy it was to give in to the rapturous ease of that much power.

As I slip inside the pipe, I let my preoccupation dissipate along with the bubbles. I need to stay focused.

The narrow pipe curves this way and that, and despite my determination not to think too much about what I'm about to do— what I must do—my body won't let me forget it. My stomach roils, and I can't calm my skittering heartbeat. Too soon, I spot a maintenance hatch above my head and am letting myself out onto a lawn mowed to uniform perfection. The sarong I tied around my waist drips even more than my hair does, but the pre-dawn light hides me well. Still, it's not inconceivable I could run into someone—a cadet back late from a local bar or an officer up early to get some training in before sunrise. I scan the area, my gaze roving over the orderly expanse of identical squat, tan buildings laid out in rows along concrete paths and squares of more short-cut grass.

Bingo! By a stroke of luck (right when I was starting to believe luck would never strike again), I've exited near the residential section of the base, and I spot what I was looking for. The pool.

As quickly and silently as I can, I pad across the grass to the pool area, deserted at this hour. Walking again—having legs after so much time Below—feels equal parts foreign and familiar. Like slipping into a favorite pair of shoes that got lost in the back of your closet for a year. I grab two standard towels, the same tan as the buildings, from where they sit folded in perfect squares in an unlocked supply cabinet next to industrial-sized sunscreen dispensers.

With one last glance around, I secure one around my body under my arms. Then I flip my head over to twist the other around my wet hair. A flash of gold enters my vision, and I stop.

I finger the smooth metallic strand in front of my eyes. My mouth tugs downward and I swallow. I can't stand the sight of it.

Moments later, the second towel is wrapped around my head and I look like I could be anyone's daughter or visitor returning from a (very) early swim.

Now ... Clay said his dad's quarters were next to the pool. All the rectangular buildings nearby look the same except for one; it's just a little bigger and just a little browner than the rest. Could it be the officers' quarters?

I make my way over, standing tall instead of slinking around now that I'm not dripping wet. I've watched the twins sneak in after curfew too many times to not have learned that a confident walk and an I'm-not-doing-anything-wrong expression are the best cover. I channel their constant cool as I read the names off the rows and rows of the building's mailboxes. McBride, Johansson, Daniels, Ericson! Number twenty-two.

When I stand in front of his beige door, my stomach flip-flops. I knock, the clunking of my knuckles against wood far too loud in the silent half-light of the early, early morning. Rustling erupts within, and with every passing second my nerves grow tighter. As the door creaks open, they're ready to snap.

"Lia?" Mr. Ericson peers down at me, his broad bulk filling the doorway and a confused expression marring his stern features. This early, he'd probably been expecting some senior officer with an emergency to be the one knocking. Not some girl he's only met once over pretentious Italian food. Urgency replaces the confusion as his thick eyebrows shoot up. "Is it Clay? Is something wrong?"

"Clay's fine. Everything's fine," I rush to assure him. The last thing I want to do is send the man into a panic before I ...

Before I ...

I should run. Right now. Make some excuse and leave. But Ondine can sense my general whereabouts through access to my magic—access I gave her. Stupid. How could I have been so stupid? If I head back toward New Meris to get my parents' help or even try to run and hide somewhere, Ondine will be able to feel it; she'll squeeze the magical bonds she placed on Caspian tighter and tighter until she kills him. Tears prick the backs of my eyes. "C-can I come in for a minute, Mr. Ericson?"

"Sure ... " he says uncertainly, holding the door open wider and stepping aside. "Clay's okay?"

I nod as I slip past him. All the furniture in the small living room looks like he bought it in the same day on one long-ago trip to Ikea, then forgot about it. The room is orderly, functional, not very homey. Still, I can picture the two of them sitting next to each other on the oversized leather couch snacking and trying to bond over a game they each only half care about. Clay and his dad. Who he's only just starting to get to know again.

That sick feeling returns to my stomach—the one I had all those weeks I sirened Clay. I thought that part of my life was over. I vowed to Clay, to myself …

If they were just threatening my life, I'd risk it. Risk running to the Foundation before they caught me or diving right into the ocean toward my parents. I swallow. At least if I died, I wouldn't die a siren. But it's not just my life. They have Caspian.

We stand at a loss, Clay's dad and I. He has no idea what to do with me here, a teenage girl he barely knows who shows up at his house before sun-up. We hover in the no-man's land between couch and coffee table. He takes in the towels wrapped around me. "Have you been swimming?" Then, when I only nod: "How did you get in here? Clay didn't bring you, did he?" He looks around the room, like maybe Clay is hiding behind the big-screen TV. Clay's a regular visitor with security clearance, so of course Mr. Ericson would think that's how I got in this early, with no one calling him to let me on base. "I thought Clay and you broke up a while back," he says, then rubs the back of his neck uncomfortably like he's not sure if that was the right thing to say.

"I'll explain everything," I lie. "I just need a minute." In another minute, he won't care about an explanation. He won't care about anything except the sound of my voice and the commands I give him.

He pulls his bathrobe tighter around his thick torso. He's a large man—muscular and hulking—but as he stares down at me, eyebrows knit together in concern, he looks like a confused, unsure little boy. It's the same expression he bore at the dinner table when he thought Clay was leaving. I look up into his lined face. This man isn't perfect. I used to think of him as a bad guy, as the guy who walked out on Clay and his mom and barely looked back. But, he's changed. Well, he's trying to change.

A snippet of my conversation with Clay plays in my ears and, for a moment, I'm back in his arms in front of the crackling fire.

"How are things with your dad?"

"Good, actually … It's kind of been the only good thing in my life

these past few months. Knowing my dad and I are working on our relationship. Knowing we finally have one."

As I peer up at him now, I see a man who's trying to be better. Before it's too late.

A man who brushes his teeth in the morning and probably enjoys a cup of coffee and heads to work every day like my parents and laughs when a friend says something funny and has good days and grumpy days ... and is entitled to make his own choices. He has a life. A life I have no right to take control of. Just because I've known Caspian longer and care about him so much more doesn't mean the life of the man in front of me is any less valuable.

Can I do it? Can I siren him?

My continued silence as I stare up at him biting my lip has put him on edge. "Lia, do you want me to call your parents?"

I shake my head no—in response to his question, to sirening him, to all of it—even as I open my mouth to sing.

Think of Caspian, think of Caspian.

The instant I think about singing the siren song, magic floods me, filling my senses, sparking to my fingertips and tingling up my throat. This isn't my magic; it's the deep well of magic I now share with Ondine and the others. It rises within me, the most powerful of ocean waves. Sparkling and comforting, welcoming and dangerous.

In another instant, it'll crash over me, enveloping me in its embrace and carrying me off to do its bidding. All I have to do is sing those ancient words I now know so well, let that melody gush forth, and lose myself in the music.

Easy. It would be so easy.

"Lia?" Mr. Ericson's voice rings out from somewhere far away.

But his eyes. His eyes are still so close.

Hazel. Earthy green with gold flecks around dark, concerned irises. They're just like Clay's.

Suddenly, the siren song isn't the only thing welling within me. Tears are, too. A waterfall of tears. And I can't stop them from coming.

You have to. Get a grip on your emotions and sing the damn song. Think of Caspian. I tell myself again. *Do it for Caspian.*

But Caspian wouldn't want me to do this.

I don't want me to do this.

I stare again at those familiar hazel eyes.

Then I turn and run from the room.

Chapter Thirty-Eight

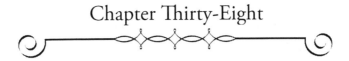

Shouting out an excuse about needing some fresh air, I tear through the back door right before tears spill from me, hot and wet down my cheeks. I catch them in my palms as they crystalize, cursing myself for breaking down this close to a human.

I hunch over my bent knees as I fight to even out my breathing. Magic still simmers right under my skin, calling out to me to use it, making me dizzy with it, so I force my consciousness back to the present moment. To this postage stamp–sized private yard off Mr. Ericson's quarters and the smell of fresh grass and the slowly lightening, grey sky. Still not close to sunrise.

I can't do it. I can't make myself siren again.

But that means Caspian will die. I can't let that happen either.

I suck in another lungful of air, shaking my head.

No. No. This can't keep happening. I can't keep getting stuck in these decisions between bad and worse ... between someone doing something despicable or having someone you love in fatal danger. I won't do it again.

There has to be a third option.

I just need to find it.

I can't leave here or she'll sense I'm making a run for it, which means I can't go get help. If I delay much longer, she'll know something's wrong. If I'm going to find a third option, I need to do it fast.

My mind spins, searching an endless sea and seeing no land in sight.

Footsteps squelch the wet grass behind me. I don't have time to explain any of this to Clay's dad.

A hand wraps around my upper arm, spinning me around.

"I just need another min—"

But the hazel eyes that stare back at me don't belong to Mr. Ericson.

"Clay?" The word escapes on the breeze, too hopeful and unbelieving to resonate. What is he doing here?

His gaze flicks all over my body, like he's checking for fatal injuries. "Are you—"

His dad clomps to the doorway. He must be more comfortable confronting his own son than me, because he says, "Clay? Now what's happening? What the devil's going on here? Do you know what time it is?"

Shooting me a quick let-me-do-the-talking look, Clay turns to face his dad. "I ... uh snuck Lia into the pool for ... y'know, a late-night swim ... "

"You what?"

"She wanted to, y'know, see the base. Kind of a private tour," Clay raises his eyebrows suggestively and understanding dawns on his father's face. "Then we ... um ... got in a fight," Clay says, nodding at how upset I look. "Can we, uh, have a minute?"

"You ... " Clay's dad flounders. He hasn't had to parent Clay in years. "I got you security clearance so you could feel at home here, not so you could ... score with girls."

I don't have time for this. How long before Ondine gets suspicious?

If I don't siren him soon, can she make me do it through my link to the magic? Will she come up here and try to force me? I should be relieved to see Clay, but I wish he'd stayed in Malibu where I know he'd be safe. The last thing I need is to get him mixed up in this and put his life at risk, like Caspian's is. I won't let Caspian die and I won't siren again, so I must come up with another option. Now.

I need Clay's dad to leave us alone so I can get Clay out of here and *think*.

Clay looks between the distress on my face and his dad with a pleading expression. "Dad, please?"

His dad scrubs a hand over his face. Takes a deep breath. Is he about to waste more precious seconds lecturing us? "Don't you dare think we won't be talking more about this in the morning," he says, voice stern. His eyes dart between us and something like relief passes over his features at the thought of escaping our teenage melodrama. "I'm going back to bed. Don't wake the neighbors."

We wait, breath held, until his footsteps retreat up the stairs. His bedroom door shuts with a click.

"Are you okay?" Clay's hands roam across my arms, my cheeks. "Sorry I said all that. I couldn't think of anything else. Last month, one of the admiral's daughters got caught with a guy in the rec room—that's what gave me the idea." His constantly moving hands reach my fists that still clutch palmfuls of hidden pearls. "What's wrong? What's going on? I woke up in the middle of the night, terrified. I thought it was a nightmare but ... "

"But what?" I have to get him out of here.

"But I felt this weird tug in my ... not in my stomach exactly but ... inside. And I knew—just knew—that you were scared. That you were in danger. I followed the tug and ... it led me here. I guess that bond between us goes both ways?"

"Clay, you have to get out of here. Now. I—I don't have time to explain, but Ondine ... she, she has Caspian. And if I don't ... she's going to kill him. I need to find another way to. Wait. What did you say?"

"That I knew you were in danger and I was scared? It's true. I drove for—"

"No! Not that. About the bond!"

"That our bond goes both ways?" he asks, raising an eyebrow. "It must. It led me to you when you were in trouble the same way it led you to me when Mel and her dad kidnapped me."

"It goes both ways … " My mind races. "Clay!" I stand up on my toes and press my lips to his, fast and grateful. "You're a genius!"

"I know," he says, smiling at the unexpected kiss. Then: "What'd I say?"

"You being here right now proves our bond goes both ways—either one of us can use it if we need to." Does that mean … It has to! I have to try.

"Right … " Clay says, titling his head and trying to follow my logic.

"What if it's the same with my connection to the sirens? Ondine designed that whole memory spell to take control of me and my magic … but what if … " I pace on the soft, dewy grass. "The bond you and I have was supposed to end when the siren spell wore off, but now it's working in a way we never expected." Clay nods, and I pace. "And the potion the Tribunal made you drink—that was supposed to only block your memories of Mer-related events, but it blocked *all* your memories of me. It had an effect we didn't anticipate."

"That's for sure," Clay says.

"So, maybe my connection to the sirens has an unanticipated effect, too. If the spell is meant to give them control over my magic, what if it goes both ways, too? What if I can use it to control theirs?" I could free Casp. And maybe, just maybe, I could break their hold on me.

His eyes widen with understanding. "How can I help?"

"What's the fastest way out of here?" I ask, shoving my handfuls of tears deep into the pockets of my wet sarong. "I'm gonna need the ocean."

If Ondine senses me running as far away from the base as I can and not stopping until I've reached an isolated stretch of beach hidden beneath craggy cliffs, all I can do is hope she comes after me to convince me to turn back. As long as she thinks there's a chance I'll still fulfill our bargain and siren before the sun rises, she won't kill Caspian. Right?

Tides. *Please let me be right.*

If Ondine comes after me now, her proximity will only make my task easier.

And that would be a blessing since this is the hardest magic I've ever had to do. I have no clue if I'll even come close to pulling it off—to breaking the sirens' hold on me and releasing the magical ropes holding Caspian hostage. But considering my other choices are letting him die or stealing Mr. Ericson's free will, I have to risk it.

"Last year, I could sense the bond stronger as soon as I got in the ocean," I tell Clay as we head to the shore. "I'm betting that getting into the water now will mean the ocean's power gives me a better awareness of my connection to the sirens." As I unwrap the towels from my torso and hair and throw them down on the sand, Clay takes off his leather jacket. I place my hand on his larger one, stalling his movement. "What are you doing?" I ask.

"What do you mean, what am I doing?"

"You have to go. Right now."

His mouth falls open. "I'm not going anywhere."

"Clay, we don't have time for this. Ondine and the others could come for me any minute. It's too dangerous." I lock my gaze onto his. "It means so much to me that you came when you knew I was in danger, but now I need you to go back home where it's safe while I deal with this."

He peers down into my face, his lips forming a thin, serious line. Good. He gets it. He may not like it, but he gets it.

"Eff that," he says.

"Clay ... "

"No. I've spent months safe at home—and I was miserable. Without you, it doesn't ... You don't have to deal with this alone. I'm here, okay? And I'm staying."

"No, you're not," I push at his arm in my urgency.

Instead of backing away he steps closer, cupping my cheek in his calloused palm. "You don't control me, remember?"

Hazel eyes bore into mine, steady and unyielding.

"I know, but—"

"Is there anything—anything at all—I can do to help right now?"

I stare out at the deceptively calm ocean, as if each little wave that crests and breaks against the sand brings them closer. "No," I say, willing Clay to run to his car and drive away from me to safety.

"Don't lie to me," he says before the word even fully escapes my lips. He furrows his eyebrows, studying me. "Tell me what I can do."

Damnit. How can he tell?

"You have to go," I shout. "I can't—" My voice breaks. "I can't worry about you."

"Yes you can. You worry about me and I worry about you. Isn't that ... isn't that what a relationship is supposed to be?" Now the desperation in his gaze, the need for understanding, matches mine as he grabs on to my upper arms and holds. "It's my decision to make," he says. "And I deserve to make it."

He's right.

He's right. All the air heaves out of my chest and shoulders. "When I ... when I tap into Ondine and the others' magic, it ... it overwhelms me. I get, I don't know, lost in it. Swept away."

The time I first accessed Ondine's power and almost lost myself to its seductive, glittering allure, the time I sensed the other girls' connected braid of magic and collapsed into Thessa's arms from the intensity of it, the time I used our newly linked powers when I restored Clay's memories and felt the dark temptation of the magics pulling me. This time, I won't only be accessing that deep well of power—I'll be trying to take control of it. Trying to grab on to stronger magic than anything I've ever known without letting it take me over. I grip Clay's hand. "I need you to be my anchor."

He nods without hesitation.

"This okay?" I ask as we swim out deeper into the ocean, the magic inside me easier to access the farther we go.

"I can handle myself," Clay assures me, his muscular arms slicing through the water. Those daily ocean swims he's been taking for months on end have honed his technique. Still, with light only just starting to leech into the sky, he must be cold.

Once we're surrounded by rippling salt water on all sides, I stop. "Here should be good."

Clay stops, too, his legs paddling beneath him. I hold out my arms and he grips my forearms right before the elbows with strong hands. I do the same, taking bone-deep comfort in the firmness, the steadiness of his touch.

Fear—fear that I can't do this, that my magic isn't strong enough, that I'll let Caspian die, that I'll die, that Ondine will come after Clay—pounds through me, my whole body reverberating with it.

Then Clay fixes me with an expression that holds none of that fear. Not a drop. Instead, it radiates all the confidence in me I lack in this moment. Hazel assurance fills my vision, offering me what I need to finally let my eyes drift closed, take a deep breath of the salty ocean air, and begin.

With a slow exhale, I release my tail, using the transformation to root myself in my own magical energy. Then I reach into my core, sensing that deep well of new magic now inside me, tempting me and terrifying me all at once. Here goes ... everything.

I shake my head, refusing to let the magic addle me. I need to find out if Ondine and the others are coming for us. And I have an idea how to do it. Earlier tonight, when I first got back to the academy and the other girls weren't in our dorm, I got a flash of the shell grotto—like I could see through one of their eyes.

Like I was in one of their minds.

None of them have ever mentioned that ability as a perk of being in their circle, and they wouldn't have been able to help themselves from showing it off to me if they could do it. Even Ondine can only use the circle connection to get a vague feeling for where the rest of us are. But the memory ritual ... that was way stronger than even the blood oath that brought me into the circle. Could opening my mind and sharing my memories with them during the ritual have created some mental link with them that they're not aware of? Ondine did say a ritual that ancient could have unforeseen effects. Time to test my theory.

I feel my way around the new magic within me and, just like Ondine taught me, force myself to see past its tantalizing sparkle—to the braided magic at its center. Six strands of power from six different Mermaids twine together, bound to each other. Fearing that Ondine will be able to sense my presence, I steer clear of contact with the thickest, brightest strand of icy blue. Instead, I concentrate on one of the thinner strands with my mind.

Dizziness churns through me, my mind's eye spinning and blurring. I'm nauseated by the time the blurry shapes condense into a scene in front of me. Dark water, speeding by fast. Two sets of fins flicking in front of me—one pink, the other ice blue, Jinju and

Ondine. That means the eyes I'm looking through are Dionna's. Can she feel my presence?

"Hurry up, Di," Jinju shouts, her voice ringing out inside my skull. *"We have to move."*

Dionna doesn't reply, but her arms move faster in front of my face—her face—as she hurries to catch up. If she sensed me, she'd say something, right? Better not push my luck. Locking onto the image of my own body, I retreat from Dionna's mind and haul open my own leaden eyelids.

Only Clay's grip on my arms keeps me upright while the world tilts around me. As his handsome face welcomes me back, the memory of what I've just seen thrums through me. Dionna, Jinju, and Ondine were swimming toward the pale glow of the impending sunrise. A dizzying glance over my shoulder reveals that same orange glow just starting to creep into the gray horizon. East. They're heading east.

Ondine knows I've deviated from her plan and left the naval base. I look up at Clay. "They're coming right for us."

Chapter Thirty-Nine

"It's your last chance to go home, to get out of here," I say. "They're after *me*, not you." Can Ondine sense he's here with me? "You can go," I say, forcing the words past my constricting throat.

Clay shakes his head. "I'm not leaving. Not when you need me." I do need him. So much that I don't ask him if he's sure or give him another out. Instead, I grip his arms harder, the muscles of his forearms pressing against my palms as I close my eyes again.

When I see that braid of power in front of me, I don't go for Ondine's magic, even though it holds my only chance at finding a way to break the sirens' hold over me. There's something I need to check on first. Someone.

Dizziness engulfs me again as I concentrate on another strand of magic in the braid and my mind's eye spins at high speed, making me even more nauseated than before. This time, the scene that solidifies in front of me turns my nausea to raw nerves.

Caspian has long-since stopped struggling; the harder he fights them, the tighter the magical bonds that hold him captive bite into his arms, chest, and tail.

No, he stays stock still as his calculating blue gaze flies around the shell grotto, no doubt searching for any possible means of escape—and finding none. Then it lands on me and glares. Hard. A strand of blond and green hair floats in front of my face on the current, and a small hand comes up to sweep it out of the way. I'm looking through Nixie's eyes.

"I'm so bored," Thessa whines in Mermese. Nixie turns to her even though I'd much rather keep watching Caspian. He didn't *look* hurt, but ... *"I can't believe we have to stay here and play guard while the others get to go with Ondine to monitor Lia. I've never been that close to shore before."*

"I know." Nixie sighs, the sound spilling from inside me. *"I never get to do anything viriss. Still,"* I get another glimpse of Caspian as Nixie looks over her shoulder, *"Ondine said guarding him is an important job."*

"Please." Thessa rolls her eyes. *"Only Ondine can release those bonds. He's not going anywhere."*

Suddenly, I'm staring at the shell-encrusted ceiling as Nixie throws her head back in annoyance. *"Yeah, you're right."* She raises her grass-green fins in front of her. *"Want to play a clapping game?"*

"Baby," Thessa mumbles.

"Am not." Nixie lowers her fins, steals another glance at Caspian, then looks away. Damnit! Why don't either of them ask if he's in pain? Don't they care at all? *"Thessa, do you ... do you think Lia will forgive us?"*

No! Did I think that too loudly? Can Nixie hear me? I hold my breath.

Apparently not because when Thessa doesn't answer, all Nixie says is, *"Well? Do you?"*

Thessa drags the tip of a shining white fin along the floor. *"When Ondine said we needed to keep our knowledge of the siren spells a secret from Lia until after the ritual, I agreed because I thought she'd understand, that she'd be ... impressed."*

What? How could I ever—

"And surprised!" Nixie says.

"Right? It's not like anyone else knows siren spells. It's such advanced magic. Think it's because she was raised too close to humans, like Ondine said?" Thessa's shoulders slump, but almost as soon as they do, she straightens them. *"If she doesn't forgive us, Lia's an idiot."*

"Thess …"

"No, I'm serious. I know you like her. I do, too. But if she can't understand how much our plan could help our kind, how important she could be … "

"Good luck with that," says a sing-song voice. *"That girl's denser than a kelp forest."*

Nixie turns around and my stomach sinks into my fins as black hair and a slender coral tail slither into my field of vision.

Thessa and Nixie both tense. *"Who are you?"* Nixie asks.

"How did you get in here?" Thessa demands.

"Don't get your tail in a twist," Melusine says with her patented mixture of boredom and superiority. *"Ondine sent me."*

Thessa and Nixie share a suspicious look.

"I visited her here with my father when I was little, so she knew I knew the way. I'm her cousin—Melusine. Surely you've heard of me."

"You're Melusine?" Nixie says with an awe that makes me want to clomp her on the head. Y'know if I weren't inside it.

"Funny, isn't it? If it weren't for Lia and this self-righteous moron," Melusine narrows her eyes at the spot where Caspian's bound form floats in the center of the room, wide-eyed and silent as he stares at her, *"I'd be the one connected to your magical circle now, and we'd all be working together so I could siren anyone I needed to in order to protect Mer secrecy."*

That's true. With all the circle's power at her disposal, how many human government officials would she have already sirened? I want to throw up.

Similar disgust passes over Caspian's face, while Thessa and Nixie nod in approval.

"*But enough about what should have been,*" Melusine continues. "*Time to focus on what is. Ondine needs you both—now. She sent me here to guard him,*" she flicks a dismissive fin in Caspian's direction, "*so you can both go join her.*"

What? No. They can't. They can't leave Caspian alone with Melusine. I don't know what she's up to, but one look in those calculating sapphire eyes confirms she's got a plan.

Thessa and Nixie don't know her the way I do, though. Still, they hesitate, and I stop breathing as Thessa opens her mouth to respond. "*Ondine told us to stay here and watch him ... *"

"*Yes, and was that or wasn't that before she told me to rush over here and send you to her?*" Melusine spaces out the words slowly, condescendingly, and pink-tinted shame creeps into both Thessa and Nixie's cheeks. Then Melusine's voice speeds up with urgency. "*We don't have time to go back and forth on this. Lia is trying something crazy that nobody expected and now Ondine needs your help right away.*"

Oh no. That means Ondine must know I left the base and have a new plan. How much of it can she sense? Does she know I'm going to try to tap into her power—our power—to break their hold over me and Casp?

"*Why didn't you help her?*" Thessa asks Melusine.

"*I haven't bonded my magic to hers.*" I can practically hear her adding "idiot" to the end of her sentence. "*Ondine said she needed the entire magical circle together to stop Lia. That's why she sent me here to play guard, so you two could join her.*"

"*What's Lia doing?*" Nixie asks.

Melusine lets out an impatient groan. "*I don't know because when Ondine—who I trust implicitly—told me there was an emergency and she needed my help, I didn't waste precious time asking a million inane questions.*"

Don't leave! I want to shout at Nixie and Thessa. *Don't leave him alone with her. Please.*

"*But please,*" Melusine continues, "*if you two would rather stay here while all the action is going down on shore and leave your sworn circle in danger, be my guest. Just don't be surprised if Ondine strips you of your magic when she gets back for disobeying her at such a crucial moment."* She pouts her lips and examines her perfectly sculpted fingernails. *"Up to you."*

Thessa grabs Nixie's hand and the two jet toward the exit. When Nixie glances over her shoulder again, I catch one last glimpse of a stoic but terrified Caspian as Melusine approaches him. He renews his violent struggles against his bonds.

I have to help him! I can't just sit pretty in Nixie's head when Caspian's in trouble. What is Melusine planning to do to him? I push myself full force out of Nixie's consciousness.

But in my haste to help Casp, I forget to picture my own body. I spin out of Nixie's mind into … nothing. Darkness closes in all around me. And not darkness like all the lights are out in the grottos because some mini earthquake everyone slept through caused a power outage. Darkness like a fathomless void. Darkness that pushes in on all sides with no sense of space or self or escape.

Have to get out, have to get out, have to get out. But how can I get out when I'm not in? When I'm not anything? I visualize my own face, my own head, torso, tail. But without knowing where I am, I can't sense how far away my body is or how to get back to it. A thought echoes soundlessly through me: If my consciousness is trapped somewhere that doesn't exist in any real place, how long do I have before I stop existing altogether? Panic, fear, powerlessness all swirl around me as I claw at nothing, until …

"Lia … Lia … " A voice calls out from somewhere far, far away.

Then louder: "Lia! Lia! Get back right now!" And something tugs at me, hard. A lifeline in the darkness. I grab on, following its pull until I slam back into my body, gasping as if yanked from the brink of drowning.

And into Clay's arms.

I clutch at him, and he holds me against his chest. "Are you all right? You turned paper white and you went all limp. I didn't know what to do, so I tried our bond again … "

"I'm okay. It was … I was … but you got me back. You did it." His hands cup my head, his fingers tangling into my hair as if doing so will keep me safe.

As soon as I catch my breath, I let it all out on a sob. "Melusine has Caspian."

Clay wraps his hands around my upper arms and holds me at arm's length so he can peer down into my face. Fear scars every centimeter of his own.

"What?"

"Ondine sent her to go guard Caspian so the other two girls in the circle could join her here. Maybe Ondine's planning some sort of spell with the whole circle after she comes to get me … tries to force me to … " I'm talking so fast that the words are getting lost. "They left Caspian alone with Melusine. And I know Melusine's up to something. I told him she was! He started talking to her at school, sitting with her … I warned him she was trying to take advantage of him, that she had some kind of scheme or something. Whatever she's been planning to do to him, she's going to do it now."

Clay curses, the burst of volume incongruous out here on the silent sea, swallowed up before it even leaves his mouth. If anyone distrusts Melusine as much as I do—more, even—it's Clay.

At the same time, both our gazes dart around us, our mouths thinning into grim lines. Without either of us saying a word, I know we're both letting the painful, helpless reality settle over us: We're too far from Caspian. There's no way we can get to him now.

Not when I still need to use my connection to the sirens to break their hold on me, then get Clay and myself to safety before they reach us. I only have one way to help Caspian now, and it's to keep going with my plan. "If I can break their magic hold on me," I bite the inside of my cheek—that's a big if, "I can try to break the bindings Ondine created to hold Caspian prisoner. Then, whatever Melusine's planning, at least he'll have a chance to fight."

"Can you really do that?" Clay asks, like I just said I planned to fly to Neverland. I don't blame him. What I'm suggesting may be just as impossible. I still don't understand much about how the connection works.

"I can try," I say. "I have to try."

Clay grips my forearms again, and I do the same to his. "I've got you." His words seep into me as my eyes close and my mind sharpens, seeking out that braid of our combined magic one final time.

"What's that?"

My eyes snap open again at Clay's words.

Now I'm the one cursing.

Until I'm not. Until all I'm doing is staring at a flash of blond and blue in the distance. Until all I'm doing is screaming for Clay to hold his breath as a massive, twenty-foot tidal wave rears up—a menacing gray wall of water—and comes crashing down on us.

Chapter Forty

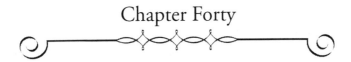

Clay's fingers slip off my forearms as water engulfs us. It fills my mouth and throat and nose before rushing out through my gills. All I can do is hope Clay had time to heed my warning and hasn't swallowed any.

I wrench my eyes open, searching the murky water for him. In the aftermath of the wave, sand swirls in front of my face and I can just make out his form ahead of me, small with distance and growing smaller by the second, his legs lashing out around him, struggling against the tide as it pulls him farther and farther away.

I have to get to him. I raise my tail, ready to smack it down with all my might and propel myself toward him. But before I can, cold hands yank my fins and I jerk backwards. Tightening my stomach muscles, I use the momentum to spin in the water.

And face Ondine.

Magic crackles all around her, her skin and even the whites of her eyes glow an eerie blue with it. I swallow. Because I bound myself to her, she can use all that magic to kill me right this instant.

"I'm so disappointed in you, Lia," she says, her exquisite, doll-like

features twisted into a sneer. *"I believed in you. I put my trust in you to save our species from discovery. And you betrayed that trust."*

"What are you going to do?" I don't bother to hide the tremor from my voice, not from someone who can read my fear as well as she can.

"Whatever I do now Lia, you've brought it on yourself by refusing to protect your kind."

"You mean by refusing to siren." The last thing I want to do is piss off the psycho with the raging powers, but I'm not betraying my people—I'm sticking to what's right the only way I know how.

"And for that, you knew the consequences. We had a deal. It is sunrise." She gestures to where early-morning sunlight illuminates the water above our heads. *"Caspian will die."*

Those words—spoken with such certainty—break something inside me. I grit my teeth as tears pour unbidden from my eyes, dozens of glimmering pearls now shining in the indigo water around us like stars. *"You mean if Melusine hasn't killed him already, right?"* I shake my head in a vain attempt to banish the pain of what I'm saying.

"What?"

"Don't play dumb with me. I'm done. I'm so done with you only telling me what you think I need to know. Revealing information in bits and pieces. I have news for you: That's not truth. It's not trust. It's control. And I've had enough of being controlled."

I picture her restraining Caspian and ordering me to siren. I picture the Tribunal stripping Clay of his memories and mandating that I stay away from him. I picture everyone in my life telling me to move on, telling me how I should feel.

I've had enough.

Lunging forward, I grab Ondine's forearms the way Clay so recently held mine and—before I can hesitate or talk myself out of it—I dive into the connection we forged with our spellcasting.

Ondine's magic pulses at the center of the braid, a sparkling ice blue I would know anywhere. I latch on to it as I would a sailing rope, and in an instant, my whole world consists of that dazzling power, glittering everywhere. So beautiful. Like Ondine. She knows so much. Surely she can't be wrong. Surely if I just do what she asks, everything will be fine. Everything will be shimmering and beautiful. If I just siren for her—what? No. No. I can't lose myself to Ondine's mesmerizing magic. I'm here to free Caspian from her hold. And to free myself. But as I search all around me, nothing stands out. No strands of specific spells, no way for me to sense how I might target those spells, nothing. I grow warm with panic. How much time do I have before Ondine manages to expel my presence? I was kidding myself when I thought I even had a hope of figuring this out. Let's face it—I've only been studying magic for a few months. My understanding of it isn't sophisticated enough for me to discern specific spells here, let alone disable them. If I could cry inside my subconscious, I would now. Tides. What am I going to do?

And why is it so … hot? It's … it's not me; it's the magic. Ondine's magic—always so icy—is hot. White hot. Like a lightbulb about to burst. I retreat until I'm once again looking at it pulse at the center of the braid. What's going on? What could cause it to …

In a flash of memory, Ondine's words come back to me from that not-so-long-ago night on the beach, when she explained why we'd need the other girls' help to restore Clay's memories:

Taking too much power from any one Mermaid poses too high a risk. Your magic is rooted to who you are, and when you cast a spell, you unleash it outward, pushing it out into the universe to do what you want it to. That is why Mer who practice magic often feel drained after an intense casting. They have overextended their own power.

Could Ondine be overextending her power? Like when my laptop gets overheated and starts burning my tail? Her magic could still be depleted from leading us in two intense rituals—the blood oath and the revamped dagger ritual to restore Clay's memories. And today she used the blood oath connection to track me when I left the naval base, she's restraining Caspian with her magic, and she just manipulated the power of the ocean—the strongest power known to Mer—to create that massive tidal wave.

She is. She's using too much magic! And now, trying to block me from accessing her power must be putting her over the edge.

There are even tales of Mer in olden days who used so much magic—sent so much outside themselves—that their bodies couldn't regenerate it … According to legend, some lost their magic for good.

I may not have a sophisticated enough knowledge of magic to figure out how to disable specific spells, but what if I could …

If she's overextended, her grip on her power is at its weakest, so … what if I could seize *all* her magic? End *all* her spells at once? Her control of Caspian, her control of me. It's like in those spy movies the twins watch where some sexy agent in tight black leather tries to disable a bomb. If I don't know which wire to pull, what if I pull them all? No, that's crazy. And dangerous.

And my only option.

That rope of magic grows impossibly brighter. Blinding. I can feel it sizzle and it scares me. It scares me more than anything has ever scared me.

I grab on to it—and scream.

Chapter Forty-One

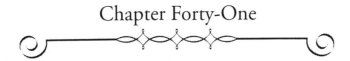

I don't know if my screams are in my skull or if they vibrate through the water that some distant part of my brain tells me still surrounds us. I don't know if the magic I'm doing now has some fancy name or if some scholar has written about it on an ancient algae scroll. I don't know if this will work because I don't know how long I can hold on.

All I know is that I have to.

Even as her power sears through me, scalding me from the inside, I pull hard. Taking it into myself with all my strength. *Don't let go, don't let go. You can do this,* I tell myself.

Ondine wanted to use magic to control me? Not happening. I may still not know much about casting spells, but all those weeks of tapping into Ondine's magic to watch over Clay—a little longer every day—means I know how to keep ahold of it, even now as it bucks and burns and makes me writhe.

Pain lances across my face. I wrench my eyes open in time to see Ondine's fingernails come up to claw at my cheek again, leaving what must be another bloody gash in their wake.

Fury contorts her delicate features, the blue strands of her hair twisting around her head in the current like snakes.

When her sharp nails don't make me stop pulling at her power, the hideously beautiful, blue Medusa wraps her hands—hands that have held mine in comfort—around my throat, their heels pressing against my windpipe and their fingers blocking my gills.

My hands compose a physical link where they grip her forearms, anchoring our magical connection, so I can't use them to fight her off—a fact she's probably counting on. Instead, I beat my tail against the current, thrashing my body to shake her off me, sending us both spiraling downward through the dark ocean.

But her vice around my throat only tightens, and soon my movements weaken, my body going limp as my vision blackens around the edges.

I can't fight her off.

Victory glints in her ice-blue eyes.

I can't fight her off *physically*. But what about magically? If all I have left is a few seconds before I black out, I'm going to damn well use them. I pour all my remaining strength into the connection, pulling at that burning, white-hot power.

Pulling.

Pulling.

Pulling it out of her and into myself. Her eyes widen to sand dollars as the last strands of magic snap and the rest of that shining rope of power catapults into my chest, coiling within me. The fingers around my throat loosen, and the eerie blue glow of her skin and eyes dims.

My ears buzz with power, so loud that Ondine's scream is silent: a gaping mouth and shocked, cold gaze. Her pale, gray-tinged form is the last thing I see as she falls away from me, sinking down into the vast void of ocean below us.

Then my vision goes dark as I pass out on a tide of roiling magic.

Chapter Forty-Two

"Unngh." My head thumps and my insides heave.

"Lia?" A cool hand melts onto my feverish forehead, and I cling to the relief it brings. "She's awake!" Rustling. Feet padding against sand, then shadows crouching around me. "Lia, can you hear me? Can you open your eyes?"

It takes seconds and years for my eyelids to lift. When they do, Clay's face hovers over me. It's quickly joined by Caspian's. And … Melusine's.

I jolt up to sitting, the sudden movement sending pain shooting through my head. "Get away from them!" I shout at her.

"Whoa, whoa, it's okay," Clay says. Melusine raises an eyebrow at me and takes an exaggerated step back. She's wearing that standard beige *siluess* from the Foundation, but tied around her damp hips is a leather jacket—Clay's leather jacket.

"What's going on?" I demand, finally taking in the scene around me. The sun shines higher in the sky now. I'm sitting on the same beach Clay and I came to after leaving the naval base and Clay kneels next to me, Caspian crouching on my other side, one of the towels

I'd taken from the base now wrapped around Casp's waist. Someone has draped the other towel over my tail. I close my eyes and breathe, transforming into my legs and tying the towel around me in case I need to chase Melusine away.

"As soon as the waves died down," Clay says, "I swam back out to look for you, but," he gestures at his legs, or more accurately, at his lack of a tail, "it took a while. It felt like a few hours." He shrugs, but anger—at the situation? At himself?—knits his brow and tightens his jaw. "By the time I reached you, you were just … floating there. I thought … "

"She's okay," Caspian says, voice steady. The two of them share a look of deep relief.

"I carried you back here, but I couldn't wake you. Then Caspian and Mel showed up."

"As soon as I got free, we took two of the school's seahorses and raced here as fast as we could," Caspian says. "I'd heard those other girls saying this was where Ondine was, and I had to get here to help you."

"But what's *she* doing here?" I glare at Melusine, whose face stays so calm it makes me want to scream. "I saw her come after you," I say to Casp. "I used the magical connection with the other girls to see through Nixie's eyes, and I saw Melusine. She sent the other girls after me when Ondine told her to so she could … " I still don't know what her plan was, but I know she was up to something. "… so she could hurt you," I finish.

"No." Caspian shakes his head, a few strands of his damp blond hair falling forward. "She sent the other girls *away* so she could *help* me. She came to help me escape."

Huh? My disbelief must register on my face because Melusine opens her mouth, as if to explain. Then she closes it again and nods to Caspian as she crosses her arms over her enviable chest. *Oh, right.* Now that we're above water, her voice doesn't work.

"After Melusine told me that Ondine planned to make you take the place they'd intended for her, as a siren," he forces out the word, "she knew I'd go to you, and I guess she didn't trust me not to get myself in trouble." He half-smiles in a sheepish, guilty way. "So, she followed."

That so does not sound like Melusine. Yes, now that the first three months of her probation are over, she's allowed free movement underwater provided she checks in once a day at the Foundation, attends her therapy sessions, and doesn't set a toe on land (so she doesn't encounter humans). But considering her past crimes, if the Tribunal ever found out she'd sought out sirens, she'd be imprisoned for sure. On top of that, those girls could have seriously hurt her if they knew she'd come to help Caspian escape. Why would someone so selfish put her own safety at risk? "She wouldn't do that."

"Yes she would." Caspian says the words slowly, like he's putting conscious effort into staying patient with me. "She did."

"Why?" Clay voices my question.

Melusine's mouth moves in a silent response. She hits her thighs with clenched fists.

"Because she and I are … friends," Caspian says. Her sapphire eyes meet his lighter ones and she looks like he just admitted they were bank robbers or murderers. Of course, she *is* an attempted murderer.

"But I saw you." An image rises up of Caspian fighting wildly against his bonds as the other girls left them alone together. "Casp, you looked terrified of her."

"I could tell she was lying. She's scarily good at it, but … anyway, I knew she wanted the other girls to leave, so I played along."

So, she did have a plan she was hiding, but it was to … help? And Caspian figured it out? He *trusted* her? "I thought … "

"Yeah, I know. But she really came to get me out of there." He shoots a grateful smile in her direction, and she nods once before looking away. I might throw up, and I don't think it's because of the waves of new magic still undulating within me. "There was just nothing she could do until Ondine's bonds magically dissolved. That's when we fled and came here. I'm guessing you had something to do with that part?"

"Did you see Ondine on your way here?" I ask.

That limp, gray form falling away from me through the water ... is she dead? Unconscious in the ocean somewhere? Powerless and on the run?

Caspian and Clay—and even Melusine—shake their heads. "We didn't see her," Caspian says.

Before I can explain that Ondine weakened herself by overextending her magic, that I seized it to end all her spells at once, Clay grips my shoulder. "Lia!" He stares at where four streaked heads rise out of the ocean.

Chapter Forty-Three

I spring to my feet and immediately have to clutch on to Clay to hold my balance; the magic flooding my system throws off my equilibrium as it rushes through my veins. Caspian, too, rises from his crouched position and takes a step forward in front of Melusine and me, putting himself between us and the figures rising from the surf.

Four sirens step out of the seemingly calm sea, their streaked hair flying behind them as a strong wind picks up. I shiver. They are part fairytale, part horror movie. Jinju, Thessa, Dionna, and Nixie carve dark outlines against the pale sky and silver ocean, their hands clasped in a perfect, impenetrable line. Only Nixie has attempted to loop strands of thick seaweed around her waist; the rest stand bare aside from their glinting, jeweled *siluesses*. A gasp sticks in Clay's throat, and he and Caspian quickly avert their gaze from the sirens.

Are they here to attack me for seizing Ondine's magic? To cast another spell against me? Against us? Clay, Caspian, and Melusine must wonder the same thing because all of us tense, readying ourselves for a battle we don't know how to fight.

Magic—rich and thick and unfathomably deep—pushes against my skin from the inside, but I have no idea how to use it. If the last few days have taught me anything, it's that I know even less about spellcasting and rituals than I thought. But these girls do. They've been studying magic under Ondine for years. I shift from one foot to the other, not knowing whether in a second's time, I'll need to flee or fight. What's their next move?

All four of them come toward us across the sand, and Clay and I grab hands, interlacing our fingers. Stronger together for whatever we're about to face.

Jinju's dark eyes lock onto mine, holding my gaze for an infinite moment before lowering, cloaked by thick lashes. All four girls sink to their knees.

Caspian shoots me a confused look. Understanding seems to dawn on Melusine, whose features now form a stunned expression as she stares at the Mermaids in front of us. What are they doing? Are they ... bowing?

They kneel in a half-circle around me. *"We've come to pledge ourselves to you, Aurelia Nautilus,"* Jinju intones, her Mermese formal.

"W-what?"

"Ondine's gone," Dionna says. *"We looked for her, but ... "* her voice breaks and she sniffs. *"Then we came here and waited for you to wake up."*

"We can't sense Ondine anywhere," Thessa says. *"But all her power is ... in you."*

"You control our circle now, connect all our magic," Jinju says, maintaining that reverent tone. Why is she ... her words combine with an image in my mind's eye of that braid of magic. Oh! All the strands of the other girls' magic wove around the central strand of Ondine's that pulsed at its center. Her magic—now mine—held it together, allowing them to draw from each other's powers. Without it, their coveted circle would disintegrate and none of them would be strong enough to cast the kinds of ancient spells and rituals Ondine

was grooming them for. *"We-we know you didn't want Ondine controlling you."* Jinju chooses her words carefully. *"Now you can be the one in charge of how we use our circle's magic."*

Me? I barely know the first thing about the magic that now fills my every pore, making me feel both unbearably heavy and like I might float away from reality all at once. I only took it from Ondine because I didn't see any other way to save Caspian, to save myself, to save all the humans she wanted sirened. I never wanted to take Ondine's place. I don't know how.

"We can help you learn to control your new magic once we're back at the academy," Dionna says, giving me a little half-smile of reassurance like she did the first day we met, when she was the first one to welcome me. *"We'll all figure it out together."*

I can visualize it. Heading back to Sea Daughters Academy, spending my days basking in the sunshine of the waterfalled lagoon and my nights tucked away in the shell grotto practicing untold magic with these girls. But the spells they're talking about—the only ones that require this much magic—are ancient rituals like the ones created by the Sea Sorceress. Dangerous rituals. Rituals like the one Ondine used that granted her access to my most cherished memories and thus the power to kill me, or like the one that required Mr. Havelock and Melusine to stab Clay so his death could serve as a sacrifice. There are reasons these kinds of spells were outlawed. I may not agree with every one of the Tribunal's decisions or all the ways they decide to mete out justice, but I do agree with the spirit of the laws I was raised to uphold. I can't lose sight of that.

Jinju's words echo at me. I'm in charge of how the circle uses its magic now ...

My head swims with the idea. I'm not ready to be in charge of this kind of power. Even Ondine—who was older, more experienced, probably more intelligent, and definitely more educated than I am—didn't use this power properly. She let it convince her that just because she could do something, she *should*. How long before having this much magic at my disposal makes me think the same thing?

I peer down at the Mermaids kneeling at my feet. They have betrayed me, conspired against me, threatened to kill me and those I love. They are sirens who have broken the law by learning the secrets to forbidden knowledge. But they are not only sirens. They are girls, girls who put their trust in the wrong person. Just like I did. And I don't want to hurt them.

But I don't want to lead them either.

I release my grip on Clay's hand and take a step toward them. Beside me, Caspian stiffens, but he doesn't move to stop me. Neither does Clay. Their trust warms me as I struggle to tamper down the icy magic enough to stay steady on my feet. When I glance over my shoulder to offer them both a small nod, Melusine studies my every move, eyes narrowed.

Turning my attention ahead of me, I take another step toward the sirens. And another. Then I step over Jinju and Dionna's clasped hands and keep walking past them.

Toward the waves.

Confusion rustles behind me as the other girls, unsure, rise to their feet and turn, their gazes boring into my back.

The magic swirls inside me with every step, making me lightheaded.

No one speaks as I stop at the shoreline, the cool water lapping at my feet. In the silence, I let the sea's call fill my ears, my heart. Crystal blue endlessness stretches out before me. It is the ultimate power source. The ultimate magic.

The new magic within me responds to it, cresting and crashing along with the waves, matching the ocean's constant heartbeat. I don't know much about spellcasting or ancient rituals, but I know where this magic belongs. And it isn't with me.

With feet firm and spine straight, I open my palms toward the mighty sea.

Nothing happens.

The magic stays with me, sparking beneath the surface of my skin, imbuing me with unnatural, unimaginable strength. I bring my focus back to the sea, to the call of the ocean all Merfolk hear—the call that tempted me every day of my life as I grew up on land. I send the magic to answer it.

Just as I pulled all of the power from Ondine while she tried to strangle the life from me, now I pour it out. My body tingles with burning ice as the magic picks up speed, cycloning through my chest, down my arms, and out my open palms.

I crash to my knees as it all flows out of me and disappears beneath the waves.

Chapter Forty-Four

Life doesn't return to normal. Even now, as I walk down a street in Malibu where I've walked a zillion times before, surrounded by the familiar trees and parked cars and passersby in designer sunglasses and flip-flops, I can't trick myself into thinking this is still my life.

"How long do we have?"

Caspian glances up at the afternoon sky. "Two hours. Then we should head back."

I nod. No time at all.

He stops when we reach the home on the corner lot. The same house Clay and I met at before, the one left empty when one of the families from the Community moved Below. "I'll meet you right back here," Caspian says.

I nod again. "Where are you going to be?"

With his head, he gestures in the direction of the Foundation. "Visiting some friends. That way our story's actually true."

I don't ask which *friend* he wants to visit. "Be careful. Please."

"Lia, she told you—"

"That she came to help you escape, that she risked missing

her curfew and violating her probation. Yeah, I know." When I interrogated her again underwater, she answered all my questions right. That doesn't mean I trust her. Not for a second. "Be careful," I repeat.

Now he's the one who nods, his sandy blond hair falling into his eyes.

"Casp ... " This is the first day we've been alone together since our fight in the lagoon, since he told me he ... I wanted to bring it up the whole way here but kept losing my nerve. Still, he deserves to hear the words. "I'm so, so sorry for the way I spoke to you when you told me not to link my magic to the others'. You were right. Obviously." Does this apology suck as much as I think it does? I need to do this properly. "I should have listened to you. You were saying something I didn't want to hear, but I needed to hear it. And I should have listened," I repeat. "I'm sorry."

"You said some things I didn't want to hear," he says, voice low. Like that I didn't love him the way he wants me to. That I couldn't accept the future he wanted for the two of us.

"I—"

He holds up a hand. "I needed to hear them, too." He rakes a hand through his hair, which is still damp from our swim here, so it smooths back from his forehead. "And ... I know you care about me."

"Of course I do!"

"When I rushed in like a fool to save you and got myself captured instead, you drank that potion to protect me." His ocean blue eyes meet my brown ones, emotion flooding them. "You chose me when it counted. You love me. I wish you were in love with me." He breaks my gaze, takes a deep breath. "But, I'll get over it." I place a tentative hand on his arm as he says, "It hurts, y'know?"

The last thing I want is to hurt Caspian. But I have, and I don't know what else to say to let him know I'm sorry, and that a part of me wishes I felt differently. Since I have no more words, I hug him. Hard.

He hugs back, and as I let go, the space between us starts to feel comfortable again. We're not totally there yet, but we'll get there.

"So, um … " He's clearly hunting for a way to change the subject. Probably a good idea.

"Um … Oh!" I say, latching on to a topic. "There's one thing I still can't figure out." I shove my hands in the back pockets of my denim skirt. I don't want to talk about Melusine around him, but I don't want her to be a point of contention between us; he needs to know we can talk about anything. "In the shell grotto, Melusine told Thessa and Nixie that Ondine sent her to get them because I was planning something crazy that no one expected. I thought that meant Ondine had somehow figured out I was going to see if our magical connection went both ways and allowed me to control her magic. But … if Melusine never spoke to her, how did she know?"

"She didn't. She made the whole thing up." I raise a skeptical eyebrow. "Really! I asked her the same thing," he says. "Her exact words were, 'Lia doing something crazy that no one expects? Pretty safe bet.'" He chuckles. I do, too.

Clay's lips are on mine the instant the door clicks shut. Hands run up my bare arms and tangle in my hair as biceps cloaked in thin cotton press against my eager palms. His tongue welcomes me, drawing me in until I'm utterly lost in his kisses, drowning in the sensations of soft lips and rough stubble. I am breathless by the time his mouth leaves mine—only to immediately find my neck, narrowing my world down to gasping electricity. He presses me back against the door and I can't get enough of him.

It's been so long.

It's been too long.

Wrapped in his cinnamon scent and his strong arms, I never want to be apart again.

Once we're both settled in the den at the back of the house and have regained the power of speech, I catch him up on what's happened Below in the last two weeks.

"Any of the other girls talking to you?" Clay asks. An image of the cold glares I get daily at the academy flashes through my mind. To them—these girls I thought I knew—I'm the one who stole away their powers.

"Not yet."

"But they didn't ... talk to ... anyone else, right?" Clay keeps the question casual, but fear lurks in his hazel eyes. If even one of them tells the authorities we got Clay his memories back, the Tribunal will come for him. Strip his memories again.

Then they'll come for me.

"No. They're keeping their word." So far. Clay runs a nervous hand through his hair. "Hey, it'll be okay," I say, taking his hand in mine. "They can't tell anyone about the ritual without admitting to performing dark, illegal magic. They don't want to implicate themselves in all this."

This whole situation has been such a mess. As soon as all that power left me, Caspian, Clay, and Melusine had to rush to hide the other girls under a nearby dock; without the magic from the circle, only Jinju could still maintain her legs. Since they were raised Below, none of them had ever practiced much.

Once we were all concealed under that dock, we struck a deal. In exchange for their silence about Clay and his memories, I agreed not to tell the authorities about their knowledge of illegal siren songs. Knowledge that would mean imprisonment or some harsh, archaic punishment none of us can conceive of.

Clay twists his thumb ring. "They still know those songs. It's ... scary, y'know?"

"Yeah. It is." I lean against the back of the couch, exhaling. "But none of them can actually siren. That's why Ondine needed me or Melusine in their circle. Now that the circle's magic is gone, they can't recruit anyone else." Clay nods, as if forcing the words to sink into his head.

"As for the rest of it … " I continue, "if they still want to study the other spells Ondine was teaching them, I can't stop them, but at least I know they don't have the power to carry them out without Ondine's magic connecting all of theirs. Doing any of those ancient spells alone would be like … "

"Like trying to play a symphony by yourself," Clay finishes.

"Yeah." Deep in thought, I twirl my hair around my finger, but when gold glints in the corner of my eye, I let the strand fall away from my touch. At least the roots have started growing in brown again. I rest my head on his shoulder and he swings an arm around me, pulling me closer against him.

"So, still no sign of her?"

I shake my head. Ondine has vanished. While we were under that dock, the others and I agreed to tell the authorities as close to the truth as we possibly could so they'd have the best chance of finding her. We told them she'd said she wanted to teach us some type of new magic, but hadn't given us any details. She'd brought us out toward the shore on a kind of field trip, saying the spell needed to be performed at dawn; then she'd swum off, telling us she'd be back, but she'd never returned and we hadn't been able to find her.

The fact that the spot she'd brought us was so close to the naval base sparked the authorities' suspicions, but if anything, it's made them take her disappearance more seriously, hoping once they find her, she'll provide answers about what kind of magic she was planning.

She's now officially a missing person, and they've launched a full investigation. If she had any contraband—*konklilis* or ancient scrolls on forbidden magic—they'll find it. The school's cooperating, letting them turn the entire place upside down. That comforts me. I don't want anything dangerous that she's collected in her long life to fall into the wrong hands. And I don't want any of it to stay where Jinju, Dionna, Thessa, or Nixie could find it and be tempted to use it. They've spent too long under her warped influence—they deserve a fresh start. What they do with it will be up to them.

"At least you won't have to deal with those girls anymore," Clay says. "I don't like the idea of them near you."

He's right. Starting next week, I won't have to endure their spite-filled silence. I'll be leaving Sea Daughters Academy to join my parents in New Meris. I told my mom and dad that since I enrolled there for Ondine, there's no reason for me to stay. One of the history teachers has stepped in until the school's board can decide on a new headmistress. The wards Ondine used to protect the school during the war are gone, but the sea's safer now, so that's okay. No one'll be allowed up top anymore, since without those spells there's not enough to ensure they're hidden from the occasional marine biologist or boater. A vivid image rises in my mind of that breathtaking lagoon, once filled with frolicking mermaids, now empty. I shrug before tears can well. Secrecy is a part of Mer life.

My parents were only too happy for me to join them in New Meris, like they'd originally wanted. Ondine's suspicious disappearance shook them. They've asked the authorities to keep them apprised of any new developments, but so far there's been nothing to report.

"It's weird to think I'll be living in a palace," I say. The palace where Clay and I both almost died at the Havelocks' hands.

"Yeah," he strokes my skin where his hand rests on my shoulder, "but it'll be really nice for you to be back with your sisters and your parents." He sighs. "I just wish you weren't so far away."

"I'm here now," I say, angling my face up toward his and kissing him, deep and lingering. But his responding kiss is laced with tension. Something's wrong. "I'll come visit any time I can get away," I say when our lips part, rushing to reassure him. "Caspian already agreed to help cover for me like he did today. To come with me and say we're visiting Amy and our friends in the Community. I should be able to make it back here every two weeks at least."

"It's not enough."

I stiffen. "Clay … " I lift my head from his shoulder, sitting up. "I know it's not ideal. I know you want to see me more. *I* want to see *you* more. But it's too dangerous right now. This is the best I can do."

"And it's not enough," Clay says again. "How ridiculous is it that it's dangerous for me to see my own girlfriend? I don't want to be in a relationship where I only get a few hours once every two weeks. And where we have to," he gestures around the small den with its closed curtains and locked door, "hide out."

The room grows cold all around me. What's he saying? "What are you saying?" The words stick in my throat. He doesn't want to … he *can't* want to … break up. Can he?

"Lia … " The regret in his voice pulls my name down at the end. *No, no, no.* "I love you. You know how much I love you." He scoots away from me on the couch, angling his body so we're facing each other. Those few inches of distance separating us stretch to a chasm. "And loving you has opened me up to this entirely different world and culture. When I lost my memories of all of it, the one thing that made me feel better—that made me feel like *me*—was swimming in the ocean every day."

"I saw you," I murmur. "Through the bond." What's he getting at?

"It's like … like I knew there was something out there. Like I knew there was something I didn't know. Something I was missing or had lost and was trying to find. I tried so hard."

"I know," I say. I rest my hand on his open palm. He doesn't pull away, but he doesn't hold mine back.

"I was drawn to it. Even before I lost my memories, I found all your traditions so fascinating and I really liked learning Mermese. But … I'm not a part of it. No matter how much I learn about your culture or how many expressions I master or how many hours I spend snorkeling or swimming, it doesn't matter. Your world isn't open to me."

What am I supposed to say to that? I can't deny it.

"And being with you while I'm on the outside of that world," he continues, brow furrowing, "Lia, it's dangerous. Really dangerous."

Too dangerous. That's what he means. Being with me is too dangerous.

"I can get sirened. I can get killed. And I don't have equal rights under your laws, so even if I haven't committed any crime, I can be forced to drink potions that alter my mind."

Shame colors my cheeks. He's right. It isn't fair. I swallow against the tears that burn my throat.

"And it's dangerous for you, too." Now he squeezes my hand. "When we were in that water and Ondine sent up that wave, I knew she was after you. I knew—and I couldn't do anything." He drops my hand and shoots off the couch. He paces, restless. "I swam as hard as I could and I couldn't get to you." A chair crashes onto its side as he kicks it over, making me jump. "I was so goddamned helpless. You needed me."

"It's okay, I'm okay," I say.

"This time. But what about next time?" He turns away from the chair to face me. "We keep getting in these situations. And for what?"

"What do you mean, 'for what?'?" Now I stand up, anger welling in my chest.

"I'm going to die."

The words hang in the air and his eyes bore into mine, challenging me to disagree when he says, "I'm going to get old and die and you're not. I know you don't want to hear it, but it's the truth. The way things are now, we have no future. Everyone knows it."

My stomach plummets as I grow light-headed. I grip the arm of the couch for balance. I can take these words from anyone else— from everyone else—but not from Clay.

"Lia, we're too different. When I knelt on that beach holding your hand and just hoping you'd wake up, this is all I could think about. Something *needs* to change."

This is it. He's going to break up with me. After everything we've been through. Everything we've risked. It's all too much for him.

And I can't even blame him for what he's about to do.

"I know so much more about your world now," he says. "I've seen the potions and the rituals and the ancient magic." Clay steps up close to me, a hairsbreadth away. His hands are cool as they cup my heated cheeks, ensuring he has my full attention. "Lia, we need to find a way to make me Mer."

THE END

Etallee Leedis (Pronunciation Guide) for Clay

Hey, Caspian—

Hope it's OK that I keep writing. If I'm bugging you, let me know. I think I've got a good handle on the last vocab list you sent (well, I've memorized it at least—you can laugh at my pronunciation later). Can you send another when you get a chance? Thanks a lot, man. *Tallimymay* (right?). Appreciate the help.

—Clay

Dear Clay,

Congratulations on your progress! I've compiled the next list for you using words you may have heard recently. Take heart in the fact that your pronunciation will improve with practice; as a general rule, just remember to elongate double vowels, let s's linger longer than you do in English, and add a musical lilt to your words. I've spelled out each word phonetically to help. I'm sure Lia will be impressed.

Best regards,

Caspian Zayle

For Review:

Allytrill: ALLEY(as in "Don't swim down that dark alley!")-TRILL(rhymes with "thrill"), noun
  - A graceful Mer dance with an upbeat tempo that is performed in pairs on formal occasions

Konklili: KAWN(rhymes with "dawn")-KLEE-LEE, noun
  - A shell imbued with recorded voices that Mer can listen to by holding the shell up to the ear; a Merbook

Siluess: SILL-YOU-ESS(rhymes with "guess"), noun
  - A traditional chest covering worn by Mer women

Spillu: SPILL-EW(rhymes with "fish stew"), noun
  - A Mer game of skill and strategy played on a board of alternating light and dark panels that are equipped with clips to keep the game pieces from floating away

Tallimymee: TALLY(rhymes with "valley")-MY(as in "Those are my swim trunks.")-MAY, noun
  - The most respectful form of thank you; usually directed at elders

Udell: U(rhymes with "woo")-DELL, noun or adjective
  - A Mermaid or Merman who has a hateful, prejudiced view of humans
  - Describing such a Mermaid or Merman
  - Describing such anti-human prejudice or behavior

For Advancement:

Allydriss: ALLEY(rhymes with "galley")-DRISS(rhymes with "hiss"), noun
- A graceful Mer dance with a calming melody and slow steps that is performed in pairs
  on formal occasions

Cicereel: SISS-ER(rhymes with "Mer")-EEL(as in the kind that lives in dark caves)
- The title of a traditional Mermese folksong meant to evoke calm seas; often sung as a lullaby

Daniss: DAHN(rhymes with "prawn")-ISS, noun
- A chancellor assigned control of an ocean principality by the crown

Domstitii: DOME(rhymes with "home")-STEE-TEE, noun
- The Tribunal; a council consisting of six members that presides over a trial and has absolute authority to pass judgement and sentencing in pursuit of justice
  NOTE: Sometimes, they fail in this pursuit.

Esslee: ESS(rhymes with "cress")-LEE, noun
- A chain of pearls made from tears shed over a specific event to commemorate or memorialize the experience. *Esslee* are cherished possessions.

Lenlitli: LEN(rhymes with "Mermen")-LEET(rhymes with "fleet")-LEE, noun
- A male participant in a wedding chosen by the groom to offer emotional support and perform various nuptial activities; a groomsman

Milliki: MILL-EE-KEE(rhymes with "sea"), noun
- A title of respect given to the member of the service staff who holds the top domestic position in a household; similar to a housekeeper who also performs culinary duties

Nii nai sillis suzallis: NEE NY(rhymes with "my") SILL-ISS(rhymes with "abyss") SOO-ZAHL(rhymes with "call," as in "the call of the ocean")-ISS, noun
- Literally translated: A pleasure to encounter you; a traditional Mer greeting

Riliika: RILL(rhymes with "gill")-EE-KUH(as in, when Lia says, "Duh!"), noun
- A ruler who is an immediate member of the royal family age twenty or older and who acts as an advisor to the crown

Urtanri: ER(rhymes with "her")-TAHN-REE, noun
- A spice rub that consists of fourteen different types of seaweed finely ground into a paste to season fish

Viriss: VEER(as in "to veer off course")-ISS, adjective
- Salty; used colloquially Below to mean pleasing or appealing in much the same way the word cool is currently used in the human world

Acknowledgements

First, I'd like to thank you for swimming with Lia out to sea and back again. It means so much to me to share her story with you.

I can't begin to express how grateful I am to my Mer Chronicles readers. As a new author, I have been astounded and touched by everyone who has embraced this series. Thank you, thank you, thank you for your heartfelt letters, emails, messages, and gifts, and for your gorgeous fan art (seriously, I wish I could draw or Photoshop like you guys)! Massive thanks to everyone who wrote a review, shared your excitement on social media, or recommended *Emerge* to your friends and family. To those of you who came to see me at events this year, I can't tell you how wonderful it was to meet you, answer your questions, and talk about these characters. Thank you all for being a part of Team Mer!

This series wouldn't be possible at all if it weren't for the very first members of Team Mer. To Jennifer Unter for her trusted opinions, invaluable savvy, and essential partnership every step of the way. To Georgia McBride for supporting this series as soon as she started reading it, for so keenly understanding every step of bringing it to readers, and for providing me with opportunities I never could have dreamed of. To Jaime Arnold for unparalleled P.R. prowess, coveted insights, and a friendly face at events.

To everyone at Month9Books for all it takes to bring tales of magic and adventure out into the world. Thank you to Shayla Crane for your feedback, questions, and critiques. Thank you to Jennifer Million and Bridget Howard for all your hard work and consideration. Thank you to Stefanie at Beetiful Book Covers for making the face of this book as gorgeous and spellbinding as I ever could have hoped for.

Special thanks to the entire team at IPG. It's because of you that readers all over can share in this story.

As someone who has listened to audiobooks for years during my morning workouts, I can't describe how grateful I am to Audible for creating such a vivid, engaging rendition. I couldn't love it more! Thank you to the extremely talented Sarah Mollo-Christensen for voicing the characters who lived in my head for so long.

To Maryelizabeth Yturralde, a Mermaid and a friend, who has rallied behind this book from the first and has helped put it in the hands of fellow fangirls, bibliophiles, and Merpeople.

To the booksellers, librarians, and educators who have worked so tirelessly and with such enthusiasm to connect readers with storytellers. Special thanks to the Immaculate Heart and USC communities, and to C2 Education.

To all the other authors who have welcomed me, offered advice, and supported this series, especially Mercedes Lackey, Kathy MacMillan, Emily France, Wendy Higgins, Gretchen McNeil, Jennifer Bardsley, Susan Dennard, Axie Oh, Jennifer Brody, E.M. Fitch, Jennifer M. Eaton, Robin Reul, Brenda Drake, Skylar Dorset, Lori Goldstein, Jennifer Gooch Hummer, and the Sweet Sixteens as well as my fellow GMMG authors.

To Lex for understanding the intricacies of magic and discussing them with me late into the night.

To Kate and Savannah for your unending encouragement and bolstering breakfasts.

To my aunts, uncles, and cousins for enthusiastically embracing this book, showing up with hugs at events, and sharing the heck out of it!

To the Saval family for being not only loving and supportive but also thought-provoking.

To my brilliant, beautiful mother Andrea, who, though she will never read this book was with me every step of the way while I was writing it—and who will be with me always.

To my strong, stalwart father Daniel, who has more heart than anyone else I've ever known and who has taught me so much.

To Simon. For being as confident and curious as Clay, and as sharp and chivalrous as Caspian. And most of all, for showing me every day what true love means so that I can write about it.

TOBIE EASTON

Tobie Easton was born and raised in Los Angeles, California, where she's grown from a little girl who dreamed about magic to a twenty-something who writes about it. A summa cum laude graduate of the University of Southern California, Tobie hosts book clubs for tweens and teens. She and her very kissable husband enjoy traveling the globe and fostering packs of rescue puppies. Learn more about Tobie and her upcoming books at www.TobieEaston.com.

OTHER MONTH9BOOKS TITLES YOU MIGHT LIKE

EMERGE
SOULMATED
SUMMONER RISING

Find more books like this at http://www.Month9Books.com

Connect with Month9Books online:
Facebook: www.Facebook.com/Month9Books
Twitter: https://twitter.com/Month9Books
You Tube: www.youtube.com/user/Month9Books
Blog: www.month9booksblog.com

She will risk
everything to stop him
from falling in love with
the wrong girl.

Emerge

TOBIE EASTON

"The most fun I've had reading in a long time!" —Wendy Higgins,
New York Times bestselling author of the *Sweet Evil* series

Two souls. One fate.

JOINING OF SOULS BOOK ONE

SOULMATED

Shaila Patel

SOMEONE SHOULD HAVE TOLD HER.
YOU CAN'T CONTROL THE CREATURES
YOU LET INTO THIS WORLD.

SUMMONER RISING

LAWS OF SUMMONING 1

MELANIE MCFARLANE